# FRÄULEIN M.

# FRÄULEIN M.

CAROLINE
WOODS

TYRUS
BOOKS

Published by
TYRUS BOOKS
an imprint of F+W Media, Inc.
10151 Carver Road, Suite 200
Blue Ash, OH 45242. U.S.A.
www.tyrusbooks.com

Hardcover ISBN 10: 1-5072-0022-6
Hardcover ISBN 13: 978-1-5072-0022-3
Paperback ISBN 10: 1-5072-0021-8
Paperback ISBN 13: 978-1-5072-0021-6
eISBN 10: 1-5072-0023-4
eISBN 13: 978-1-5072-0023-0

Printed in the United States of America.

10  9  8  7  6  5  4  3  2  1

**Library of Congress Cataloging-in-Publication Data**
Woods, Caroline (Caroline Courtney), author.
Fräulein M. / Caroline Woods.
Blue Ash, OH: Tyrus Books, 2017.
LCCN 2016034235 (print) | LCCN 2016046191 (ebook) | ISBN 9781507200223 (hc)
| ISBN 1507200226 (hc) | ISBN 9781507200216 (pb) | ISBN 1507200218 (pb) | ISBN
9781507200230 (ebook) | ISBN 1507200234 (ebook)
LCSH: Sisters--Fiction. | Choice (Psychology)--Fiction. | Mothers and daughters--Fiction.
| Family secrets--Fiction. | Berlin (Germany)--Fiction. | South Carolina--Fiction. | BISAC:
FICTION / Literary. | GSAFD: Mystery fiction. | Historical fiction.
LCC PS3623.O6752 F73 2017 (print) | LCC PS3623.O6752 (ebook) | DDC 813/.6--dc23
LC record available at https://lccn.loc.gov/2016034235

This is a work of fiction. Names, characters, corporations, institutions, organizations, events, or
locales in this novel are either the product of the author's imagination or, if real, used fictitiously.
The resemblance of any character to actual persons (living or dead) is entirely coincidental.

Many of the designations used by manufacturers and sellers to distinguish their products are
claimed as trademarks. Where those designations appear in this book and F+W Media, Inc. was
aware of a trademark claim, the designations have been printed with initial capital letters.

Cover design by Sylvia McArdle.
Cover image © GettyImages.com/michelangeloop.

*This book is available at quantity discounts for bulk purchases.*
*For information, please call 1-800-289-0963.*

# DEDICATION

For Colin and Camille.

# PART I

# BERLIN, 1923–1931

*The world may very likely not always think of them as they think of themselves, but what care they for the world?*

Grimm's Fairy Tales

# BERNI, 1923

At St. Luisa's Home for Girls in western Berlin, birthdays were observed, not celebrated. Berni's eighth, which fell in the winter of 1923, came and went with neither singing nor candles on a wooden *Geburtstagskranz*. Instead, the nuns burned money.

"They treat us like livestock," Berni hissed into her little sister's good ear that morning at breakfast. They were eating dry slices of *Vollkornbrot* with nothing to improve its taste: no meat, no butter, no jam. "Kannst du mich hören?" This was Grete's least favorite question, but Berni could never help asking.

Grete, who was five, tugged a lock of blond hair over her left ear. It was smooth and pink as a shell, with fewer grooves in it than in other ears. "I can hear you," she muttered with a glance at the sisters' table. "You needn't speak so loudly."

Berni took a bite of bread and wrinkled her nose, tasting a distinctive tinge of fish. On Friday mornings, the stink of pickled herring seeped into everything in the refectory: the girls' hair, their bread, their thin gray dirndls. Having served breakfast, the cook and her staff peeled open tins of Voelker's fillets to prepare a meatless dinner of herring salad. The one aroma that could cut through the fishy air was the comforting smoke from burning pine logs. But that winter the stack of firewood in the circular rack had dwindled.

"If we had parents," Berni said, mouth full, "we'd be eating jam, cookies, tea—"

"Hush," whispered Konstanz, who sat on Berni's left. "I have a father, and he always said children need nothing more than potatoes to survive."

"I am sure he didn't serve you frozen milk." Berni tilted her cup and glared at the sisters, who ate knackwurst and drank coffee at an elevated table, their faces hidden by the lily petals of their cornettes. They didn't seem even to notice that today, for the first time, there was no fire at all. For firewood you needed money, and the sisters' money, it seemed, was no longer any good.

Each Friday the firewood man arrived just after morning prayers, when the girls had their hands folded in their laps, their eyes active. Sister Maria Eberhardt, the reverend mother, waited for him beside the back door of the refectory with an envelope of cash.

Over the course of the winter, the envelope had grown larger and larger. On the first of the new year, Sister Maria paid him with a box full of money. Then a basket. Berni had heard the term "inflation," but she didn't understand what it meant or why it happened. She didn't yet know that panic and hysteria were driving Berliners to vice, to risk. Her world was still small; what she knew was the slap of a bleach-dipped rag against the bathroom floor, the chill of chapel marble under her knees. From history class, she knew there had been a Kaiser and now a democracy, but as a Catholic—a minority in Berlin—she should not forget the pope sat above everyone else.

She had asked Sister Josephine, her favorite, about inflation one afternoon after mathematics. "Oh, child." Sister Josephine spun Berni around, pulling her braids into long, dark ribbons of hair. "We have been trying to repay England and France since the end of the war."

"Then why does there seem to be *more* money floating around, piles and piles of it?"

"Because there's a man in an office cranking a printing press, trying to make enough to repay the Frogs. You must quit this nasty habit of chewing the ends of your plaits, Bernadette. You look like a wild orphan."

If anyone else had said this, Berni would have balked. The word "orphan" was taboo among the girls. They were daughters of St. Luisa. They were Lulus.

Konstanz gave Berni a jab, and Berni looked down to see a yellow cardboard cone in her lap. Both of them watched the sisters eat as Konstanz passed it to Berni under the table.

The cone was a *Schultüte*, the gift parents gave their children on the first day of school. As Berni's greedy fingers dug inside, her eyes drifted over the long tables and benches, settling on Hannelore Haas, an eight-year-old who'd arrived the day before. Her eyes were swollen from crying. As had been happening to families more and more frequently, Hannelore's parents had been unable to support all their children, and so they left their eldest here. Giving her the cone was almost cruel, Berni thought; it suggested this place was just like any other school, though as soon as Hannelore saw it she must have recognized it for what it was.

Of course, the other girls had immediately seized Hannelore's parents' parting gift. Nobody was allowed to think she was special just because her parents were alive. Emboldened by Sister Maria's absence from breakfast, they'd been passing it from table to table. By the time it reached Berni, the toys and school supplies and most of the wrapped candies were gone. She dug out a chocolate-covered nut, then glanced once more toward the sisters before popping it into her mouth. When she looked up, Hannelore's glazed eyes were fixed on her.

"Don't," Grete murmured, but Berni bit into the chocolate, and her eyelids fell shut. The flavor, a bit bitter, stung the sides of her mouth and set her molars buzzing. The nut crunched into a sweet, oily paste. She could *see* the flavors, somehow, painted on her closed lids: magenta and yellow and aquamarine. When she opened her eyes to the whitewashed brick walls, the bare bulbs dangling from the ceiling, the gray of the girls' uniforms and black cluster of nuns, she almost couldn't believe this dull vision was the real world.

"Try one." She pressed the cone toward Grete. "They aren't paying attention," she added with a nod toward the sisters' table.

11

Grete shook her head, her blue eyes wide with fear.

"You have to. The chocolate, it's—it's a carnival. It's May Day and Christmas together."

Again Grete refused, and Berni pinched her lightly on the arm. If they were caught with Hannelore's *Schultüte*, they both knew Berni would be in trouble, not Grete. The sisters scarcely noticed Grete. Sometimes it seemed even to Berni that her sister had been crafted from less substantial stuff than she was, that God's brush had a little less paint on it when he made Grete, his clay mixed with a little more water. She was pale and petite, with weak hearing; there was nothing weak about Berni. The sisters said she must have had a bit of gypsy in her, with her dark coloring, her big feet and hands, her restless energy. All the proof Berni and Grete had that they were related were the shallow clefts in their chins, and their name. They were called Metzger, not Kirchhof or Ostertag, names the sisters gave to foundlings. Later, Berni promised, when they left St. Luisa's, they would find other Metzgers. It would mean something.

"Fine," Berni whispered when Grete refused again. "More for me." The girls on the other side of Grete groaned.

*"Ruhe bitte!"* The refectory door swung wide, slamming the opposite wall.

Chairs shifted and spines straightened. Berni pressed the cone against her leg, willing it to disappear.

The reverend mother stood in the doorway with a wheelbarrow. A woman thick of neck and skull, Sister Maria taught six years of Latin to every child who came through St. Luisa's. As she passed, Berni strained to peek inside her wheelbarrow and saw that it was stuffed with crisp new money. Sister Odi leapt from her table to waddle behind Sister Maria, picking up bills that had fluttered to the floor. When Sister Maria reached the back door, she stood and put her hands to the base of her long spine, straightening it in a series of cracks. Berni waited, holding her breath, for the firewood man to knock on the door. It did not take long.

"Come in," Sister Maria said, standing impassive beside her wheelbarrow.

Berni had expected him to gasp at the sight of all that money, but he merely looked exhausted. Sister Maria had turned the wheelbarrow around so he could grasp the handles.

"This'll buy you one log." He cringed a little, inspecting her face, awaiting censure.

"He said they can afford only one log!" Berni said into Grete's left ear. Grete nodded and swatted her away.

Sister Maria rose another few centimeters, her forehead level with the firewood man's. According to rumor, she had been everything from a boatswain's daughter to a lady wrestler in a traveling circus before taking the vows of the Order. The man shrank in her presence; the hand that held out the one dry log shook.

"We agreed on the price just last night," she said, her voice firm.

"The price has already changed." He scratched the back of his neck. "Most likely it has changed as we stand here. Nothing I can do about it."

"These are children, *mein Herr*. They will freeze to death without a fire."

"You know how things are, Sister. Madness."

Berni could feel every girl in the room watching Sister Maria, waiting to see what would happen, eyes blinking in unison like those of a giant spider. "Keep your log," Sister Maria said after a long pause. "God bless you in this difficult time."

The man handed Sister Maria a few slivers of kindling without a word. After he had gone, Sister Maria stared at the kindling and the pile of cash. "Sister Odi," she barked. "Take all of this and put it in the fire."

"All of . . ." Sister Odi said, sputtering a bit. "You don't mean . . ."

"It won't do us any good as money," Sister Maria said, flicking her hand over the wheelbarrow. "We might as well use it to light the kindling."

Sister Odi reached into the pile of money and looked at it as though she wasn't quite sure what it was. Gingerly she tucked a handful into the fireplace. Then she lit a match. Berni hovered a few inches above her bench to watch the bills curl and crumble, licked by the flames. A few banknotes skirted across the floor, lifted by a draft.

"What a shame," Berni whispered. "They have so much money they can burn it. They might as well have given some to me, to us."

The side of her vision went black. Berni turned to see Sister Maria looming, draping the girl across the table in the deep folds of her double sleeves. The odors of incense and lemon soap wafted from the fabric. "You should not be in awe of money, girls," said Sister Maria, her gray-green eyes fixed on Berni's.

Behind her the phrase *Iudicate egeno, et pupillo*, the guiding verse of the Order of St. Luisa, was painted on the wall in Bavarian script. The sisters translated it as "Defend the poor and fatherless." Berni knew *iudicate* could mean "defend," but it could also mean "judge." Sister Maria insisted the two were interchangeable.

"Remember," said Sister Maria, "where your treasure is . . ." She held out her hand.

"Where your treasure is," Berni said, completing the scripture, "there will your heart be also." She handed the *Schultüte* to Sister Maria. Across the room, Hannelore yelped.

• • •

Later, in the dormitory, when Berni opened her pockets, Grete was horrified to see the bills crumpled up inside. "Oh, Berni, how could you? You're already in trouble!"

Berni unfolded one pale pink banknote, holding it taut between her fists. "Look at this, Margarete. *Eine. Million. Mark.*"

Grete's eyes widened. "But where would you spend it?"

Berni let Grete trace the scalloped patterns on the money with her fingertips, then stashed it all in her pillowcase. It would only upset Grete if she told her she longed to use the money to take her to a real ear doctor. Sister Lioba, who worked in the infirmary and performed annual hearing tests using tuning forks and whispers, knew nothing.

Grete said, lip trembling, "They'll never choose you for the academy if you misbehave."

"*Ach!*" Berni shrugged, pretending not to have thought of this. Every year the sisters chose a handful of teenage girls to attend a private Catholic academy in Wedding, run by Ursuline nuns. It was the girls' only chance, besides finding a husband, at a better life. "I have years until then, to become a model child."

After the lights in the dormitory went out, the girls slid under Berni's quilt, leaving Grete's bed empty. Grete put her face in the crook of Berni's neck. "Tell me a story."

For years they'd slept beside each other, even though the sisters liked to arrange girls by age. They'd come to St. Luisa's when Berni was four and Grete two, after their mother died and they could no longer stay at her cottage in Zehlendorf. Berni remembered the smells of her mother's home best: cedar chests opened in winter, nutmeg shaved over hot milk. As a baby, blond Grete also had a milky scent, and a fear of thunderstorms; as soon as she could toddle, she'd climb from her trundle into Berni's carved wooden bed.

At times, Berni could not help feeling that her real life was a kind of river she was always running alongside, searching for a place to leap back into the water and be carried along by the current, back to her mother, Trudi. It was Trudi's elder sister, a spinster whose name Berni would no longer utter, who had dumped them at St. Luisa's.

She'd come to live with them when Trudi fell ill with pneumonia and saw her through her death. The aunt stank of something briny and woke late every morning without feeding the girls. The last time they'd seen her, she'd been crying in the reverend mother's office, hanky to her nose, saying she couldn't do it anymore.

"Are you certain, Berni?" Grete asked once, chewing a fingernail. "That wasn't our mother who gave us to the sisters, after our father died. Was it?"

"Hush! Mother can hear you in heaven." Of course it hadn't been their mother. Berni could vividly remember the first time she'd seen St. Luisa's. It sat on a bleak corner in otherwise affluent Charlottenburg, gray as a prison, with rows of too-small windows. The trim, painted strenuous red, gave the building a stressed, weeping face, and Berni had known instantly they were in trouble. She'd given their aunt a good kick in the shin.

"Tell me a happy story," Grete whispered now. Under the bedcovers her feet tickled Berni's shins, her toenails poking through her holey socks.

"Once upon a time there were two sisters, Snow White and Rose Red. Schneeweißchen preferred the hearth and home; Rosenrot played outside and gathered berries for their mother."

"No," Grete said. "One about *our* mother."

"Ahem. Once upon a time, in Zehlendorf, there lived a young woman who raised squab in a shaded dovecote in her backyard. She had two little girls who slept in the attic under the eaves: Bernadette and Margarete, one tall and raven-haired, one fair and small."

"How did the dovecote smell?"

"It smelled foul, and so the mother planted wildflowers all around it." Berni had recited the story so often she could see discarded feathers on grass. "One day, a magician came to the house. The young mother held baby Grete against her side and took Bernadette by the hand. 'Choose the whitest birds you can find,

16

my sweet, the ones with the most magic,' she told Bernadette. The magician took them away with a sweep of his cape."

"She was a kind mother."

"Very kind," Berni said. She did not have to recite the next part of the story, the one they knew best. Their mother had been very kind to introduce them to the magician; she did it to hide the real reason she raised their beloved doves, which was for meat.

• • •

So much money. Berni dreamt about it, woke up licking her lips. She felt it crunch between her fingers, under the sheets.

She didn't tell Grete what she intended to do until Thursday evening, when Sister Maria marched out on her weekly mission to feed the poor and Berni's accomplice, Konstanz, met them in the dormitory. "Sister'll be out until eight, at least," Konstanz announced. She had wide green eyes and a willowy build, more fairy than child. "You aren't going to tell, are you, Grete?"

Grete had both hands over her ears, the corner of a blanket in her mouth. Berni knelt down, close to her face. "Nothing bad will happen. She has so much money she can burn it." She couldn't explain her need to possess something, anything, even if it did turn out to be worthless.

"Why must you always put us in danger?" Grete tilted her watery eyes toward the ceiling and sighed. "Every night I wish the next day will be quiet, every night . . ."

Before long, Berni was pulling Grete down the quiet corridor. Konstanz led the way, grabbing corners as the girls slid through the halls. At last they reached the east wing, where they tiptoed past the wooden doors to the sisters' rooms. Berni put her arm around Grete, whose face had turned the color of bathwater, as Konstanz worked a hairpin into the lock. When finally the handle gave, Berni entered the room quickly and lifted the shade. Gray evening light illuminated the cot, the desk, the heavy crucifix. Sister's laundry was folded atop her sheet.

"I don't know why, but"—Konstanz's eyes widened—"I never would have imagined they wore underwear." Some of the bloomers were even faded pink, large and dainty at once. On a rough wooden table sat a teapot and tiny mug. Berni opened the pot to peek at the stiffened tea bag inside. She ran her finger over the edge of the cup to feel the greasy print of the sister's lip.

"Let's go," Grete whispered. Berni pretended she hadn't heard.

"Look at this." Konstanz threw off a radio's cover. It looked like a large wooden jewelry box with black dials. "It's a TRF set. My father had one." She began to adjust the reactor.

"Come, Grete." Berni picked up the desk chair by the rungs. "You need to be closer to the sound." Grete glared at her, face deep red, as she took her seat.

When a song burst out of the radio, they all leapt back. "Turn it down, turn it down!" Berni cried. She yanked Grete's hands from her ears, trying to get her to smile.

"And now," a voice announced when the music faded, "Frieda Pommer and Max Zuchmayer singing their popular duet, 'If I Could Choose Again.'"

A lively tune began: horns, strings, accordion. Konstanz leapt into the middle of the room, landing soundlessly as a cat, and curtsied; she would be Frieda Pommer. She put one hand on her hip and glided her mouth over the words as if she'd heard them all her life:

A skinny man approached me to see if I'd be his bride.
A poor man with a good heart said that heart was free, but lied.
I'd gladly dance with either, but I'm already obliged
To a portly chap in uniform who has something to hide.

Berni was enthralled. The lyrics did not make her think of politics, only of men and marriage, of dancing and wine. She and Konstanz kept their shrieks silent and clapped without sound. Konstanz twirled and goose-stepped, and when Max began to sing, Berni stood.

She could not have said where the idea came from. If she had known how Grete would react, or what would come after, she never would have done it. She wasn't even sure how or when she'd learned what made men different from girls, but she snatched a rolled-up stocking off Sister Maria's bed and stuffed it into her underpants.

Konstanz put her hands over her eyes, giggling. Then Frieda looped back to the chorus, and Konstanz threw back her head. She and Berni linked arms, and Berni thrust her little crotch this way and that, hands on her hips like a Prussian soldier, the sock forming a bulge under her skirt. She had tears streaking her cheeks, her tongue pumping silently in her mouth.

Round and round she and Konstanz went, in dizzying circles—the dull Spartan room a blur, the only color the shockingly intimate laundry on the bed and the bright yellow of Grete's hair, until—

The radio's volume shot sky-high, blasting Frieda Pommer's voice throughout the building.

Berni whirled around. Grete's sticky fingers held one of the dials, and her mouth was pressed shut. She stared past Berni, at nothing. Berni had completely forgotten her as she danced.

Konstanz cried out, covering her ears. Berni tore the stocking from under her skirt and whipped it at the bed, then slapped Grete's hand away and shut the darn thing off. Too late; she could hear the sisters' doors opening, could hear their alarmed voices.

"If you wanted me to stop," Berni murmured, "you could have just said so." But Grete wouldn't answer. She wouldn't meet Berni's eyes, not even when Sister Odi burst triumphantly into the room.

# GRETE, 1931

They were stopped on a corner of the Kurfürstendamm, the busiest shopping street in the city. A place where they very decidedly did not belong, Grete thought. Their clothes gave them away; donated dresses did not grow at the same weedlike pace that girls did. Strings hung from Berni's broken hem, and still the fabric did not cover her knees.

Berni didn't seem to notice. Her hand shielding her eyes, she had the optimistic, faraway look of a sea explorer. She held the last of the three boxes of communion she'd been asked to deliver to churches in west Berlin, Grete the red cash tin. Berni had been ordered to return to the home in time for lunch. Grete was not supposed to be out at all.

"Can you read the time, Grete-bird?" Berni pointed to the clock on the Memorial Church, its stones blackened with city pollution.

Grete squinted up at the gold numerals. For a moment, she considered telling a lie to get Berni moving. "Eleven thirty," she said honestly. "We need to go home, Berni."

"Eagle eyes!" Berni bent down so that her lips touched Grete's earlobe. "That means we have time," she said in a low voice, affecting an Eastern accent, "to visit Libations of Illyria."

A blade of fear stabbed Grete's stomach. "Please, no. Let's find St. Matthias, then take the U-Bahn home before anyone notices I'm missing." She leapt back when an omnibus lumbered to the curb, sending oily water toward her shoes.

Earlier in the day she'd been peacefully changing beds in the nursery when Berni burst into the room. Grete would join her, she declared without asking, on her communion-delivery adventure. It was something to celebrate, Berni insisted: the sisters entrusting her with the communion wafers the Lulus baked, worth more than a pfennig apiece, meant they were on the verge of choosing her for the academy.

Grete had given her usual excuses, knowing they would not deter Berni: she had to carry soiled sheets up to the laundry, she had a Latin exam to study for. Tomorrow, Sister Maria would fire questions at her in Latin, standing behind the dais so that Grete could not see her mouth. Her only hope was to study until she could recite the whole dead language in her sleep, and here was Berni, pressuring her to go on one of her larks. But Berni promised they'd practice this evening; she'd have Grete speaking like Julius Caesar by the end of the night.

"Come, one more detour," Berni said now, shielding Grete from two women in trousers walking and smoking, moving at breakneck speed. "I'll buy you a pretzel."

Bells tinkled, and a young man rode by on a bicycle. He tossed some change into a homeless veteran's cap. Grete had seen only the thin white arms of the cyclist's companion, clasped around his waist. Watching them, Berni's face took on a look of naked yearning. It seemed she longed for those pale arms to belong to her.

Grete pulled at her sleeve. Berni had to remember they weren't both Rose Red. Somebody had to be Snow White. "I must prepare for Latin."

"This is more important."

"You always say nothing's more important than schoolwork." In a matter of weeks, the sisters would choose three girls out of Berni's class of forty to study with the Ursulines in Wedding. For months Berni had been struggling to behave, to polish her shoes, to bite back crude comments. Around the sisters she smiled so broadly she'd developed an eye twitch. Why would she risk that now?

Berni shook her head. "They sell real potions at Libations of Illyria—love spells, strength tonics. I'll buy an elixir for luck." She patted her pocket, which jingled. "I've enough change saved for both of us." To show she'd won the argument, she began to walk up the boulevard so quickly that Grete had no choice but to scramble after her. Berni's long black braids flagged behind her, the plaits of a little girl; on Berni's gangly, sixteen-year-old figure, they reminded Grete of garlands tacked up long after Christmas.

Grete tried to keep up with her, dodging pedestrians. The Ku'damm was packed with people. Behind iron gates, cafés crammed table after table onto the sidewalk to enjoy the damp May weather. A waiter with a tray bent to show the Viennese strudel, the *obsttorte*, the black forest. Two delivery boys in aprons hauled loads of pink flowers down the restaurant's cellar steps. Grete's mouth watered; she smelled coffee, browned onions, custard.

"Everyone looks so angry," she said breathlessly, when she'd caught her sister.

"That's the Berlin sneer. Watch." Berni affected an exaggerated frown and strolled with her shoulders thrown back. "You have to hold your *Schnauze* high."

Graffiti was everywhere, even in this neighborhood; someone had defaced every National Socialist poster adorning a Litfaß column. When the girls stopped at an intersection, Grete pointed to a row of perfectly trimmed hedges on which *KPD* and *BLUTMAI* were scrawled in white paint. Berni chuckled. "Serves them right for trying to make shrubs behave like walls. If I had a garden, I'd let it grow wild."

"But what does that mean? What does blood have to do with May?"

"It's for the anniversary, I'd imagine." Berni worked her lower lip over her teeth. "Some troubles between the police and Communists. The demonstration turned . . . heated."

"Did anyone die?"

Berni drew a long, impatient breath. "We aren't political. We don't have to worry. *Wait!*"

The passing motorcar honked its horn at them, seconds after Berni yanked Grete off the curb by the back of her collar. "I heard it," Grete said, clutching her throat, though she hadn't. She'd heard the horn, of course, but not the approaching engine. "You have to *look* into the street before you cross, little bird." "Everyone does," Grete muttered.

. . .

It would have been foolish to tell Berni what happened at this year's physical exam. Grete had hoped somehow her hearing would improve with age, that thirteen would be a magic number, but Sister Lioba had declared her ears, if anything, were getting worse.

In her left ear, Grete had heard enough of Sister Lioba's whisper to be able to repeat it: "Hoppe, hoppe Reiter, wenn er fällt, dann schreit er." But in the right, she could only feel the little blasts of breath. She did her best to guess, filling in the next two lines of the nursery rhyme. Sister shook her head. "It will only make matters worse if you lie, Margarete." She glanced heavenward as she said this, indicating what might be the source of Grete's problems.

Grete already knew the blockage inside her ears kept her at a remove from God. At Mass, she watched the concentration and piety on the other girls' faces as they listened to the sermon, while she was distracted by the echoes of the organ, the odor of incense, the pressure inside her ears. Sometimes she wondered if God was punishing her or her parents, since she'd had problems hearing little things since she was born. Birdsong had always eluded her unless she stood directly under a tree. Raindrops jumped noiselessly in their puddles.

The intermittent ringing, however, hadn't always been part of her life. It began when she was five or six. "There's a faucet left on somewhere," she had complained to Berni. "A pipe is running.

Don't you hear it?" In time Grete realized the high-pitched sound belonged only to her, and that it tended to appear most often when she felt scared or nervous.

"You shouldn't mind if people know about your ears," Berni tried to reassure her. "You can't help that any more than I can help my hair becoming knotty."

Grete shook her head. Berni *could* help it if her hair tangled. Other people could and would hold it against her if she were a mess. And they'd hold Grete's deficiencies against her, too. Of course they would.

"You have lost the high frequencies in the right ear," Sister Lioba had announced at her last physical, "though the lower ones seem present, for now." She wrinkled her nose so that Grete could see the black hairs. "It may be progressive. Time will tell."

That spring, the words *it may be progressive* had become the rhythm of Grete's life. She vowed to develop her other senses before they were all she had left. When the sisters took them on a hike in the Grunewald, Grete smelled smoke half an hour before Sister Odi spotted a farmer burning his fields and hustled them to the train. She spied an osprey's nest spraying off the corner of a building in Sophie-Charlotte-Platz. And at Mass, when the tip of Father Radeke's finger lingered on Konstanz's lip as he gave her communion, Grete lowered her face but not her eyes and told no one, not even Berni.

• • •

"This is the address," said Berni, her face uncertain. They'd stopped in front of the eight double glass doors of Fiedler's department store.

Grete's gaze scrolled up the enormous façade, its windows a code: a row of triangles, a row of circles, a row of squares. "A department store?"

Berni shrugged. "Sure," she said, though Grete could tell she wasn't.

Three security guards in black-and-gold uniforms stood together between two sets of doors. In the shining glass, Grete caught her sad reflection: her overwashed blue dress and limp, pale braids. Berni stood almost a foot taller. Beside her Grete felt stunted and anemic, like the albino frog they'd discovered in a gutter, which Berni declared would be picked off by a bird in no time. At thirteen she looked no different than she had at age nine. A late bloomer, Sister Josephine called Grete, like the hickory tree in the yard. "Berni matured late as well," she'd say, "and look how tall she's gotten." This did little to comfort Grete. She had a feeling she'd never measure up to her sister.

"Come on," Berni said, gripping the polished brass doorknob, and before Grete could argue, she found herself inside the store.

For a moment, they did not move. They gazed upon a maze of velvet-draped tables. Jewelry, crystal, and leather shone in the soft light. In the middle of the marble floor a bronze goddess held scales in the middle of a fountain. Berni pointed up. The arched ceiling, three stories high, was made of stained glass. Grete watched a saleswoman reach languorously for a silk scarf. Everyone in here moved in a kind of trance, it seemed to Grete, the un-hurry of the rich; it took a moment to figure out which were people and which were mannequins, so uncannily did they resemble one another.

"Look over there," Berni said, and before Grete could ask where, Berni was on the move. In the far corner Grete saw a passageway labeled in gilt letters: Libations of Illyria. She began breathing quickly. Perhaps the wealthy really did have access to liquid magic.

They had to pass through a tunnel of exotic plants, ferns that offered caresses. The air smelled floral, fruity, sweet, strong—how awful the dormitory toilets would be after this! When Grete opened her eyes, Berni had stopped in a plant-laden cave of sorts, in front of a glass case. Behind it was a young woman in the same black-

and-gold cap the doormen wore, but with silk stockings and a fitted jacket. Looking bored, she dabbed her deep plum lips with a tissue.

Berni had her hands on the top of the case, inside which were bottles of all shapes and sizes, some with long delicate necks, some with tasseled ionizers. Grete saw nothing miraculous. Instead of Luck Tonic or Courage Elixir, there were Spirit of Myrcia and Essence of Lilac.

The shop girl used a nail file to nudge Berni's hand off the case; it left a steamy print. Her hair was artificial red, too shiny to be real, and her large nose was twisted to the side in amusement. Grete realized in horror that poor Berni had been duped. This was where rich ladies bought their toilet water, nothing more. She had never experienced *fremdschämen* for Berni—usually it was the other way around—and she felt the world tip on its axis.

"Berni," she whispered. The shop girl licked her teeth, waiting. "We can leave now."

Berni cleared her throat. With a fingernail she tapped the glass. "Where are the potions?"

The salesgirl took a breath and paused, then opened her mouth in a wide grin. Her teeth were yellow and crowded. "They're all potions. Would you like to try the Oriental Lily Nectar?" When she talked, a string of saliva like spider's silk linked her upper and lower incisors. She produced a deep purple bottle with a cap shaped like a flower.

"What does it do?"

The salesgirl's forehead wrinkled momentarily. "What does it *do*?" She inserted a dropper into the bottle, then squeezed it twice on Berni's wrist. "This perfume is extracted from the blooms that grow around the Taj Mahal." Her voice was deep, deeper than the average woman's, and as long as Grete watched her lips move, she could hear her voice better than she could Berni's. She put a drop on Grete's wrist as well. "Want to know the price?"

Grete hesitated a bit, then sniffed. Perfume, ordinary perfume. "Berni . . ."

Berni put her nose to her wrist and inhaled. "Very nice. But no, I don't want to know the price." She was sixteen, too old to believe in magic. Yet she sounded so desperate that Grete longed to hide. "I want to know where the real libations are."

The salesgirl tilted her head, and finally Grete could see the brown eyes under her cap, alarmingly large and quick. "You'll get the true fragrance after a little. Let the bouquet develop."

"Tell me where you're hiding the real stuff." Berni took one of her long, heavy arms and draped it around Grete's shoulders. "What do you carry for hearing loss?"

Grete's face suddenly felt hot under the fluorescent lights. So this was Berni's purpose. She should have known.

Berni cupped her cheek and said, eyes filled with worry, "Don't you want to be able to hear Sister Maria during the Latin oral?"

Whenever she had a problem, Grete thought, shutting her eyes, Berni swooped in to solve it. Bullies were vanquished, spills cleaned. Even when Grete could glimpse a solution, Berni would pluck it from above her, as though snatching a feather from the sky. The one thing she'd never been able to attain for Grete was a normal ear.

The salesgirl looked confused. Delicately she ran a hand over her red hair, petting it, as if to confirm it hadn't gone anywhere. "Look," she said. "I've humored you enough."

"Berni, this is stupid." Grete yanked her sister's hem so hard she felt a seam tear. Berni froze, looking down at her, her face wrought with failure, and for a moment Grete wished it had worked. If only she could allow Berni to cure her. She opened her mouth to say something—but what was there to say?—and then she heard high heels on marble.

The salesgirl straightened up when a blond woman appeared. She wore a short red coat and black leather gloves. Her eyes were as dark as the gloves, saucy and round. "Darling," the woman said, reaching for the salesgirl. They kissed on both cheeks. "How's the new job?" The salesgirl's face turned the color of her hair. "Old hat."

"I can wait my turn," said the blond woman, smiling politely at Berni and Grete.

"We're finished," the salesgirl snapped. "They aren't buying anything, is that right?"

"No," Berni said, her voice cracking a little. "You don't have what we came for."

The blond woman looked closely at Berni and Grete, taking in their shabby dresses, the worn shoes, and her face rose and fell in pity. Berni crossed her arms. Nobody but Grete saw the salesgirl produce an ivory and gold phone out of nowhere. She dialed one number and murmured something Grete could not hear into the receiver.

"Berni," she whispered, lifting her sister's dark braid. "We have to go . . ."

"I have a good one for you," the blond woman said to the salesgirl, accepting an amber bottle. "Why are the Sturmabteilung uniforms brown?"

The salesgirl hesitated. Berni answered for her. "Something to do with shit stains?"

Grete's mouth fell open. The woman began to laugh. Then one of the doormen came crashing through the plants, a big man, white-eyebrowed, his face florid. He lifted his chins at the salesgirl, who nodded with satisfaction toward Berni and Grete. The blonde woman turned in the act of squeezing the ionizer at her throat to watch him take each girl by the arm, and Grete thought she heard her say, "Oh, for goodness' sake!" as they were ushered away.

Grete squeezed her eyes shut and stumbled beside him so that she wouldn't have to watch the tranquil salespeople and shoppers disturbed. She mumbled to herself, practicing for her Latin test. *Decem, viginti. Trentrigintata.*

"Pick up your feet." The man's breath smelled of ham. "I won't carry you up the stairs."

Berni's voice: "I can carry her."

*Octoginta. Nonaginta.* After this, they would be in such trouble. Berni would never be chosen for the academy.

Berni began to cough, the sound deep-throated and animal. It echoed in the glassy space, and the man told her to hush. Outside rain fell gently, little more than mist. The doorman let Grete cower behind Berni, but he kept his grip on Berni's arm. A few times she spasmed, hand to her mouth, suppressing the quakes of her lungs.

"You girl . . . know better . . ." In the noise on the street, Grete lost parts of what the man was saying, but watched in a panic as he tapped the lid of Berni's white box.

"We didn't steal anything." Berni's voice, very close to Grete's left ear, squeaked a bit. "It's the host. We bake it at St. Luisa's, then take it to the churches."

His chin puckered in disbelief. Grete could imagine the sisters' reaction when they were returned to the orphanage by the police. *Let's run, Berni,* she wanted to shout, *let's just run*—but she couldn't form the words, and she knew even if they ran it would do them no good. Everything was over now, all their dreams, all Berni's good behavior erased in one poor decision. Why hadn't she been strong enough to tell Berni no?

A voice cut in, saying something Grete couldn't hear, and she whirled around to see the blond woman in the red coat had joined them on the sidewalk. "There's no need to harass these girls." She leaned in between Berni and Grete. "You don't have to show him anything, Fräulein," she said. Her skin smelled of citrus. "Don't let him tell you otherwise."

"Remind me how this is your business," the doorman shouted. A drip of water fell from the canopy onto his face, and Berni snickered. He grimaced. "We catch thieves all the time."

"Well, if they did steal something I can pay for it. I have plenty of money to share." The woman opened her white rectangular purse and pulled out a smaller rectangular wallet.

"We didn't steal!" Berni ripped open the cardboard box. With her grimy hands she rifled through the disks of bread. "We're on our way to St. Matthias. I swear on the Bible."

Grete put her hands to her mouth. She wasn't sure which was worse, the swearing or the desecration of the Host. The woman looked down at Grete and said, "It's all right, my dear, God won't smite you. It's just a bit of bread in a box, after all."

Bread in a box? But it wasn't; it was the ultimate gift. Grete scowled at the ground, at the backs of Berni's shoes.

"And there are only a few marks and a handful of pfennig in the red tin," Berni said. "Go ahead and count it. We'd be the poorest thieves in the world."

The doorman looked back at his two colleagues, neither of whom moved to help. Finally he made a dismissive motion with his arm and said something Grete couldn't hear.

"Come on," Berni said, hugging her so closely around the shoulders that Grete had to walk sideways. Rain fell steadily now; she felt it dripping down the center of her scalp. Ahead of them, the pointed spires of the Memorial Church were wrapped in fog. Grete felt Berni sigh and realized she was staring not at the church but at the Gloria-Palast movie theater. Through its arched doorway Grete could see burgundy carpets and crystal chandeliers; above the doors of its café was a giant plaster pretzel.

Just before they reached the U-Kurfürstendamm station, someone stepped in front of them: the woman in red. She stood there hugging her square white purse, her lips poised in a little smile. An umbrella dangled from her forearm.

Berni jumped apart from Grete and curtsied. "Thank you for your help."

The stranger took Berni's chin into her bare hand. "Where do you two come from?"

"St. Luisa's Home."

"That makes you orphans." She replaced her glove, smiling, working her fingers into the leather. "I had a feeling. You have that look." She tapped her cheek twice, and as if by magic, a dimple appeared. "Determination? Desperation? A little of each? What were you doing in Fiedler's, if I may ask?"

"We were looking for potions," Berni said.

A smile broke over the woman's face. "Magic potions?" She moved to open her umbrella, but then she held it out to Berni. "You take this. I don't have far to walk."

Grete stared at the brilliant blue silk, imagining what the sisters would say if they strolled into the orphanage with it. "Oh, thank you, but we can't," said Berni, coughing into her sleeve.

"I'm not offering it for keeps. I'll come so that you can return it. St. Luisa's, right? And your names are?"

"Bernadette Metzger. This is Margarete Metzger, my sister."

"And I am Fräulein Schmidt. How do you do." She pressed the umbrella toward Berni, smiled, and walked away so there could be no argument. Grete's toes uncurled inside her shoes.

"She was beautiful," Berni said as they watched Fräulein Schmidt stroll up the Ku'damm, her bottom twitching from side to side in her slim skirt. When she was gone, Berni fiddled with the clasp and slid open the umbrella. They each took hold of the black lacquered handle.

Grete gasped. "What will we tell Sister Maria when that lady comes for her umbrella?"

"Oh, Grete, she's never going to come," Berni said.

This filled Grete with relief. She watched Berni look wistfully up at the brilliant blue-purple silk and metal spokes. She'd loathed hearing Berni swear, but more than that, she'd hated the way Berni's face had lit up when she made that woman laugh. They stood still, twirling the umbrella above them for a moment, before Grete asked her to point the way to St. Matthias.

# BERNI, 1931

"Well. Bernadette Metzger! You're wondering why I called you here."

"Yes, Reverend Mother." Berni sat on her hands, perched on the chair in front of Sister Maria's desk. Her feet jiggled and twitched beneath her as she tried to keep the upper half of her body calm and respectful. She associated this office, with its dark walls and massive desk, with punishment; her knees smarted at the memory of kneeling on rice.

Sister Maria lifted a hand, wide and bony as a duck's foot. The gesture seemed a kind of blessing, and Berni held her breath. "You will be proud to learn that we, against our better judgment, perhaps, have decided to send you to the Ursuline Academy for further study."

Berni focused on the painting of the Virgin above the mantle so that she would not shriek. The Blessed Mother looked peaceful as a pond in her comforting blue cloak, her hands spread open and shaped like doves. "Thank you, Sister Maria. I won't let you down." Somehow Berni kept her voice even. Inside her mind, flowers burst into bloom. Birds took flight.

Sister Maria hadn't yet smiled. Her upper lip pointed down in the center like a turtle's beak. "Do you know why we at St. Luisa's are in the business of teaching girls Latin and history, Bernadette? Girls elsewhere learn only dressmaking, home economics. The liberal education, most people say, is for boys."

Berni shook her head. Her knuckles pressed the backs of her thighs. She still could not believe she'd been chosen. She longed to leap from her chair so that she could tell Grete and dance in the yard.

"The Order decided long ago that you girls should have a chance to learn men's subjects. Most of you will never use them. Yet we expect those of you who study with the Ursulines to continue to prosper. How do you think *you* will use your education?"

This was easy to answer. "I will start a school for the deaf," Berni declared.

Sister Maria leaned over the desk, bringing her broad face into the light. "I see." Her expression was benevolent for once, though there was something behind it Berni could not read. "I will not mince words: I did not choose you for your good behavior. The opposite, in fact. But I could not argue with your academic performance. You seem to do well on examinations, and you are aware the girls who attend the Ursuline Academy sit for the Abitur, the university entrance exam, the same one boys take."

*University.* Berni nodded vigorously.

"Each young lady who fails the exam," Sister Maria continued, "proves to the men of Germany that women have no place taking it. Do you understand?"

"I understand." Berni squirmed. The reverend mother had already told her she needed to take school seriously.

"Good. I have faith in your ability to control your baser instincts."

"I will." Another question lingered on the tip of her tongue, something she knew she should leave for another time, but she could not help asking. "And Grete? Surely if I go, you'll send her in two years? She's a better student than I am."

Sister Maria retreated, pulling her hands into her cowl. "Poor Grete. After she failed the last exam in Latin, I asked her what her favorite subject was. Her response? First aid. It would be a shame to continue putting pressure on her academically, don't you think, Berni?"

Berni tried to keep her voice calm. "Who's pressuring her?"

Sister Maria shrugged. "You don't need a diploma to specialize in *Kinder, Küche, Kirche*, and we both know that's where she's headed. She's a delicate one."

Berni felt her face grow hot. "She enjoyed first aid because she's interested in medicine, not in just being a wife."

"Don't say 'just' a wife, Bernadette. There is nothing wrong with this path. Grete has homely sensibilities; anyone can see that. And if she doesn't find a husband, she can stay here."

Berni's fingers and the tips of her ears were still tingling with the first good news, yet a weight grew in the bottom of her stomach. "Stay here?"

"Yes, we'd be happy to have her join the lay staff. You, with all your energy, may think this the worst place in the world, but I assure you, it is not." Sister Maria pointed upward. "God has a plan for each of us, large and small. Who would pollinate flowers if not the humble bee?"

*But we are not humble bees. We are Metzgers.* "Grete's more than capable. She simply can't hear well, but it's only bad in one ear." It was a relief to say this aloud. Berni waited for a reaction from Sister Maria, but the woman did not blink.

"That's why her voice sounds funny," Berni continued, her voice rising, "and why she doesn't do well in class. If you look closely you'll find she reads and writes better than I do."

The lamp flickered. "I'm aware of this," Sister Maria said shortly. "It's why I'd encourage her to seek another path."

Now it seemed as though the Virgin in her gilt frame was looking past Berni, not at her. She put her hands over her face and then her ears, trying to banish the little voice inside that told her this was true: Grete would shrink and cower at the academy. Berni's breathing grew faster and faster. The reverend mother knew. Sister Lioba must have told her. They knew all about Grete's ears and had never done anything about it.

"Berni. Look at me. You cannot let your ambition set her up for failure."

"You're punishing her!" Berni said at last. She stuck her hands back under her knees to keep them from flying about. "How can you punish Grete because she can't hear well?"

"Punish!" The reverend mother shoved her chair back. Her eyes, and then Berni's, flitted to the corner where she kept a switch. "We at St. Luisa's have been nothing but charitable to you. We've offered both of you shelter, food, an education. Orphans live on the streets and work as prostitutes. Now I've just told you that your sister is welcome to stay here indefinitely, as long as she needs a place, and you accuse me of trying to *punish*?"

Berni shook her head. All her life, she had believed there was indeed a place for Grete and herself, a home, hazy at its edges, with a fireplace warmth at its center. It would be theirs, theirs alone, and once they found it all would be *gemütlich* forever.

On shaking legs, she stood. "If you hold Grete back, simply because of her ailment, I—I will never go to Mass again."

Sister Maria's mouth opened. For a moment, nothing but air wheezed out. "You'd commit yourself to the devil, thinking it would save your sister?" She came around the desk. "Do not poison your sister's spirit, girl."

"Poisoning her?" Berni's throat felt dry all of a sudden. "Not me! Not me!"

"Come here, child." Sister Maria locked Berni's elbow in an iron grip and tried to force her to expose her backside. She was strong, but so was Berni. Berni tucked her thighs, squirming away from the slap. In the process, she twisted Sister Maria's arm. She heard bones creak.

"Hold still—you devil child!"

The room darkened, and Berni wondered if the devil truly had taken her. Sister Maria dove for the switch, but Berni got there first. She stood poised to fight, legs splayed, the whip dangling from her right hand as the reverend mother watched, panic in her eyes.

Berni meant only to scare Sister Maria, to make a noise, to show *she* was in charge now. But as she brought the switch down hard on the edge of the desk, its tail end lashed the sister's face, catching her on the ear and across her cheek. Sister Maria's hand flew to her face, and her eyes widened and filled with tears. As they stared at each other she reminded Berni of the toddlers in the nursery who'd cry in stunned silence in the wake of a nun's slap, and she realized then that Sister Maria was a mere human; they all were.

In the stillness Berni knew she'd destroyed everything, all she'd worked for, all her hopes for herself and Grete, in a single moment. She howled, and threw down the switch; before Sister Maria could grab her arm, she gave the desk a kick. The lamp crackled and went out, and Berni ran down the hall toward the stairs. As she sprinted, she thought about the black mark her shoe must have left on the desk. A Lulu would be the one to clean it.

• • •

Berni barely slept the night after she whipped Sister Maria. Grete had known something was wrong, but Berni had simply turned the other way and stared across the row of beds, unblinking, until dawn. When morning came, she knew, she'd be hauled back to the office and sentenced. It would almost be a relief.

But when the call to rise came, nothing happened. Breakfast, Berni realized with a shiver, would begin with the Angelus, and she'd vowed to stop praying unless Sister Maria relented about Grete and the academy. "You go," she told a puzzled Grete. "I'll be in the refectory a minute behind you." Instead, she wandered for the rest of the day. Bell after bell rang, and for the first time she noticed how the home would thunder with hundreds of feet and then go quiet again, during prayer, chores, and meals.

Her stomach growled. The air in the dormitory began to feel close. At four, the recreation hour, she snuck down into the courtyard, hoping to find Grete before word spread. The girls she passed in the corridors avoided her eyes, or perhaps she was imagining it; she hoped she was.

She hadn't taken two steps out the door when she felt two rough hands seize her arms. She turned to face Hannelore Haas, who had been waiting years to get revenge on Berni for stealing her *Schultüte*. She must have known nobody would stop her now.

"Go ahead," said Berni. Tears were already pooling in her eyes.

Hannelore's blows came quickly, the first grazing Berni's temple, the second landing squarely on her eye with a loud *pop*. Berni's head snapped back on her neck, and for a minute she saw blackness and stars.

She lay on her bed with a cold rag to her eye when Grete came, wringing her hands.

"It's not true, is it, Berni?" Her lips looked white with fear. "You didn't."

"It's your fault," Berni cried, her eye pulsing. The washcloth fell to her lap, and Grete gasped. "Why did you tell Sister Maria you liked first aid? It will be disastrous for us if we don't figure out how to be independent, completely disastrous, don't you understand?"

Grete backed away a few steps, her lip trembling, and Berni's anger fizzled. She reached for Grete. "Never mind, little bird. I'm sorry. So it won't be the academy. It will be something else. I will mend this." She felt Grete shiver. "Don't worry."

• • •

The next day began the same way. When Sister Odi blew her whistle at the front of the dormitory, every girl leapt up, bare feet on the cold floor, except Berni. Sister Odi left her alone. She stayed curled against her pillow, eyes squeezed shut, until she felt someone large and soft plop onto the mattress behind her. She heard the creak of Sister Josephine's knees.

"My dear Berni. My spirited child. It is not too late to repent. This silly disagreement between you and the reverend mother—you should not allow it to consume your soul."

She felt a cool hand against the burning skin of her neck. "Silly? She's against us, Grete and me. She doesn't care. Why should I sit behind her at Mass and pretend she's holy?" Why, she thought, burrowing further into her blanket, should she be the one to give in? The hand withdrew. Sister Josephine seemed to be thinking. Finally she said, "You're wanted in the office. I'm told you're to bring your hidden contraband. Tread carefully, Berni. If you won't take the rest of my advice, at least do this. Tread carefully."

Berni waited until Sister Josephine had gone to sit up, rubbing her eyes. She trudged listlessly back to the scene of violence, the umbrella bumping against her thigh as she walked. She felt like a used dish on its way to a sink of hot water.

She was surprised to find the woman from Fiedler's department store sitting in the office, wearing a green dress and a tilted hat of black felt. When she turned her head, her blond hair swished. She gasped when she saw Berni's eye. "*Du Lieber!* What's happened to this child?"

Sister Maria worked her lower jaw back and forth. The thin red welt running from her earlobe to her chin looked painful. "Bernadette, can you explain your appearance to Fräulein Schmidt?" Her mouth spread smugly, and Berni knew then she'd been in the courtyard and had done nothing. She touched the puffed skin of her eye. Her fingertips felt very cold. Flatly she told Fräulein Schmidt that three girls had held her down and beat her.

"That's what they always say." Sister Maria chuckled. "The fights are never their fault."

"Don't you at least want to ask who hit her?" Fräulein Schmidt asked. "Or call in witnesses?" Berni tried not to grin.

"Berni," said Sister Maria, sounding tired and irritated, "you have something that belongs to Fräulein Schmidt?"

Fräulein Schmidt smiled and thanked Berni when she handed her the umbrella.

"All is settled," Sister Maria said. "You may go, Bernadette."

Before Berni could leave, Fräulein Schmidt grabbed her forearm. "Tell me," she asked the reverend mother. "What do you know of her parents?" Sister Maria froze as Fräulein Schmidt went on. "Are they alive? Do the families ever reclaim the girls?" Berni's heart thudded. For a moment even she thought this woman had gone too far. "Fräulein Schmidt," said Sister Maria. "We do not examine the backgrounds of the girls we raise. Each one starts out the same—humble, as we are all humbled before God."

The two women locked eyes in silence for a while, and then Fräulein Schmidt peered up at Berni from under her asymmetrical hat. "Why don't you wait outside for a little while?"

Berni did as she was told, coughing, dabbing pus out of her eye with her sleeve. Finally, the door opened, and Fräulein Schmidt's slim figure emerged. "It's been decided. You'll come live with me."

The words sounded too good to be true. "Live with you?"

Fräulein Schmidt flexed her fingers, then pulled back a glove to check her watch. "Yes. I live in Schöneberg, on the southern side of Berlin. I have an extra room to let."

Berni hesitated. "The sisters will let me go?"

"Darling," Fräulein Schmidt said gently, "they don't want you corrupting the others."

• • •

In the early morning Berni nudged Grete as soon as she saw a hint of pink through the windows, then went to scrub her face and teeth. When she returned, she found Grete sitting atop the blanket, still in her nightclothes. Her childlike legs, warm and wrinkled from sleep, were curled atop the one wool cardigan Berni planned to smuggle away. She'd been told she could take only one skirt and one blouse, and in the night she'd packed the same for Grete.

"Get dressed," Berni whispered, stroking her sticky hair. "Today we begin a new adventure." Slowly, Grete complied.

Sister Maria waited in the corridor to escort them outside; she did so in silence. The welt on her face was beginning to scab. At the door to the yard, Berni felt a tug at her heart when she saw that Sister Josephine would see them off as well. "I must be getting old," she said, her plump face streaked to the chin with tears. "It seems only yesterday you two came in as babies." She allowed Grete to tuck under her arm, so that Berni could no longer see her face.

After only a minute, a muscular black motorcar growled under the arched entryway to the courtyard, the grille in front as tall as Grete. Fräulein Schmidt hopped down from the driver's side, her red lipstick stark against the flat scenery. "How do you do, Bernadette?" she said, disregarding the two nuns, who seemed ruffled in her presence. "Oh, and Grete! Little Grete, what are you doing here?"

"She's coming with us," Berni said.

"I see. I hadn't realized. Well—all right. I can make space."

Berni turned to Grete, excited now: the last obstacle to their departure had been lifted. The adventure could begin. But Grete hadn't let go of Sister Josephine. This was to be expected; Berni had known there would be some resistance, that Grete needed persuading. She dug through the fabric of Sister Josephine's cloak to find her sister's piping-hot face.

"Come on," Berni said, a frog in her throat. "It'll be fine."

"I'll start the Maybach," Fräulein Schmidt said with a nod to Sister Josephine, and she walked toward the car. A little whimper came from under Sister Josephine's sleeve.

Berni pressed her lips to Grete's ear. "Come now. If we need to escape, we can." The engine started behind them, with terrible timing; it lurched and wheezed.

"I can't," Grete said, her voice tiny. "How do we know what she'll do with us?" Berni wanted to shake her, to force her to see this was their best chance.

Sister Josephine laid her gnarled fingers on top of Berni's and nodded. "I'll make sure she's taken care of, Bernadette." She glanced toward Sister Maria, who stood apart from them, her hands hidden in her cowl.

Berni looked from the black car to Sister Maria, then back to Grete and Sister Josephine. It had started to drizzle. Their faces were wet. Berni kissed Grete's cheek. "There's nothing to fear, little bird. We will be together." Grete remained still, her face squeezed into a grimace. Berni felt as though she'd swallowed an egg. The engine of the car roared behind her. She reached into the pillowcase and took out Grete's blouse and skirt, her white-bristled hairbrush, and finally, after a moment's hesitation, the sweater.

"You'll join me soon," Berni whispered into Grete's ear, then kissed the lobe. "I will not be far from you."

"Bernadette." Sister Maria had called her name. Reluctantly, Berni went to her and looked up at the thin hard line of the sister's mouth, the shape of a crow flying. "If you remember anything about us, remember the values we've taught you," Sister Maria said. "You will see. The devil comes in many forms. Some are not as obvious as others."

What did this mean? Berni hadn't the stomach to ask, or to thank Sister Maria for her advice. "I—" She took a deep breath. "I am sorry, Sister." The words did not come out as sincerely as she'd hoped, but at least she'd spoken them; she'd done it for Grete's sake.

She went to kiss Grete one last time, then climbed into Fräulein Schmidt's motorcar. Through the scratched window she watched Sister Josephine hold tight to her frail blond sister.

As they drove away, Fräulein Schmidt cracked a silver lighter to her cigarette. Berni shut her eyes, already wondering whether it was she or Grete who had made a mistake.

# BERNI, 1931

"This, as you can see, is the parlor." Fräulein Schmidt leaned against the long velvet divan. "I plan to bring the dining table out and convert that room to your bedchamber. The parlor wouldn't look as empty then, *nicht?*"

Berni stepped around the room, touching everything. The intricate plasterwork around the windows cracked a bit under her fingers. In the corner a cello leaned under a portrait of a woman with a rose pinned at her throat. A bowl of figs sat on an end table next to a lipstick-stained napkin and a pile of stems. "I do not think it seems empty," Berni said. The spines of Fräulein Schmidt's books felt worn and well used. Most were collections of sheet music, but Berni also saw volumes of poetry, Virgil's *Aeneid* in the original Latin.

"They told me about you and the academy," Fräulein Schmidt said behind her. "You don't need to go to school to be educated, you know. You can be an autodidact."

"Yes," Berni murmured, more to herself than to Fräulein Schmidt, "it will be a fine place to bring Grete." Her sister was all Berni had spoken of during the car ride, which would have been exhilarating if she hadn't been so distracted. She'd apologized for Grete's timidity around strangers, which she assured Fräulein Schmidt was not personal; she expected Grete to join her here in a matter of weeks.

"I'll allow you to stay a month without paying rent," Fräulein Schmidt said. "But after that I will begin to charge you for the room. A pittance, really. I don't need much money; my father left me this place when he died. He didn't want to, since I'm not married." When she smiled, Berni noticed one tooth in front was slightly darker than the others. "He said at least I'd earn an honest living as a landlady. But so far I am running more of a charity than a boarding house. You might say I've created a home for lost girls of my own."

The last part made Berni shiver. "Where will I get rent money?"

"Oh, there are plenty of things you can do. You can run a coat check, or sell cigarettes, as Anita does—you'll meet her in a moment. And you should call me Sonje, you know. I use the informal *du* with everyone. Though I'm not as Socialist as some of my friends. I like chocolate and eiderdown too much. And these." She held out her cigarette, which was wrapped in jade paper and had a gold tip. "Would you believe these little beauties cost nearly a mark apiece?"

It was all starting to make Berni's head swirl: the smoke, the information. She felt someone's hand on her back and moved aside so that a petite woman with a tight mop of pinkish curls could get to the table; in one sweep she cleared the fig stems and napkin. "Bernadette," Sonje said, her hand on the woman's shoulder. "Meet Frau Pelzer, our housekeeper."

Frau Pelzer shook her hand so hard her shoulder popped in its socket. "Don't tell me you're another picky eater," she said, showing her gold fillings when she laughed.

A housekeeper? Berni could barely stammer a greeting, she felt so overwhelmed. This woman would cook for her? Clean up after her? There had to be a catch. She put a hand to her forehead. "I'm sorry, I—I'm not feeling well."

"Do you need the toilet?" Sonje asked pleasantly, and Frau Pelzer grunted, "I'm not finished bleaching the tiles."

Berni stumbled into the little hallway with its worn red rug. She opened the first door on her right, which turned out to be a linen closet. Instead of holding sheets and towels, the shelves were stacked with cigarettes, cartons of cigars, tins of loose tobacco with bright labels, like tea.

"You can stay in the bedroom on the left," Sonje called to her. "But—ah—Berni—"

Berni put her hand on the knob. What she needed to do now was cry, loudly and messily, into a pillow. But there was already a girl with bright red hair sitting on the bed reading a magazine, her long legs crossed at the kneecaps.

It was the perfume salesgirl, Berni realized in horror, from Fiedler's. "You!" she cried.

The girl snapped her legs underneath her. "You? What are you doing here? Sonje!"

Sonje appeared on the threshold, arms crossed. "Berni, Anita, I hope you'll at least try to be friends, or cordial roommates."

Anita gawked. "She's sleeping in here?"

"Only until I can convert the dining room to a third bedroom."

"I need air," Berni muttered, and she ran out of the room, past Frau Pelzer, who laughed throatily as she yanked open the main door to the apartment. She sat on the front steps of the building, her hands over her ears. A pile of yellow horse dung gathered flies in the road in front of her. Sonje's street, which sloped downward at a steep angle, looked completely unfamiliar. Alien territory, though Berni had walked it with Sonje just minutes before.

• • •

For dinner Frau Pelzer served pickles, crackers, and tinned fish. "Sorry for the cold meal, girls," Sonje said over a newspaper. She had several papers spread over the table.

Berni had to wring her hands to keep from grabbing all the food. She couldn't remember the last time she'd eaten. She'd have bolted it down if Anita hadn't been watching her closely.

"Something to read, Berni?" asked Sonje. "Perhaps *Germania*, that's the Catholic Centre Party's paper. Or *Berliner Tageblatt*, for Social Democrats. Ah, here's *Deutsche Zeitung*, my personal favorite." She smiled. "The rag of the anti-Semites."

Berni recoiled. "Your favorite? That's disgusting."

Anita dabbed her mouth, leaving black cherry smudges on the tissue. "She's Jewish, you pointy-head," she said. "She's joking when she says it's her favorite."

Berni considered this for a moment, wondering if she'd ever spoken to a Jew before. She knew better than to check for horns under Sonje's hair; the sisters had told the girls this was a myth. It was Anita who interested Berni more. Powder coated her skin like new snow, making the landscape flawless but stark, a harsh contrast to the scarlet wig. Her eyebrows were delicate as cricket legs, her jaw broad and lips full; they became a deeper pink as she ate and abraded them with bread. She tossed her pilsner down and slammed the foam-laced glass on the table. "What the hell are you looking at?"

"Nothing."

Anita's laugh was a high, nervous staccato, a bird's warning. "Your new friend needs to practice her manners," she told Sonje.

Sonje folded back a page of her paper. "Oh, you were staring, too."

After dinner, Berni dallied in the parlor, waiting for Anita to go to sleep. It was out of the question for Grete to join her while they still had to share a room with Anita. She'd have to put her sister off until Sonje found a bed for the dining room.

Before Sonje turned in, she handed Berni a slim red hardcover. "You should fill your mind with genius before sleep. Have you read Rilke?"

Berni opened the book to a well-read page. "Ich bin auf der Welt zu allein . . ." She shut the book with a bang. "No." She *was* feeling "too alone in the world," far too alone to read Rilke.

"Hmm." Sonje looked over the titles in the hallway bookcase. "Aha! Reliable Nesthäkchen." She handed Berni *Nesthäkchen and the*

*World War* by Else Ury. "I loved these as a child. But don't stay up late. Tomorrow Anita will take you to the Medvedev, to learn to sell."

"To sell?"

"Cigarettes."

Berni shrugged. She took the book into the bedroom, where she was disappointed to find Anita fully dressed, glowering at her over the mattress. Her knobby fingers hovered over her buttons. "I bet you'd like to see me nude. You wait in the hall. I'm not a lesbian like you."

"I'm no lezzie," Berni said, familiar with the word; it was a favorite accusation among Lulus. She waited outside the bedroom, feeling Hannelore's fist against her eye with every beat of her heart. When she went in she found Anita wearing a nightgown, her enormous eyes protruding from the top of the quilt. Not only had she left her wig on, but she also hadn't taken any steps to excavate the makeup. Berni climbed in beside her, lying on the very edge of the bed.

"Aren't you going to change your clothes?" Anita asked.

"Aren't *you* going to remove your hair?" For years Berni had wanted nothing more than to get rid of this old dirndl, and now she clung to it. It was the last dress Grete had seen her in. She lay back and opened the book. A smudge of what looked like red jam sat in the upper corner of the page. Nesthäkchen, the doctor's daughter, was complaining to her grandmother that only boys were allowed to fight in the war.

With every flip and flop Anita made, the mattress creaked. "My sister and I had a rule," Berni said, yanking the quilt her way. "You choose a position and then you stay there."

"Another word about your sister, and I'll scream."

Berni ignored her. She read until her eyelids drooped from exhaustion. She did not want to be alone with her thoughts for long.

• • •

The Medvedev, on the other side of a horseshoe-shaped park near Sonje's apartment, was a dim Russian bar filled with more afternoon drinkers than Berni had expected. Men slumped on stools, and Anita prowled among them with a little tray. "Walkure . . . Walkure . . . Gold tips. Walkure No. 4," she whispered in their ears. Berni watched in disgust as Anita's fingers curled under the men's hair. Some kissed her hand; some groaned, rolled their eyes, and pulled out the requisite bills. Most seemed more interested in the radio, which was tuned to a Socialist broadcast.

"I go home for supper," Anita said later, counting her cash as they leaned against the wall, "then return for the evening shift. That's when you get the good tips." So far she seemed to enjoy playing Berni's guide, treating her as if she knew nothing.

Nobody had mentioned Anita's job as a perfume girl at Fiedler's, and Berni felt a little bit of wicked satisfaction when she asked Anita why she wasn't needed at Libations today.

Anita sniffed. "I don't work there anymore. As they put it, 'the novelty had worn off.'"

Berni was trying to figure out what this meant when she noticed Lev, the Medvedev's owner, making sharp gestures at Anita from the front of the restaurant. Anita slipped her money back into her pocket and sighed. "He doesn't like me counting it in front of customers."

It was then Berni noticed the girl tucked inside the coat check. She had a round face and big, sad eyes; she looked like the littlest matryoshka doll in a set. Ignoring Anita's protests, Berni crossed the room to talk to Lev. He eyed her suspiciously underneath wild eyebrows that fanned toward each other like dove's wings.

"Tell me," she said. "Are you hiring coat check girls?"

He took her in: the gray dirndl she refused to take off, her greasy black braids. "You are not coat check girl material."

"Not me, my sister. A little blonde angel." In the coat check room, Grete would still have to see what went on in a place like this, but at least she'd be secluded. At least she'd be safe.

Lev sneered. "Mischa is my daughter. Believe me when I say I do not even *need* to hire a coat check girl, especially this time of year. But I have to keep an eye on her, is that right?" A stream of Russian poured from his mouth, and the girl pursed her lips.

"Let us see if you can even sell a cigarette, eh?" he said to Berni, crossing his arms. She stomped back to Anita and grabbed at her tray. "Let me try."

"What?" Anita's left eyebrow, penciled red, rose an inch. "I haven't taught you—"

The strap was already over Berni's head. She approached the bar, holding out a single box of cigarettes with a red airplane on the cover; she realized, when she turned to see Anita and Lev smirking at her, that she hadn't a clue how much each of them cost.

"Josetti, *meine Herren?*" she asked men who ignored her. "Smooth and . . ." Every sad face at the bar already had a cigarette in its lips, dropping ash. She moved on to the tables. "Come on," she told one particularly hard-looking man with great loops of dark skin under his eyes, "you're making yourself look cheap."

"Piss off," he said, looking toward the radio. "I'm trying to listen."

She tried offering the tins shaped like bullets, the one with a winged victory goddess on the box, but nobody gave her a second look. She was ready to give up when she felt someone palm her ass as she passed his table. Not a pinch or slap, or even a grab, but a long, slow swipe, covering both sides of her derrière. She whirled around to see a younger man wearing the broadcloth cap, but clearly German, not Russian.

"Relax," he said, "I'll put something in your tip bowl."

Berni reached down and pressed her thumb into his eye.

The other men at his table started laughing as he shrieked, covering his eye, calling Berni every obscenity she'd ever heard, plus some new ones. Lev and Anita came running. "Is there blood?" The man pried his eye open as Lev murmured, "Let me see, let me see."

"He touched me!" Berni spat. "On my bottom, like he owned it!" She could tell Anita was trying not to laugh. Their eyes met, Anita's sparkling. Soon the two of them had collapsed into giggles.

"What is this girl's name?" the man spat. "Better not see her again, Lev, or I swear—"

"Her name is Berni," said Lev, "and she is only training, *mein Herr.*" He glared at her with his hand on the man's shoulder.

"Berni!" Now the man began to laugh, still holding his eye. He whispered something to his companions. "You should not hire another one, Lev, they're nothing but trouble."

"No, no." Anita laughed lightly. "Berni, it's short for Bernadette, not Bernard."

Everyone except Berni laughed together now, and she felt a prickle of panic. What were they talking about? "How's my given name your business?"

"Calm down, honey," said another man at the table. "When a big girl like you runs around with a *Transvestit,* well, people are going to get confused."

"*Transvestit?*" Berni looked from the men to Anita. Anita was hiding her face behind her cupped hand, and her shoulders were shaking, but she made no sound.

The table of men were laughing so hard they'd dropped to their knees. Berni growled. She'd had enough of letting all of them get the better of her. "*Transvestit,*" she said to Anita. "If you don't tell me what it means, I'll tell Sonje."

All color had drained from Anita's face. Her hands shook as she yanked her skirt down, giving Berni the feeling the joke was on her as well. Even Lev seemed to be in league against them, now that his customers were laughing and happy. "Here," he said, trying to lift the hem of Anita's skirt. "Show her. Show her!"

Anita pinched her knees together. Her face became a mask of panic, her eyes wild, and Berni remembered a time she'd seen a group of men in an alley with a cornered dog, kicking it for fun.

She took off running, out the door and into honking traffic. She ran over the mottled lawn of the park, past a group of picnickers opening champagne on a blanket. After a minute she realized someone followed her. She heard a pair of ridiculous high heels slapping the path, heard Anita's breath wheezing closer and closer behind, but she did not stop. She ran as though lions were chasing her.

She burst into the apartment to find Sonje on the telephone; she took one look at Berni, murmured a goodbye, then hung up. "What is the matter?" she asked, standing up when Anita came close behind, panting. Each breath sounded like a cry.

"I want to leave now," Berni said. She felt heat coming from Anita. "The men at the Medvedev said Anita was a *Transvestit* and that I was too. I don't want to catch what she has."

"I don't understand, Berni. Of course you aren't . . ." Sonje put two fingers between her eyes. "Berni, I—my God, I never did explain, did I? I thought it was obvious . . . my, my." She tapped the table. "You won't catch what she has, *nicht*? It's how she was born."

"This is *not* how I was born," Anita said to the floor. "It's how I made myself."

"Oh yes, yes of course," Sonje said.

Berni looked from one to the other, her face and fists growing hot. "Fine, speak in riddles. I don't care. Just take me back—get me away from—from *her*."

Sonje sighed and sat back in her chair, arms crossed. "Goodness, Anita, is there anything worse than aggressive stupidity?"

The corner of Anita's mouth twitched.

"Goethe," Sonje told Berni.

Berni stamped her foot and ran for the bedroom. She began gathering her few belongings into her pillowcase: one hairbrush, a pair of underpants. The problems of her previous life seemed so simple now. The sisters, frigid as they could be, had never managed to make her feel so ignorant, so foolish. Why hadn't she tried harder to cooperate with them?

After a moment she heard the front door to the apartment slam, and then a soft knock at her bedroom door. "Go away," she called.

Sonje stood on the threshold and watched her for a while. "So, you are leaving already."

"I am."

"Your life has not been easy, Berni." She took a seat on the bed. "I thought you might understand her. Your parents are dead. Hers are alive, but they feel their son is dead."

Berni covered her ears. She saw the veins in Anita's hands, her hollow cheeks, the wide jaw and skinny neck. "You let me share a bed with a boy!" she cried. "And the men thought I was, too, since I ran around with a—*Transvestit*."

"There is no boy here," Sonje said softly. "She is Anita. She desires men, same as me, same as you. You don't call her 'boy.' It's *sie*."

Berni's head spun. Did she desire men? "That's ridiculous."

"Bernadette, if you leave us, where would you go? I won't let you live on the street. And I don't think you can return easily to the sisters."

"They'd take me," Berni said, but she wasn't sure.

Sonje did not say anything. They listened to the wall clock, which seemed to Berni to grow louder with each tick. Finally Sonje cleared her throat. "I had a chance to attend an academy myself as a girl, a music conservatory. My father was a composer, and to him I was more a protégée than a daughter. After the conservatory rejected me, he would not speak to me." She picked a thread on the quilt. "He must have known I'd blown the audition on purpose."

"Why?"

"I don't know. Why do we sabotage ourselves? I suppose we each had our reasons." Sonje stood and flicked dust off her skirt. "I found Anita two years ago," she said in a hardened voice, "unconscious under a nightclub table. Try to imagine how she'd react, hearing us discuss the opportunities we've had the luxury of throwing away." When she left she closed the door to the bedroom, plunging Berni into darkness.

• • •

A few nights later Sonje took both of them to the Tingel-Tangel in Mitte to meet her lover, Gerrit. The air inside was thick with smoke, shot through with electric theater lights, but they soon found him at a round table close to the action. A girl performed a contortionist piano act onstage, back-bending over the keys.

"Pleased to meet you," Gerrit said as he took Berni's hand. Like Sonje, he used the *du* form. "Comradess Berni."

"You as well," Berni said, taking a seat. She wasn't sure what to call him—Comrade? His peaked canvas cap sat on the table in front of him, and his shirt was coarsely woven. His face, however, had a raw smoothness suggesting a recent shave by a skilled barber, and his fair hair looked clean. Too well-groomed to be a real Communist, Berni thought, though his attractiveness certainly didn't seem to bother Anita. She sat with her back to the stage, her lashes fluttering at him like fervent moths.

Today Anita had offered to lend Berni clothing in what seemed a peace offering of sorts: a skirt and Bemberg stockings made of rayon. "Much better than real silk for preventing foot odor," she'd said. She looked slightly disappointed when Berni chose to borrow wool jodhpurs and a gray cloche hat from Sonje.

The men's voices at the Medvedev echoed in Berni's ears: *another one.* Did wearing trousers make her a *Transvestit?* If so, she didn't care. She'd had her fill of ugly dresses long ago.

Four beers appeared on their table, and Berni passed one to Anita, receiving a slight nod in return. For the past few days she and Anita had been polite to each other, if stiff. Berni had begun sleeping on a pallet on the floor of the dining room. Yesterday Anita had taken her to the Silver Star, where Berni had done much better selling cigarettes. Shockingly, everyone there seemed to treat Anita as if she were normal; there were even others like her. Still, Berni found she could not help looking for the boy beneath the girl. Even now, as she watched Anita paint her lips Coty dark, she stared at the faint ghost of hair on her upper lip.

"How did you come to befriend Sonje?" Gerrit asked Berni, his arm interlaced with Sonje's. Berni explained briefly why she had to leave St. Luisa's.

Sonje tittered and said something about Berni's moxie, but Gerrit shook his head. "Those nuns," he said, "send the academy the girls they think worthy of joining the middle class. Your sister, with her defect, wouldn't make the cut."

"Enough politics for now," said Sonje. Berni watched the stage. In St. Luisa's she'd have slapped anyone who said "defect."

Gerrit went on as the pianist completed her solo. ". . . defenders of capitalism are loath to allow proletarians a hint of social mobility. You should be proud you refused them."

Should she? She missed her sister. Today she felt the sting of her absence more painfully than ever before. She tried to think what the girls at St. Luisa's would be doing this evening. Bible story time with Sister Josephine; it seemed so distant from the Tingel-Tangel that it might have been happening on another continent.

Berni's beer felt cold in her hand and in the pipes of her throat. She watched a stocky emcee appear at the corner of the stage, followed by a spotlight that adjusted itself a few times. "Ladies and gentlemen, let's turn our attention to the mech-an-i-cal."

Six young women chugged onstage in a little train, wearing military jackets and sheer hose. "We hear it everywhere—everything's become too mechanical. Transportation. Communication. Even the act of love!"

The girls thrust out their hips to a drumbeat. Someone whistled.

The emcee tugged his bowtie. "My friends, Berlin is healthier than it's ever been. Look at how productive we are. We make coal. Rubber. Steam!" Six little clouds of white smoke puffed up behind each girl's rear end, and in unison, their eyes popped. The crowd laughed and clapped. Berni turned with mouth open to Anita, who shrugged as if to say she'd seen it before.

"Love in Berlin has become mech-an-i-cal, they say. But we know our city still has its beating heart." Now each of the dancers ripped a panel off the chest of her military jacket, revealing six round left breasts.

Berni was enthralled. She couldn't help it. Those breasts! Each a perfect sphere or cone, the faces above coldly beautiful, captivatingly stoic. She peered over her shoulder to see the crowd's reaction through the dim smoky air, and jumped when she found Anita crouched behind her. "Tell Sonje I'm headed to a party."

Berni glanced toward Sonje, who had her face tucked against Gerrit's. "Why leave now?" she asked Anita. "The show's just started."

"I'm through with this tired old bit," Anita said, and turned away with a flounce.

Berni took pulls of her beer, growing bored and embarrassed by her tablemates' necking. By the end of the routine, the dancers were wearing very little. When finally Sonje resurfaced, she glanced toward the exit, then pulled Berni close. "Anita auditioned for this dance line once." Around them, the crowd burst into applause. "You can see why she wasn't chosen."

The alcohol was beginning to make Berni feel dizzy, and very sorry for Anita. "I'll just make sure she's okay," she said and stumbled out, bumping the backs of chairs as she went.

She found Anita standing on the curb, one bony arm flung out to hail cabs. "So," she said, sucking the end of her cigarette. "You'd like to see the real Berlin." She yanked Berni's arm down when she tried to signal a car. "We want a cyclonette. Cheaper. Look for the cabs with three wheels." Eventually they found one, and Anita gave the driver an address. They drove past the opera, then under the Brandenburg Gate, which glowed pale purple.

"Sonje likes to pretend she's so modern sometimes, she and Gerrit looking at tits."

Berni hadn't heard Anita criticize Sonje before; it felt a bit titillating. "Well," she said, to be contrary, "I thought the show was clever."

"Clever? Come on, it's a tit show."

"It's satire. A commentary on modern life."

Anita snorted. "Satire. No matter how they try to dress up *Girlkultur*, my friend, it's naked girls on a stage."

Berni paused. Should she let on that she knew Anita had auditioned? "Look," she said after a while. "I'm sorry I ran from you the other day. At the Medvedev."

Anita shrugged, picking lint off her stockings. "It doesn't matter. I don't like it either, what I am." They were almost to the other end of the Tiergarten now, and Anita's expression lifted. She pointed toward a stately, darkened building. "But I won't be this way for long. There's the Institute for Sexual Science, have you heard of it?"

"They cure homophiles?"

"In a manner of speaking. They can make a man into a woman."

Berni stared at her, nearly speechless. "You mean they'd—they'd cut it."

"Snip, snip." In the electric city glow Anita's face went from soft and angelic to sharp and sly. "Then I'll find a handsome Gerrit of my own. All I need is a Gerrit. I don't have expensive taste, like Sonje. I don't need someone like Herr Trommler to take care of me."

"Herr Trommler?"

"Who do you think owns the Maybach? Not Sonje. Pretty women like Sonje always have a daddy. Trommler . . . *ach*. Picture a man the size of a Holstein steer."

Berni had thought of Sonje as independent. The news of Trommler depressed her.

"We'll get out here," Anita called when they arrived at a row of tenements. At the door, she tugged on her skirt a few times, then rang a buzzer. Berni could hear the party before she reached the flat, could feel it through the soles of her shoes. Inside they were met with a blast of heat and dark. Perspiring people danced: men with women, men with men, women with women.

A man in bloomers mopped at the exotic rug, his hairy, pale thighs showing under the ruffles. "Anita!" he shouted over the music when he finished. He was dressed as a baby, in a bonnet, with a rattle and pacifier hanging around his neck.

"Max," she purred, "I didn't know we were to come in costume." Her shoulder and chin seemed drawn to each other by magnets.

Max's belly brushed Berni's hip. "But you are in costume, dear. You're Anita Berber."

Berni thought the costume comment wouldn't go over well, but Anita fluttered her false eyelashes, draping a long-fingered hand across her bony chest. "Max, I go by Anita Bourbon. *Der Berber*, may she rest in peace."

"Who's Anita Berber?" said Berni, and Max and Anita both squealed in disbelief.

"She was a famous nude dancer and actress," Anita told Berni. "Taken from us too soon."

"Some say of a sex accident, some of an overdose." Max put his pacifier in his mouth.

Anita handed Berni a drink that sparkled and excused herself to talk to another man in a fox fur with claws. Berni stood by the wall, glad to have something in her hand. She watched Anita's friend produce a vial from his purse, and from it he and Anita took a miniature spoon and put it in their noses. Anita caught her watching. Her lips formed the words *don't tell Sonje*.

Berni nodded and found a seat on one of the satin sofas. Next to her a girl and boy were wrapped around a pipe with a glowing orange end. The boy elbowed Berni, his eyelids with their white eyelashes drooping. Pale orange freckles dotted his cheeks and elfin nose. "It's your turn."

"Karl," his companion whined, "we don't have much more."

The pipe smelled like Eastern spices. "No, thanks."

Karl waved the pipe in front of Berni's face. "This will make you relax."

How different from a cigarette could it be? Berni inhaled and handed it back to Karl.

"What about him?" Karl pointed to Anita, who stood alone now, peering over the tops of people's heads, looking for someone. "Isn't that your friend?"

"*Her*," Berni corrected him. She felt suddenly protective of Anita. "It's her. *Sie*."

Karl blinked slowly. "I don't understand."

Berni's mind had slowed. She looked at the men's clothing on the girl beside Karl, at the outfit she herself had chosen, the jodhpurs and suspenders. They weren't called "he," but Anita was "she," and Anita was "she" all the time. Berni watched Anita's dark nervous eyes dart around the room, and a sad thought came to her: *How complicated Anita's life is* . . . She looked so vulnerable that Berni would have stood and embraced her if her legs hadn't turned to lead.

Berni watched, as if through water, as the baby-man approached Anita and put his hands on her thighs, rubbing up and down roughly, as an ungainly child might pet a cat. Berni took another pull off the pipe when the boy put it to her lips, surprised to find that she did relax. Karl kissed her on the cheek. She shut her eyes and felt very good indeed, and for a while, wrapped in Karl's pale arms, she forgot Anita.

Berni did not wake until someone threw her arm around his neck. His elbow went under her knees, and as he lifted her against his chest, she smiled, happy for someone to carry her somewhere. Her eyes opened and she caught a hazy glimpse of a dark beard where she'd expected the smooth curve of Karl's jaw. But then, from far away, she heard Anita's voice: *Not her, that one's sixteen, and hasn't been touched deeply yet.* Then Berni was put back on the cushion, and then she was left alone.

Just before she was engulfed in sleep, a thought came to her, perhaps the first clear thought she'd had since she arrived at Sonje's. Incorporating Grete into this life would be difficult. As difficult as weaving a satin ribbon through burlap.

# SOUTH CAROLINA, 1970

The fly had grown comfortable enough to entwine its back legs and let down its sucker. Janeen could have killed it, if she had a swatter; instead she watched it take minuscule gulps of a buttermilk biscuit. For a minute she wished she had one of those machines from the movies, through which she and the fly could switch bodies; how gladly she'd trade her slouching frame in its elephant-leg trousers for a pair of wings! She gazed out the banquet room's lone window, aching to buzz past the moss-draped oak outside and take to the skies.

Her mother rested a large hand on Janeen's shoulder, bringing her back to the buffet at the luncheon following her father's funeral. An impromptu receiving line had formed. Yet another neighbor had made a forced nice comment about how big she'd grown, something wildly inappropriate to tell a five-foot-ten seventeen-year-old.

"Here we are," her mother, Anita, murmured close to her ear, her cologne thick in Janeen's nose. "Another vulture. Lacey!" she greeted the next sympathetic well-wisher.

It both amazed and irritated Janeen that her mother, who wasn't even a born-and-bred American, played this game so much better than she did. "Southerners will tolerate some eccentricity, as long as they can make of you a sort of pet," Anita had said just that morning as she buttoned her white polyester shirt, a purchase from the men's department at Sears. "To a few, I am their German pet."

Janeen felt fairly certain she, herself, was nobody's pet. Lacey Callahan, mother to the junior prom queen, approached her with the same bless-your-heart smile her daughter had perfected, her teeth hard and white as squares of gum. "Oh, he was a wonderful man, y'all," Lacey cooed. "So . . . jolly. I thought you might've buried him with a tumbler in hand. My Lord, never saw the man without his drink!" She laughed behind her fingers, the nails Pepto pink.

Janeen might have slapped Mrs. Callahan if it hadn't been for Anita, who tapped her chin. "An interesting idea, but as you saw earlier, Remy opted for cremation."

Mrs. Callahan's smile cracked a little. "I—yes. I *was* at the service, o'course."

"Of course. Biscuit?" Anita asked, reaching for the one the fly had been nibbling. She plopped it on Mrs. Callahan's paper plate.

As Mrs. Callahan melted back into the crowd, Janeen's teeth shredded her chapped lips. How many people in this room had really known her father? How many cared he was gone? "I can't do this much longer," she murmured to her mother.

Anita squeezed her around the shoulders. "At least we are not wallowing at home, *Liebchen*. And this crowd is making your father in heaven laugh."

*In heaven.* Janeen felt her stomach flip. Her father, who had been perfectly well seven months ago, was in heaven. And here she and her mother were, smiling sadly as people they hardly knew filled their plates with pasta salad.

Then she noticed a scruffy little man lingering beside a fake ficus tree, a young girl on his hip. She crossed the room in ten strides, never taking her eyes off of him. He wasn't much taller than she— the height came from her mother—and he looked a bit frightened as she gazed down into his eyes.

"You came," she said breathlessly, unsure if she should hug him. "Everett. Maisy. You're the only family who came."

Her mother had warned her not to expect any of Remy's Louisiana relatives to show. They were notorious homebodies— "Hermits, almost," Anita claimed—who Janeen saw but once every five or ten years. But she had made a point to call Everett, her father's favorite cousin from childhood. She peered into his face now, trying to find any trace of her tanned, swarthy father in his features. With his thinning hair and sad-dog eyes, Everett Lefevre was at best a watered-down version of the man she'd lost.

Everett hefted Maisy on his hip. He'd borrowed a shirt for the occasion, she could tell; the seams fell far below his shoulders. Tears welled in her eyes. "A cryin' shame, all of this," he said. "And you so young."

Janeen swallowed. "I'm not so young," she told Everett, and she meant it. She felt like she'd been zapped overnight into middle age. She touched Maisy's small white shoe. "I'm sure glad you're here."

"Daddy told me not to touch the vase," said Maisy.

"The vase?"

"She means the urn," Everett whispered.

For a moment Janeen couldn't look at them. Everett slid Maisy to the ground, and Janeen felt his arm go stiffly around her, then drop. At least he seemed genuinely sad, unlike the others in the room, who appeared anxious to make their tee times.

"A shame your daddy isn't here to give you comfort. Ironic, I guess."

"Ironic?" She looked down; Maisy had pressed a tea tassie into her hand. "Ironic how?"

"Maybe that's not the right word." He tugged his collar. "I meant because the same thing happened to him, you know, and he just a little older than you."

The pecans in Janeen's mouth turned to stones. "I didn't know he was that young when Granddad died."

"Well, sure. His daddy had the same thing, early cancer of the prostate. Runs in the family. I'm lucky it's my mother who was a Moore . . ."

Janeen half-listened, watching Anita. Her hair had grayed significantly in the past year. She wore it as short as Mia Farrow's in *Rosemary's Baby* and dressed in men's shirts and trousers, never a bra. Her flat chest, she quipped, helped her "support" women's lib. She had her hand on Mr. Beecham's shoulder—the owner of the restaurant where Remy had worked for twenty years.

"Did my mother know about this? About Granddad having prostate cancer, too?"

"Uh, I'd think so." Poor Everett seemed to know he'd stepped in something. "Your father would've told her, right? When they talked about their families?"

"My mother wouldn't have told him about her family." Anita acted as though she had no history, as if she'd washed up on the shores of America fully formed, like Aphrodite, or a piece of sea glass, broken and beaten but remade into something better. "And she tells me nothing."

She left poor Everett in midsentence and strode toward her mother. She didn't even acknowledge Mr. Beecham. "I'm walking home," she announced, drowning out his platitudes.

*"Liebchen."* Anita lifted a damp, dark curl off Janeen's forehead. Now that they were close, Janeen could see red at the corners of her brown eyes and around the rims of her nostrils. But when had she wept? She'd been stiff and erect as a lightning rod throughout the service. "Do not run off alone. We have been invited to Charlotte's for supper. They will close the restaurant tonight in honor of your father, so that we who knew him might dine together, reminisce . . ."

"I'm sorry," Janeen said in Mr. Beecham's direction, without meeting his eyes. As she fled her mother managed to grab her fingertips, calling her name. Eyes closed, lashes wet, Janeen wrenched herself free, knuckle by knuckle.

• • •

A few mornings after Remy's funeral, Anita went back to work.

"I do not think I need explain, *Liebchen,* why I must return so soon to the library," she'd said the night before as they watched television. "We need money, for one. Also it will be good for me to have my hands busy. You will see, when you return to lifeguarding. It is a shame you aren't in school right now."

"Yeah. Would've been nicer of Daddy to die in the fall." Janeen stuffed her mouth with the last of her TV dinner.

"Janeen, for hell's sake!"

"Mutti, it's 'for heaven's sake.' No one says 'for hell's sake.'" A newspaper lay on the ottoman in front of Janeen; she tented it in front of her so that her mother wouldn't see she was about to cry. Anita would only act dismissive. *"Chaneen,"* she would croon in her accent, "it will all be okay." It was not supposed to all be okay. They were supposed to be sad. To be angry. To throw things.

"Heaven, hell, whatever it is. You know what I mean." Anita got to her feet, the long bones in her toes cracking, and went to adjust the rabbit ears. Onscreen, Marlo Thomas had her toe stuck in a bowling ball. The laugh track echoed. "You have been acting as if your father's death is my fault. And I think it is a bit unfair, considering I am mourning him too."

Janeen said nothing, staring with glazed eyes at the U.S. section of the paper. On the third page was a photograph of a father and daughter on a beach. The man was swinging his little girl by the arms, and the girl's head was thrown back, her mouth open in adoring laughter.

"If you become lonely tomorrow, Janeen, have lunch with me in Shortleaf Park." Anita ran her hand over her head, leaving rake marks in her short, sweaty hair.

Janeen said nothing. She took a second look at the man and his lucky daughter. They'd been photographed from a distance, and the image was grainy. Then she noticed the second photo that accompanied the article, one of a fair, hawk-nosed young man in a black cap and gray jacket, silver bars on his collar. A swastika on his sleeve.

She sat up, knocking her fork to the carpet; she ignored her mother's squawk. "Neighbor Claims Missing Man Is Former Nazi," the headline declared. Henry Klein, the man in the beach photo, had been missing for over a month. Before his disappearance, a woman had reported she recognized him as Klaus Eisler, a former officer in the SS intelligence service.

"Huh. Look at this." Janeen spread the newspaper down on the ottoman. "A Nazi was living in Florida."

"Psst," Anita replied, pretending to spit. "May they catch him and string him up by the little hairs." Her eyes flitted briefly toward the article. Then she did a double-take. She brought Janeen's arm closer, her fingers cold and rigid. In the blue light from the television, her face seemed drained of color.

"Mutti," Janeen murmured, "did you know this man?"

"Did I know him!" Anita rolled her eyes and snorted, horselike, but Janeen noticed that the hand holding her tumbler of schnapps seemed to shake.

"It says he grew up in Berlin, like you."

"Berlin is a large city, *Liebchen*, didn't you know?" Anita squeezed her dark eyes shut once, twice, as though she were using her lids to erase what she'd just seen. Her mouth set itself in a hard line. "It is time for me to fall asleep, and so should you. Stop reading this nonsense."

"Okay," Janeen said, her eyes on the page.

"And it would not hurt if you would take a minute to clean out the refrigerator in the morning." With that, she'd gone to bed. Janeen had stayed on the sofa for hours, waking only when faint light began to creep under the drapes. The newspaper lay over her lap like a blanket. Her fingers and the side of her face were stained with black ink.

That morning, alone in the house for the first time in she didn't know how long, she opened the refrigerator. It smelled terrible.

Casseroles wrapped in aluminum foil or plastic were shoved in every which way, behind which she and her mother had let fruit and vegetables molder, a carton of milk turn lumpy. A hastily wrapped block of Cheddar bore green spores. Science experiments, her father would have called them.

At the back of the top shelf, Janeen saw why her mother couldn't bring herself to throw out the spoiled food. There was the final pie her father had baked, peach crumb. Late at night, after they'd come back from the hospital, her mother had been taking tiny bites directly from the dish with a fork. Now white fuzz dotted its surface.

Janeen stared at the glass dish for a while. Her father's last pie. His blunt fingertips had crimped the edges of the crust. He'd softened the peach cubes in butter and brown sugar. Come fall, the apples on her father's favorite scruffy tree would rot on their branches. Come Thanksgiving, there would be no bourbon crème, no chocolate pluff mud pie. A vision flashed past: Janeen and her mother parked glumly in front of a Christmas special, freezer meals on their laps. Silence between them. For a minute, she couldn't move.

And then she could. She yanked the dish from the fridge, took it to the garbage can, and shook it until the pie went *splat* across the top of the trash. The underside of the crust looked naked and exposed, shattered into a dozen pieces. She put her wrist to her forehead, breathing hard. Anita had never been sentimental or delicate, but she should have known Janeen wouldn't want to do this by herself.

Anita's own father had passed away when she was a girl. Shouldn't she have understood? All she would say about it was that she'd lost her parents at a very young age—too young to remember, she said. Too young to grieve?

• • •

For a while that afternoon, Janeen lay on her stomach in the spare bedroom, which would have been her sibling's if her parents had another child. Instead it hosted their record player and her father's rarely used banjo.

Lately, she'd been dying for a sibling.

Their house was a ranch, the windows low enough for her to watch blue-black birds nip insects off the tops of the grass. Through the screens she could smell pine resin and, from the salty flats of the Lowcountry, a hint of brine. The grass needed a trim, the tops of scattered blades turning to seed.

Tending to the yard had always been her mother's job. She was the only woman in the neighborhood who could operate a lawnmower, which she did with vigor as she chain-smoked. As a kid, Janeen had sometimes wished her parents would fit in better, that they'd act like normal people. Like squares. Most people's parents were squares, even though they tended to be ten years younger than hers. Remy and Anita had gone to outdoor concerts and sat on blankets holding hands. On more than one occasion they'd come back smelling of pot. Her father baked. Her mother was a librarian's assistant who tinkered with their cars in her spare time. When they danced together at weddings, they'd always joked that she liked to take the lead.

People in Pine Shoals always assumed her mother was a war bride, but her parents had met in a bakery in Atlanta right after the war. Her mother had just been let go from a munitions factory, and her father, back from France, had taken the morning shift at a bakery.

Every day at five o'clock in the morning, before anyone else arrived, her mother would be waiting outside the door. Face gaunt, her hair chopped at uneven angles, she'd mumble her order: apple streusel and a coffee. After weeks of watching her stare out the window and take long bites of cake, Remy sat down at her table, and immediately she moved to put on her jacket.

"Must leave," she told him abruptly. "I must go."

At first, Remy had found her rude. And when he heard the accent, the one they'd mocked and cursed on the battlefield, he'd almost left her alone. But then he noticed how her long-boned hands—the nails painted red, but shredded, chipped—shook on the Formica, her cup rattling against its white saucer. "Just let me finish my coffee," he said. "We don't have to talk."

At this, she seemed to relax. After a while she cleared her throat. "From where I came . . ." she began, and he flinched again at the accent, "people have cup of coffee and cake in afternoon, then, walk. You will walk with me, in the park?" She smiled, her teeth crooked and gapped, and he realized then how lonely she was.

That first day, she taught him a word in German: *Waldeinsamkeit*, the sensation of being alone and content in the woods. "But you aren't alone," he protested as they strolled through Piedmont Park, a few blocks from traffic. "I'm spoiling it." And she smiled at him and told him it was sometimes possible to be alone together.

As a young child, Janeen would request this bit of family lore at bedtime, brushing aside *Cinderella* or *Sleeping Beauty* in favor of her parents' romance. But as she grew, questions surfaced. Why had her mother been so sad? Why did she work in a factory? Where did she go before Atlanta?

Her father's answers were short: because she missed the people she had to leave in Germany; because she wanted to help America win the war; New York City. Ask your mother, he'd say when Janeen pressed for details. But her mother never told the story.

Lying on the floor of the spare room, Janeen tried reading a dime-store mystery for a while to take her mind off her parents. The words blurred on the page. Finally, at two, she plunged into the heat to get the mail. The envelopes scorched her hands a little, like cookies from the oven. She leafed through catalogs and bills; at the back of the stack was a letter addressed to Anita Moore. There was no return address, but the stamp had been canceled in Manhattan.

Something about it sent a shiver down her arms. She took the envelope up to the music room, where her record still droned, two male voices harmonizing sweetly. She sat on the round rug, staring at the envelope.

It was the handwriting, she realized after a minute, and the goose bumps spread to her scalp. It looked exactly like her mother's. It was as if she'd sent a letter to herself.

She hesitated for another second, then turned it over and ripped open the flap. The letter was written in German. She nearly folded it and put it back into the envelope, but she could make out the first line, and the second—what else were all her years of German class for?—and before she knew it, she'd read the whole thing.

Dear Anita,

It is only fair that I begin with an introduction. Though I go by Margaret now and use my ex-husband's last name—Forsyth—I am the girl you knew as Grete Metzger. Berni's sister. I will understand if you stop here and throw this letter away.

By now you will have heard the news about Henry Klein, the one they are saying is Klaus Eisler. His resurfacing will no doubt have taken you back to the past. In remembering the Eislers, you perhaps have remembered me. This is why I felt I must write. For far too long I have let Klaus and his actions speak for me. It is time I speak for myself.

I write to beg forgiveness. It's too little, too late, I know, but since I cannot tell Berni—and many others—that I am sorry for what I've done, I will tell you.

Every day I'm consumed with regret. I consider small decisions, small mistakes. When I stayed at St. Luisa's instead of climbing into Sonje's car. When I shouted you out of the

Eislers' courtyard instead of accepting your apology. When I found your address I faced another decision. Would I write to Anita and explain, burden her with my apology, or remain silent? Would I ask what happened to Berni or stay forever in the dark? I know it is no good to open old wounds, but I choose to ask.

All these years I've been able to think of nothing but Berni. I wonder if you feel the same. You knew her better than I did. You were her true sister. There is so much I would tell her if she were alive. I'd tell her I loved her, first, and I would do my best to explain what happened between Klaus and myself.

Please accept my gratitude, Anita, for all you did for Berni that I couldn't. If you are willing to correspond, I'll write again. If not, I will disappear.

Should we never speak again, I wish you the very, very best.

Grete

The record player whirred and whirred; it had reached the end of Side A.

Janeen's entire body tingled. There it was, in black ink: Klaus Eisler, also known as Henry Klein. The man in the newspaper. The man Anita had pretended not to know.

Janeen felt sick. Why would her mother have lied about knowing him—an officer in the SS? Had he been her mother's boyfriend? Or worse, had he been her—Janeen's stomach lurched—colleague? She'd heard her mother say before, in passing, that the Nazis had been able to seize the minds of all kinds of people. What if she'd been talking about herself?

Janeen sat up shakily. She unwrapped a root beer barrel from a cut-glass bowl on the bookshelf and sucked it to think. She read the note again, then a third time. Anita had stood in the Eislers' courtyard. She'd been a "true sister" to someone named Berni. Janeen found herself feeling oddly jealous. Her mother had lived an entire life without her, one she knew absolutely nothing about.

She bit the candy in half, grinding it smooth against her molars, and tore a page from her notebook. She wrote very little, so that she would not reveal her limited German:

Dear Grete,

I will listen. That is all I can promise. I'll look for your letter.

Anita

Janeen read it over and nodded. It was the only way to find out the truth—she couldn't ask her mother. This woman would respond and confirm that Anita had been no Nazi. Of that Janeen felt certain. Almost certain.

This was how she justified sealing the envelope. Before she could change her mind, she ran the reply down to the mailbox. She waited, breathing heavily, until she saw the mailman loop back around, drawn by the raised red flag.

# PART II

# BERLIN, 1932–1933

*We take them [the youth] immediately into the SA, SS, et cetera,
and they will not be free again for the rest of their lives.*

Adolf Hitler

# GRETE, 1932

For over a year Grete lived at St. Luisa's without Berni, and in that time she allowed the other girls to stream around her as a river wears down a stone. It was easier not to talk, not to risk entering conversations she might not be able to hear. By the summer of 1932, she knew the other girls had forgotten she existed. They thought of her as inanimate, a bench or forgotten hymnal.

The plan had been for Berni to find an apartment for them to live in together, and that would have happened long ago, according to Berni, if it weren't for the Depression. "I can barely make enough money selling cigarettes to support myself," Berni said on her most recent visit, avoiding Grete's eyes. "In St. Luisa's, at least you know you will be fed every day."

Sister Josephine helped facilitate their meetings. Every month or two she sent Grete on an errand, to get soap flakes or cherry juice for her gout. Like clockwork, Berni would appear outside the store. How she and Sister Josephine communicated was a mystery.

"If you have so little money, why are you smoking?" Grete snapped. Her sister's excuses were growing tiresome. Sometimes she wondered if Berni was having too much fun to burden herself with a deaf little sister.

The changes in Berni disturbed Grete. First her hair had been chopped to chin length. Then she began wearing ties. She used suspenders to hold up trousers made for men. Her hair became shorter and shorter, combed wet like a boy's, and her laugh changed; it became deep, hoarse, a smoker's laugh. Whatever had caused this metamorphosis, it had nothing to do with Grete, and she both hated and feared it. The same unease she had felt with Sonje Schmidt, she felt around Berni now.

Until Berni did something like this: as soon as Grete mentioned the cigarette, she ground it under the worn toe of her brogue, then tossed it into the street. "There. That was my last one!"

Grete could not help but smile. It was raining, and the paper bag she held was beginning to soak through. "I have to go. This afternoon we're cleaning the *Gymnasium*."

Berni's face darkened. "Soon, little bird. I promise. Soon . . ."

A passing car swallowed the end of Berni's sentence, but Grete could have filled it in: *Soon I'll come for you*, or *soon we'll be together.* Another empty promise.

• • •

One morning in June 1932, two things happened that had never occurred before. Rain fell through sunlight, and a man came to see her.

"The devil is having a parish fair," Sister Josephine said when she passed Grete's table, gesturing toward the window. When Grete looked up, she saw long droplets streaking the glass. The sun cast blurred rainbows on the floor. In the doorway, Sister Odi and Sister Maria Eberhardt conferred with a man in his late thirties or early forties. He wore shabby clothes but carried his thin frame erect, and he twisted his hat in his hands as he spoke to the sisters. All three of them turned and looked straight at Grete, and her throat constricted.

A hush fell over the room as Sister Maria led the man, who dragged his left leg slightly, to Grete's table. Neither of them sat. "Margarete, this is Herr Eisler. He would like to have a word with you."

Even if Grete wanted to say anything, she couldn't have; from the moment she'd seen the man she'd known he was here for her, to take her away to an asylum or sanatorium for the deaf, or worse.

He looked down at her with gentle eyes. His hair had receded on the sides, but there was plenty in the center and the back, wiry auburn hair that needed a trim. "Let me see you, Margarete. Don't be shy." He spoke good, unaccented German that belied the tattered clothing.

Sister Maria shook her head. "No, *mein Herr*. This is how you have to talk to her." She leaned close enough for Grete to count capillaries on her nose and shouted, "Herr Eisler wants you to work for him!"

Grete blushed. Work for him? There must have been some mistake. She cleared her throat, and then she cleared it again, and finally, out came a little croak: "Par—pardon?"

Sister Maria righted herself and patted Grete's shoulder hard. "You see, *mein Herr*? This is what you and your wife would have to endure."

Grete fixed her eyes on a knot in the wooden tabletop, her face burning.

". . . too much of a hassle, I think, for Frau Eisler, with two children and a household to run. Can I introduce you to one of our older girls? There's Ingrid, and Gertrude—"

Herr Eisler shook his head and knelt close to Grete so that she could see the field of faint scars where shrapnel had implanted along his neck and jaw. "You do have experience cleaning? Doing what a maid does, Grete?" There seemed a bit of a wink in his expression, as though he invited her into his confidence. She looked down at his hands, broad, rough hands; she resisted the urge to place hers into one of them.

He would think her dumb if she didn't answer, but Sister Maria was gripping the soft saddle between Grete's shoulder and neck. Did she have a maid's experience? St. Luisa's was ostensibly a school, for lost girls; everyone knew without being told to downplay the scrubbing, cooking, sweeping. By now it had been six months since

Grete had seen the inside of a classroom, except to clean it. As the economy worsened—4 million unemployed, Berni said repeatedly, as though Grete hadn't heard this herself—Sister Maria began hiring the girls out as domestic workers, to a *Gymnasium* for upper-class young men.

"I do not do this to punish you girls," Sister Maria claimed. "You must work because I know of no other way to feed you. And you are building character and humility."

At the *Gymnasium*, Grete wasn't sure she'd built character, but she'd gotten to know the smell of *boy* quite well, detectable under the bleach she spread over the floors: grass and rubber balls, sweat, ham and potatoes, and something else, especially in the showers, something she could not name. She also learned the feeling of large-soled shoes on her back, the shoes of students who teased and tortured the little working girls.

With Sister Maria's fingers against her collarbone, Grete whispered, "I haven't done any work as a maid, *mein Herr*. Just a bit of cleaning."

He laughed. "A bit of cleaning is probably more than Frau Eisler had done, before she became my wife. Come work for us." He looked up at Sister Maria and shrugged, sheepish, as though he'd disobeyed her. "Grete can start in two weeks."

She could only nod. Sister had to answer for her. "Thank you for providing this young lady with a place to go. We're quite disturbed when our girls depart without attaching themselves to a proper chaperone."

Herr Eisler shook Grete's hand and put his hat on. She wished everyone would stop watching her so that she could shut her eyes and try to remember everything, to convince herself it had really happened.

• • •

A few weeks later, she walked over the wet streets of Charlottenburg in a new coat—new to her—holding the little carpetbag Sister Josephine had given her. The old nun had promised, tears in her eyes, to get word to Berni about Grete's new position.

Bells sang, dismissing parishioners to enjoy the Sunday afternoon. A rare sun shone hot and yellow on the puddles in the gutters. This did not resemble the Berlin that Sister Maria had described, not at all.

"You know nothing of what's out there," she began unceremoniously, when she called Grete into her office the day before. "Civil war." Her lipless mouth pressed itself white in her ruddy face. "Tell me the chancellor's name," she demanded.

"Brü—Brüning, Reverend Mother. The Chancellor is Herr Brüning."

"Wrong. He was sacked. Now it's von Papen. A Catholic, but not a good one."

Grete blinked. She'd been unaware there was such a thing.

"He's Herr Hitler's puppet, and he has destroyed the Republic. He lets the SA—the Sturmabteilung, paramilitaries—run wild. That's what you'll see out there, men dressed up like soldiers, batting one another on the heads." Sister Maria went to the window and looked out. "Do you know what the Nazis think of nuns? They say we aren't doing our duty to the Vaterland. Never mind I've raised hundreds of babies. If the Nazis force their way in, they'll rape us and call it good for the Reich."

Grete put her hand over her mouth, her ear buzzing. What a word, and from a sister's mouth! Sister Maria turned to watch her. Her fat neck shortened as she puffed up her shoulders in satisfaction. "You see, Grete. This ugly world will eat a girl like you alive."

"The Eislers will look after me," Grete said. Of course Sister Maria would try to throw water on her happiness. "I will be safe."

The old nun stared for a while, sitting back in her chair, her eyes narrow and glassy. "For all our sake, I hope you are right."

Grete saw no signs of civil war as she wandered Charlottenburg. She passed a fountain and felt its spray, then a BMW store with dormant neon lights. Eventually, she found Seelingstraße, a street where the trees' branches touched in the middle, and then number 36, where a thin woman held open the door. The woman beckoned to Grete from across the street, then whisked her into the vestibule, where they stood and stared at each other for a moment.

"I am Frau Eisler. You're Grete? You're here to work, *nicht?*"

Grete felt guilty for having imagined Herr Eisler with a prettier wife. Frau Eisler had a long chin that curved upward like the toe of an elf's shoe. Her skinny body seemed concave; her breasts sloped toward her belt. Her arms were all bone but somehow held a fat child.

"Say hello to our new maid, Gudrun." Gudrun had her face buried in her mother's limp blond hair. When she turned around to pout, Grete saw that she was beautiful: a ten-year-old angel with golden ringlets, pudgy flesh, and a rosebud mouth.

"*Guten tag*, Gudrun," Grete said. Gudrun answered with a *harrumph*, and blew a raspberry at Grete when her mother turned to climb the stairs. Grete set her jaw.

At apartment 301, Herr Eisler opened the door before his wife could knock. "Grete. Welcome." When he smiled or spoke, Grete noticed he showed more bottom teeth than top, and she fell in love all over again. "I see you've met Frau Eisler."

"Yes, Herr Eisler." Grete blushed to speak his name.

"Not Eidler," said his wife. "You're saying it wrong. Eisler."

"Gisela," Herr Eisler whispered, looking at the floor.

Frau Eisler opened her lips and hissed, "*Eissss*ler." Spittle flew from between her teeth.

"I'm sorry." Grete tried harder. "*Eisss*ler."

Herr Eisler gave his wife a look and told all of them he had to go to work in the factory. "Night shift," he said. "It was all I could pick up." His wife deflated, letting Gudrun slip to the floor. Before she reached up to kiss him, she turned to Grete. "You can wander through there, past the pocket doors, and put any belongings on the lofted bed in the children's room."

"But that's my room," Gudrun cried, and her father hoisted her into his arms.

A window was open in the bedchamber, through which a breeze gave life to the transparent curtain. Grete watched it float up and down a few times and timed her breathing to its waves. She would try harder. She would listen closely. She would gain the love of this family.

There were three beds, two of them bunked, and she threw the carpetbag up onto what she presumed was the loft. Quickly she climbed the wooden ladder to peer at the mattress. The ceiling would be a few inches from her face as she slept, but it did not occur to her to complain.

She wandered back out into the little hallway. The apartment's furniture did not manage to fill the space. There were only three chairs around the dining table, where Frau Eisler now sat with Gudrun. Before Grete could think of something to say, Frau Eisler handed her a hammer.

"See the dining chairs here? Turn one upside down. We are going to remove their seats."

Grete stared at the hammer. Had she heard correctly?

Frau Eisler laughed, showing overlapping teeth. Thin dimples appeared, and Grete saw how young she was, barely over thirty. "You think I'm joking, *nicht*? Our family hasn't had good fortune these past couple of years. When Klaus was a baby and Herr Eisler was a bank teller, we bought this flat and furniture. Now . . ." She caught her breath and put her hand on her forehead and then her mouth. "Now he works on an assembly line. And poor Gudrun has never known what it's like not to struggle." She reached for the girl, who sat on the floor, and Grete couldn't help but put her arms out to Frau Eisler in the same gesture of comfort.

"We press on!" Frau Eisler burst, bright-eyed. She dropped to her knees and clutched one of the chairs by the legs, turning it over so that Grete could see where the leather cushion attached to the seat. The wood underneath, pale and untreated, was stamped with the manufacturer's initials. "Pull out these little nails that hold the leather on."

"But, *gnädige Frau.*" Grete swallowed, found her voice. "I'll ruin the chair."

"Just take the back of the hammer like this. It'll slide out easy." Frau Eisler popped the first shiny nail head and let it roll in her palm. She smiled with the corners of her mouth down. "I almost forget that these chairs were a wedding present. Herr Eisler didn't want me to do this. He'll be at work for another ten hours today. At least."

What had happened to the fourth chair? Why did she insist on doing something her husband didn't want to do? Grete knew better than to ask questions. She took the hammer and slid her first nail out with ease.

"We'll make house shoes with the leather, for Gudrun," Frau Eisler said. "And for you."

"For me? Oh, I couldn't."

"Of course you will. I won't have someone who works for me going around barefoot. Besides, you'll make them. You can sew, *nicht?*"

"Yes, Frau Eisler."

"*Eisler,*" she said. "I am very glad to hear it. You'll never learn anything more valuable than how to take care of a house."

Grete worked until she had a pile of nails. With the chairs denuded, Frau Eisler suggested they test them by sitting and sharing a bit of rum torte that her neighbor had baked.

"We won't be having a large dinner tonight. My husband is of course working, and Klaus will be out on a forest excursion." Frau Eisler's face glowed. "Klaus is my seventeen-year-old son. He's a good young man, keeps a paper route. He's also in a club like the Wandervogel."

They split the rum torte with Gudrun, "Just we women," Frau Eisler said, handing her daughter the lion's share.

Crumbs stuck to Grete's dirndl. She could not believe her good fortune.

• • •

In time, Grete found clues to the Eislers' past. In a drawer, she found a stiffly posed portrait of Herr and Frau Eisler with a young Klaus and a toddler sister and baby brother that she could only presume had died. Nobody mentioned them, but their deaths explained the gap between Klaus's and Gudrun's ages. The loss of the middle children, Grete came to discover, had given Klaus the placid confidence of the last remaining gladiator, Gudrun the sour disposition of the overly coddled.

The family tragedy might also have contributed to Frau Eisler's neurosis. She and Grete completed all indoor chores together, beginning with the laundry; once a month they hauled coal up to the attic and boiled a cauldron of water in which they washed all the sheets, tablecloths, and towels. But any errands that required leaving the apartment—returning the laundry key to the custodian, taking out the garbage, purchasing groceries—she asked Grete to do.

On the rare occasion that Frau Eisler did venture out, she walked quickly and muttered under her breath. "Whore-lids," she said one day when she and Grete passed a drugstore boldly displaying diaphragms in its window.

When they saw girls who smoked cigarettes and wore short haircuts, she told Grete these were "Germany's wasted youth."

About the Jewish Bolsheviks, whom she blamed for the country's recent plummet back into economic turmoil: "They've sodomized us all."

The city was going into the shitter. Since the Social Democrats had gotten their way, they'd become as big in the head as any Kaiser. They'd added six new boroughs to Berlin and were trying to make it the most licentious place in Europe, worse than Paris, worse than London.

"Where are the good, decent Germans?" Frau Eisler would cry, to which Grete replied, "We are right here." She listened to this kind of talk for hours, saying little, and afterward Frau Eisler would apologize—they'd driven her to speak this way. She was only using their words.

• • •

Grete saw little of Herr Eisler, who worked long hours at the factory, or of Klaus, who woke early to deliver newspapers before he attended classes at his *Gymnasium*. Klaus frightened her. She could hardly find her voice when he wasn't around, and when he was, she went mute.

Every night, after the kitchen gleamed from her efforts, she changed into her nightgown in the darkened pantry. When she climbed the ladder to the loft she felt his eyes on her skinny bare legs. Once she turned over in her bed and caught him staring up toward the top bunk, eyes reflective, like an animal's.

When he left for school in the morning, she breathed a sigh of relief.

Once she overheard him arguing with his parents at breakfast. Their voices came through the window to the balcony where she stood watering the sun-starved flowers. Down below was the shadowy *Hof* at the center of the building, where people kept bicycles and shared gossip.

"I'm a man now. I shouldn't have to share my room."

"Maybe he is right," said Frau Eisler. "It's already crowded in there with Gudrun."

"We cannot send her away," Herr Eisler replied firmly. "It's the least we can do in times like these, to give one more soul a place to rest at night."

Grete's fingers slipped around the neck of the watering can. She'd drenched the geraniums. Water drained from the pots and splashed on the courtyard below. Two ladies sitting in chairs, smoking black cigarettes, looked up at her and cackled.

• • •

One evening in early September, she dawdled in taking out the garbage. It was a humid night, white clouds still visible as little puffs against the darkening sky. Thus far it had been an unusually warm summer, and the heat was still oppressive, working rancid smells from the stones on the floor of the alley, the odors of damp bricks and cooking fat. She waited down here sometimes, her only solitary place, unpleasant as it was, and tried to fix her speech. She said it a few times aloud: *I wish you were my parents.*

Grete wasn't stupid. She knew she was only their hired help. But there were signs, details she detected if she paid enough attention. When Herr Eisler was home for dinner she sometimes brought her stool to join them at the table. They took her to church once a month, and even though it was a Lutheran service, the gesture touched her. In some ways, they were beginning to see her as part of the family.

*I wish you were my parents.* There was no way of knowing if she'd pronounced it right. She dumped the trash into the canister.

"Grete!"

Frau Eisler stood at the top of the fire escape, in boots with laces untied. Grete slammed the metal lid onto the trashcan, which toppled over. All sound in her right ear stopped when Frau Eisler scrambled down the stairs, and Grete saw the folded paper in her hand.

"Why did we receive a letter addressed to Fräulein Metzger? Who is Berni?"

The greenish-black, mildewed walls of the alley seemed to tilt inward. A letter from Berni! She wrung her hands to stop herself from grabbing it. "She's my sister." She bent to pick up the galvanized metal garbage can.

"Why does she tell you to take the subway to Schöneberg? We cannot train a new maid, Grete. Don't lie to me. It will cost you your dinner."

Grete's heart pounded. "There's no plan for me to run away, Frau Eisler. I'm sure she's just inviting me to visit." She'd never seen the apartment in Schöneberg. More than anything, she wanted to read that letter.

Frau Eisler tucked it into her pocket and gestured for Grete to follow her back up the rickety metal staircase and into the apartment, where Gudrun sat slurping a glass of milk. She smacked her lips together after each gulp, letting out a small "ah."

"Good girl," said Frau Eisler, cupping Gudrun's blond curls. "Now, tell me. What does your sister's husband do?"

Grete inhaled, thinking. The room smelled of turnips gratin growing crisp and brown. She had made the dinner herself, put the sliced root into the oven in a pan of milk and shredded hard cheese. She'd braved the dark root cellar.

There was no choice but to be honest. "She doesn't have a husband, Frau Eisler."

Frau Eisler stared. "She lives *alone*?"

"Not alone, with a woman named Sonje Schmidt."

"She's Frau Schmidt's maid?"

The girls at St. Luisa's had the same questions, but Grete had no answers for them. They'd come to their own conclusion: Berni had become a loose woman. "Fräulein Schmidt may have adopted her," Grete said now. Sweat gathered at the collar of her dress.

"I'm sure she didn't adopt a teenage girl. If Berni isn't a maid, what does she do?"

Grete's fingers fluttered to her earlobe. "She sells cigarettes," she said, and Frau Eisler's eyes got big and round.

"Oh, child." Frau Eisler's face constricted in horror and delight. "She cannot be up to any good." She pulled chairs out so they could sit. "Do you think she is a whore?" There was a bit of strange pleasure in her eyes.

Grete winced. She had heard the word before, many times, from a chorus of cruel and desperate girls. *Whore. Whore, just like your sister.* Frau Eisler took Grete's silence the way she wanted to and sat back with a grin, stroking her chin. "Whores should know their place, *nicht wahr?*" she said. "She should know not to write to a respectable house like this."

"Whores should know," Grete echoed, miserable. She longed to melt through the porous seat of the chair. But Frau Eisler gazed down at her with pity and understanding. How different this conversation was from the accusatory shrieks of the orphanage girls, the judgmental silence of the sisters, save Josephine. Suddenly Grete felt the most sincere love for Frau Eisler, so powerful that it took her by surprise. Words poured out of her mouth, too quickly for her to consider how they sounded.

"*Gnädige Frau*, you have to know how sad my sister has made me. For weeks I thought she'd return, but she didn't. I saw Sonje Schmidt's car in my sleep, whenever I shut my eyes. I kept waiting for it to return, but it didn't, and my sister became a stranger. Sister Josephine took me into her lap and held me when I cried. I wondered if I should have gone with her after all—"

She'd forgotten Gudrun, who interrupted her with a laugh. "You're too old to be in someone's lap."

Her mother shushed her, her attention on Grete.

Grete breathed heavily, exhausted from so much talking. "Sister Josephine told me my reward would come. It has, in the form of your good family. I want to be here, rather than . . . in Schöneberg." She wanted to say more, about how respectable they still were in their poverty. She wanted to say that she prayed for Herr Eisler at night, for his pension to be restored, for his crumpled leg and scarred skin to heal.

At the same time, she desperately wanted to see what was in Berni's note.

"Shh, very well, Grete, very well." Frau Eisler smiled with lips shut, satisfied. "Throw that whore's letter away and draw some hot water for Gudrun's bath. That's the last of any talk about this sister. Throw the letter away now."

Her legs shaking, Grete walked as slowly as she could to the rubbish bins by the back door and unfolded the letter without a sound.

My little Grete-bird!

How I have longed for your face! I am glad you found work (difficult these days!) and shelter and have broken free from the shackles named Maria and Eberhardt.

Are you happy now? Are you well fed? I cannot wait to hear that all is right with you. You'll see my address on the envelope. I'm a U-Bahn ride away, my sweet—come see me for cake and *kaffeeklatsch*. We'll add a splash of bitters and toast life outside St. Luisa's. Where I can even write the word "bitters" in a note to you, ha-ha!

I cannot wait to kiss your cheek.

With love, Berni

Another day, the thought of cake and coffee might have whet Grete's appetite rather than her jealousy. But how could the prodigal Berni be so naive to assume nobody outside St. Luisa's read one another's mail? Grete shivered at her sister's professions of love, coming right on the heels of a conversation in which she'd let Frau Eisler call Berni a whore. Tonight she would dream of the black car's taillights again.

# BERNI, 1932

Though Berni was still too young to vote, Sonje asked her to come along when she cast her ballot in the federal parliamentary election in July. "Girls your age can't remember a time when women were denied suffrage," she said after she voted for the Social Democrats, as she and Berni hurried through the protestors, sign-holders, and leaflet-pushers outside. "But you should never take it for granted."

"Believe me, I don't." Berni wouldn't admit that until now she hadn't thought much about the German woman's ability to vote; as a Lulu, she'd felt about as influential as the rats who ran under the city streets. Any rights she now found she had, she treated with wonder.

"Good," Sonje said with a wink. "Now let's celebrate."

They took a taxi to Unter den Linden, the stately boulevard that ran between the Brandenburg Gate and the Museumsinsel. Berni followed Sonje to a restaurant with outdoor seating on the grassy park between the two lanes of the street. Before they could sit, Sonje drifted from one table to the next, kissing people's cheeks: a pug-nosed woman in ermine, three reporters in rumpled flannel suits and oversized hats, a young couple whose slick black pinscher sat beneath the table, still as a statue.

"What do you think the mood is at the Hotel Kaiserhof this afternoon?" asked the female owner of the pinscher, speaking of the Nazi headquarters. Berni noticed her dog trembling slightly, his eyes fixed on the table.

"Desolate," said Sonje right away. "They're finished."

All except Berni murmured their agreement: the Nazis could not have convinced enough people to vote for them. "No one who has read *Mein Kampf*," Sonje said, unwinding her gauzy scarf, "will forget Hitler's lunacy about Jews, despite their efforts to hide that before this election. Curious how they left the word 'Jew' out of their plan for job creation, *nicht?*"

"Well, they can't say out loud their plan to create jobs is to take them from Jews," said the woman in ermine.

One of the journalists snorted. "Let us hope those in the provinces have the same common sense we do in Berlin. It'll be up to them."

Berni thought she saw something pass over Sonje's face—a flicker of fear—and then she recovered. "Come, Berni. I'm famished. I'll be back tomorrow, gentlemen," she said, tapping her fingernail on the journalists' table, "to toast the Nazis' loss."

They followed the patient waiter to a table with wicker chairs, afghans draped over the backs, and despite the heat Berni put hers on her lap. It seemed unwise to waste anything that came free. Typically she and Anita ate saveloy sausage from street carts, or sat at counters that sold yellow pea soup for a handful of pfennig and offered free bread. The waiter returned in a moment with two shimmering pillars of beer, a white cloth draped over his arm. This did not seem the sort of place where you might stuff bread into your pockets.

Bread. It had been on Berni's mind all morning, because of the Nazi posters: "*Arbeit, Freiheit und Brot!* Adolf Hitler will provide Work and Bread!" The slogans were so simple, yet so appealing—Berni wasn't sure how Sonje couldn't see it. In contrast, the Socialist flyers showed a man wrestling with a snake, its scales branded with the words "Ten-Hour Day, Slaughterer of Workers." What did the 4 million unemployed care about a ten-hour workday when what they had now was zero?

Tomorrow, Berni thought, glancing up through linden branches at the gray sky, everyone in this café might find him- or herself in a very foul mood. When she clinked glasses with Sonje, the gesture felt hollow.

"I believe my friends think you're my lesbian paramour," Sonje said breathily, leaning over the table. "Don't look now, but they're staring at us. I feel very avant-garde."

Berni ran a hand over the short hair at the base of her neck, kitten-soft. When she wasn't working she wore trousers, wool blazers, men's scarves. She'd very deliberately cultivated the *garçonne* appearance, and it didn't bother her when people mistook her for a lesbian. Something about it made her feel more grown up. "Shall I give you a little pinch on the bottom as we go?"

"Depends on how much I drink. Ah, there's the board with the lunch specials. Schnitzel! Vanilla ice cream with cherry sauce! Lunch is on me. Order something substantial."

"I can't let you buy me lunch. I'm late on this month's rent already."

Sonje fluttered a hand. "It's nothing. I'll just put it on the account."

"Ah." Berni let Sonje summon the waiter and didn't protest when she declared they'd both like the special. An account at a restaurant like this could only belong to one person, and Berni felt a little queasy to think the meal would be covered by the invisible Trommler, Sonje's "close personal friend." Berni hadn't yet met him, but she knew Sonje would disappear into a hotel with him for a weekend every now and then.

"I don't know how you do it," Berni said after a while. "Carrying on with Trommler, and with Gerrit. Doesn't Gerrit become jealous?"

Sonje made a face. "Gerrit is a Socialist. He thinks it's grand I'm taking advantage of a rich bastard like Trommler," she said, though Berni found this less than convincing. "Look, we women have made strides, but we still have far to go. We can vote, yet we still hold only a small minority of seats in the Reichstag. More of us live independently, yet we're limited to clerical jobs." She took a few large sips, and half her beer was gone. "The sexes aren't treated equally, so it's not unwise to get a bit in return from your affairs with men. You offer them your bed, they offer you something too."

"Do you even believe in love?" Berni asked. "Or is the term out of fashion?"

"I believe in love." Berni waited for Sonje to say that she loved Gerrit, but she didn't. "I was engaged to be married once. Before the war. I think that's why my father left me the flat, you know. If my parents had any idea I wasn't to start a family, they would have sold it."

"What happened to your fiancé?"

"What do you think? He was gunned down at the Marne." Sonje mashed a sardine into a piece of toast from the basket on the table. "He was the only one for whom I enjoyed playing cello. Usually it felt like performance. With Jakob it was communication. I'd play, the cello between my legs, he'd lie on his back and listen . . ."

From across the patio, Berni made eye contact with the pinscher and had the distinct feeling neither of them wanted to be there at the moment. Sonje would interpret her silence as pining for some boy who'd gotten away from her, but she was thinking of Grete. They hadn't needed words to communicate, either: a certain scowl, a little chirp, one lowered eyelid could convey a world of meaning. The doubts that visited Berni daily, like a commuters' train rolling faithfully into the terminal, came into her mind now: what if Grete *wasn't* safer working in someone's home than living with her, Sonje, and Anita? Or worse—what if she was learning to communicate without words with somebody else?

Berni shook her head and saw the dog mimic her gesture. Grete's situation would be temporary. Berni had already saved a couple hundred marks. A few hundred more and she'd be able to pay the first few months' rent on a new apartment. She'd been careful not to mention any of this to Sonje and Anita. It would be impossible to explain without insulting them.

"Look at me," Sonje said finally. "A mess! Best to keep your lovers a bit distant, see?" She downed the remainder of her beer and lifted a finger in the waiter's direction. "Speaking of, Berni, are there any men—or women, I never know for certain with you—in your life?"

"A few here and there," Berni said, toying with her napkin. In fact, there was one, but he was too poor; Sonje would never approve. Berni tried changing the subject. "We're near the library," she said, taking a sip of beer and looking eastward. The statue of Frederick the Great on his horse looked small enough for her to pinch between her fingers. "We should check out some books when we're done eating."

"*Jawohl*," said Sonje. A break came in the clouds, and weak sunlight poured over their table as the food arrived: pork schnitzel fried golden brown, piled with mushroom sauce, haricots verts in vinegar, carrots and potatoes, green salad. The meat sizzled against Berni's tongue. When she swallowed, the food caught in her throat, as though Trommler's coins lodged there.

• • •

For much of the afternoon, Berni forgot the election. At the library she checked out Erika Mann's travel memoir and a book of erotica. She came home to find Anita in a silly mood, dancing to jazz, wearing a bluish drawn-on mole on her cheek. ("It's my day off," she said by way of explanation.)

Berni allowed Anita to experiment with the shape of her eyebrows as she read aloud, lingering on sensual scenes to draw massive sighs from Anita. Meanwhile, summer rain pummeled the drainpipe outside her window. She heard Sonje get changed and leave the apartment, but she didn't bother to ask where she was headed. When finally Berni went to the looking glass she had to laugh; Anita had drawn a look of perpetual surprise on her face, the left brow subdued, the right raised in question.

It was still light outside when news of the election came over the radio. Berni and Anita were stretched out on the parlor rug, arguing over the movie star cards that came in their cigarette tins.

"You want Elissa Landi, Conrad Veidt, and two Rena Mandels— for *one* Marlene Dietrich?" Berni cried. "This is what they call robbery."

Anita fanned herself with the red-and-gold card in question. "But it's not just any Marlene, darling, it's Marlene in her white tuxedo. Think how gorgeous she'll look tucked in the top corner of your mirror."

Berni studied Rena Mandel, whose face was everywhere lately because of *Vampyr*. Finally she sighed and handed the cards over. "I don't plan to keep Marlene," she said. "I'm sending her to Grete."

Anita dropped her head to one shoulder, an inquisitive bird. "To Grete. She hasn't even answered you, *nicht*?"

"She will," Berni replied, wishing once again she hadn't told Anita about the letter. "She is preoccupied. Once she settles into her new position, she'll have time to reply."

Anita shook her head. "Your sister is all you talk about, your sister, your sister, and yet you never bring her here and let her work as the Eislers' maid. Like Frau Pelzer!"

"Keep your voice down," Berni snapped, glancing toward the kitchen. She could hear water being poured into a pan. "Frau Pelzer can hear you."

Anita rolled her big eyes and handed Marlene over, holding on for a second longer than was necessary, making Berni tug. They listened to the radio drone for a moment, neither of them, it seemed, paying attention to the words. After a while Anita looked up and bit her rouged lower lip. She still had the false mole decorating her cheekbone. "Have you told Grete about me?"

Instead of responding, Berni ran her finger over Marlene's blond hair, her wide-brimmed white hat and black bowtie. She pictured Grete pinning it to the wall of her austere bedroom. "Of course I have," she said, but of course she hadn't.

They heard footsteps in the hallway, clicking rapidly toward the apartment, and in a burst of humidity Sonje barreled in. She went straight to the radio, which had been droning without their notice, and turned it almost all the way up. She shimmied out of her rain jacket and left it on the rug, where it began darkening the weave, and when she noticed Anita stick her fingers in her ears, she yanked them out.

"Listen," she hissed.

". . . most surprising result is the National Socialist Party's gains in the Reichstag. The Nazis have added one hundred and twenty-three seats, bringing their total highest of any party. Still, they do not hold a majority. The leaders of the pro-Republic parties, now pressed from both sides by the NSDAP and KPD, have insisted they will not cooperate . . ."

"It was those fools in the countryside," Sonje declared.

". . . Nazis received thirty-seven percent of the popular vote . . ."

"Illiterate hicks," Anita added.

Berni said nothing. Of course Sonje wouldn't want to think anyone in her beloved Berlin had voted for Hitler, but Berni had seen flags in people's windows, demonstrators in the parks. She studied Sonje's discarded umbrella, leaking dirty water onto the floor, thinking of Grete. Grete wouldn't know what any of this meant; Berni would have to write and explain.

"Oh, no. Oh, no."

They all turned to see Frau Pelzer standing in the doorway to the kitchen, clutching a damp dishtowel to her mouth. Her lips had turned bluish-white. "Oh, this is not how I thought it would go," she cried, wringing the towel.

Sonje stepped toward her and took her arm. "Let's not worry yet," she said, though she, too, looked pale. Her hair, usually curled in perfect waves, lay damp on her shoulders, and she had runs in her stockings. "Let's see if they manage to get anything accomplished."

"Who did you vote for, Pelzer?" Anita asked, her chin in her hand, the trading cards still spread in front of her on the floor. They looked silly now, a child's game.

Frau Pelzer blanched further at the question, and for a moment Berni wondered if she'd faint. "I—I leave the voting to my husband, I'm afraid . . ."

Sonje had been patting Frau Pelzer's arm, gazing at the floor; Berni noticed her wrist stiffen, her eyes sharpen. Frau Pelzer's nostrils quivered, and Berni felt a stab of sympathy for her. Clearly Frau Pelzer didn't want a Nazi government. Besides, Sonje herself had just been lamenting the amount of power German men still held over their women . . .

Anita began to say something, but before she could, Berni leapt to her feet. She made her voice loud enough to drown out everyone else. "I think we should all go to a nightclub."

"Before they shut them down," Anita grumbled.

"Especially you, Frau Pelzer," Berni said, louder. "The boys'll swoon over you." She knew Frau Pelzer would never accept, but the invitation did the trick; the housekeeper began cooing and hiding her face in her apron, making such an adorable show that Sonje relaxed and joined in teasing her. She had a pair of crocodile pumps Frau Pelzer could borrow; Anita offered lace garters. They'd drink schnapps until the sun came up, Sonje promised. They'd eat roses dipped in ether.

Anita jumped to take Frau Pelzer's hands. "Do you know 'The Lavender Song,' Pelzer?" She pulled the housekeeper into the middle of the room, kicking Sonje's coat aside. When Anita danced, she looked like one of the orangutans in the monkey house at the zoo: all arms and skinny legs, her hands and feet enormous. She sang while Frau Pelzer blushed and blushed:

We're not afraid to be queer and different
If that means hell, well, hell, we'll take the chance.
They're all so straight, uptight, upright and rigid
They march in lock-step, we prefer to dance.

Frau Pelzer kept one hand to her flaming cheek, bright spots on her décolletage. Berni knew exactly what she was thinking: what would her husband think if he could hear this song, could see her dancing?

They were all laughing, Anita and Frau Pelzer tangled in a waltz, Sonje draped across the arms of the velvet chair, when Berni realized the news broadcast had ended. The radio had switched to an advertisement for Coca-Cola GmbH. The spell was momentarily lifted, and everyone seemed a bit giddy. Sonje and Frau Pelzer both started pointing to Berni's face.

"Berni," Sonje cried, as though this was the first she'd noticed them. "Your eyebrows!"

And just to keep them laughing, to keep the subject light, Berni waggled them and did a little jig.

# GRETE, 1932

"Don't even think about dropping this off with that Jew on Damm Bismarck," Frau Eisler said one morning as she handed over her husband's gold watch. "Go to Scholz's. We have to put the money back into our own economy."

Grete didn't know what she meant by their own economy, but she took Frau Eisler at her word. She had taught Grete there were Jewish goods, shoddily constructed, and then there were German goods, which made better investments. There was Jewish haste and German diligence. Before, Judaism had meant little to Grete. It was simply different, like the Lutherans. She'd had no idea the Jews were driving small German businesses bankrupt. Arzt's, the Jewish grocer she'd been buying eggs from, and the German one she switched to after Frau Eisler caught her, seemed about the same. But after Frau Eisler's lecture, Grete never returned to Arzt's.

The only Jew she knew lived right across the hall: Rachel, who worked for Frau Schumacher. Frau Eisler sniffed about her and said you couldn't be too careful about theft, but Grete had heard Frau Schumacher say she'd never employed someone more hardworking.

A few nights after Berni's letter arrived, Rachel appeared at the back door to the Eislers' apartment, the one that led down to the alley, holding a cardboard butcher's box.

"*Abend*, Margarete. Is there anything you can trade for a chicken thigh?"

"I don't have anything extra. I'm sorry."

"Please, please." Rachel was perhaps sixteen, with thick brown hair and a full bust that strained against her blouse. Her brow was beaded with sweat. "You know what I need."

Grete inhaled. She knew Rachel had an ailing brother, a veteran. Some nights, long after Frau Schumacher and her elderly mother were asleep, Rachel worked the coatroom at Halle der Rosen and gave the extra cash to her family. To keep the old ladies oblivious in their beds, she snuck Fleischmann's yeast into their after-dinner milk to aid digestion and make them drowsy.

"You're making soup tonight, Grete? You can use both the meat *and* bone."

The Eislers hadn't had meat in five days. "All right. Wait here."

"Thank you," Rachel whispered, too quietly for Grete to hear. Grete felt sorry for her, and for her brother. Rachel had alluded to amputations. But every time Grete traded with her, she knew it should be the last. Frau Eisler would never approve.

• • •

Frau Eisler, Klaus, and Gudrun trickled into the dining room at dinnertime. Klaus set Gudrun down on her chair, and Grete came in slowly, holding an iron cauldron. The chicken thigh, baked and shredded with skin and fat on, had made a neat little pile next to its bone, which thickened the stock. But the meat had practically disappeared in the thin soup.

Klaus sat at the head of the table, his pale eyes lively from hunger, and Grete dished him the fullest bowl of soup, slightly meatier than the ones she handed Frau Eisler and Gudrun. Lastly, she gave herself a tiny helping, went to the pantry, and opened the window. Children in the *Hof* called out songs. She dipped her spoon into the bowl.

"Come sit with us, Grete!" Grete could hear the bread in her mistress's mouth. "Gudrun wants to be in my lap!"

Grete reentered the dining room shyly, avoiding Klaus's curious stare. She felt him watching her eat for a little while until he turned, with a bored blink, to his mother.

"A photographer stopped me on the street," he said with his mouth full, "and asked if I would model for a pamphlet. The pamphlet will be called 'Facts and Lies about Hitler,' and I would be an illustration of our youth. The man said I was a fine specimen of Aryan manhood."

"What vanity!" Frau Eisler leaned on her elbow to admire Klaus and spoke loud enough for people outside to hear. "They want you to serve as an example of German beauty! Imagine!"

Everyone at the table took a moment to study him as he ate. He had pale hair, a high forehead, heavy-lidded gray eyes, and tapered fingers with pink knuckles. His nose pushed proudly out and then hooked down, bringing to mind the Prussian eagle. He turned his hands upward, and Grete noticed a dark mole on his palm. She stared at it, transfixed. It seemed a queer place for a mole, as though it were a mistake.

"Model of Aryan manhood!" Frau Eisler cried. "Men aren't supposed to think of such things. I hope you haven't already done it."

Gudrun opened her wet lips and indicated that she wanted more soup. "But Mama, Brother doesn't look like a Pole, and he doesn't look like a Jew."

"The simple wisdom of a child!" Frau Eisler cleaned the girl's face with her apron. "No more for you, we must save some soup for your father."

Gudrun narrowed her eyes at Grete. "She's eating. The maid." Grete coughed on a burnt piece of turnip and looked down. In just a few minutes, she'd drained her shallow bowl.

"Mother," Klaus said. "It pays twenty marks."

"Klaus, my boy, no! You cannot allow someone to photograph you like a common whore. How do you know this photographer is really working for Hitler? He may want to sell the photographs for unclean purposes and then you'd be no better than"—she tapped her fingernails together—"Grete's sister."

"Pardon?" Klaus burped lightly into his napkin, then turned to Grete with, once again, just the slightest spark of interest. "What does she mean?"

"My sister sells cigarettes," Grete said, her voice foggy.

Frau Eisler sputtered, "And surely that's not all."

Grete opened her mouth, but no sound came. She realized now she'd jumped a train in allowing Frau Eisler to think Berni was a whore, and that there would be no stops. Frau Eisler bore holes in her with her stare. To contradict her would have been disastrous.

"You must tell us more," said Klaus.

"She sells champagne and cigarettes—"

"And?" prompted Frau Eisler.

"And she's a whore." The lie came out easily. The other three looked at her, waiting for her to go on, and she told the first story she could think of. The more fantastical she made it sound, the easier it was to say. "And my sister dances. Onstage. In a show where women wear only feathers. Men in the audience pay her."

"To do what?" Klaus implored.

The ringing had begun in Grete's ear, loud and sharp.

"Klaus," said Frau Eisler, "can't you see you're embarrassing our Grete?"

"That is truly repellent," said Klaus. "What else do you know about the whore?"

"Grete's sister's a whore," Gudrun said. Fat, pretty Gudrun. Grete tried not to imagine rolling her down the back stairs into the garbage cans. Under the table she pinched her own hand.

But Frau Eisler shifted her off her lap and, to Grete's surprise, told Gudrun to fetch a damp cloth to wipe down the table, normally Grete's duty. Gudrun stomped away, and Frau Eisler gave Grete an encouraging smile. This was the first time anyone, even Berni, had given her such an audience. The sound in her ear actually seemed to subside. More words came.

"My sister has made herself permanently sterile," Grete said. She wasn't even sure this was possible.

Klaus laughed. "She did us all a favor."

Gudrun, who'd been sullenly wiping under everyone's forearms, repeated the word again—"Whore!"—and Frau Eisler and Klaus laughed. Grete tried to join in, but her mouth felt cottony. She sensed she was on the right side of the joke this time—wasn't she?

They were all laughing when Herr Eisler came in, and everyone froze. Frau Eisler stared, horrified, at the near-empty soup pot.

"A nice family scene," he said. "I'm not sure I approve of the subject matter, though." He kissed Gudrun's head, causing her to wriggle with pleasure.

Grete leapt from her chair, jostling the table.

"No, Grete," he said. "Sit, please! I'm not hungry." Frau Eisler watched him with a wrinkle in between her eyes. He kissed her and dropped one hand onto Klaus's shoulder, then dragged his leg around the table and dug his thumbs into Grete's back. The pressure radiated through her body. "Do you enjoy life here?" he asked, close to her ear.

"Ja, natürlich." Grete knew he was thinking of her salary, how frightfully small it was. He paid her with scarcely more than shelter and food. Had Frau Eisler not been watching closely, she would have told him how lucky she felt that he had chosen her.

"We were just hearing tales of Grete's sister," said Klaus.

"Oh? And what does Grete's sister do?" Herr Eisler leapt at Gudrun, his hands up like claws. "Is she a lion tamer?" Gudrun tossed her blonde head and giggled.

Everyone left the table a few minutes later, and Grete went to the sink with Frau Eisler and took a dish brush from her hand. "He's a superior man," Grete said softly.

Frau Eisler worried her hands together and headed toward the bedroom. Grete cleaned the kitchen and dining room alone, finishing after all four Eislers were tucked into bed. It was her duty, naturally, but it was also her pleasure.

• • •

On her next free Wednesday afternoon, Grete found herself in Schöneberg.

The neighborhood looked nothing like what she expected. She had prepared for throngs of thieves, homophiles, beggars, prostitutes, old men who'd grope her or worse. The buildings were smaller and closer together than in Charlottenburg, and she saw more people on bicycles. The odors were different, stronger perhaps, some foods she didn't recognize. She turned the corner at a dense hilly park and took a breath of damp summer air.

She'd woken that morning with an ache. She had been sleeping on her stomach, and a dull pain on the right side of her chest had woken her. She crept to the toilet and peeked down into her shirt to find a grotesque sight: one swollen nipple. One small breast. Only one. The other remained as flat as it had been since birth, no more than a freckle on the skin. It figured she'd be disfigured, lopsided, in this way. How long would she be able to hide it?

Berni's street, Pfrommerstraße, intersected a much grander avenue at an old hotel, white marble with balconies. So it was a fine neighborhood after all. Perhaps Berni worked at the hotel, Grete thought, until she came close and could see no light behind the front doors of Haus Julen. The hotel was closed, dark, with dead vines staining the stone.

On Pfrommerstraße she encountered a young woman pushing a black pram and a group of men in nice suits. She stalled for a while across the street from Berni's building, wiping her palms on her skirt and shivering. Nine concrete steps lined with fat stone railings led to double black doors labeled in brass: 455 and 457. Grete stared at the door to 457, unable to believe it held Berni. And then it opened.

"Yoo hoo!"

As soon as she appeared, it was all right.

"Hello!" Berni's head and arm waggled out of the partially open door. "What are you doing over there?" Grete felt something tighten and then break loose inside of her.

"You're going to wake the neighborhood," she murmured as she approached the stairs.

"Let them wake!" Berni's cheeks were bright pink. "Watch, those steps get slippery." Grete was relieved to see she wore a dress, a boxy black silk dress with house slippers and a long strand of fake pearls, a few cracked in half. She put her bare arms out and gathered Grete in. Her skin was warm, her heartbeat fast and heavy. They stood that way for a long time.

When they pulled apart, Grete sniffed and touched her eyes. "Ber-Berni? I'd like—"

"What? What will make you happy?" Pieces of Berni's hair stuck to her face.

"Just that. To call someone *du*."

"You have no one to call . . . ?" Berni's face collapsed, then recovered. "We'll call each other *du* all day, my darling. *Du!*"

"Du!"

"*Du!* Shall we go indoors? We are living in a police state now, after all, ha!"

Inside, they studied each other for a moment, grinning. Grete took in Berni's hair, short as ever and dyed blacker. Her eyebrows had been plucked and redrawn into vermicular commas. Her face, fortunately, had not changed: pudgy and freckled, with chocolate brown eyes. Grete tapped her finger in Berni's cleft chin, and Berni echoed the gesture on hers.

"Let me take your jacket," Berni said. "My God! Are they feeding you? It's not in style to be *this* thin!"

"Don't grab my arm like that. Of course they feed me. You know how times are."

"I know all too well," said Berni. "Here, up, up."

They followed a patterned blue carpet up a narrow staircase, down a hallway—Grete smelled foreign food again, smoky and sweet—and then Berni put a key into a door. The apartment's parlor spread wide before them, its bay window facing the paler brick walls of the *Hof*, with a cushioned seat full of magazines. The furnishings were old-fashioned like the Eislers', dark and heavy but stylish, more expensive, nothing missing here: a floral divan, an orange leather armchair, and a coffee table piled with newspapers and coffee cups.

Grete followed Berni through the dining room, which held a twelve-seat table extended too many times; it sagged in the cracks. She could hear a radio in the kitchen: Wagner segued into Margo Lion. A cheery female voice with no sense of pitch sang along with the lyrics. Grete tried to step quietly. She didn't want to see anyone else.

"Here's where I sleep," Berni announced, pulling aside a curtain. "Wonderful sunlight in the afternoon. This is a two-bedroom flat, really; Sonje has the large one, Anita the small, and mine used to be the dining room—you can tell from the windows—but it's good to have my own room, *alles knorke*."

Berni spoke the *Berliner Dialekt* now, saying *ick* instead of *ich* and using slang Grete didn't recognize; she'd have said something were she not overwhelmed by the room where her sister lived without her. The walls were striped in mauve and white, with roses on the white parts. A chair rail went nearly all the way round the room, stopping where a stained outline revealed the ghost of a cabinet. The room smelled of cinnamon and something else culinary.

Berni showed her the sleeping pallet on the floor, covered by a gray blanket. "They say it's good to sleep on something hard." She yanked the curtain back over the threshold; there was no door. Then she pushed a pile of clothing off her chair, offered Grete a seat, and knelt in front of her. "Isn't it marvelous to be out in the world? Last week I saw the Graf Zeppelin float past the cathedral. Scared me half to death before I realized what the thing was! But I want news from you. How is my bird?"

Grete put her hands in her lap. "I'm growing a breast."

Berni sat still for a minute. Her brow wrinkled, and she swallowed, the corners of her mouth trembling. "Singular?"

"Stop it!" cried Grete, though she could feel laughter bursting within her, too; it felt good. "It's not funny."

"But it is," said Berni, wiping her eye, her legs curled underneath her. "Oh, Grete-bird, how I've missed you. Let me see this breast."

"No." Grete crossed her arms.

"I have a feeling you'll get another one to go with it."

Anxious to change the subject, Grete searched her mind for a question. There were so many that she had trouble choosing one. "Where did you get all these clothes?"

"There are others who live here, and we share. Now! Let me offer you a slice of sauerbraten. Growing breasts requires sustenance."

That was the smell: beef round marinated in vinegar. Looking upon the tender meat, its dark coffee-colored glaze, Grete nearly fainted. "You don't need to give me some," she croaked.

"There, a wafer for you, a wafer for me. And some meat."

The biscuit, faintly sweet, crumbled in Grete's mouth. Berni pulled the vanity stool over to the foot of the armchair and put the plate on a small table. Meat. *Fleisch.* Grete stared at it: two melting slices with deep black skins, veins of precious fat. She consumed it without utensils, like an animal. Apple kraut, too, deep red from beets, sharp with onions, stained the tips of her fingers pink. A few cold potatoes in white sauce—those went down in three gulps.

As her belly filled and Grete came out of her fog, she became more aware. Berni hadn't prepared this meal. Who had? A maid?

Berni had more money than she let on. Her claim that she couldn't support Grete as well was only an excuse. But why did she need one?

Before she could ask, Berni began firing questions at her. She wanted to know if Grete slept in a bed, if the Eislers were kind to her. She wanted to know, truly, was she well fed?

Grete responded between telltale growls, her belly unused to consuming so much at once. She did have a bed, her employers were kind, and she ate better than most of Berlin.

"Grete." Berni stood and leaned over the chair to hug her. The smell of cinnamon grew stronger, with a bit of armpit sweat that was not altogether unpleasant. "I am sorry we've been apart for so long."

Right then Grete's molars made the unhappy discovery of a piece of gristle. The combined effect, the snap of the gristle and Berni's words, sent a shudder through her. Why was it that sometimes an apology made everything worse?

Grete spit the white morsel into her napkin. "What do we do now?" Her voice came out strained and desperate. If someone had mentioned the Eislers to her then, she would have had only a vague idea of the outlines of their features. At the moment they had no more dimension than Gudrun's paper dolls. They could not compare to the live face in front of her.

"We save every pfennig. We work and work until we have a little pile of money, and then we look for rooms in a boarding house together."

"What about here?" Grete said, ignoring the fact that she had no desire to get to know any of Berni's neighbors. "This is a boarding house."

Berni's lips twitched. "You don't want to live here. It's not the place for you."

Grete thought of Frau Eisler calling Berni *whore*, and her stomach dropped.

As though she could read Grete's thoughts, Berni said: "Tell me. What's your mistress like? Is she pretty?"

"She is not particularly pretty, but she's . . . respectable."

"What are their political affiliations? I ask because . . ." Berni didn't finish her sentence. A clock in the parlor began its tinny song, and she looked toward the hallway. "It's late. The Eislers will wonder where you are."

"Berni." Grete took Berni's hand and examined the residue underneath the nails. Bluish-black tar—cosmetics—and a deeper yellow-brown stain—tobacco. The cracks in Berni's palms were red. She had written something on her skin and then smudged the ink. Grete could make out the number *2* and the letter *L*. "Berni," she said again. She looked into Berni's brown eyes. The whites were clear, alert. A question waited at the back of Grete's mouth, but she could not bring it out.

Berni lifted the fine blond hairs out of Grete's face. "I'll write you again. If that Frau Eisler complains about you getting mail, tell her to go shit in her hat and pull it over her ears."

Grete couldn't help but laugh. She tried to read the look on Berni's face—guilt? Yes, that, and something else—but then she heard a shout in the street. Berni ran to kneel under the sill, and Grete followed. They watched four Hitler Youths in brown sprint past. A group of men followed, running at top speed. Something glinted in one of their back pockets: the barrel of a gun. Another man followed on a motorbike, making the glass vibrate. Berni covered her ears.

"It was better when they only threw rocks," she said. "Do you know about all this?"

"Yes," Grete breathed. "Poor Horst Wessel."

"Poor Horst Wessel?" Berni gave her a funny look. "Horst Wessel was a thug the Nazis made into a martyr. Don't tell me you fell for that song." She chucked Grete's cheek. "Come on, I'll take you home. You may not be safe."

They went down the fire stairs. Grete wondered for a moment what made Berni avoid her housemates, but then she had nothing to think about but balance as they rode toward Charlottenburg on Berni's black bicycle, Grete perched on the seat, Berni standing on the pedals. It had begun to rain. Grete squinted and held on to the stem. Berni took her through the labyrinth of tenements off the main streets, and she caught glimpses of the alleys and interlocking *Höfe* of Berlin. The people here were invisible, but their odors announced themselves: sewage, pickled cabbage, motor oil.

Berni let her off a block from the Eislers' building. "We will be together soon, Bird."

Grete nodded, but she'd heard this every time they'd parted in the last few years, and the words had lost their meaning. She watched her sister pedal away, still standing though the seat was free. She felt a sudden panic. She'd been given a safe ride home, but nobody would do the same for Berni.

• • •

A few nights later, Grete sat up quickly in the dark. A sound had woken her. She saw that the windows were open; a breeze puffed the pale green curtain, through which she could make out a silhouette crouched on the balcony. She gasped, shut her eyes, shrank into a ball. Klaus would know what to do; she looked for Klaus and found that his bed was empty.

After much steeling of nerve, she whispered his name. Her voice was strangled with phlegm. "Klaus. Is that you out there?"

His long-nosed face appeared against the curtain. "Shh. Come down here."

"But Gudrun," Grete said, heart pounding.

"She won't wake. Climb down the ladder."

Grete put her bare feet on the wooden rungs two at a time. She passed Gudrun, slumbering with her mouth open, clutching the doll she'd scalped that morning. The hair was strewn about the floor. Grete felt sure she was the only one who noticed how much rubbish this spoiled child generated. Uneaten food, little wrappers, torn cards and valentines.

She put a shaking foot on the sill. Klaus's thin arms and legs were bent into the wrought-iron cage surrounding the bedroom window, a space about five feet in height and eighteen inches deep. He held a cigarette between his lips.

"Come out here." He offered her a dry hand, and when their palms touched, Grete felt a zing. She lowered one foot, then the other, onto the iron bars; her ankles could easily have fit through the spaces between them. Her foot touched fabric. Klaus had tied something to the bars. She found her balance and glimpsed their reflection in the darkened windows across the courtyard, two figures standing above the red, black, and white of the Nazi flag.

*You're political*, Grete wanted to say, but instead she gripped the front of her nightgown so that he wouldn't notice her new development and looked down. The slate mosaic floor shone in wet squares of black, mauve, and green. The area was empty save for forgotten wet laundry. One lost stocking curled on the ground like a snake.

"I can't sleep. This evening we had a *Heimabend*," Klaus said, as though a "home evening" explained everything. "At our group leader's house. There's another parliamentary election coming in November. We have to maintain the momentum Herr Hitler began building last month. Did you know Hitler was the only one who predicted the current economic crisis?"

Grete flushed. She couldn't admit aloud that all she knew of Herr Hitler was that he'd run for president in March and lost. She was surprised to hear he'd gained "momentum" in the meantime. Fortunately, Klaus didn't wait for her to reply. "It's a headline in the papers I'm delivering tomorrow," he said. She wanted to ask what paper he delivered, if he worked for the Nazi Party, and if that was why she'd never heard him mention payment. But he went on. "Herr Hitler knows how we can get out of this, too, if people would listen. Lower taxes on farms, raise the wage. Think, Grete—farmers could afford to grow more corn, more beans, raise more livestock. Meat for dinner after an honest day's work. Does that sound good?"

"It does," she said in her small voice. "It does sound very good, Klaus."

"I wish my father could see it. Righting the wrongs of Versailles should matter to him more than anyone."

"Your Herr Papa is busy and troubled, *nicht*?"

"He is lost. Our veterans try to work, but others have taken their jobs. We mustn't look down on them, though, even the homeless and maimed. They, too, are part of the Volk." He looked intently at her now, his eyes white-shiny in the light coming from the moon. Grete felt dizzy. She opened her feet to steady herself, still standing on the knots in the Nazi flag. A breeze picked up her nightdress, and she remembered that she wore nothing underneath it. Her left nipple throbbed a bit, only the left.

He cocked an eyebrow at her when she pressed her skirt to her legs. He so clearly wanted to look like a man, his cigarette dangling from his lips. She found it touching.

"How old are you?" he asked.

"Almost fifteen."

"I see you with your rosary in bed. Why are you Catholic?"

Why? He might as well have asked why she'd been born, why her eyes were blue.

"You can be anything you want," he continued. "I wonder who your parents are. They look to have had good blood."

"I know who my parents were," she said quickly. "My papa was in the war, too." She knew what Berni would say if she were here, the story she'd trot out. She'd tell him about everything, from the blackbird that nested in the eaves of their mother's porch to the color of her stocking garters. "I had parents," she repeated, her voice thin, her skin prickling. Speaking to him in reality felt quite different from the make-believe conversations she had with him when she was alone in the alley. She was irritated with him, she realized, for implying she didn't know her parents, and she opened her mouth and asked a question. "Why are *you* a Nazi?"

Klaus's cigarette dropped a tube of ash. "Would you want to hand over half your wages to France and England? Under Hitler, we'd stop paying reparations."

"I see," said Grete. Sister Maria's warnings about civil unrest came back to her then, and she gasped. "You have to be careful, Klaus. In the streets."

"I know. It's not about punching someone's face. It's about changing minds." He began speaking about the failed Republic. The Social Democrats were weak, he said; they were able neither to tame the radical Socialists nor to learn from the strength of the Nazis. He spoke of blood, good German blood, tainted from the outside and from within. She watched his bird's profile as he spoke. The tip of his nose dipped with each consonant, pointing toward his mouth on words like *Vaterland*. With his skin greenish in the moonlight, his body frail from lack of food, and his face marred by the deep circles under his eyes, he looked unhealthy, even bloodless. She ached to give him some of her own blood, transfuse it, let him drink it.

"Maybe you should think about joining the BDM," he said finally.

"What is that?"

"The Bund Deutscher Mädel. The Hitler Youth for girls. I wonder if maids are eligible." He offered her the end of his cigarette, half of which she took into her lips, nearly burning them. "Hungry?" he said, amused. "Don't eat it."

The odor reminded her of Berni. She pulled so much smoke out of it that it burned to nothing, and Klaus dropped it through the bars. Grete waited for the sizzling sound when it touched the wet slate, but heard nothing.

"Are you?" he asked.

"Am I what?"

"Hungry."

"Of course. What I mean to say is, your family feeds me as well as they can—"

"*I* am hungry. What do we have in the pantry?"

"I'm sorry, Klaus. We have nothing but spices, a jar of salt."

"Say that again. Just the last word."

She tried to look away, but he pulled her chin up so that they were face to face. "*Salz.*"

"Why do you speak that way? Your voice is all in your nose. You didn't say the end of the word—it's *salz. Salz.* You're missing that *–tz.*"

"Salz."

"You can't hear everything, can you?"

She took a long breath. She had never really spoken about this to anyone except Berni, but when she saw that his face registered only concern, no mockery, that his undivided attention was on her, a sob slipped out of her mouth. "It's only going to get worse!"

He tilted his head to the side. "How do you know?"

"The nurse, at St. Luisa's." She sniffed, brushing a tear from under her eye. Her ear whined. "She told me it might be pro— progressive."

"She said it might be? Well, that means it might not be."

She nodded and took a breath, and then she told him everything: that her right ear buzzed and hummed and rang. That today when she woke, she heard only silence on that side for at least an hour. She explained, words coming faster now, how she monitored the placement of everyone in a room. How she tried to keep his mother, at all times, on her left. How the little sounds escaped her: breaths, rustles, hisses.

He scratched the fine hairs on his chin. "Perhaps someone hit you very hard when you were young. Had you thought of that?"

Yes, she'd thought of that.

"One of the sisters, maybe?" he said.

The sisters had struck children from time to time, but Grete couldn't remember anything that would have destroyed her hearing. She couldn't answer.

"This won't do, Grete. If your left ear can hear, there isn't any reason for you to speak that way, don't you agree? You can hear me now, *nicht*? *Salz*. You're saying 'salth.'"

"Salz."

"Let me show you." Klaus held onto the bars overhead to steady himself, and then let one of his hands go. It seemed to take forever to reach her mouth, for his dry fingertips to land on her lips. With his other hand—he now had to balance his feet on the bars—he grabbed her wrist and placed hers on *his* mouth. In between her fingers, she felt his warm, tickling breath. His lips were smooth and wet and soft.

"Feel how I speak," he said. Sharp bursts of air escaped his lips as he enunciated. "Say *fleisch*."

"*Fleisch*," she said, beneath his touch.

"No. Let go of this foolishness. Focus on the end." She focused on his eyes instead, pale and luminous and pointed directly at her. "It's all in your mind. *Fleisch*."

"Fleisch."

"Better." The mouth under her fingers thinned into a smile. "You can hear the difference?"

"Ich kann!"

In her excitement she'd forgotten to lower her voice, and they heard Gudrun stir. Grete gasped. She and Klaus, strangers yesterday, stood with their hands moistened by each other's mouths. She'd forgotten to cover her chest; the one swollen bud pulsed like a new heart.

They dropped their arms at the same time and laughed nervously. Grete tugged the neck of her nightshirt. Klaus pushed aside the bedroom curtain, warned her not to wake Gudrun, and helped her over the sill. He followed her inside, where they climbed into their beds.

# GRETE, 1932

By day, Grete and Klaus remained strangers, particularly when his mother was around. He pretended she didn't exist, and she shrank in his presence.

But at night as Gudrun snored, by candlelight in the corner of their little bedroom, they practiced. Klaus had found one of Gudrun's discarded childhood puzzles, a set of interlocking wooden blocks carved with the alphabet. He and Grete went through them one by one, spending more time on the ones that gave her trouble, *K* and *F* and *scharfes S*. She had never felt such freedom and acceptance. While Berni had always tried to solve Grete's problems by taking them off her hands, Klaus seemed to believe Grete could be taught to work them out for herself.

Herr Eisler announced that he'd lost his job at the factory on the first of September. This came as no surprise; his wife had been praying for that very thing not to happen for weeks. Grete stood sniffling over the sink that morning, peeling a potato. What would become of her now? Would Berni take her in? And could she leave Klaus?

She gave a start when Klaus appeared at her shoulder. He had a bag of newspapers strapped to his back. "Dry those eyes," he said.

"But your parents—"

"They aren't looking to the future. Our campaign worked last time and will again." He gestured over his shoulder, to the copies of *Der Angriff.* "The Party earned thirty-seven percent of the votes in the July election. Two hundred and thirty seats in the Reichstag. Do you understand?"

"I'm not sure," she murmured, focusing on a stubborn crust on one of the dishes.

"Next time it will be even more." Klaus took a sip of coffee from the white cup in his hand. The window was open before them. Someone had brought a radio into the *Hof* and was listening to a broadcast in English. Grete watched Klaus's jaw tighten. He cursed.

"What is it?" she asked.

He shook his head. "The BBC's telling the world about our troubles. If I were a fighting man I'd go down and set our neighbors straight."

"You can understand English?"

*"At schools, very good English I learn."*

Grete was impressed. "What did you just say?"

He took one of the serpentine potato peels sitting inside the sink and dropped it into his mouth. "I said I'm hungry."

She blushed, watching him eat the raw peel. They listened to the broadcast a little longer, Klaus muttering, "Brazen."

"Grete." Frau Eisler had burst into the kitchen, her arms and hair splayed like pale tentacles, and Grete and Klaus sprang apart. "We'll have to pay you double next week. We won't be able to complete our mortgage payment if we give that much to you this Friday."

An uncomfortable moment passed. Frau Eisler and Klaus stared at Grete, and she felt even more blood rush to her face. "Of course," she said. "Do not worry about paying me."

Frau Eisler closed her eyes and nodded once. Klaus yawned and peered into the courtyard, finishing his coffee, and Grete went on peeling, her face on fire. She composed a letter to Berni in her head. *I must see you. Tell me where and when. It is urgent, sister.*

• • •

The following Wednesday, without waiting for a reply from Berni, Grete took the U-Bahn to Schöneberg. Aboveground, she watched a pair of painters plaster an advertisement for "Back to Nature" body powder on a Litfaß column. The girl in the ad wore a short skirt and had a wide smile. She held a lily in one hand and a compact in the other. "New Woman!" the copy shouted, "Use your senses!"

A Negro girl in an advertisement. *Whoever thought such a thing would help sell powder?* That was what Frau Eisler or Klaus would say. As Grete waited for traffic to clear, she watched the men cover her shiny brown calves and vulgar pink strappy heels with transparent glue. Her legs were quite beautiful and reminded Grete of horses' limbs.

When she rang the bell at the boarding house, she heard a shout inside, and finally someone ran down the stairs. The door opened. Fräulein Schmidt stood there drying her hands on a towel. "Oh, hello, Grete. Can I help you?"

Grete swallowed. Why did she care that Fräulein Schmidt remembered her name? This was the woman who'd taken Berni away. Grete should have reviled her, but she had to admit she was lovely. Her curls were such an unusual shade of strawberry blond. Grete cast her eyes at her tiny feet and mumbled, "May I please see Bernadette?"

"Berni? Oh, I imagine she's out somewhere. I've wondered about you, dear thing. Would you like to come in for tea? A slice of strudel?"

That was the warm-apple scent emerging from the house. Grete thought of the strudel and cream she'd seen the sisters eat on Easter. "No, thank you. Do you know where I can find her?"

Fräulein Schmidt's forehead wrinkled. "Have a warm dessert and tea and wait for her here. English-style tea, mind you. I serve English-style tea."

Grete hesitated, her mouth watering. Fräulein Schmidt's full lips pursed in satisfaction, and in that gesture she reminded Grete of someone, she looked like someone else—Rachel. Fräulein Schmidt, she realized with fear, was Jewish. "Tell me where Berni is, please."

Fräulein Schmidt looked her up and down. "All right. I believe she's at a restaurant." She told Grete to look for Berni at the Silver Star Club, in Mitte, just outside Potsdamer Platz.

On her way, Grete tried not to think what Berni might be doing in something called the Silver Star Club at midday, midweek. She passed the line of taxis and piles of luggage outside Anhalter Bahnhof, then walked through Potsdamer Platz, where music lured daytime shoppers toward leather goods and cologne. Rich, childless women, Frau Eisler said, who were too self-centered to save their money. Finally Grete found the club next door to a jeweler. In the window, a pair of gold handcuffs inlaid with rubies and emeralds lay on a red velvet cloth. Her reflection in the glass, by contrast, was the same gray as the city. Behind her, a smudge of brown, red, and gray. The SA were marching past, singing.

*Blood must flow, blood must flow! Blood must flow as cudgels fall, thick as hail!*

Some pedestrians stopped, and a good number of them booed. One of the marching boys dropped his flag so that the pointed end was like a bayonet and lunged at a man and two women. Grete flinched. What had she heard Klaus say about the SA—that they were brutes, but necessary? Their ranks had grown to four times the size of the emasculated army, enough for the country to defend itself if necessary. Defense wasn't pretty, according to Klaus.

The doorman at the Silver Star hardly looked at Grete, his eyes on the departing boots. She was glad to get inside the velvet curtains, and then she took a breath and the heavy cigar smoke hit her. She felt trumpet blasts in her gut. The music was terrible, lawless, no better than the horn blasts and backfiring cars she'd left outside. She would have fallen to her knees had someone not run up and grabbed her upper arms. Berni's breath was hot in her ear.

"Sister, what are you doing here?" Berni took her wrist and yanked her through the bar, which passed in a blur. Women stood on tables twirling pistols and rope lassos, their buttocks half-exposed by blue bloomers. A band of black men gyrated onstage.

"Ouch—Berni, ouch! Let go!"

Berni flung her at a chair between the stage and the kitchen doors, then got down close to her face. "I'm working and I don't have time for this. Here." She reached into the pocket of her black half-apron. She wore a maroon silk bodysuit similar to a bathing costume with white pumps that reminded Grete of little ducks. Her shoulder strap had been torn and tied in a knot. Berni pried Grete's fingers open and stuffed some cash inside. "Buy yourself a U-Bahn ticket and lunch. Get lunch before you go home, and eat it all yourself. Do you hear me?"

Grete thrust out her jaw. She opened her hand and counted five marks.

"Sit outside, under . . ." Berni said something that was lost to the music. "Listen! Have a beer like a big girl, and forget everyone but yourself for an hour. Then go home before dark."

Grete felt faint. The band began a mocking, unpatriotic version of a traditional German song. Their legs flew this way and that as though they were made of rubber. There were foreign men making a ruckus at the bar. The coat girl in the corner had a bruise blooming around one eye. "Berni," Grete said, "what are you doing here?"

"I told you. I'm a cigarette girl." Berni reached into her pocket and produced a little tin, on its face a blond goddess in a toga holding a torch. She glanced up when someone said something Grete couldn't hear, and a look of unmitigated fear passed over Berni's face.

At first the figure in front of Grete's unfocused eyes seemed beautiful, a woman of movie star stature, dressed in the same uniform as Berni, but her hair, hat, fingernails, and shoes were all the same shade of tomato. She moved so much that Grete couldn't get a good look at her—she dipped her red beret over her eye and winked at Berni, then looked over her shoulder at Grete and sniffed with her big nose. Something in the gesture seemed familiar, and Grete's stomach growled uneasily.

"Come over here, Berni's sister. We have grapefruit."

Grete looked helplessly to Berni, who nodded after a moment, indicating that they should follow. *Who is that*, Grete mouthed, and Berni responded only, "Anita."

They followed Anita's hard haunches to a little table with a bowl of pale yellow fruit in the middle, the linen littered with shoe prints. A telephone marked with an enormous number 16 sat beside the bowl. Anita smiled at Grete and tossed a grapefruit from one hand to the other. "Nice to see you, Margarete." She began to giggle, hiding her face from Grete so that she could look at Berni and whisper something.

Berni rolled her eyes. "And now we're all friends. Grete-bird, we have work to do, and I'm sure you do as well. I'll show you out."

"What kind of hostess are you?" Anita said. Grete watched her pierce the grapefruit rind with one curved scarlet nail, releasing a fragrant spray. There was something obscene in the way she split the pale skin. She gnashed the fruit with her crowded yellow teeth, and Grete remembered. Fiedler's. Libations of Illyria. Horrified, she turned toward Berni, who glared at the tabletop as if she knew she was a traitor.

"Have some." Anita gestured toward the bowl. She spit a fat grapefruit seed onto the table, where it lay like a slug. "You look like you need it, kid."

"Grete," Berni said, taking her hand. "How is everything at the Eislers'? Truly."

"Why must you keep asking me this? All is well." No way would Grete give Anita the satisfaction of hearing how the Eislers suffered. "I am very fortunate to work for such a man."

Anita laughed toward Berni again, and Grete felt panicked to miss part of what she said. ". . . sweet how . . . loves Herr Papa, isn't it, Berni?"

Berni stood. "All right. I believe it is time for you to go, Grete. Say farewell." Grete couldn't resist glancing at Anita one last time, who narrowed her eyes, before Berni rushed her toward the back, past waiters in tired tuxedos. They barreled through a door with a circular window into the dark, clean kitchen. One chef sat on a stool, asleep sitting up. Berni crossed the tile as though she knew exactly where she was going and found a door. They emerged in an alley between the bar and the jewelry store.

"Why did you do that?" Grete asked, rubbing her upper arm. The dim sunlight and cool air, she had to admit, felt very good.

"Did you really want to sit there with Anita?"

"No. How can you befriend her, Berni?"

Berni rolled her eyes. She unhitched a velvet purse from under her skirt and opened its clasp. "I'll give you some more money, to tide you over until next time."

Relief overtook Grete. "I do not want you to think I came for money." But of course she had; she'd planned to ask for a little, just this once, just to give Klaus what he needed. And why shouldn't she ask Berni for it? She lifted her chin. Berni owed it to her, the prodigal Berni who had enjoyed herself while Grete suffered.

"I don't think you came just for money. But I can see you need it." Berni looked very tired and defeated. "I wish it had gone better with the Eislers."

"All *is* well with the Eislers." How dare Berni act so superior, she of the champagne and cigarettes? How sinful, how indulgent she was. How sloppy in choosing her friends. She and Anita partied while Klaus and his family, and much of Berlin, suffered.

Now that they were outside, the noise contained in the club, Grete could think better, could speak better. "Why have you turned your back on goodness? You've become what they say—do you know what people say?"

Berni crossed her arms and pursed her lips.

"What do people say?" Anita had opened the door to the alley. The music surged and fell away. Grete shrank back. Now she could see that Anita's face powder did not match the olive skin of her throat. There was something else, too: her neck and chin were oddly grayish.

"Well, go on," Berni said.

"They say—" Frau Eisler's voice came in and out of Grete's mind. *Whore-lids. Greedy, idle women.* "A girl's virtue is the most important possession she has—"

"You hear this from his wife, eh?" Berni spat. "Fascinating. What else does she say?"

"The German family is—is the basis of our economy, and the family is centered on virtue." If Klaus could see her now; she was pronouncing everything wrong. She thought of their letter games. "You know this, Berni. You know from Sister Josephine."

Berni's face faltered. Anita took a step closer to Grete, who continued. "Without virtue, a girl is *nichts aber der Müll.* To be thrown away like—" Grete stopped.

Anita's breastbone gave it away. There were blemishes, a delta of shorn hairs in the middle of her taut chest. Grete put her hand to her mouth. When Anita caught her looking, she covered her sternum. "Don't stare at me. Why are you staring like that?" She glanced toward Berni. "I understand now, Berni. She thinks she's too good for us. And so do you."

"Anita—" Berni started coughing, the unhealthy bark that Grete had heard many a late night in the orphanage. Without thinking Grete put a hand on her back, finding ribs closer to the surface than she'd expected. "She didn't mean to insult you," Berni croaked to Anita, but it was too late. Anita's arm was quick. She had encircled Grete's wrist in her big palm. Berni, still coughing, tried to stop her but doubled over, hands on her knees.

What came next seemed to happen very slowly. Anita took Grete's hand down and then up, under her hem, toward the tops of her legs. She guided Grete's fingers into her crotch, where Grete felt something she had never touched before: a naked penis and a pair of warm testicles.

To her horror, something twinged between her own legs.

Then Berni was between them, pushing them apart. She had Anita up against the wall of the Silver Star. "You're crazy! You're crazy! She's an innocent!"

Anita was laughing, a bit too loudly, as if she knew she'd done wrong. Grete sobbed into the crook of her arm. Her fingers tingled. Her head pounded. "I'm no innocent. I'm no innocent anymore." She heard Anita's heels clicking away, toward the street.

"I'm sorry," Berni whispered. When she came close she smelled like Anita, like liquor. "She was showing off, can you see? Showing off! She doesn't know how to make a joke."

"*She?*" Grete cried. "A joke?" She took off running. Behind her she thought she heard Berni sob. The afternoon had grown dark; the department stores in Mitte were igniting their fluorescent towers. Taxi headlights flickered in the mist. She ran toward Charlottenburg and safety, Berni's money in her pocket, in the opposite direction from the way Anita had gone.

• • •

That Sunday, Grete prepared a feast for the Eislers. She woke before dawn to complete her chores so that she could spend all day cooking. She was meticulous. She did everything perfectly. She had never seen a meal like it before in her life, not even on the sisters' table. But she had imagined eating one like it so many times that she knew she could create it. The dinner came straight from her dreams.

The sausage itself came from Rachel. Grete had given her the money with an order: pork links, butter, rosemary, which Rachel fulfilled. Grete cooked while the Eislers were at church. Zarah

Leander's voice trumpeted from the radio. She could not help but dance in the kitchen as she fried the sausage with sliced potatoes and a purple onion. She'd woken in the middle of the night with a pain; her right breast had begun to bud. Not everything about her would be lopsided.

To sweeten the evening further, Herr Eisler came home to eat. Just before dinner, when his wife asked nervously if there would be enough food for him, Grete could reassure her. Oh yes, she had plenty of sausage, split down the middle, the insides caramelized brown, the skins perfectly seared. She had intended to eat one herself, but by the time Sunday arrived she decided to give the extra to Klaus.

He initially refused. "Are you sure you just want potatoes for your dinner?"

"Yes, yes." She gave him a long look, all her gratitude for what he'd done for her speech, she hoped, written across her face. He raised his eyebrows.

Grete had borrowed a fourth chair from Rachel as well; fortunately, nobody asked where it came from. She poured herself a glass of weak tea from the pot at the center of the table, and beer for the others. "Eat," she said as though she were the host, adding neither "sir" nor "please." And they did. Even Gudrun professed it delicious. For once there was no talk of politics, not a single frightening news story or reiteration of the priest's homily. Nobody asked Herr Eisler how his search for work in the East had gone this week, though he hadn't been home since Wednesday. A happy hush fell over the table until the plates were clear.

"This must have cost us dearly." Frau Eisler wiped grease from her lips. "Are you sure we can afford to dine this way?"

"Please don't concern yourself," Grete said. "The cost should not worry you."

Frau Eisler beamed and lightly pinched the soft part of Gudrun's arm, as though the child would already have plumpened. Nobody else asked how she'd purchased the food, not even Herr Eisler. He and his son shoveled it into their mouths as though they'd never eaten before.

"After dinner," Frau Eisler asked Grete, "won't you join us in some parlor games?" Her usually wan face had taken on a glow, especially when she looked at her husband.

"Oh, yes, after I finish washing the dishes," Grete replied.

"I'll help you," said Herr Eisler. He and his wife both smiled benevolently at Grete, and she felt she could not be happier.

After the dishes were cleared, Frau Eisler called them into the parlor. She lay on the floor, her crooked body stretched out on the thin woven rug. She had unpacked half of a box of dominoes. Gudrun, her legs and arms slung across a chair, had begun to whine. "I don't want to play Chicken Foot. I hate that game."

Nobody listened to her. Herr Eisler worked a newspaper puzzle with his bad leg crossed underneath the good one and a pipe in his mouth. Frau Eisler constructed a foot of dominoes in the center of the carpet and invited Grete to join her when it was ready. Klaus drew in his sketchbook, and Grete, face flushed, perched on the edge of his chair to look over his shoulder. Between his charcoal-smudged fingers she watched a mountain emerge, dark pines, a deer in the foreground with eight-point antlers.

"That's beautiful," she said, her voice loud and clear. His parents looked up to see her sprawled across the back of his chair, and Herr Eisler smiled.

"Come play with me over here, Grete," said Frau Eisler.

Grete's ear remained silent through the domino game. The Eislers, for once, weren't even indulging Gudrun. The little girl's face bloomed red with sweat, and the short blond ringlets around her face were stuck to her skin. Finally, at about nine o'clock, the child began moaning and clutching her stomach. Grete watched Frau Eisler's eyes flicker toward her daughter, and her heart began to beat quickly. She would have done anything to draw her mistress's attention away. She would have said anything they wanted to hear about Berni.

"It was the sausage," Frau Eisler concluded after she pressed a palm to Gudrun's forehead, and Grete knew the fantasy evening had come to an end.

"How well did you cook it?" Herr Eisler asked kindly.

"I—I . . ." Grete stuttered, struggling to speak correctly with Klaus at her shoulder. "Didn't it seem well cooked? I'm sorry, sir, I should have tried the meat."

"*Fleisch*," Klaus whispered. His mother gave him a puzzled look.

"I feel perfectly well," Herr Eisler said.

"Well, Gudrun does not," his wife replied. "Grete, take her and give her a cool bath."

That night Herr Eisler, Frau Eisler, and Klaus turned in at the normal hour, while Grete sat with Gudrun as she retched into an old chamber pot. Every time she was sick, Grete cleaned her face with a cool, wet towel and then carried it down to the alley, gagging. Each time she returned she found Gudrun calling out, loud enough to wake her family.

"Grete, Grete," she moaned, curled on the kitchen floor. "Why did you leave me?"

"Hush," Grete said, exhausted, emboldened by their isolation. "You're going to wake the others. Shut your mouth and try to sleep."

This was punishment, Grete knew. She never should have gone into a place like the Silver Star expecting that she wouldn't run into trouble. God knew she was unclean now. What did He think of Berni? Her thoughts roiled late into the night as Gudrun continued to heave, long after her stomach was empty.

Finally Grete awoke, a sour taste in her mouth, unaware until now that she'd drifted off. Gudrun was gone. Grete sat up so quickly that she collided with the dark shape in front of her, and found her damp head pressed into Herr Eisler's chest.

"Let's put you to bed, sweetie." He let her stay close to him for a moment. "Gudrun went to bed on her own." His voice was gravelly, deep; she could feel it resonating against her.

He carried Grete into the bedroom. Through the fog of her ear she thought she heard him thank her for cooking them such wonderful food. He climbed the ladder to her loft and placed her head on the pillow. "I'm sorry," she whispered.

"For what?" Herr Eisler said. "Children are sick all the time."

She shook her head. "I did something wrong. I ordered the sausage from Rachel, across the hall. She must have poisoned us." A tear slipped down her cheek.

Herr Eisler paused for a moment. "Rachel did not poison us, Grete. You were right to ask her to buy groceries for you. It is what neighbors do for one another. Who told you to be suspicious of the Jews? Klaus?"

Grete couldn't answer. She began to weep silently, so hard her shoulders shook. He touched her head, then crept out of the room. After he'd gone she could still feel his arms underneath her shoulders and knees.

• • •

In Monday's mail a letter arrived from Berni. Another came Thursday, and then the following week, two more. There was no use hiding them from Frau Eisler, who opened the first one and read it aloud, looking to Grete for her reaction.

"She's asking you to run away with her. Look here: 'Meet me at the Charlottenburg station, and bring everything you own. I can explain everything, and we can be together.' What's the meaning of this, Grete? Have you always intended to abandon us?"

Grete took the envelope without a word. The return address was still Sonje's, in Schöneberg. Slowly she tore the letter, envelope and all, in half. "I will never live with that creature," she said quietly, knowing Frau Eisler would think she meant Berni. After that Frau Eisler handed her the envelopes unopened, as though she could tell there was no risk of Grete running off with her sister, or even writing back.

Klaus kept the radio in the parlor on all the time now, making the apartment feel busier than usual and connected to something bigger. It helped distract Grete. While she canned fruit or ran a brush over the floors, she would forget Berni and Anita, but a minute-long break brought everything back.

Weeks went by, becoming a month and more since she'd seen Berni, and the letters slowed to a trickle. One afternoon in November, Grete stood at the table teasing pie crust out of a half a scoop of flour and a bit of butter. Klaus sulked in his bedroom; the Party had lost votes in the election. Grete felt relieved, though she didn't entirely know why and didn't tell Klaus. Apple pie would cheer him. She had four apples peeled and cored when children began shouting in the *Hof*. Frau Eisler came in, dusting off her hands, and followed Grete to the window. They looked down on the top of a shiny scarlet head. Grete clapped her hand over her mouth.

Frau Eisler sprang back, eyes wide. "Is that Bernadette?"

Grete shook her head.

"Someone needs to shoo that whore away from the children. I'll get Klaus."

"No, no, *gnädige Frau*. I'll go talk to hi—her." Grete could hardly hear her own voice over the thud of blood in her earlobes. "No need for anyone else to come."

Grete took a trash bag with her to act as a sort of shield. When she got down to the courtyard it was empty, except for Anita. Empty chairs and cups sat on the ground. Everyone had gone inside to watch. Grete made a wide circle on wobbling ankles. Anita stood still, a red pillar.

"Listen, mouse. I'm here to tell you that I'm sorry." Anita looked away and took a few deep breaths. "All right? Now will you stop ignoring Berni's notes?"

Grete winced. An apology was not what she wanted; for once in her life she wanted silence, oblivion. "Please, be quiet. I'm begging you." She looked around. The building stayed troublingly quiet, its incessant radios turned down. Laundry flapped overhead, spraying bleach-smelling drops.

"I've offered you an apology. For Berni's sake, I admit." Anita took a step closer, and Grete shrank down. Up close, Grete could see makeup caked solid pink on his sunken cheeks. "You don't know how lucky you are, to have such a sister."

"I knew my sister once. I don't know her now."

"You don't know her? Let me offer you some knowledge."

*Erkenntnis.* It was a word Grete and Klaus had practiced, with its troublesome final *s*. She shook her head, but Anita continued. He gave a tiny poking scratch under the side of his wig. "How did Berni learn your address, the Eislers' names? How did I find my way here?"

"Sister Josephine told her." Grete turned her back. With Anita behind her she could understand fewer words. She looked up at the gray sky crisscrossed with clothing. Klaus's flag hung limp beneath the Eislers' balcony. Their windows were open.

Anita was saying something about the sacrifices Grete had made for the Eisler family. His waxy-scented lips came close to Grete's good ear. "They should be grateful to Berni, too."

When she shut her eyes and covered her ears, she could pretend Anita wasn't there.

"Are they? Do you praise Berni's name together?"

Perhaps nobody else could hear him, either.

"Does Frau Eisler know it was Berni who got you this position?"

Grete spun around. "That's not true." Herr Eisler had chosen her over anybody else, the day the sun and rain appeared at the same time. A miracle. *The devil is having a parish fair.*

Anita had his large hand on Grete's shoulder, in the manner of someone offering help. "Why do you think the man singled you out? How else would he have known you?"

"Because . . ." *Because I was special, they loved me, they saved me from hardship.*

Anita moved his hand to Grete's upper arm, gentler now, his touch lighter than Sister Maria's had been that day. "He came in and asked for you by name." His tone was finally almost kind, his voice low. "Because he is Berni's lover."

Grete did not have to have heard that term before to understand what it meant.

"She wanted to see you break free from that orphanage. She did the best thing that anyone has ever done for you. Now do you see why you should respect your sister? Grete?"

Grete heard roaring now, in her ears and in her brain. Her fingers went to Anita's hand and picked it off her arm. This was Grete's own fault. She'd lied about Berni to entertain Frau Eisler and Klaus. And God had made it true to punish her. She squatted down, hugging her knees. Anita hovered above her and said things she could not hear. She squeezed her eyes shut.

Herr Eisler, a man near forty, had touched her teenaged sister. Hands that had helped her carry groceries, that had smoothed her hair, hands that had lifted her to bed had also—

She sobbed quietly. It seemed a secret league existed between men and girls like her sister, one to which Gisela Eisler and herself would never belong. That was what had Anita and Berni laughing in the nightclub. Picking her head up a little, Grete looked at Anita's stubbly legs, bony chest, painted face. Twitching, insecure eyes.

*Why, look at this poor cross-dresser. Look at this pitiful boy.* The Herr Eislers of the world had made them all fools.

Their eyes met and held each other for a long while. "Grete . . ." Anita finally whispered.

Grete sprang upward like a cornered animal. "Trash, trash! *Müll!*" she cried, shaking the garbage bag at the intruder, and Anita cowered backward, stumbling on his high shoes. "Leave! Go away, and tell my sister I will never see her again! Go away, dirty trash!"

"Trash?" When Anita recovered, he spat on the ground. "Is that the Eislers' swastika flag up there? They're the ones with blood on their hands. Mine are clean." He held up his pale palm, the fingers long and skinny.

"Go away!" Grete sobbed. She ran for the alley, the leaking trash bag leaving sweet-smelling liquid on her skirt, and stumbled on a slab of slate. Her knees smacked the ground. When Anita tried to help her up she said, "Go to hell."

Anita laughed. "You think you're noble, begging Berni so that you can take care of your precious Eislers. But all you've done is give that lech some of his money back."

Grete took another lunge, tears streaming. They tussled, but Anita overtook her quickly, and Grete ended up flat on her back. "Listen to me. Listen!" Anita cried, struggling to keep Grete still. "It is Helmut Eisler's fault!" he shouted. "He's the grown man, he should know better than to love your sister—"

Your sister—

Your sister—

His shrill voice bounced from wall to wall as a breeze entered the *Hof*. The swastika flag flapped a feeble acknowledgment. The Eislers' thin curtains rolled in soft waves.

Something seemed to have gone out of Anita. He let go of her arms, then made a sober assessment of the trash bag and Grete's skinned knees. "I suppose I . . ." He caught his breath. "I suppose I've done nothing more than make a mess for Berni."

Grete turned away from him, leaving the trash scattered on the ground. She walked toward the alley and did not look back. By the time she reached the apartment, the door to Frau Eisler's bedroom was closed.

That night, before Herr Eisler returned, Frau Eisler came to inform Grete that she'd be sleeping in the kitchen. It took her a few days to find a cot. Grete slept on the floor in the meantime and tried not to listen to the argumentative tones coming from their bedroom. The terror and loneliness she felt that first night faded a bit, however, when someone began hiding alphabet game pieces in her blankets. The *K*, the *F*, the *scharfes S*.

None of the Eislers would look her in the eye after Anita's visit except Klaus, who encouraged her to attend Hitler Youth meetings for girls, even as his mother began the search for a new maid.

# BERNI, 1932-1933

"And you, Fräulein?" The man cleared his throat. "Er—*mein Herr?*"

The faraway sound of Anita's laughter reached Berni's ears, and she realized the doctor was talking to her. She tore her eyes from the window. Disrupting what would have been a picturesque view of the Tiergarten were squadrons of Hitler Youths, marching in protest outside the Institute for Sexual Science. Fat, wet, early December snowflakes had been falling for nearly an hour, but that hadn't stopped them. They were beginning to make loose snowballs and throw them at passersby who wouldn't take their pamphlets.

Somewhere in this cruel city, Grete was alone, and Berni could not reach her.

She looked at the doctor, a nervous man with a thin mustache, parted precisely in the middle just like his hair. In the beginning, when Berni had been in a better mood, she had giggled about him with Anita. He had never addressed Berni directly before.

"Excuse me, *Herr Doktor*, I'm not sure I heard you correctly," said Berni. "Did you just call me *mein Herr?*"

"I'll call you whatever you prefer," the doctor replied, clearing his throat. "I've just finished with your friend for the day. I thought you might answer some questions."

Berni tilted her head, puzzled. She had been coming to the institute for over a month as the researchers studied everything they could about Anita, from a handwriting sample to measurements of her skull, trying to decide whether she'd be a good candidate for surgery. It was something Anita wanted so desperately she was willing to ignore what Berni considered the frightening mechanics of the process. Just one year prior, the famed Lili Elbe had died as a result of sex change operations performed at this very institute.

"Me!" said Berni, laughing. "I am already a woman. I'm here because Anita's afraid to go past the Nazi pigs by herself." Initially, Anita had also lured her there with the promise of free contraceptives, but Berni did not even want to think about that anymore. "Oh, and I enjoy your books." On her lap she held a book on naturopathy and an illustrated volume of erotica, neither of which she'd been able to concentrate on. "Do not waste your time on me, Doctor. I'm normal."

She put her head down, and out of the corner of her eye she saw Anita grimace. Then she hid behind her hair, which had finally grown long enough to brush her shoulders. Tossing the red wig aside, she'd debuted her hair triumphantly the week before: shiny, thick, brown. Tucking her real hair behind those ears was, Berni knew, a significant milestone.

"But of course you are normal," the doctor told Berni. "Everyone is an intermediate of some kind. No such thing as a 'full man' or 'full woman.' This is what we have set out to prove, what will help us dispel fear!" He shook his fist. "Without fear, we can change the laws persecuting homosexuals! Now"—he uncapped his pen—"if we could open a file on you, it would add to our research . . ."

The doctor, Anita, and two busts of Socrates and Sappho in their shelves all watched Berni expectantly. The room with its heavy draperies and plush furniture would have seemed less a hospital than an upscale library, were it not for the cases of wooden phalluses and Japanese sex toys on display along the walls. Berni shut the books on her lap and pushed them away from her. "You don't understand. I prefer men." *One in particular*, she thought with a wince.

The doctor made a note on his chart. "You are still a variant, Fräulein. Look at what you're wearing."

Berni pulled at the lapels of her secondhand dinner jacket; with it, she wore trousers and shirtsleeves. Her hair was still very short— she liked feeling air tickle the backs of her ears—and she kept it sleekly styled, a tortoiseshell comb peeking out of her breast pocket like a fey young gentleman.

"These are the clothes I feel comfortable in. Nothing more."

"Sartorial habits reflect your inner nature and even your hormonal makeup. People like you are valuable to us—you show the natural variation." The doctor grinned, showing rodent-like teeth. "All the better if you are a heterosexual."

"There is no *if.* I am. I told you, I'm normal." Berni began wrapping her scarf around her neck. "And I have somewhere to be."

"Let her go," Anita told the doctor, examining one of her fingernails. "Berni has just experienced heartbreak. She is not quite herself."

Berni wanted to argue—heartbreak had nothing to do with it, she *was* herself, and that was just it, she was normal—but she'd already insulted Anita enough. "I really do have an appointment," she said quickly when the doctor stopped her to give her a few brochures.

"The least you can do is hand these out," he said. "Counteract our friends outside."

Berni read the title aloud: "What Must Our Nation Know about the Third Sex?"

The doctor nodded, stroking his mustache. "We suggest all variants give a copy of this to loved ones so they can understand."

A wave of nausea passed over Berni. She had to leave then, right away, with hardly a goodbye for either the doctor or Anita, who looked panicked all of a sudden at the prospect of exiting the institute alone.

Downstairs, a group of people of indeterminate gender clustered around a string quartet. A plate of cake and fruit sat out on a table in front of a crackling fireplace. Berni's stomach growled, but she had to keep moving. Outside in the cold, she took long, deep breaths, stinging her throat. The Hitler Youths in the street noticed her, and from the portico she could see their eyes and ears prick up like a pack of guard dogs.

*Give a copy of this to loved ones.* That, she realized now, was the problem. That was why she couldn't answer the doctor's questions. She didn't want to be a "variant," an "intermediate," a member of "the Third Sex." She wanted to be the kind of person with whom her sister would feel comfortable again.

The snow had stopped and was already starting to melt along the edges of the grass. As she approached the protestors, Berni had to remind herself once more: the Nazis had suffered a crippling defeat in the parliamentary elections. Yet here they were, not even a month later, swarming the gate of In den Zelten 10. Boys, she saw as she came closer, they were only boys, with grim little mouths and pockmarks on their cheeks. Still, she felt a pang as she imagined Anita going down this path by herself.

The tallest among the boys, his face long and pointed as a dachshund's, stepped in her way. "Fräulein," he said, sneering openly at her clothes. "Take this." He pressed something into her hand, laughing to his friends behind him. "The bitch needs it," she heard him say.

"Here," she replied, slapping the Third Sex pamphlet against his chest, startling him so that he had to take it. "It's a trade."

She ignored the torrent of obscenities that followed her, walking with her hands in her pockets past the row of embassies strung along the Tiergarten. Outside, chauffeurs and butlers warmed waiting cars or, for those diplomats who appreciated pomp, fringe-footed draft horses attached to *Droschken*. She crossed into the park and found the spot where she'd planned to meet Helmut, beside one of the ponds.

Church bells dinged on the other side of the embassies. He was fifteen minutes late.

She looked out at the water, opaque gray and calm. The bare white trees were like veins on the darkening sky. The Nazi flyer, she realized, was still balled up in her hand. Prodded by a sort of masochistic curiosity, she opened it to find a brochure praising the role of the housewife, urging women to leave the public sphere.

> *She* cannot feel spiritually satisfied if she must divide her attention between her *duty* to bear children and other distractions: the pursuit of income, political action. The world of the home may seem small and limited, but in it *she* will be relieved to find her microcosm . . .

*She* was illustrated glowingly as an aproned, dimple-elbowed *Hausfrau.*

Berni chucked it to the ground, producing a squawk from one of the three swans who dug their beaks through the silt on the bank. Half-buried in the mud was a metal bowl full of swollen kibble. The one who'd honked at her flopped its head upside down.

*Heartbreak.* It had been a month since she'd seen Helmut. She'd been to the Eislers' building the week before, looking not for him, but for Grete. In the alley she found a girl carrying trash down the fire escape, a stringy girl with hair the color of under-ripe rhubarb. She'd admitted she worked for the Eislers, but she claimed to know nothing of Grete.

Helmut's wife must have found out about her and sent Grete away. That was the only explanation. Berni didn't like to blame other women, but hell, in this case, she would blame Gisela Eisler. Helmut had alluded to the fact that his wife was a Hitler supporter.

"Berni!"

Goose bumps broke out over her skin when Helmut came close and said her name again: "Berni." His voice, deep and resonant, made her toes curl in her boots. "I'm so sorry, darling, I was trapped behind a motorcade. Berni, look up. Look at me. Are you all right?"

"I didn't ask you here for lovemaking," she said, watching the muddy pond. "Where's Grete? Did you fire her?"

"Berni, look at me."

She looked instead at his Adam's apple, which pulsed apologetically. She pushed him hard on both shoulders. "What have you done with her? Of all times, these . . . where is she?"

Her eyes stung with tears she thought might freeze. Helmut wiped them with his thumb. His mouth hung open, showing his bottom teeth. At one time she'd loved watching him speak; when he did, only the lower lip moved up and down. She'd liked to chew that lower lip.

"I'm sorry," he said. "I know it seems Grete's been punished for what you and I have done. She's safe, though, she's safe. Bernadette—"

She kissed him. She couldn't help it. She shut her eyes and let them roll back in her head. His scent enveloped her, divinely familiar. A voice in her head criticized her for letting him overpower her, for falling under a man's control.

*No*—she pressed her mouth to his, so hard she might make his lip bleed. Her own desire, not Helmut, was what mastered her.

• • •

The smell of him, the taste of his aftershave, brought her back to a scene not six months earlier, in bed: Helmut playing the glockenspiel of her vertebrae, tapping softly with the tips of his long fingers. "Have I told you, my darling, I played in a festival band. Pretend I'm holding the mallets. Da, da, dum . . ."

"You're a musician?" she murmured into her pillow. They'd thrown the windows open to let in the breeze, and the swish of street cleaners' brushes drifted in. The beginning of the morning's light touched her ceiling. When she and Helmut were together they did not sleep.

He turned her over and kissed her, pulling her bare chest to his. "I was, in another life. You've made me feel reborn."

"Don't get too sugary with me. I'll throw you out."

"Speaking of sugary." He went, naked, to the jacket he'd hung on her chair. She admired his long body, even the hollow spot in his left thigh where a bullet had pierced the muscle. He produced a gift: a hat with a glass-eyed bird on it.

"You silly man!" She flung her arms around his neck, kicking the hatbox off the bed. "Do I look like the kind of girl who wears a hat like this and favors pink ribbon? I'm practically a boy. I don't know what you see in me at all."

"You're like a great city house." He draped a piece of her short hair behind her ear. "You're a big townhouse with all its lights on."

"I can't accept an expensive gift. No matter what it is."

"Why not, my darling? If I could I'd give you everything." Those urgent brown eyes. That bottom lip. She loved him. She couldn't help it. He began kissing her again, his elbows on the pillow, framing her head, his hands up in her tousled hair. This made it worse, because now she'd have to interrupt him. It would be obvious she'd planned what she said next.

"I can't take something like this when my sister still suffers in the orphanage." She'd known this would tug at his heart. He began kissing her all over, as quickly as he could. The stubble of his beard felt exquisite on her shoulder.

She tried to keep her mouth free of his so that she could talk. "Grete's been scrubbing floors to keep St. Luisa's afloat. It is brutal."

"Nobody has enough money these days," Helmut murmured against her skin. "My God, you are smooth and fair."

"You should see her. Tiny, blond, fragile. She'll never survive in a factory. She should be someone's maid. I can't sleep until I know she's all right."

She said it just like that, so that he would think it was his idea, and she refused to feel guilty about it. Grete would help him in return, making Berni no Sonje, and he, no Trommler. They loved each other, or at least they loved the time they spent together. She accepted no money, no gifts, and even helped him choose presents for his wife (*Drachenfutter*, they said, laughing—treats to appease the dragon). When they dined together they ordered pickled herring and crackers at cheap counters and split the bill. She didn't worry about what this indicated, in terms of his finances. She didn't think until it was too late about who would come last.

• • •

"Darling," Helmut murmured now in the cold park, his lips wet and warm against hers.

As they kissed, Berni felt her body thaw, her mind awaken. This man had taken her affections and promised protection for her sister, and he'd failed her. She pushed him away and wiped her mouth. "Gisela knows?" Above her head, the bare branches of the Tiergarten trees seemed to claw their way closer.

Sympathy and confusion crossed his face. "Yes, of course Gisela knows."

"Why 'of course'?"

"Well, you told her, didn't you, my darling? I heard a girl came to the *Hof* and yelled about us. I thought your conscience had urged you to do it."

"What kind of fool do you think I am?" It had begun to snow again, frozen little drops that hit the hard ground and pinged upward, and Berni's teeth chattered so hard she thought they might crack. When Helmut reached for her, she held him at arm's length.

A girl had come to the Eislers' apartment complex, yelling about Helmut and herself? A lie from Gisela, of course. "You can't seriously believe I'd do such a thing."

He lifted his collar, hunching his shoulders around his neck. "All this time I've wondered why you'd do it, and it has been difficult for me to forgive, but now I—"

"Difficult for *you* to forgive! Where is Grete?" She began pushing him again, shoving him in earnest toward the mushy bank of the pond. "Where is she?"

He slipped a little, his heel hitting the icy bank, and held up his hands. "She's safe, Berni. She's in Potsdam. She works for my elder sister, Mildred. Mildred's well-off and infirm. She doesn't speak. She relies on routines. It's good work for a girl like Grete."

"Potsdam." Berni's legs felt unstable. "What do you mean, a girl like Grete?"

"One who cannot hear well. There's no sense in pretending it's not the case." Gently he rubbed her shoulders. "My son keeps in touch with her, Berni. He says she's happy."

"Your son? What does your son want with her?"

"My son is a good young man." Headlights beyond the park illuminated his reluctance.

"But?"

A jet of white breath shot from Helmut's lips. "Klaus is as nationalist as they come. You should have seen him and Grete, when she lived with us, singing the songs. She helped him roll the newspapers he delivered, tied the twine around them in bows."

Acid rose at the back of Berni's throat, but she laughed, hard and loud. "Now I know you're lying. What else have you lied about? What can I believe? Oh, God!"

"Grete and Klaus grew close, Berni. I believe that's one reason Gisela was ready to see her off. But it's harmless. They're young. And they think they're patriots."

"I am as young as Klaus," Berni said. It was something Helmut had never wanted to mention, and she watched him duck his head in shame, tuck his bare hands into his coat. "Give me her address so I can be through with you," she said, something breaking within her. She was shuddering so violently now that her breastbone ached.

Helmut reached for her, and at first she flinched, but then he held up a pen. His hand was warm, cradling hers, as he wrote the address in between the lines of her palm. He stared into her eyes as he curled her fist closed. "I've been forwarding her your notes. Give her time, Berni."

She yanked her arm backward, staggering a little. "Don't you dare give me advice about my family, you weak man. Go set your own son right."

His jaw tensed. "You never cared about my family when you had me in your bed."

"You've never cared about anyone but yourself," she said, taking a big breath, "and fuck me, I'm only seeing it now."

She was already walking away when she delivered her *Treppenwitz*, her body moving stiffly, unnaturally, because she could sense his eyes watching her go. Knowing she could run back and kiss him at any moment made her feel like she was dragging her legs through sand. A double-decker bus waited for her on the edge of the Tiergarten, and she sprinted for it. Inside the windows were fogged, the seats crowded, so she went up to the second level. The bus began to move, lurching Berni toward the seats all the way in the back. The metal seat chilled her skin, her blood. Snow pelted her cheeks. Gisela knew. Gisela could have told Grete.

When she disembarked in the spider-shaped square of Nollendorfplatz, the Hercules fountain had been turned off. The electric streetlights were coming on, one by one, each with a corona of mist. She told herself if she raced to the other side of the square by the time the last lamp popped on, then Grete wouldn't have found out.

She didn't make it.

By the time she arrived at the apartment, snot had pooled beneath her nose, and she'd lost feeling in her fingertips. Frau Pelzer had gone home for the night, leaving one lamp burning in the parlor. Berni kicked the door shut with a bang and dropped her coat on the floor, then collapsed into a dining chair. A platter of fish pickled with pink peppercorns sat underneath a plate. She watched ants swarm a discarded crust of bread.

The door to the apartment swung open, and Anita bounded inside, skin bright red from the cold. "You didn't hear me calling? I was right behind you in the square." Her face was split by an earnest, vulnerable grin. "They've offered to give me free beard epilation at the institute."

Normally Berni would have teased her gently—she had never heard Anita mention her beard before—but she remained motionless, her eyes fixed on the table.

Anita fell into the chair opposite her and tucked her hair behind her ears. "They've signed me into a therapy group as well, to meet on Thursdays—"

"Wonderful. Now you'll be expecting me to go with you every week."

Anita's big eyes, their lashes curled and blackened, blinked sadly. "I can only guess that the reason you're being so horrible is that Helmut has ended it. You're better off without him."

"What do you know?"

"Have you . . ." Anita reached for the wick of one of the candles on the table and pinched it off. "Have you heard from Grete?"

"I haven't. She still won't return my letters. But Helmut tells me she is in Potsdam, working for a vegetable of an old woman."

Anita exhaled. "So she's safe."

The word *safe* made Berni twitch. It was the second time today she had heard it. "As if 'safe' is all that matters." All the trouble, she had been thinking lately, had begun with Anita.

Anita's smile faltered. "Well, it is something. Knowing she's cared for."

"She was *cared for* by nuns." Berni stood, the chair legs groaning across the wooden floor. "That is not all she needs." She couldn't remember feeling so tired. She longed for her bed, where she could cry in peace, really let it out. The sound of pumps clattered behind her, and Anita came to block the entrance to Berni's room, still brimming with energy.

"Come, I'll put on some music and you can forget Helmut."

"Why did you do it?" Berni snapped.

Anita's face crumbled. For all the effort that went into the sculpted eyebrows, the stained lips, she could do nothing to mask her emotions. "Do what?" Her voice cracked a little.

"Do what? Do what? Put my sister's hand on your—"

Anita exhaled. "I've told you I'm sorry. I don't know what came over me."

"A lot of good your apologies do me now."

"But I am sorry." Anita stiffened. "You forget I don't see my own family. Not ever. I don't even try to write. You—you forget."

"Is that what you meant to do? Drive a wedge into my family so we'd be the same?"

"No!" Anita grasped Berni by the arms, trying to get Berni to look at her. "That was never my intention. But we can be the sisters now, Berni. The doctors will make a real girl of me, just like Grete. And *we'll* be the sisters."

Berni shoved her aside. As though Grete's gender were the only thing that mattered. What Berni wanted to do, even more now than at the Silver Star, was throw Anita at the wall, really hurt her. Instead she blew through her curtain, into her cold room. In the distance she heard sirens. She drew the drapes over her windows to shut out as much light as possible, then got into bed without bothering to wash her feet. When she opened her eyes Anita stood on the threshold, rubbing one leg against the other like a fly.

"Go away," Berni croaked.

Anita sat on the edge of her pallet, shoulders hunched. She breathed a few times.

"When I was a child," she began, her voice low, unaffected, "all I wanted was a Käthe Kruse doll. The one with brown yarn hair and a red calico dress and apron. I wanted that doll so badly. I'd seen little Käthe sitting in the window of a fabric store near my mother's house. A fabric store, not a toy store, because they meant to encourage mothers to make doll clothes for their daughters. My mother wasn't much of a seamstress, but I thought that sounded so lovely."

Berni rolled over so that she could look at the ceiling and listen. A string of sirens had whined past and then faded, and all she could hear now was Anita tracing stars on the quilt.

"Every year when my mother asked what I wanted for Christmas, I said, 'Käthe Kruse, Mutti. Käthe Kruse.' She said it was wrong for boys to play with dolls, that I'd be teased, that I'd be beaten. I was beaten anyway, I told her, so I might as well have Käthe. Instead I'd get wooden blocks, a train on a string. My little sister, Birge, got a blonde Käthe a few years later. She let the hair unravel and turn dirty. Sometimes I kept Birge's Käthe under my quilt. I knew if I'd been a girl there'd be *Puppen* under the tree with my name on them."

"And what was your name?" Berni whispered.

The response was barely audible. "Otto."

*Otto.* Berni formed the word with her mouth, giving it no sound.

"Maybe I mixed up your sister with mine," Anita said.

They passed a while in silence. Then Anita got up and went to her room. Still Berni hid, burrowed in her blankets.

January 7, 1933

My dear Grete-bird,

I am always let down when Christmas is over, not because I will miss it but because the season is never what I imagine it will be. These past several years I've spent the months leading up to the holiday imagining this will finally be the Yuletide you and I spend together, that I'll have figured out a way for you and I to set up a life of our own. We're not a week into the new year and I already feel hope rising; you'll read enough of these letters that you'll finally forgive me, and either I'll come to Potsdam or you'll return to Berlin. Would you be fine starting out in a shabbier neighborhood, if it means we can live on our own? Kreuzberg? Yes? Good.

You won't believe where I've spent this afternoon. I'm at a sort of museum. A museum of vice, I suppose. The titles of the books in the shelves would make you blush. Anita is here having an interview. She's a candidate for an operation that would turn her from a male to a female. Because someone must be cautious I've warned her not to hope too high. But I do have hope for her.

I know Anita is the reason you're angry with me, and you probably never want to hear her name again. As I've mentioned, I don't blame you, and I've given her hell. But I think we might need to forgive her, Bird. It's taken me a long time to see it, but she hates who she is so much that she's willing to risk her life to change. Can you imagine knowing you were Margarete and looking down and seeing . . . Hans? It baffles me so thoroughly I think I can forgive. But I won't until I have your permission. Won't you write and tell me what you think?

Whenever it snows I think of you, because I wonder if it's snowing on you, too. Of course it is; you're not so far away. I'm sharing the waiting room sofa with a lovely older woman with beautiful white hair. She's reading *Der Zauberberg* and keeps stopping so that she can read a line or two to me. Here is a good one: "Tolerance becomes a crime when applied to evil."

This woman and I are so peaceful, with the manservant bringing us water from a crystal jug, she with her Mann and I with my copy of *Faust*, that I can almost forget the nincompoop boys picketing outside. Hitler Youths. They come here every day. Shouldn't they be working, or attending school, anything other than harassing these people? You agree, yes?

This old woman is fiery and candid and has just told me she's been celibate most of her life. I plan to try that myself. Already I have been wearing my worst underwear when I go out with Anita, just to be sure I don't sleep with anyone. I thought you should know.

With love,
Bernadette

• • •

February 10, 1933

Dearest Grete,

We are living in strange times. With all of the elections last year and the last-minute changes in chancellors and all the resignations, I think I (and most of us) hoped we wouldn't hear about politics for a while. Now old Hindenburg has reached into his hat and pulled out Charlie Chaplin—excuse me, Herr Hitler. I know a lot of people are waiting to see how he'll fail. Sonje insists this is the best thing that could have happened, because the debt and unemployment are too much for anyone to handle. She says Hitler will get himself launched out of the chancellor's office in a few months, just like von Papen and Brüning.

Still, the Nazis seem to be working fast. I don't know how it's been in Potsdam, but here we had tens of thousands of SA parading down Unter den Linden holding lit torches on the night of the 30th. It was, I don't know—convincing. I do not mean they convinced me to worship Hitler; far from it, but the parade made the appointment seem to mean something. I know that's what they intended, but still it frightened me, though I wouldn't tell Sonje. I'm telling you. Are you frightened?

I'm writing in a café and can hear someone lecturing on the radio, but I can't tell which of them it is. They've put speakers in Nollendorfplatz. A constant stream of Hitler's and Goebbels's voices comes at you as you're waiting for your tram, or as people queue for theater tickets. I don't know what they think they'll achieve other than general annoyance. So much of the message is hate-based, about the Jews and the way they sabotaged us in the war, that old story. Occasionally there's a line about abortion, how it's caused by women wearing trousers, and I have to laugh so that I won't cry.

A boy has just run past with a swastika band on his arm. I understand the appeal the Nazis have for children, non-Jewish children, that is: parades, firelight, drums. And for men, particularly brutish, un-intellectual, unemployed men. Now they're told to put on black boots, carry flags and torches, and feel important. It's the women I can't understand. The Nazis make no secret of the fact that they intend us to leave the professions, the universities, even the conversation to men. And still the women flock to Hitler. You see them pressing their bosoms to his car windows when the motorcades pass. *Subjugate us!*

What are they thinking?

Write about the weather if you prefer not to answer that. Or write just to say you're alive.

Your Berni

• • •

March 1, 1933

Grete, when I saw the Reichstag burn I cried your name. Even though I know you are miles away, I worried you'd be caught in the flames. That is how often you are still on my mind.

They put van der Lubbe in custody *toute suite*. The police work quickly. However did they manage to catch this Socialist boy, the lone madman, within a few hours?

They've called Sonje's friend Gerrit in for questioning twice now, to interrogate him about his feelings toward the government. Brave Hitler, outlawing the political parties of his enemies. Who knows what dangers, what terrors we'd be subjected to if we were allowed to continue to think on our own? The Communists were planning a massive uprising, it seems, beginning with van der Lubbe lighting that match. Now, for our protection, bars like the Medvedev have been shuttered. Anita and I will never have the chance to be corrupted at the Eldorado, or to listen to the "deviant" radio channels; they have gone to static. Forget about any newspapers but the Nazi ones. Do you remember Sister Maria teaching us about *habeas corpus*? In our country people can be detained and held without trial now. All for our protection, thanks be to Herr Göring.

It hasn't yet been a hundred days since I saw you, but that was another lifetime. In this Third Reich even our letters are read for our protection, our telephones monitored, for our protection. *Guten morgen*, Herr Letter Censor! Thank you for your protection!

I hope you are safe and in good health. My offer to meet, anytime, anyplace, still stands.

Your Berni

• • •

May 12, 1933

My sister, I hope you are well and safe.

Just weeks ago, Anita learned she'd been accepted as a patient at the institute I told you about, in the Tiergarten. She'd been accepted for surgery. She might have become what she always wanted. Well, the Hitler Youths who were protesting outside have finally breached its unholy doors. The doctors have fled.

And the protestors have stripped the library of its unclean books. They have gathered them in a heap and burned them in the plaza in front of the opera. I went to see, and stood at a distance to protect myself from the flames and to keep myself from jumping into the fray. There was paper everywhere, young hands greedy to get it into flammable piles. A river of unruly paper, like nothing I'd ever seen. It slithered out of their hands and spilled down the sidewalk as if trying to escape.

I saw Rilke verses burn, Kleist's essays. Anatomy texts. They even burned the black-red-gold flag, the flag of the Republic. They had a bust of Dr. Magnus Hirschfeld, founder of the institute, on a spike.

Shouts, laughter, shrieks, mania. No more words to describe it. I tasted the ash of Anita's and so many others' hopes.

I don't know what else I can say that can be both intimate and public, now that everything is both. No more words. They've all been burned.

Take good care of yourself, my sister, always, always,

B.

# SOUTH CAROLINA, 1970

"Come, Janeen, you can tell me now. Have you been here with a boy?"

"No," Janeen grumbled, walking her bicycle beside her mother's as they crunched into the gravel parking lot of the Hollis tract, a swamp of ancient bald cypress and tupelo on the eastern edge of town. "I've only come with Dad."

She waited for her mother's face to change, for some note of sorrow upon hearing Remy's name, but Anita only nodded. She jabbed her kickstand with the toe of her espadrille. "I have heard it's a popular place where people *park*, if you know what I mean."

"I *know* what you mean," Janeen said, watching her mother carefully extricate the urn, its lid taped shut, from the basket on her handlebars.

A few weeks had passed since her father's funeral, and they'd come to the swamp to scatter his ashes. Anita seemed to think they'd been sitting around too long. "We need to free him, *Liebchen*. We must return him to the earth. Ashes to ashes, et cetera." It had been Janeen's idea to leave him to rest in a place he'd loved. Her mother would've been happy to spread him in the park in the center of town and be done with it.

Janeen followed Anita through the entrance to the unfinished boardwalk, ducking under the caution tape into the pea-green air of the swamp. Closed to the public until a dispute between loggers and the county could be resolved, the waters were teeming with bass and catfish.

Maybe coming here hadn't been such a good idea, Janeen thought as she stepped gingerly over the boards. Everything gave her pause, reminding her of the last time she'd been here with Remy.

The overturned blue canoe floating in mud: he'd wondered if they could salvage it. Crude messages scratched in the boardwalk's posts: they both had blushed and pretended not to see.

Her mother barreled ahead on the winding walk. "Careful," she called as she shimmied down the trunk of a fallen tupelo that made a bridge over the water. Her long thighs gripped the bark. "It is a bit slippery."

Janeen inched down the log in an awkward sidesaddle, glancing warily at the urn. "You be careful, Mutti. Don't drop him."

"I won't, *Liebchen*. Iron grip."

Finally, Janeen's thigh touched her mother's, and she stopped. The skin of algae beneath them lay perfectly still. The enormous bases of the cypresses' trunks, some a thousand years old, looked like the humped spines of dinosaurs rising from the yellow water. A haze of tiny insects hovered at the surface.

Janeen could hear her mother breathing and the eerie *kill-deer*, *kill-deer* of plovers in flight. For a minute she watched a white egret take long, slow steps on its wire legs. She glanced at her mother, who squinted out over the swamp. Her nose was dotted with pale brown freckles. For years Remy had urged her to wear a hat, and Janeen noticed now that she'd finally put one on: Remy's LSU baseball cap. Janeen reached for her mother's hand.

"Okay," said Anita. She turned the urn upside down and dumped the ashes straight into the water, as though she were making instant soup.

"Mutti!" Janeen shrieked. A bubble rose to the surface as her father disappeared. "What in the world—"

"What is it?" Her mother actually looked perplexed. "This is what we came to do, *nicht*?"

"But I wanted to . . ." How could she explain to someone who had no sentimentality whatsoever? She needed to weep, to scatter him gently. She had a Robert Penn Warren poem folded in her pocket that she wanted to read aloud. "I thought I'd say a few words," she mumbled, embarrassed. Her mother just blinked at her.

"What did you wish to say? Please, sweetheart, he can still hear you."

"Forget it." The moment had already passed, and she'd never get a chance to retrieve it. Her eyes burned with tears.

They watched a pair of yellow warblers cross frantically from tree to tree, flapping madly then coasting, flapping then coasting. When Anita spoke again, her voice had softened. "I am sorry, Janeen. I'm not good in moments like this. They don't bring up Germans to be light and fluffy, hadn't you noticed? We are a hard-boiled people."

A chill ran through Janeen's bones, despite the heat. For two weeks she'd made sure she was first to the mailbox every day, yet she hadn't received anything from Margaret Forsyth. In the meantime, she'd seen little updates about Klaus Eisler, or Henry Klein, in the news. He'd been spotted in Virginia, then Delaware. The more information about his background emerged, the sicker she felt: Eisler had been special assistant to Heinz Jost, chief of SS intelligence in foreign territories and later the leader of the infamous Einsatzgruppe A, responsible for the murder of tens of thousands of Lithuanian Jews. While Jost had been convicted—and later pardoned—for crimes against humanity, Eisler had vanished from Europe at the end of the war.

"But is that the worst way to be?" Anita continued, startling Janeen back to reality. "We cannot dwell on your father's death, or we will fall into the vortex. It is like leading a horse—you cannot turn back to look at him, or he will never move forward."

Janeen considered this for a moment. "Who's the horse in this scenario? Me?"

Anita chuckled. "I think we both are, *Liebchen*."

"I can't put Dad behind me like you can."

"I am not saying I've put your father behind me. I have never put anyone I cared for out of my heart."

The boggy scent of the swamp overtook Janeen, stirring her stomach. A little itch of a thought came to her, and before she could control it, pushed its way out her lips. "But you had to leave everyone you knew in Germany."

Anita grew very still and sat tall on the log. The toe of one of her shoes dipped into the water and drew absentminded circles in the algae. She cleared her throat and said something, her words lost in the birdsong and the warm breeze rushing through the leaves.

"Pardon?"

"I did what I had to." Anita's nostrils flared. She removed the baseball cap; underneath, her dark hair was soaked with sweat. She ran a hand over the back of her neck. "Sometimes we must convince ourselves we no longer care for the people we once did."

Her words sounded callous, and convenient, and Janeen might have said as much had her mother not turned to her with flashing dark eyes full of anger and grief.

"Those were end-of-the-world times," Anita said. Her lower jaw came forward. "You are a lucky child, having never known such. Now"—she pointed toward the boardwalk, the urn tucked in her elbow—"let us go; you're in my way."

• • •

Janeen waited to get up until her mother had gone to work the next morning. When finally she went down to the kitchen, she found Anita had left her half a pot of coffee and some soft bananas, as well as a list of chores. She ate a banana, then watered the trees in the little backyard orchard her father had kept and pulled weeds from the beds. By lunchtime she was ready to trim the creeping fig that grew up the risers of the front steps. She'd finished two of them when she heard a friendly honk behind her.

When she stood she felt the static charge to the air. Clouds rumbled overhead. The mailman had parked at the end of their driveway. He waved at her, probably expecting her to come say hello—he was the father of one of her kindergarten classmates—but she waited until he'd put the letters in the box and driven off. The air around her felt thick, giving her the sensation of swimming toward the mailbox. When she yanked it open she heard the grind of rust.

There it was: a fat envelope postmarked in Manhattan, with a handwritten return address this time. East Seventy-Eighth Street . . . she ran her finger over the delicate script.

Skin tingly, she dropped the pruning shears on the lawn and took the letter up to her room, closing the door. She tore open the envelope and spread the pages over her mattress. She realized now that a little part of her had hoped this letter would never come, that she'd be able to continue believing her mother was the same woman she'd always thought she was. It wasn't too late, of course. She could ignore this. She could return it to sender.

She opened her eyes. The name Klaus caught her eye, right on the first page, and she shivered.

Dear Anita,

You have sent me a life preserver. You do not know what it means to me, to be able to say the things I should have before. I know I punished Berni with silence, and the fact that you have chosen not to answer me with silence is the greatest gift.

The last time you and I spoke, in the Eislers' courtyard, you urged me to look past our differences and write to Berni. I'm sorry to tell you I failed. For the two and a half years that I worked for Helmut Eisler's sister, Mildred, in Potsdam, I could not find the strength to answer Berni's letters. I worried she'd want to see me, and after hearing that she'd been intimate with Helmut Eisler, I knew I would not have been able to look her in the eye.

At Aunt Mildred's I could disappear. She lived alone in a three-room unit above a delicatessen, and she never looked at or spoke to me once. All day she blinked at the wall and licked her lips. The first night, when I took her housedress over her head and lifted her arms to run a washcloth underneath, I cast my eyes down. Within two days I could bathe and clothe her without hesitation. Numbness and nurture: this was my first taste of my future profession.

I talked to Mildred, though she didn't answer, and I practiced my speech. Klaus had attempted to teach me to speech-read, and he'd helped me learn to feel rather than listen for my own voice, parts of which were lost to me. But the speech-reading was mostly a lost cause. German is a dark language, most of its sounds uttered deep in the invisible throat. I had to learn to anticipate what people were saying, to fill in the gaps.

At Mildred's I was free. I was lonely. I read Berni's letters, and I treasured them, even though I offered her as much interaction in return as Mildred offered me. Not long after the Third Reich began, she stopped writing, finally discouraged by my silence, and my only connection to the world became Klaus Eisler, and at his urging, my BDM troop.

I was no Hitler Youth star. The one area in which I excelled was first aid, mainly because I was immune to disgust. Our leader made me first-aid girl, and the others treated me as I was accustomed to being treated: as a servant. And the Nazi indoctrination, which increased after 1933, made me uneasy. Our leader lectured on eugenics: Why deny humans the science that had made our dogs smarter and faster than any other dog on earth? The other girls ate up the material like caterpillars on leaves.

I did not mention my doubts to Klaus. I wrote how proud I was to serve Hitler. We had grown far more affectionate in letters than we had in person. Distance had an intoxicating effect. Within five letters we called each other *du*.

*There is a way for you to go to school again, my dear,* he wrote one day, shortly after my sixteenth birthday in August 1933. *Ever wanted to work on a farm?*

*A farm?* I imagined dirt and plows, the dizziness I felt in the sun. *Am I suited for that?*

*You can't stay at Mildred's forever. Consider the* Landjahr. *It's for the best of the Hitler Youth, girls and boys. I would do it myself if I weren't already vetted by the* Sicherheitsdienst. Landjahr *graduates are first in line for trade schools and colleges. You could go to nursing school after you complete your duties.*

I shook my head; they'd never choose me. But I read the end of his note over and over again. I can recite it by heart:

*I imagine what you have become, little Grete's face with a womanly shape. At night I think of your fingertips on me.*

I found Aunt Mildred dead one morning in February of 1934. The cords in her neck were stretched out, her eyes open and teeth bared, caught in the act of biting for one more second of life. I stared at her for a long time. Then I washed her body before I called the hospital.

The Eislers did not attend her funeral. They'd resented her; her money was in a trust they could not touch until now. But even before this, they had moved to a nice new apartment beside the Grunewald. Herr Eisler, through Klaus's connections, had a new position as a custodian, with a salary and pension. I cringed to imagine him cleaning toilets, but Klaus celebrated over putting his parents' creditors in their place. Jewish bankers, I assume, who'd been after the Eislers for years. Hitler had made such loans defunct.

*Does this mean your father has come to support the Party?* I wrote, because I knew this had long been a concern of Klaus's. He didn't answer; he told me much later that I should never have put such a thing in writing.

Knowing full well I had no chance of being chosen for the Landjahr, I approached our leader anyway, at the next sports afternoon. My palms and thighs were dusted with sand, and my tongue felt thick and clumsy in my mouth. Our *Gruppenführer* tweeted her whistle for a water break, then glanced at me, her face broad, freckled, and clean. I greeted her with "Heil Hitler."

Before I could say anything, she put a hand on my shoulder. I wished she'd look at me, instead of gazing out at the field with athletic pride on her face, but I gathered enough of what she said for my mouth to drop open. She told me she'd mentioned my "leadership potential" to the higher-ups in the Party.

The only area in which I could remember having led was medical training. I do not know how I formed words. "I have considered the Landdienst."

"Excellent," she said. "They need medic girls in the country service, too. I'll put in the paperwork." The water break was over; she looked off toward the field and blew a sharp blast on her whistle.

I was stunned. I'd have felt more like celebrating were it not for the sense that she anticipated my question, that somebody had put in a word for me ahead of time.

I suppose you will want to know about my current life. I am a professor of nursing. I teach pathophysiology lectures. I have a daughter who lives in London, and I have never been to visit. We have grown distant. We have always been a little distant. My son is still at university but does far too much to take care of me. Neither knows anything about my youth in Germany.

My ex-husband, Charles, is a former war journalist. We met in a refugee camp in Zurich in 1942. I had been there three years, by way of Stockholm in 1939. Charles found me at the bedside of a woman whose baby we were trying to turn. The version was successful, but when the baby was born she sobbed and sobbed, screaming that it looked like its father, and asked us to take it away. Later we learned the father was in the SS.

I'd scarcely noticed the photographers, but while I was at the sinks, Charles caught an image of me that would find its way to an American newsmagazine. In the photo my apron is dirty and hands yet unwashed. I'm staring straight into the lens, sheepish, tired. After he took it, he put the camera down and told me I looked like I needed lunch.

Charles introduced me to America, where I started in the first year of nursing college, even though I already had a degree. Nobody asked where I'd been trained to insert catheters and stitch episiotomies. Nobody asked who taught me to draw blood from even the deepest veins. That was how our marriage went as well: no questions asked.

The closest we came to discussing my past was when the photo in the field hospital reran in a big magazine for the tenth anniversary of the war's end. I gave an interview to go with the photos, and the writer asked a few questions about Berlin. He asked what I knew about the concentration camps.

Of course I told him I'd heard of them. I said everyone had—and some readers didn't like that. Dozens of Germans wrote to the editor to insist that they'd had no idea.

But that was where the interview ended. I sat waiting for him to ask if I'd participated in any substantial way to assist the Third Reich. For weeks I'd been thinking about this moment, and I'd prepared an honest response. The writer searched in his pockets for a smoke and asked whether we planned to have another child, something like that, and Charles, who sat beside me, took over. Neither of them wondered how I'd contributed to make Hitler's dreams become reality. How could I, they must have thought. I was only a girl.

The Landdienst program sent me to a farm in Silesia run by a family named Winkler. When we stopped at Dresden someone sat beside me on the train, a handball enthusiast with thick thighs. "Wonderful," she said, "what we're doing for Germany. Saving our breadbasket from the Poles."

"Yes," I said, wishing she'd sit somewhere else. "I suppose so."

A huge group of young people arrived at the farm, and Herr and Frau Winkler fawned over us and embarrassed us terribly. Frau Winkler wore a clean dress but was missing teeth on the sides. Her husband was equally sun-browned and simple. That first evening they slaughtered a pig larger than I, and we drank so much beer that none of us felt well in the morning.

The Winkler farm was on the small side, just under thirty acres. We stayed two kilometers away in another, larger house. The Winklers grew sugar beets and golden Raps flowers, from which they made rapeseed oil. When the Raps bloomed, the fields ignited in brilliant yellow underneath the blue country sky. Our primary duty was to convert some fallow fields near our group house. I helped yank out rows and rows of old beetroot. I discovered I could handle far more physical labor than expected, and I wished my BDM leaders and Klaus could see me work.

Life had never been so easy, so prescribed. I began to wonder about my plan to become a nurse. Perhaps I'll stay here forever, I thought. The farm could be my place.

One night, when we'd all had a little too much ice wine, a group of girls gathered to go walking. The rest of us were turning down our beds, or brushing the smell of campfire out of our hair; these girls snickered and stage-whispered, pinching their cheeks. I knew where they were headed. These were the ones who kept photographs of Adolf Hitler under their mattresses, their lipstick prints on his ugly mouth. They'd confused their Führer-lust and all that talk about "good blood" into an insatiable desire for the boys in our camp.

Disgusted by them, I went outside to take a real nighttime stroll. Alone I walked, through abandoned rows of dry brown corn, my head buzzing from the wine. To the left of the field, the surface of a small pond shone black and stippled. I suspected anyone watching me could have seen the white of my blouse from miles away, glowing blue in the night.

My pace quickened. I felt chased, even though each time I turned around, nobody was there. I began to run. I ran until I felt my insides would bleed. When I finally collapsed onto the soft earth and turned around, I was alone in the middle of the large field. It was Berni who'd been chasing me. I'd seen her in the excited, amorous faces of those other young women. But those were Nazi girls, of course, who would have called her, and you, whores and deviants.

For a long while I'd pushed both of you from my mind. In escaping you I felt I'd escaped everything that scared me about life. Sex. The feelings for Klaus that I fought. The confusion over Herr Eisler and Berni. Now I saw that was everywhere, and what a fool I'd been to judge Berni and you. I thought of your particular struggle, Anita. Berni had urged me to consider this, in her letters, and I had shut out any empathy until now. Now it came flooding in.

I lay on my back, crying. In the sky there were so many stars, so many more than in Berlin. I looked at them for a long time. When finally I went to wipe my tears on my sleeve, I noticed something pink in the dirt. My fingers plucked it out. It was a tiny mitten, for a girl of four or five. It hadn't been out there long; the yarn was still bright. I turned it inside out and looked at the little knot someone had tied when she finished. I thought about the fingers that would have tied that knot.

The Winklers had no children.

I looked around at the land, frozen in blue-white. The abandoned fields. The large farmhouse, adjacent to this field, which had been conveniently available for us to inhabit.

I told myself it wasn't possible. The Winklers? Would they have stolen someone else's . . . and where would that family have gone? Where would they have been *sent*? I felt something form in my stomach, like a fist of lead.

Now that I'd found the mitten, I began to see other signs: a chest of delicately crocheted afghans I found in the farmhouse where we stayed, a ledger at the bottom of my drawer, written in Polish. The leaden fist remained in my stomach for the rest of the time I spent in Silesia. As I went on with my duty, and when the following winter I began nursing school, it grew more painful, despite how I tried to pretend outwardly that it wasn't there.

I returned in 1935 to a Berlin I didn't recognize. I hadn't been there since Hitler became chancellor, so I hadn't seen the parades of adoring crowds packing the sidewalks, their children in swastika sweaters. I hadn't seen the massive swaths of red all over the Brandenburg Gate and the new offices the Party had usurped in buildings all over the city. When my taxi rode past the Silver Star Club in Mitte, I saw dirty snow drifted against its boarded-up doors. Outwardly, the city seemed to be in better order. I heard Hitler had "cleaned up the party," tamed the SA, though it would be years before I heard the full extent of the Night of the Long Knives. There were fewer homeless on the streets, fewer soup kitchens. The weather seemed to have improved. Even the sun worked for Hitler.

There were other, more troubling, changes, of course. Signs outside businesses declared the owners would not sell to Jews. There were whispers about Dachau, but when people claimed it held only criminals I allowed myself to believe them. Hitler supporters, particularly those whose lives had improved, had answers like this for everything. What did it matter if a Jewish woman couldn't buy her eggs from this grocer if there was another downtown that let her in? What harm was there in denying Jews entry to the civil service, when they could pursue other professions?

*I* was one of those people who benefited from measures such as the "law against the overcrowding of German universities." While in Silesia I'd gotten the news that I'd been accepted to nursing school. The excitement brought back old conversations and dreams I'd shared with Berni, and I vowed to contact her as soon as I'd settled in the dormitory. I bought new white leather shoes with the tiny bit of money I'd saved from my *Landjahr*, and had my hair cut the way I knew Klaus liked it. My goal, as always, was to please him. We were eighteen and twenty-one, a nursing student and an officer in the SD, the intelligence branch of the SS. We could marry. But I didn't see him for a while; they needed his assistance in securing the Rhineland. I wasn't sure exactly what he did, but he made it sound innocuous. Gathering information, he called his work. Getting to know the local population. *The 1930s will go down in history,* he wrote, *as the years in which Germany restored what was rightfully hers.*

*Take care of yourself,* I replied. *My dear young soldier.*

*Ours is a peaceful revolution. We are simply reclaiming what is ours.*

I thought of the pink mitten, and of what the girl on the train had said about our breadbasket and the Poles. I did not mention it, though. I anticipated the day he'd see me in my new gray dress, my white bonnet, the shiny black cross pinned at my throat. I wrote that thanks to him, nobody in Silesia had even mentioned my speech. Thanks to him, I had a shelf of medical texts and journals, which I read late into the night, fascinated.

The day I learned there was such a thing as nonprogressive hearing loss was one of the best of my life. I decided—on my own, as I didn't dare consult anyone else—that I had mild conductive hearing loss in my left ear, moderate in my right, and that my tinnitus was most likely linked to anxiety. Conductive hearing loss, my books claimed, could be partially remedied via something called a hearing aid, a device nearly the size of a telephone. I couldn't imagine ever daring to use such a thing, but I had answers. I felt as though the sun shone more brightly upon me than it ever had before, that someone had arranged a parting of the clouds, finally, just above my head.

My elation faded when I thought of Sister Lioba, the one in charge of the infirmary at St. Luisa's, and her callous pronouncement that I might or might not become deaf one day. I wondered how many hundreds of girls had passed through her "care" since I'd left, and I vowed to become a different kind of nurse.

As for Berni, I was too cowardly for the direct approach. I waited outside your apartment building one foggy spring morning, trembling. After thirty minutes a girl came out, reed-thin, her greasy black hair hanging ragged underneath her hat. I almost didn't recognize her, but I saw the way she walked with her shoulders thrown back, and I followed.

By the time we reached the S-Bahn station at Julius-Leber-Brücke, I still had not found the voice I needed to shout to her. A train approached; I could see the cone of dim light on the mist. This was it, otherwise she'd get on and leave me. I pushed my way through the crowd, toward the lone figure kicking pebbles onto the track, and I cleared my throat.

"Berni!"

I wasn't sure she heard me until I saw her back muscles stiffen, and she whirled around. She lunged at me with teeth bared, because at first all she could see was my uniform. And then she recognized me. The back of her index finger landed on my cheek and she said, "Grete-bird."

There was so little we could say to each other in that listening crowd. I wanted to tell her that I'd realized what hypocrites people could be. I had to say, somehow, that I no longer blamed her for sleeping with Helmut Eisler. Finally I thought of a safe topic: "I'm going to a nursing college." She'd always wanted it for me, and I thought maybe she'd celebrate.

She didn't answer right away. The train closed its doors, leaving only a few of us on the platform. Her eyes darted over my clothing, my brown coat, the pin on my neckerchief.

With two blistered fingers she held my *Landjahr* badge, the green triangle.

"Yes, Grete-bird, I can see." She leaned in close to me, so that I could feel her skin's warmth on the left side of my neck. "Helmut told me you'd turned nationalist, and I defended you. 'Not my sister,' I told him. I said you'd never become Hitler's whore. Yet here you are."

I took a step back. Even with that leaden fist in my stomach reminding me of all I'd seen, I resorted to my old defense. "You're jealous of me."

Her body seized, and her laughter turned to coughing that worsened so quickly she had to lean over. I could diagnose it now: my sister had chronic bronchitis.

"Berni," I said, "you need to go somewhere with fresh air." I reached for her, forgetting what we'd both just said, and I put my hand on her back. "The weather in Silesia—"

Her coughs subsided, and she embraced me. Crushing my ribs, she whispered in my ear that all she needed was a way to leave Germany altogether. *Damn Silesia*, she said, *and damn all of Germany*, and I panicked inside, though I knew nobody else could hear her. She said that if she had the strength to do it she would take every last good citizen with her, and—this part chilled me—she said that if I had any sense left in my Nazi brain, I would leave as well.

After that, I did not see Berni for a while. I dropped a bottle of Prontosil in the mail for her—my professors sang its praises, hailed its German inventors—spending a week's pay on it, and I prayed she would not throw it out. I would not find out for some time, because in that year she, too, did not write or reach for me. I thought about our last conversation frequently, trying to find any meaning or reason in it other than the truth. Because I knew in my gut exactly what she meant when she said "whore," and I knew she was right. Signs were everywhere, and even I could not ignore them for long.

For one, there was the nursing school curriculum. In the BDM I learned first aid: splinting broken bones, resuscitation techniques, and dental and bodily hygiene, all of which I imparted to my troop in monthly presentations. I could see nothing but positive results from this sort of medical training, and naively expected that my nursing program under the Nazi regime would be the same. But our instructors focused exuberantly on what they called "ground-breaking measures in institutional and curative care." Within the first few weeks of school, they handed us charts detailing the protracted suffering—at great cost to the Volk—that patients with physical or mental handicaps endured. What did those patients deserve? *Peace*, the pamphlet claimed. And we would be trained to give it to them.

"What does this mean?" I whispered to Lise, the beauty of our class with her gleaming black hair and elegant figure. I chose the wrong girl to ask.

"It's law," she snapped at me. "They passed these racial hygiene initiatives three years ago. Where have you been?"

Although the government had not officially "euthanized" anyone yet—that would come later—I soon realized forced sterilization had been going on all over the place. What was their justification? People unfit to have children burdened the Reich. Among ordinary instruction in obstetric, orthopedic, and pediatric nursing, we learned how many dependent babies we accumulated each year because of syphilitic prostitutes and idiot pimps.

When our teachers spoke that way I broke out in cold sweats, thinking of Berni. When they used the phrase "genetically deficient," the tinnitus in my right ear reminded me of my secret. I felt dizzy, often, in class, and had to get up frequently for a glass of water. At night I would sit bolt upright, and vow the next morning to warn Berni and you, and Fräulein Schmidt, who I knew was Jewish, to find a way to get out of the country.

By the light of the morning everything would look different. People still took dogs for walks and planned birthday parties. *Look how calm they are,* I thought. Could our country really be edging toward a cliff? Could a government turn against its citizens? I reminded myself of all that had drawn me to the Nazi movement to begin with. The sense of family and belonging it seemed to promote. The Jobs-for-Germans initiatives. National Socialism wasn't all bad, I told myself; there were simply fanatics at the margins who would never realize their goals.

And maybe the sterilizations that had already happened had been welcome. People did opt for them all the time. As for euthanasia, I had a hard time imagining it would ever happen.

An ardent Nazi called Schaller, a gaseous and warty man who would have been called a spinster had he been a woman, taught our anatomy class and did nothing to hide his lust for girls in crisp uniforms. Of course any girl who had joined the Party and wore badges had an A from Schaller, just as we automatically had a C or below in Fräulein Angstadt's geriatric care class, brave Fräulein Angstadt whom they sacked the following year.

That spring semester, Herr Doktor Schaller leapt headfirst into racial theory. He gleefully pulled down a chart showing heads in profile, with measurements of skull and nose and brow that were supposed to determine bravery, laziness, and malice. He showed us the "Nordic" type, whitewashed with baby features, the "Dinarian," Roman-nosed, the "Jew," a caricature that looked like no person's face I'd ever seen.

Herr Doktor Schaller proclaimed the Dinarian type thoughtful and serious, because the rendering looked like Hitler. "But the Nordic," he said, "is the ideal. And there's only one Nordic type I can see in this classroom."

I began sinking in my chair.

". . . And that's Grete," he finished, his glance gleaming in my direction.

"She's no Nordic!" cried Lise, whose face had broken into splotches as soon as he pulled down the chart. She tucked strands of her dark hair back into her bun. "Aren't they supposed to be smart?" She imitated my speech, dropping the *s* and *z*. I was mortified to hear that a problem I thought I'd fixed had not been fixed at all.

The class's laughter soothed her initially, but she would not be satisfied for long. She cornered me on our walk home to the dorms that evening. "Just wait," she told me. "Wait until they find out what you really are."

One evening in summer that same year, 1935, I had just prepared a cold dinner for myself in my little room when I heard a knock at my door. I opened it to find a young towheaded orderly, his hands clasped behind his back. The sight of him made my stomach drop.

"Margarete Metzger? You are wanted in the medical director's office."

My heart pounding and knees weak, I walked to the far wing of the hospital. I passed every exit but did not dare run out. As I walked my breathing became erratic, and phlegm drained down my throat. Twice I had to stop, put my hand on the wall, and catch my breath.

When I arrived I knocked softly. All my skin tingled as I pushed that door open.

The room was dark, lit only by one lantern on the director's desk. Herr Doktor Schaller leaned back in his chair, a folder opened in front of him. When he saw me he beckoned me inside, removing his glasses. "Please, have a seat," he said, but I couldn't. I stood at the far corner of his desk and waited.

Schaller shut the folder and simpered at me. He'd been somewhere sunny for the weekend; his nose and the tip of the fleshy wart on his cheek were tinted scarlet. "Margarete." His whitish tongue performed a staccato of my syllables. "Mar-gar-et-te. Do you know why you're here?"

I shook my head no, but surely he could see guilt on my face, welling in my eyes. I knew why I'd been called here alone. I knew what he'd expect of me, in exchange for his silence about my deficiencies. I wondered seriously if I could do it—lower myself, desecrate myself, to save my own skin. Spit gathered at the back of my mouth. I closed my eyes, teetering a bit on my feet, thinking of all I'd said to you and Berni, all my unfair judgment.

"You've been reported," the doctor continued, in a manner that showed this had little consequence for him. He might have been letting me know a library book was overdue. While I stood there with palms perspiring, he poured himself a short glass of something brown and lifted it to his fat face. When he'd downed his drink, he tapped the folder on his desk. "The Gestapo received a tip about you, and they were gracious enough to allow your friend to intervene."

My friend. He meant himself. The intimacy of the term made me want to choke. But I'd heard the other word, the one that mattered: "Intervene?"

172

Doktor Schaller's eyes flitted over my shoulder. I jumped when I felt movement behind me. A tall man in a black uniform had been standing against the bookshelves the entire time. Someone to arrest me, of course, and I nearly produced my wrists for him right then. As he stepped closer, the light hit first his smooth lower lip, then his strong nose, then the gleam of his eyes. I could not breathe as he removed his cap with its shiny brim, his gaze locked on mine. He had grown much taller since the last time I'd seen him—almost three years before—and his jaw, neck, and hands had all become those of a man. He inclined his head toward me, a hint of a smile in the corner of his mouth. His hair had darkened from blond to sandy brown.

"*Guten abend*, Fräulein Metzger," Klaus said.

The fear rushed out of my body. I felt a surge of love, warm and sweat-inducing. Despite what I had begun to feel about his uniform—even despite the sterilizations, the pink mitten, Berni—I felt unbelievably, unbearably proud that such a man had come to my rescue.

Schaller sat back and interlaced his fingers. "Officer Eisler is here because one of our students had a concern about your racial identity. She seemed to think you were secretly Polish, possibly a Jew." He and Klaus both laughed.

I could not join them. Secretly Polish. Not hearing deficient. How stupid, I thought. All Lise had been able to consider was race.

"I must say, you have an unusual accent," said Schaller. "Not Polish, though, eh?"

Klaus answered for me, as my tongue felt thick. "Our Grete is a fine little Aryan."

"Evidently. But you can never be too careful," Schaller added. "Plenty of Jews walking around with blond hair these days, dyed or otherwise. It's a good thing you have a friend in Herr Eisler here, Margarete."

"Thank you," I whispered to Klaus.

"It was nothing, Fräulein," Klaus said, flicking invisible dust off his sleeve. "All I had to do was produce your file and the matter was cleared."

The doctor shook a finger at me. "Why hadn't you submitted the proper forms? You weren't listening when I explained the new racial background checks, were you?" I shook my head, and he slid my folder across the table to Klaus, winked, then told us we were free to take our leave. Klaus put his hand on the small of my back and held open the door.

We were quiet on our walk to my dormitory. I felt rattled, exhilarated, as though I'd stood too close to the train tracks when a locomotive blew past.

Beside me, Klaus took big steps, my file tucked under his arm. I could not believe this was Klaus, here in the flesh, in my building. Now in my corridor. Now, at the door to my bedroom. My shaking hands took what felt like hours to find the right key. After I unlocked it he tipped the door open with one finger, and I went in under his arm. Inside my room he placed his black cap on the desk and turned on the study lamp. He strolled around my room, his large steps covering it in an instant. He took up so much space that I felt dizzy in his presence.

We stood in the middle of the floor, staring at each other. His pale skin glowed in the dim light; his shoulders were broad. When had he become a man? And in that time, had I, too, become a woman? My thoughts were a woman's; I wanted to run my fingertips over his smoothly shaved cheeks, to unbutton his jacket and see his chest.

"You saved me," I whispered.

He nodded and pulled out my desk chair. When he sat his long slacks drew upward, showing black socks and a sliver of skin. He ran a hand through his short fair hair.

"You must be very careful when you speak, my Fräulein Pole," he said, grinning. "You were lucky this time, *nicht?* You must continue to work on your pronunciation. The Hereditary Health Court has the ability to sterilize anyone whose genetics pose a threat to the Reich."

Had I been thinking clearly, I might have noticed the respect in his voice for the words "Hereditary Health Court." To Klaus, they were not the problem. I was. But so overwhelmed was I with gratitude, with relief, that I fell to my knees in front of him, my cheek on the woolen knee of his pant leg. Patiently he stroked my head. "You silly one. Don't you want to read your file?" His hand moved to play with the sweaty hair at the base of my neck.

"My file?" I'd been so focused on Klaus having saved me that I hadn't considered what sort of evidence the Gestapo had on me. Klaus lifted me to my feet so that I could take the folder. I was so distracted that I glanced over the pages inside without reading them.

"You must read," Klaus urged me, his face alight.

I shuffled feverishly through the papers as Klaus watched. There was an application signed by my *Ringführerin*, recommending me for country service, and a copy of the certificate declaring I'd completed the *Landjahr*. I dreaded reaching the back of the file, where I'd learn everything Berni had told me about our background was untrue. But Klaus kept pressing me to look, and finally I reached the two oldest documents: my birth certificate and the admitting papers from the orphanage.

I sank onto the bed. The first detail I noticed was that I'd had my birthday wrong all these years: instead of August 15,

I'd been born on August 19. Born at home, to Frau Gertrude Metzger, wife of Joachim, son of farmers. A midwife in Zehlendorf caught me.

Our parents lived in Zehlendorf. I read it again: Zehlendorf. We, their two daughters, lived there until January 1919, when someone—I could barely read her signature, but it began with a *K*, not our mother's *G*—took us to St. Luisa's. Our mother had been dead since the end of 1918.

Our aunt! It was our aunt who'd taken us to St. Luisa's, not our mother, as I'd always feared. Berni had been right. A sense of *Gemütlichkeit* overtook me as I remembered her unwavering faith in our parents. She shared those stories with me so that I, too, would believe. How I missed my parents, whom I never knew! How I missed my sister!

I was sobbing into Klaus's shoulder; he'd joined me on the bed. I realized I didn't care about their origins. I wish I had known them, whether they were Catholic, Jewish, fair, dark, bourgeois, proletarian. Klaus held me as I mourned them, and I clutched at him, clawed at him, still looking at the names of my parents and conflating my grief for them with my love for him.

I moaned into his shoulder. "How can I thank you? How can I ever . . . ?"

"Shh," he said, his thumb on my chin. "We will find a way."

I wiped my chin on my sleeve and tried to catch my breath. "I must share this with Berni. It will protect her, too. She'll have to register to become a citizen as well, won't she?"

His pale eyes, which had been droopy, almost drunk, sharpened. He nudged me off his shoulder, squared his face with mine, and held my wrists. "I will not have you torturing yourself over Berni's choices. She's a grown woman. Nobody is forcing her to be a prostitute."

"She isn't a prostitute." I couldn't keep the edge from my voice, even though I feared I'd ruined the moment.

"Don't defend her, Margarete. She nearly destroyed my family."

"You're right, of course," I said. "Of course, Klaus. But I wonder . . . the Hereditary Health Court. Anita, Berni's friend, the—the one who dresses like a woman. Will they go after him?"

"If 'Anita' doesn't mend his ways, then yes, I think they will go after him." Klaus wiped my tears with his thumbs, a didactic expression on his face: patience and impatience mixed. "Nobody wants unnecessary violence. In the case of a *Transvestit*, like 'Anita,' there doesn't have to be any. He and your sister are Aryan, thus part of the Reich. I'm sure the authorities' approach would be rehabilitation. You see? You don't have to worry."

He'd moved his hand to my lips. That old gesture, his dry fingers against the hot breath of my mouth, stirred me. My eyes rolled back. They were tired of crying, and I was tired of fear.

I did something that would have been nothing to you, nothing to Berni, but set off explosions in my little mind: I kissed the rough tips of his fingers. I used my tongue. When I opened my eyes, I found his face closer to mine than it had ever been. Our noses touched, and a thrill like a small electric shock jolted my nervous system.

We breathed heavily for a moment. I could taste his breath. His lips moved forward half an inch, and then they were on mine. We began to kiss, slowly at first, his lips sliding over mine. His breath tasted yeasty and sweet, like beer. Our front teeth clicked when he opened his mouth.

I made a noise, something between a moan and a sob. Could this be happening to me, in my plain room? If only

2

he would stop for a moment! I needed him to stop so that I could make sure I would remember it later. I pulled away and gazed at him, up into his face, to be sure of him. He smiled at me; he knew how long I had been imagining this. I tried to swallow, but there was a lump in my throat. I was on the verge of crying again, though now I didn't know why.

I heard something like violins inside my head as he came back down to me and his tongue touched mine. Explosions happened within me, in my throat and heart and thighs. My hands were on his warm neck and the soft back of his blond hair. His went around my waist, to my breasts. He pulled me onto his lap and I could feel the stiff shape in his pants. My thumb lingered on the button on his waistband.

Then, just as quickly as it had started, he stopped. He got hold of my wrists, turned me around and put me in the chair so that I sat and he stood. His face returned to its characteristic smoothness.

"We will find a way for you to thank me, Margarete." A note of gentle rebuke crossed his face. "Not like this."

He left me throbbing all over, stunned, sitting there in my dark room alone. I went to the mirror and studied my swollen lips, which felt as though he'd stung them. My throat ached from crying. Yet I went to bed that night feeling hopeful. If he planned to find a way for me to thank him, that meant I would see him again, and that was all I could think.

Too late Janeen heard a rattling, and before she could gather the pages strewn all over her quilt, her mother had burst into the room. Quickly Janeen sat up and wiped her eyes, coming back to the present. Outside it was pouring, the rain drumming the roof and splashing on the sills of her open windows. Her mother looked at them and tsk-tsked.

"I have been thinking about what you can do this summer," Anita began, crossing the room in a few big strides to yank the sashes down. "It may do us both good if we visit colleges next month, *nicht*?" She looked at Janeen strangely. "My God, you are hyperventilating. What is the matter? What are you reading?"

Janeen wasn't fast enough to hide it. In a second her mother was standing over the bed, rifling through the pages.

"What is this? This is—" Anita read a few words, mumbling them to herself. Then she closed her eyes. Her entire body swayed, as if a wave had hit first her head, then her chest, then her hips. "This is for me."

Janeen shook her head vigorously, still unable to speak.

"It is. You have been reading my mail." Anita grabbed for the stack of pages in Janeen's grasp, but she held tight to them.

"Are you . . ." Janeen couldn't begin to ask the question. "It's for Anita," she said, her heart pounding. "It's for someone named Anita, but maybe you're not Anita. What I mean to say is that this might be a different Anita."

Something flickered over her mother's face. "What do you mean?"

Janeen took a long, unsteady breath. The letter was written to an Anita who had been a transvestite. It couldn't be for her mother. Yet there was so much in it that felt familiar. "Who's Berni?" she blurted out, her voice strained. "What happened to Berni?"

Her mother swayed on her feet. "What? Who told you that name? *Die Wahrheit sagen!*" She yanked the remaining pages out of Janeen's hands. "We are going to forget this, as soon as you tell me where you got it. Tell me."

Janeen couldn't. She put her face in her hands. Through her fingers she watched her mother stumble toward the door, and for a horrible moment she knew what would happen. Anita would take the letter to the garbage. "You have to read it!" Janeen cried. "You have to tell her what happened to Berni!"

Her mother paused on the threshold but didn't answer. The back of her trim head, the erect carriage of her shoulders, were regal yet terrifying, eerily calm. She stalked out of the room and slammed the door shut behind her.

Janeen waited a moment, breathing hard. She'd been weeping, she realized, for Grete and Klaus. What kind of monster was she? Klaus Eisler, the man who'd murdered Jews, the man who'd come to rescue Grete in his SS uniform—she'd been able to taste his lips.

Through the wall she heard an uncannily familiar sound: the screech of rusted iron. Where had she heard that sound before? It brought to mind Christmas, her father bent over their rarely used fireplace, wondering how he could open the damper . . .

She bolted into the living room in time to see her mother toss the decorative logs aside and throw the letter onto the grate. Janeen cried out to her as she lit a match and threw it atop the first page. It caught a corner, which curled up and blackened. Janeen clawed at her mother's shoulders, shouting to her to pull it from the flames. But Anita was too strong for her; she held Janeen back with one firm shoulder. Kneeling behind her mother's back, Janeen watched in horror as another page lit.

"Please, Mutti," she said, sobbing. "Please, take it out. You need to read it—to read about your parents. Please!"

A low groan leaked from Anita's lips, and she fell forward. Janeen lunged toward the fireplace and dragged out the paper, blowing on it, lifting clouds of white soot. Grit went under her fingernails. She left the singed pile on the bricks and sat back on her haunches, panting. Rain still pummeled the roof, darkened the sky outside. She could hear it dripping down the chimney. Her mother had her face in her hands.

Janeen felt stunned, as though she'd just suffered an electric shock. Neither of them had spoken since "your parents"—she wasn't even entirely sure why she'd said it. "You could have told me," she spat, her voice high-pitched and bitter. "You could have *warned* me."

Anita glanced up, her face tear-streaked. "But I had to leave it behind me, *Liebchen*. You were an American child. I didn't want you to have to even think of all this—"

"No, dammit," Janeen said, and now she could barely get the words out. "About Daddy. Why didn't you tell me?" Her stomach lurched. "His father had it too, Mutti. Prostate cancer. His father had it. You never tell me anything."

Her mother's mouth constricted. She swallowed a few times. "I had to worry for twenty-five years." Her voice wobbled. "But it is not always true that what kills the father kills the son. I didn't want to think his day would come. Why would I let my little girl worry the same?"

"It wasn't fair. You should have told me. *He* should have told me. Instead I had to be surprised, blindsided—" Janeen tried catching her breath; she was truly hyperventilating now. In her mind's eye she saw her father packing her lunch on their last normal morning; that afternoon they told her he had cancer. She'd whined she was tired of tuna fish. Seven months later he was dead. "Who expects their dad to die when they're seventeen? I could have prepared, I could have done more with him . . ." Her breaths came in great gulps. "I would have . . ."

Anita came toward her, arms outstretched, making shushing sounds. "I know this now. I'm sorry. I am sorry."

"I would have been . . ." But Janeen could no longer talk. She covered her mouth with her hand, then leapt up off the floor and ran to the bathroom. Her teary face stared back at her in the toilet water, puffed and red. Her mother's reflection appeared behind her, and then Janeen retched more violently than she ever had before. It all went into the bowl—her mother's secrets, her father's death—and when she had finished, she felt better.

For a while they sat on the linoleum as Anita held her, cradling her forehead in one large, cool hand. Janeen let herself melt into her mother's chest. Slowly, slowly, they rocked together.

"Perhaps you can go for a little drive?" Anita finally asked, and Janeen nodded.

Through the octagonal window beside the door, she saw that the sky had cleared. It was orange and purple. Outside she gulped lungsful of the cooling air before she and her mother got into the car. The streets were wet, the blacktop pungent. Nightcrawlers wriggled in hot little pools along the road. Their neighbors' houses, shielded by trees like ladies peeking from behind fans, revealed people lighting charcoal grills or washing their cars. Their normalcy felt startling to Janeen; it was almost an affront to everything she and her mother had endured.

Fireflies grazed the tops of the spartina grass along the path to the gazebo in Shortleaf Park. A summer chorus of clicking locusts, lawnmowers, traffic, and birdsong surrounded them, thick as the humid air. Janeen took a seat on the wooden bench, Anita across from her. Janeen watched her mother reach over the gazebo railing for a lily past its prime, its petals like elephant skin. She plucked the bloom from its stem and lifted it to her lips. Her pale Teutonic skin was flushed with exertion.

Finally, she spoke. "I have told you I do not remember when my own father died. But I do. I remember when my mother received the news. Trudi . . ." She looked at the ceiling and frowned. "She used to tell me that my father, Joachim, was out winning the war. You see, unlike Grete I did not need my Nazi file to confirm who my parents were. I always knew."

Janeen's breath caught in the roof of her mouth. A minute passed before her mother continued.

"When I was a girl in Berlin, I was called Berni."

There was something Klaus had said about Berni, a word he'd used; it lingered on Janeen's pursed lips, but before she could ask, her mother said, "Listen." The blush-colored lights around the perimeter of the park went on, one by one, as Anita began to speak.

# PART III

# BERLIN, 1935

*Jove spoke, and Ceres felt sure of regaining her daughter. But the Fates would not allow it, for the girl had broken her fast, and wandering, innocently, in a well-tended garden, she had pulled down a reddish-purple pomegranate fruit, hanging from a tree, and, taking seven seeds from its yellow rind, squeezed them in her mouth.*

Ovid, *The Metamorphoses*

# BERNI, 1935

Berni was on her third cigarette of Trommler's visit; she needed something between her fingers, something to do with her mouth. The air above her head was translucent, a sickly blue. The room was dark. Sonje had installed thick curtains to keep out the neighbors' eyes.

The radio switched to Nazi-approved music: "Sieht eine Frau dich an." Trommler hummed a little. "My dears, the worst part of the regime change is nearly over! I've had personal audiences with Herr Göring—"

Trommler and Göring, together: Berni rolled her eyes toward Anita, imagining giant troughs where the powerful elephantine men of the city congregated. Anita stared straight ahead, half-hidden behind the rubber plant, her dessert untouched. Ever since the burning of the Institute for Sexual Science, she had not been herself. Her laughter, even the nervous kind, had all but disappeared.

"Once they've established *Gleichschaltung*, which naturally involves growing pains, the fist will open . . ." Trommler unrolled his thick fingers and grinned at Sonje. He was as Anita had first described him: an enormous man of about sixty, whose clothing clung tight and smooth to his girth. His wide upper lip seemed flattened by a previous mustache, the way land is after a glacier. "Then I'll sell the flat back to you, expecting unlimited visitation, of course, ha-ha!"

Sonje smiled wanly. So far, he hadn't seemed to notice Berni's scraped wrists, the bruise on Sonje's lip. He burped and pointed at the empty doily atop his dessert plate and nodded at Berni, who brought over a wedge of cake teetering on the knife, his third slice. Her finger wobbled as she used it to slide the cake onto his plate:

mousse, raspberry crème, sponge. He had brought it over since the closest bakeries now refused to deliver to Jews. Their upstairs neighbor, Frau Anwalt, had revealed Sonje as such.

"Gracious, my girl, you're all a-tremble," Trommler said to Berni, resettling himself in his armchair and brandishing his fork with the flourish of a violinist.

"Perhaps our Berni is a bit hung-over," Sonje said with a thin smile.

"The young and their nightclubs!" he trumpeted, in a burst of crumbs.

"*Prost*," said Berni, tilting some liqueur into her mug. "There aren't enough nightclubs in existence to get me drunk anymore. I stayed in with Anita last night."

Anita did nothing to corroborate this lie. She refused to speak to Trommler, even though Sonje had asked them repeatedly to be courteous to their new landlord.

Berni had barely had time to process the news that the flat had a mortgage before she learned Trommler would be buying it from Sonje. Complications with Sonje's new loan officer—it was no longer legal for the previous one, a Jew, to work at the bank—were, as she put it, "smoothed" by Trommler. She had taken that little bit of equity and sewn it into the linings of quilts and coats.

A voice interrupted the song on the radio: ". . . a bloody scene on the Ku'damm last night as Jewish rioters . . ."

Everyone froze.

"Not the way to respond," Trommler muttered, "not if they know what's good for them."

". . . screening of the foreign film *Pettersson & Bendel* was interrupted, first by jeers and catcalls, then by violence, in what appeared to be a planned public disturbance by Jewish agents provocateurs . . ."

Out of the corner of her eye, Berni saw smoke coil from Anita's nostrils. Last night they hadn't been to the theater to see *Pettersson &*

*Bendel*, nor to protest; they had tickets for Lotte Reiniger's animated *Papageno*. The Nazis might enjoy Mozart, Sonje had said, but she and Reiniger would not let them ruin *The Magic Flute*.

They hadn't heard a sound from the adjacent theater until the men burst through the doors, not in full uniform, but it was obvious: brown pants, heavy boots. Any dark-haired or Roman-nosed men were yanked away by their collars. Outside the men were stopping cars in the street, smashing windows, yelling "Jew!" as the police stood aside, fretting with their dogs' leashes. As they fled, Sonje had turned to Berni, her mouth opened in a shout, and Berni saw Anita on the ground, the knees of her stockings torn, clawing at an SA man's neck.

Sonje's nose quivered. Berni gripped the arm of her chair. All Trommler had to do was look at Sonje, notice her bruised lip, and ask where she had been last night.

Instead he fixed his small eyes on Berni. "You have your papers in order, don't you? Makes no sense not to for an Aryan girl. You'll spare yourself a great deal of trouble."

Berni could feel Sonje and Anita looking at her, and her lips tightened. It wasn't her fault she could join the Volk without a forged ID or genealogy-for-pay. All she had to do was go to St. Luisa's and ask for her birth certificate. But she hadn't. Not yet. "Anita lives underground, I live underground," she said, leaving Trommler to sputter and cluck.

• • •

Jewish cabaret, the Nazis proclaimed, was dead. As evidence they had places like the Cabaret Finck on Grunewaldstraße, once a dark place, witty and elegant. It was now renamed Weingut Keller and plastered with the kind of faux Bavarian decor that made Berni sick: oversized beer steins flowing with papier-mâché foam, fake purple grapes, wooden benches in place of the little round tables, which had seemed somehow too French. Its new name wrapped around the front and side of the building in block letters as though inscribed by a giant calligrapher's pen, and the new owners had hung swastika flags on both façades and from the upper story, beside the neon signs advertising Radeberger Pilsner and Fetzer's bratwurst.

Berni and Anita worked at the Keller, Berni upstairs, Anita down. The Finck had gone underground the way Sonje had, hiding behind Aryan owners; a secret stage in the cellar, available only to those in the know, maintained a repertoire of political satire. The stage manager, Hansi, hid his homosexuality behind sexist jokes and free drinks for Nazis, who were shown only the main floor. Hansi loved the theatrics of playing dress-up for conservatives, and made Berni come to work in a ruffled blouse and gingham dirndl. It was a sad irony that Anita longed to trade places, play the Überfrau. She had repeatedly turned down the role Hansi offered her in the cellar show: Arno Breker, Hitler's favorite sculptor.

"I look nothing like him," she complained. "The insult!"

Hansi's skit involved Hitler instructing Breker and Speer to erect an obelisk in the Lustgarten. "Higher!" Hitler would say. "Higher! Higher!" as the set grew, with Speer eventually adding a domed top and round base, until the three stood back gazing at a statue of Hitler's cock, shouting, "Magnificent! Perfection!" Hansi could not stop giggling about it. "I just need a Breker," he'd add, and Anita would storm out.

One warm August afternoon, as Berni and Anita dressed for work in the staff room at the Keller, Berni tugged the empty spaces in the blouse where her bosom was supposed to spill out. "One day I'm going to burn this getup," she said, "and dance naked around the flames."

Anita tugged at her stockings and said nothing. The walk to the Keller was always hard for both of them. Anita refused to hide her face, putting Berni on her guard, forcing her to look at the people they passed on the street, really look at them. It seemed impossible that people could still find things to laugh about as they waited for trams or bought sausage under the red umbrella of the Koschwitz cart. Bureaucrats lay on blankets in the park beside the Rathaus Schöneberg, tipping back after-work beers. "Hitler's weather," as people called it, was also their weather. They were Berni's peers, professionals who sat behind desks while she wiped lipstick from glassware. Every blonde reminded her of Grete. She'd seen Grete at the subway station in March, wearing a Nazi nursing uniform. Berni had tried not to think about her since.

*We're the sisters*, Anita had told Berni once, and lately Berni had been trying to adopt this as truth. Anita was her sister now, the one to be protected, and she was, Sonje worried, becoming unmanageable. Too angry. Too defiant for her own good.

Berni wrapped a floral choker around her neck. "I look like a donkey tarted up as a parade horse," she said, producing a tiny laugh from Anita, more of a grunt.

"At least you'll see sunlight as you work."

"And Nazi faces."

The side of Anita's mouth lifted in a slight smile. "Some look ripe to bite in those uniforms. What I'd do to them with some whips and spiked boots . . ."

"Stop!" Berni cried, clutching her side. "You're terrible."

Anita adjusted her stockings once more, then removed a pack of cigarettes from her apron and put it in one of the cubbies on the wall. "For our break." She glanced at the mirror and sighed. "Off to the dark place, where they put things like me."

"Don't be dramatic." Berni meant it to sound lighthearted, but seeing Anita's reaction made her feel like one of those girls in the park.

She waited only a minute after Anita left, then slipped on her pants and blouse and stamped into her oxfords without untying them.

She scribbled a quick message and rolled it to about the thickness of a cigarette, then pulled one from the pack in Anita's cubby and replaced it with the note: *Felt sick. Went home. See you there for dinner.*

The cigarette behind her ear, Berni crept into the dining room. She hated leaving Anita alone. *See you there* was a hopeful message: it meant *don't spend the night out with strangers.*

"Leaving so soon?"

Hansi stood behind her with arms crossed, one foot tucked above the other knee, a faded apron tied round his waist. From the kitchen came the smell of burnt sausage.

"My cough is bad today—" Berni let out a weak hacking sound. She put her hands to her neck, then her belly. What had she written in her note? "My stomach . . ."

"Save it. I haven't the patience. Brigit will have to cover your tables." Hansi looked at her over his round glasses. "Next time you miss work, there'll be trouble."

• • •

Berni walked quickly from the U7, head down, watching her plain shoes strike the sidewalk in front of the Café Royal. The sweat on her neck went cold as she looked around. Could this be the street on which she'd spent her childhood? The trees, once giant, now stood no taller than the tops of the three-stories. She passed the laundry with its yellow façade, a display of clean bloomers and underpants pinned to a clothesline in the window. As a girl she'd found this titillating, but it now seemed vaguely sad. The French-doored balconies she and Grete had coveted looked the same but for the swastika flags. Splashes of red pocked this street like a rash.

St. Luisa's stood at the end of the street. No flags. So much had changed everywhere else, Berni thought, while here all that had happened was the chestnut tree had grown a few feet. Its bark looked leprous, marred with green summer fungus. Berni listened, expecting to hear the shouts of a thousand girls coming from the courtyard, but there was silence as she knocked.

A girl of about thirteen, her hair in a kerchief, answered. "May I help you?"

The door was only open a crack, the girl's pale nose poking through, but now Berni could hear it, the buzz of this little hive. The hum gave her a burst of energy, and she stood straighter. "I'm here to see Sister Josephine," she said, praying her favorite hadn't died.

"State your purpose?"

"Sister Josephine was my math teacher. I'm paying a visit."

A bit more of the girl's face emerged, her dark brows lifted in the middle. "You're here for your records, *nicht*, to prove you aren't a Jew? No need to beat around the bush, you're far from the first."

"What? No." *To prove you aren't a Jew.* There it was, in crass terms. Was that why she'd felt the need to be secretive?

The girl sighed. "If you want your records I can send you to the office. If not I can't help you. Sister Josephine is teaching now."

Berni paused. "Fine. Yes." She followed the girl into the main hallway, past the marble staircase, toward the refectory. She stared at the dusty metallic radiators, the worn wooden handrails along the steps, the oversized cross above the double refectory doors. There may as well have been grooves worn into the floor; if she followed them, she half expected an eleven-year-old Grete would be sitting there, huddled on the bench.

She was swallowing hard by the time they passed a classroom. Through the window in the door she saw a dozen girls gazing toward the board. Their hands went up in unison.

"Bernadette Metzger."

Berni and the girl turned to see Sister Maria Eberhardt walking toward them, carrying a silver pitcher of water. She looked at Berni as though she'd seen a ghost.

"You can leave us, Jacinta," Sister Maria said, though she still looked alarmed and didn't take her eyes off Berni. "You came for your paperwork, Bernadette? Why?"

*Why?* Berni blinked. Surely Sister Maria couldn't be unaware of what was happening outside. "Why, Sister?"

"Shh. I'll take you to the office. That'll be *all*, Jacinta," she called after the girl, who lingered ahead of them in the hallway, peeking over her shoulder.

Stunned mute, Berni followed Sister Maria toward her office. The nun took long, masculine steps, her wide flat feet showing in their comfortable shoes, and Berni was struck by the comfort and nostalgia she felt watching this woman whom she'd hated as a child. At the office, Sister Maria shut the door behind them. Berni took a seat in the chair in which she'd sat when offered the chance at the academy.

Sister Maria poured them each a glass of water. "I was under the impression you and your sister didn't need help from us."

Berni took a sip. "What do you mean?"

Sister Maria took in Berni's hair and her men's shirt. Berni expected her to hold forth about lifestyle choices, but she didn't. "Grete seems to be well connected, don't you think?"

"You've seen her?"

"Haven't you?"

Berni looked at the tiny stained-glass window she had once thought so beautiful. Light shone dully through its lily and cross. "I bumped into her at the train. We didn't speak long."

"I see," Sister Maria said quietly. "Then you know she's studying to become a nurse."

Berni shrugged. Choice words from their conversation at the train station echoed in her mind. *Whore*: she'd accused Grete of being Hitler's. *Jealous*: Grete's old fallback. And, of course, Berni was. The unfairness overwhelmed her. Her sister, a nurse. Herself, a waitress. Afterward Grete sent her a bottle of antibiotics in the mail, for her cough, just to show how much more she knew than Berni did. The bottle had gone in the trash.

"She came here in late May," Sister Maria continued, "to inquire about a job. Grete thought she might finish her practicum here; apparently one of her professors had suggested it. Naturally we had to turn her away."

"Why 'naturally'?" Berni asked, feeling reflexive prickles of irritation under her arms. "Why did you 'naturally' have to turn her away?"

"Because of her Party membership, of course. More than that: she'll be one of their nurses when her schooling's done. She could join the SS. I'm sorry if this is the first you've heard of it, but my guess is you knew?"

Berni bit the edge of her glass. "I knew," she said. "What did you give as a reason you couldn't hire her?"

"I told her she lacked the proper qualifications. We couldn't tell her—or any of the others who came in Nazi uniform, of course— the truth. They'd have gone straight to their superiors."

Berni knew how Grete would have taken this rejection. She felt an echo of it now, in her stomach. "You made it seem personal."

"Bernadette, I'm here to keep our girls and our church safe." Sister Maria lifted her glass, using her other hand to steady a tremor in her wrist, the first feeble gesture Berni had ever seen her make. "I'm not the bad wolf, even though you think I am. It wasn't easy to choose girls for the academy." Her tone softened. "The best moments were the ones in which we told an unlikely girl we were giving her a chance. But even that sometimes didn't go as planned."

Sister Maria looked hard at Berni, who studied the floor, her shoes. After a minute, Sister Maria sat up straight. "Now then. Your paperwork."

"I don't even want to see it." Berni slouched in the chair. "Why should I cooperate? Why obtain papers to prove I'm not Jewish?"

"There are Jewish Germans who would give everything they had to be in your position. Think of it that way." There were deep grooves above Sister Maria's eyebrows, as if the thumbs that formed her had pressed down the clay. Berni shivered as she waited for her to find the file.

Later she couldn't remember saying goodbye or the exact wording of Sister Maria's parting warning to her, something about staying alert and secretive and mentally guarded. All she knew was that the folder was in her hand. She opened it under the chestnut tree in the front yard, certain Sister Maria watched from one of the upper windows. When she'd read the file she nodded once, then walked away, heat pulsing in her earlobes.

Her file shouldn't have affected her; she'd never doubted who her parents were. Still, at home she went to her room and cried until she coughed her throat raw. She stayed in bed three days, her emotion taking on the symptoms of influenza: dizziness, a weight on her chest.

There would be trouble if she missed another day of work: that was what Hansi had told her, and he turned out to be right. On Berni's second day in bed, Anita left the Keller after her second shift with two Dutch tourists, men in flannel suits with an outdated sex guidebook. Hansi had overheard her boasting that she could show them which boy-bars were still open. "That girl," he said sadly. "She'll never pass up an opportunity to play queen of the scene."

That night the Gestapo made a sweep of homosexual clubs in Berlin. Everyone inside was arrested.

# BERNI, 1935

After one night, Sonje and Berni could tell themselves Anita had escaped, that she'd holed herself away in a hotel room with a wealthy foreigner. It had happened before.

As days went by without word from Anita, Berni found it more and more unlikely that she hadn't been taken. She couldn't tell Sonje she'd ridden past Anita's favorite bar, Der Regensturm, on her bicycle, and had seen the boarded-up door, the sign: *Closed Due to Moral Turpitude*. Crudely painted swastikas marred the glass and brick. She'd gotten off to search the sidewalk for spots of blood, but all she'd come away with was someone's small beaded purse, emptied of cash. Sonje was right—they couldn't just call the police and ask if a young man with long hair and women's clothing had been arrested. Anita had no paperwork; you could not follow up on someone who did not exist.

After eight days Trommler telephoned Sonje and finally proved himself useful: he'd learned where they'd taken Anita. She'd been tried two days after her arrest in a closed court and found guilty of sodomy and prostitution. The judge had pronounced her a traitor to her race. For reformation she'd been sent to the Columbia concentration camp in Tempelhof.

"Well?" Berni said. "What's Trommler going to do about it?"

They were sitting at the dining room table. A piece of wurst had turned to jelly in Berni's mouth. Nobody said anything when she spat a chewed-up mess of pink into her napkin.

Sonje looked toward the window. Strips of late-summer sunlight peeked around the corners of the black curtains. Frau Pelzer held the coffeepot, its neck drooping. They'd all heard of KZ Columbia: its damp basement cells, its interrogation rooms.

"He thinks you should write to the commandant of the camp," Sonje said into her cup. "They've booked her as Otto Schulz, of course. You can pretend you're Otto's girlfriend."

"Not a bad idea." Frau Pelzer recovered and began to pour more coffee. "Tell them you want to make more Germans with him. That's the whole issue, *nicht*?"

"Yes, that's the idea," said Sonje, her voice low. She put her pointer finger on the table and drew lines with it, as if they were in a war tent, outlining their strategy on a map. "You claim Otto's your lover. Then Anita has a character witness."

Berni threw her napkin at the table. "Trommler's suggestion is for *me* to do something? Where are his connections now? What if it brings the SS to our door?"

She closed her eyes. Right now Anita would be curled against the stone wall of her cell. She'd refuse even to look at the others, to eat, to use the chamber pot the six men had to share. Constipated and dry-lipped, she'd shield her face so nobody could see her week-old makeup and greasy, tangled hair. What would the other prisoners do to her? What about the guards? Berni could imagine the look on the guard's face on the day he finally opened the cell to announce that Otto's girlfriend, Bernadette, had promised she'd get him out of those silly clothes for good. *You mincing son of a bitch*, the guard would say with a wink and a slap between Anita's shoulder blades. *Still like getting your shit pushed in? Poor, poor Bernadette.*

"You're a fool," Berni told Sonje. "You sold your flat to Trommler so that I could write a damned letter."

"I sold the flat to Trommler so the bank wouldn't take it away," Sonje replied. "Don't be obtuse." They looked at each other. Then the doorbell rang. The sound sent a staticky zing through Berni's bones. When it rang again, the three of them leapt into action. Berni ran to the parlor to hide Sonje's valuables: an heirloom clock and a gold footed dish went under the sofa, along with a small urn that hid at least a hundred marks. Frau Pelzer put the cello on the balcony, then went to the door and peered through the hole. *A man,* she mouthed.

*Nazi?* Sonje replied.

Frau Pelzer shook her head and at Sonje's signal opened the door a few inches. "May I help you?" Berni could see leather shoes, the creased knees of a suit.

"Won't waste much of your time, *gnädige Frau,*" a pleasant voice said. "My name is Josef Grotte. I'm collecting for the Jewish Winter Relief."

Sonje went to the door. "Do come inside, please. We have neighbors who listen."

Quickly he stepped over the threshold. His hands were covered in wiry fur, even the knuckles, and a bit crept out the top of his collar. "If you ladies have spare clothing, household goods, anything will help. We have thousands of families to support now."

"I can give you a little cash, if that's all right," Sonje said, accepting her purse from Frau Pelzer. "You've caught us at a lean time, I'm afraid."

"Bad times for everybody," said Herr Grotte. "I hear Herr Göring's had to start forming his personal medals out of nickel." Frau Pelzer gasped. "Forgive me," he said. "I find humor to be the best form of resistance."

Sonje's mouth twitched into a smile. "Frau Pelzer, I think it would be best if you turned on the radio." Frau Pelzer huffed into the parlor, and after a moment, a Chopin waltz filled the room. Herr Grotte closed his eyes, his hairy fingers moving through the air. "We will appreciate any donation you can make, of money, of time. We've begun preparing people to emigrate."

"Emigrate," Sonje repeated. "Leave everything behind. Their language and land. Give Hitler what he wants."

Berni held her breath. She and Sonje had had this conversation as well. With the violence against Jews, the indignities Sonje had to suffer, the answer seemed simple to Berni: leave Germany. Sonje and Anita had every reason to apply for passports and hop a train to Paris or London. Whenever Berni mentioned this, Sonje asked why she didn't consider doing the same, and Berni could not answer. Deep down she knew it had something to do with a lingering hope, something to do with Grete.

"We've already had to abandon much," Herr Grotte told Sonje gently. "Those on the extreme side of the *völkisch* movement won't stop until they take everything we own."

Sonje rolled her eyes toward the ceiling. "Hitler will burn himself out, Herr Grotte."

A voice came over the radio then, to pronounce that the composer of the previous piece was the "German" Frédéric Chopin. Frau Pelzer pretended to spit on the floor. "German, my foot," she said. Herr Grotte smiled.

"I hope you are right," he told Sonje. "But in case Hitler stays for a while? We must prepare. He is our enemy, but so is pride. Men who've lost their jobs aren't keen on starting over. But the women! Ready to take on anything. Ready for a new life, in Palestine, wherever their families will be safe."

Berni's eyes drifted into the parlor, its shelves stocked with books and sheet music. Out on the balcony, the cello waited for someone to pick up its bow. Finally Sonje nodded. "I could show the women how to be music teachers. I could show them how to read and write."

Herr Grotte stepped forward and took her hand in both of his. "I speak for the entire bureau when I say we are grateful for your support, ever so grateful."

When he'd gone, Sonje turned to Berni. "You liked him, did you? You liked his ideas?" she said. "The Nazis are our enemies, but so is pride, eh?"

"Oh, yes," Frau Pelzer said, oblivious to the look that passed between Sonje and Berni. She swirled her brandy, sloshing a bit on the floor. "I thought that was very good."

• • •

That night Berni couldn't sleep. She lay awake watching shadows move across her ceiling, listening to Sonje tune her cello. Long, resonant notes pulsated the floorboards. After a while the noise stopped, and the light coming under Berni's curtain was put out.

She crept out of bed. On blue stationery, she wrote a letter to the commandant of the concentration camp. She described her purifying love for "Otto," her ambition to become a *Hausfrau*. Six children, she said she wanted, or seven. Eight. She pushed her words to the point of parody so that if Anita saw it she could at least laugh.

Before she signed it, she wrote one final line:

Send my dear friend home to me, so that he may become who he really is.

• • •

August cooled into September without word from Anita. Berni's back began to ache from sleeping in a nervous ball. Sonje seemed to age years in a matter of weeks. Streaks of white hair appeared at her temples, wiry as cats' whiskers.

On the night of September 15, 1935, the Reichstag put a new set of laws in place regarding Jews. For Jews and Germans to intermarry or even for young German women to work in Jews' homes was now *verboten*. Extramarital relations between Jews and Germans had a new name: *Rassenschande*, "defilement of blood." When Berni commented that at least Sonje wouldn't have to worry about Trommler climbing onto her anymore, Sonje became very still. Berni hadn't considered what this might mean for their arrangement.

Frequently now, on her walks to and from work, Berni was stopped for her *Ahnenpass*, the document St. Luisa's had made possible, which proved she, her parents, and her grandparents were Aryans. She couldn't stand looking at the thing, seeing her face surrounded by swastikas. She couldn't get the words out of her head: *Here to prove you're not a Jew?*

"May I go, please?" she asked one evening after two Brownshirts stopped her at Bahnhof Schöneberg. She'd been staring at the warning sign above the tracks.

*Achtung Germans: Electrified Rail! Jews are Welcome to Jump!*

The man holding her pass had dark brown eyes. His beard grew so dark that it made the skin of his jaw sandpaper-thick. She wanted to shake him. He plucked her cigarette from her lips and ground it under his boot. "Get some proper clothes for a lady, understand? You're begging to be assaulted in those tight pants. Heil Hitler!"

"Heil Hitler," she said, keeping the words down in her throat. The old Berni would have kicked him, or tried to pop out his eyeball. They'd turned her into a milksop.

At home she found the apartment empty; she ate a stale pretzel roll and sat at the table to wait for Sonje. Finding Sonje out always made her uneasy, even though Sonje ran errands regularly, visiting Trommler in his *pied-a-terre*, teaching at the Jewish Relief Agency.

Berni had no idea she'd fallen asleep until someone grabbed her shoulder. She sat up with a gasp and a moan. "You've gotten a letter," Sonje said, holding out an envelope.

"News of Anita," Berni said breathlessly.

Sonje shook her head. She handed Berni the letter, then went into her room.

Berni, I need to speak to you. Everything has changed, and I see now you were right. Come to the Lustgarten at two in the afternoon on Wednesday. Meet me beside the third tree after the Dom, on the sidewalk. Come alone. We do not have to speak of Helmut Eisler. I just want to see you. Most sincerely yours, Margarete

Berni's heart pounded against the edge of the table. Today was Tuesday.

*I see now you were right.* Part of her wondered if it would take only a few embraces, some tears, a few days together in mutual confession. They'd be sisters again. In time, perhaps, she could wring the Nazi from Grete like water from a towel.

• • •

The following afternoon Berni hurried through Alexanderplatz, peeling off her raincoat. Shallow puddles shone bright yellow. The sky behind the terra cotta tower of the old Rathaus was blue as a songbird's egg. All of it, painted far more brilliantly than any street artist's watercolor, gave her a feeling of buoyancy and hope.

The Spree even looked blue for once, an opaque slate blue, the water level high. It wasn't until Berni stepped onto Kaiser Wilhelm Bridge that she saw and heard the crowd gathered on the island. The museum island, the navel of the river, held the Lustgarten, which Hitler had converted from a green park to a paved venue for rallies. Thousands of people pressed together on the concrete. Long red banners on spikes bobbed over their heads. Berni could see the speaker clearly, waving his little arms, spitting and stretching his trout's mouth wider with every word.

". . . My brethren, what is meant by the International? 'International' means funds from all over the world land in Jewish pockets. 'League of Nations' means rule by international banks. The Jews have put nationalism out of fashion. It is time we stand up for ourselves!"

The crowd roared. Berni turned, pushing against the stream as people scratched and clawed at one another to get closer, to raise their little flags higher. She was back out on the street with her hands on her knees, catching her breath, when a pair of trim gray shoes stepped in front of her and waited. Berni looked up into the face hovering over her, shielding her from frantic passersby, and drew in her breath.

It had taken distance and time for her to be able to recognize how alike she and her sister were; she was stunned to stare into her own face under a brown nurse's veil and a crown of dark blonde hair. Berni had the uncanny feeling that she was one of her sister's patients, looking to her for reassurance. In her trim brown uniform and white collar, she *was* reassuring, except for the expression in her eyes. They seemed, as ever, alarmed.

"I have missed you," Grete said, and Berni reached for her, her hand hovering close to the stiff white collar, fastened at the neck with a black pin. More pins gleamed on the lapels of her jacket. The crowd behind them began chanting *Sieg Heil!*

Without a word Berni took Grete's hand and pulled her over the bridge, back toward the reassuring Marienkirche steeple. She stopped at a railing overlooking the Spree and slumped beside a pair of chained bicycles. "Why would you bring me here?" Her earlier optimism had disintegrated. "Trying to get me to join the Party?"

"It is safer to disappear in a crowd." Grete sat beside her, their backs to the stone railing and the sun. She tilted her good ear toward Berni. "It is good to see you, sister."

Breathing hard, Berni watched more people running, their faces eager, toward the rally. "You wrote to say I was right."

"You were," Grete said quietly. "More than you know."

"More than *you* know. They've taken Anita into custody. For moral turpitude."

Grete looked down at her hands. A bit of ink was smudged on her middle finger. They listened to geese honk in the river beneath them. "I never thought any of this would be possible. At the farm I tilled soil. That's it, Berni! And then, when I returned . . ." She puffed out her cheeks and closed her eyes. When she spoke again her voice sounded high and nasal. "They've given me new eye charts, based on color. Not vision. With the new laws I'm supposed to categorize every patient's race. And the feeble ones . . . a pregnant woman came in. She committed an armed robbery ten years ago and was found to have a low IQ. The doctors insisted we . . ."

Across the river, the speaker's voice was drowned in cheers. Fat tears ran down Grete's face. Berni imagined her sister handling a tiny fetus, skin translucent, bones like eggshells. "Can't you refuse to cooperate?" she asked finally, knowing full well this was no option.

"Nobody can refuse. Especially not me. *I'm* deficient." Her voice turned bitter. "I tried to go to St. Luisa's, to work there, but they wouldn't take me. I am still worthless."

"You aren't worthless. Look at you, a university student. I serve beer."

Grete wiped her nose with the back of her hand. Her feet were splayed on the pavement, her uniform's skirt getting dusty. People were beginning to notice the pair of them sitting together, the blond, trim nurse, the obvious outsider. "We need to walk," said Berni.

They pushed their way back toward the Alex, Grete's head drooping low. When Berni leaned in to whisper something she realized she'd placed herself on Grete's good side without even having to think about it. "Sister Maria is afraid," Berni said into her ear. Their cheeks brushed, Grete's sticky from tears. "She thinks you're one of them."

"I am one of them," Grete murmured.

"No you aren't, darling. You were misled. Now you must lead yourself out." She looked around again at the bright sky, the evaporating puddles, the red Rathaus tower. "There are ways to get foreign visas. We could be in a new country by spring."

Grete pulled Berni against a store's glass front. "There's danger in speaking this way!"

Berni was breathing quickly. The answer, at least, hadn't been *no*. "Just apply for a passport. Say you're going on holiday." All the particulars could be sorted out later.

"Klaus will know."

Hearing his name made Berni feel as though she were being dipped, slowly, in ice. So they still saw each other. "I thought we wouldn't speak of the Eislers. What, does he work in the passport office?"

"No, worse. He's in the SD. He looks for emigration requests, transfers to foreign accounts. No one may leave with more than seven percent of his property."

Berni felt like stamping, shouting, clawing at the air. "And people."

Grete wiped her eye and nodded slowly. "Yes, he looks for traitors to the Reich. I know it's bad, Berni. But there is more to Klaus. He's done good for me—"

"Look," Berni said, interrupting her; the last thing she wanted to hear was a list of ways Klaus had helped Grete more than she had. "Do you want to go with me, be sisters again? Or do you want to force more abortions?"

Grete's hands flew to her face, covering it up, hiding everything. The top of her brown-cloaked head shook hard. Berni leaned in to shield her when a large group pushed past them, flapping their flags, chanting. "We're leaving. But first you have to promise me: no more Klaus. Request a passport and stay away from him. *Kannst du mich hören?*"

"We can't talk like this! I can't. It's dangerous . . ." The ends of Grete's words blurred. "I have to go, Berni. I'll—I'll do all that's necessary."

"When you have your passport, telephone me: Sonje Schmidt in Schöneberg. If Sonje answers, hang up. We'll need a code so I know for sure it's you and you know that it's me. Breathe three times into the receiver, like this, before you speak." Berni pursed her lips and huffed, three sharp blasts. "I'll do the same."

Grete nodded, her face troubled. "All right," she whispered. Berni tapped her on the chin, at the center of her dimple, and Grete gave her a sad smile. It took only a second for her to vanish into the crowd.

# BERNI, 1935

By late October, fear of the Nuremberg Laws became too much for Frau Pelzer's husband. German girls under the age of forty-five were forbidden to work in Jewish homes, but rumor held that any relationship between Jew and gentile provoked suspicion.

Frau Pelzer lingered at the door, her face red, a large cardboard box in her hands. "I've left you the medium stockpot. You've three bags of egg noodles in the pantry. It's not so difficult to boil them. And remember to heat the gravy."

Sonje laughed and put her hands on Frau Pelzer's shoulders. "We'll be fine! Don't worry about us. Berni and I may not be domestic, but we can manage." She tugged one of Frau Pelzer's faded red curls. "Lucky woman. Your husband must think you look thirty, to be so worried."

Frau Pelzer pressed a wet tissue to the underside of her nose. "But who will do the shopping for you, *gnädige Frau*? You know they don't allow—you know the nearest groceries aren't available to you anymore."

Sonje's upper lip lengthened momentarily. "We'll be fine. Berni will shop for me."

"Berni, bah! She'll waste your money on caramels and English bacon!"

Berni tried to laugh. "Come, Frau Pelzer, tell us your age, finally. We know it's more than forty-five."

A hint of a smile appeared on Frau Pelzer's face, and she shook her curls rigorously, tittering *nein-nein-nein-nein-nein*. Before she left she pulled Berni close. "You'll tell her I said goodbye?" she whispered.

Berni didn't need to ask who she meant. "I will," she said, trying to sound convincing.

• • •

The following week Berni left the door of the icebox ajar all night, leaking water into the kitchen. She and Sonje woke to the odor of spoiled milk. After nearly an hour of cleaning, Sonje threw up her hands. "That's it! I'm hiring a Jewish girl from the agency."

As if on cue, a knock sounded at the door. Berni and Sonje froze, looking at each other.

"The candy dish?" Sonje murmured.

"Hidden under towels in the closet. What about the quilts?" The cash was all Berni cared about. Without it, she didn't stand a chance of leaving the country. She'd heard nothing from the passport office since she'd turned in her application, and she'd heard it might take some greasing of the clerks' palms.

Berni gave Sonje a minute to check on their cash-laden blankets before she opened the front door. "Hello," she said. When the person didn't respond: "Hello?"

A boy had arrived at their house. He had very short, almost shorn hair, and he wore an ill-fitting pair of trousers and a yellowed shirt. He didn't answer Berni, but kept his head down, staring at the worn doormat. He was very thin, his hands long and veined. Berni noticed his lips were purplish and chapped. A bruise drained down from his left nostril.

The sight of him filled her with fear. "Can I help you?"

He lifted his heavy lids just high enough for her to see dark liquid pupils. Her hand flew over her mouth. Sonje pushed past her, grabbed the boy by the shoulders, and yanked him inside. She locked them all into the room and shut the black curtains. When she flung herself at the boy, her arms went all the way around him, and he crumpled like paper.

Sonje brought Anita to the sofa. Her face hadn't moved, and she hadn't said a word since she entered. Berni knelt on the floor in front of her, along with Sonje, the two of them as quiet as they'd be kneeling in church. Sonje fell to pull off Anita's shoes and socks. The bare feet were pale, the bottoms blistered. Sonje began rubbing them vigorously, bringing back the color.

"You're safe, my God, you're back, you're safe," Sonje murmured.

"Anita," Berni said finally, and when she said the name Anita quivered, trying to keep her battered lip from trembling.

"What have they done to you," Sonje murmured.

Anita's hand went to her head, to the short hair above her ear, pulling at tufts of it, her face blank and blinking, as if she'd just now realized they'd stolen the brown tresses she'd taken so long to grow. Berni put her face on Anita's knee. The trousers smelled alien and stale, like urine. Anita's body seemed to warm, and Berni felt her slacken a little.

Finally Anita spoke, her voice the same: breathy, soft. "What have they done to *you?*"

Sonje's mouth hung slack for a moment before she began to laugh, a little too loudly, touching the white parts of her hair. "You mean this old thing?" she said, fanning out the plain dirndl she wore to the Winter Relief Agency. "Can't even begin to explain, my darling. I'm teaching piano."

Anita gazed down at her, eyes twinkling in her sunken face. "Then it's true what they say. The women of Germany have awoken to the wholesome values." She looked at Berni. "And you. Splotchy skin, hair every which way. It's reassuring to see some things haven't changed."

They all ended up on the couch, pressing Anita from both sides. Berni felt like weeping, and laughed to cover it; it was hard to believe this living, pulsing body belonged to Anita and was safe and alive. She did not tolerate their embraces for long. "You haven't given my room away, have you?" Her walk reminded Berni of a cricket with a bent leg. She hobbled a little, favoring one foot, her joints thrown out at angles.

Sonje followed close behind her, biting a nail. "When did they let you out?"

"Five days ago," Anita said after a pause. Hearing this made Berni feel ill. She watched Sonje wring her hands. Berni opened her mouth to ask where Anita had stayed all that time, and the beginning of a word came out, but Anita flung out her arm. "I need to be alone!"

Sonje rubbed her eyes, then stalked into the kitchen and began aggressively scrubbing the inside of the icebox. When Berni passed Anita's room the door was open. The figure in its shirt and pants was curled motionless on the bed, facing the wall, toes pointed.

• • •

Within a week, Gerrit came to the apartment to take Anita's photo for her forged passport. "Thank you for coming at such short notice," Sonje murmured as the two of them kissed, stiffly, on each cheek. "It's been too long."

"It has," said Gerrit. He nodded toward Berni, who sat on the sofa's arm. He'd ended his affair with Sonje when Trommler bought the apartment. Sonje had bashed him a little, said he'd never been a true revolutionary. He'd been born too rich, and his looks had made him too vain. Yet here he was, unpacking a camera from a lunch sack, risking his neck to forge some of the most sought-after documents in the Reich.

"Look at this." He let Berni hold the rubber stamp he said he'd cut himself, the eagle holding the circular swastika above the name of their district. "Just like the passport office."

Anita burst through the door of her bedroom, Sonje on her heels. Anita had on a white lawn blouse and a tweed skirt. She grabbed a chair from the dining table and dragged it across the parlor floor. "Is this okay?" she asked Gerrit. "Or more light?" She got up and flung open the blackout curtains. They all blinked. Berni could see a woman on the telephone, trimming her toenails, in the apartment across the way. Birds chirped.

"Nice to see some signs of life," Anita muttered.

Berni laughed. She felt weak-kneed and grateful. Here was Anita, not Otto, her old wig fitted to her head. She'd taken scissors to it, cut a blunt fringe, trimmed the ends to chin length: a red Cleopatra. "You look wonderful," Berni said, breathless.

She did, and she didn't. The wig looked artificial, stark; it couldn't compare to her lost brown hair. Her makeup caked on patches of uneven skin, and her bruises had turned yellow, but her eyes shone like jet beads. She sat straight and tall, hands clasped on one knee. "Well?"

"Well?" Berni echoed, irritated at the way Sonje and Gerrit were looking at each other, as though they were the parents. "Take her photo."

Gerrit hesitated, then lifted the camera and snapped off a few shots.

"Anita, please," Sonje said softly. "We've discussed this. You know it's the only way."

"You just think your new friends won't let their children go with a *Transvestit*," Anita said, posing, her chin drawn to her shoulder. "So tell them I'm a woman. Nobody will know, will they, Gerrit dear?"

"What children?" asked Berni, looking from Sonje to Anita. She noticed now that Sonje had something in her hands, a white shirt.

Sonje crossed her arms. "Two of the women I've met through the agency are sending their children abroad with student visas. Apparently students don't count against the U.S. immigration quotas. Anita can travel as their tutor."

Berni was stunned. "Where will you go?" She almost asked if Sonje's connection could get her a visa as well, but remembered she would have to ask for two.

Quietly, Sonje explained the plan for Anita's escape: in three or four weeks, she and three Jewish children, two of whom were Herr Grotte's nieces, would board a train bound for Liège and cross the border at Aachen. Later a ship would take them from the Hook of Holland to New York City.

"Anita," Berni said, breathless, "you could be in New York before the year's end!"

"Not me, I'm not allowed to go. But *Otto* is."

Sonje twisted the garment in her hands. Berni could see now it was a man's shirt. "Anita, please. It is for your safety. No one will believe Anita Bourbon is your real name."

"Then call me something else. Anita Freytag. Anita Samstag! Anita Metzger, use Berni's name. Whatever you want! I won't be Otto just because it makes everyone else more comfortable, including the damned border patrol."

Anita hid behind her hand, its knuckles bluish-red and scabbed. Gerrit looked down at his camera, pretending to fix something. Berni went to her and knelt down.

"New York City!" she whispered into the tuft of wig over Anita's right ear, smelling dust motes and talcum powder. "Think of the adventures you'll have, with no fear of the SA."

Anita lifted her head. Charcoal drips ran from her eyes. "The laws there are even worse than ours. The blackmailers run rampant." She swallowed. "Get me a tissue, please."

After Anita dabbed off her makeup, she removed everything, unceremoniously, right in front of them. Averting her eyes, she pulled down her blouse, her movements robotic as a patient's at the doctor's office. The plain white shirt looked no more natural on her than a hospital gown.

Otto Schulz looked into the camera with a hollow, blank expression. Gerrit took three shots, then put his camera away. No one would meet one another's eyes as Anita got dressed.

CAROLINE WOODS

• • •

Time began to speed after this. October rushed toward November and the opening of Hansi's latest secret play, a satire about the Nazis' ban on Yom Kippur prayers. Berni took Anita's place waiting tables downstairs for the opening performance. The actor playing Hitler foamed and frothed as the Jews onstage shut their eyes, reciting the words in their heads.

"We need space!" he screeched, grasping at air, wrenching it down. "*Lebensraum*! We Germans have been unfairly crowded from the space you hoard inside your *minds*!"

"I have to say," Hansi whispered the following afternoon as he slid next to Berni to put a mug under the tap. "I'm grateful the race laws don't apply to us."

"How can you say that?" Cold foam ran over Berni's hand as she watched the group of idiots at her table, young SS officers, huff their hot breath on spoons and stick them to their noses. One of the men, a big-skulled blond, caught her eye and pointed to his empty glass. She twisted her face into a smile and held up a finger: *one minute*! "I'd think you'd have sympathy for Jewish-German couples," she murmured to Hansi. "Given your situation."

"Child, Paragraph One-seventy-five has been on the books all my life." Hansi filled a second glass with porter. "I'm no stranger to discrimination by law. I have sympathy for people in mixed marriages. But am I glad my affliction isn't something visible in my bloodline? Yes."

"Whatever you say." Two mugs in each hand, Berni crossed the floor to the long table at the center of the dining room. The tail of a blue and white Bavarian flag brushed her hair as she lowered the beers onto the table. She wanted to rip it from its flagpole.

"Smile," the young SS man said, taking his mug from her. "They can't be so heavy, can they, Fräulein?"

213

"She looks sturdy enough to me," one of the girls added.

Berni stood still for a moment. Slowly, she pulled her lips back from her teeth.

All at the table erupted in laughter, averting their eyes. Spoons clattered from noses. "*Ach*, Fräulein!" they cried. "Put them away, put them away!"

"That's it," Berni murmured to Hansi behind the bar. She scratched at the lace around her neck. "I'm taking a smoke break."

Outside the sky had turned purple, two strips of pale blue and gold behind the roofs across the street. Winter was coming. Her fingers were clammy against her lips. Ash fell on her gingham skirt; she let it stay there a moment, burning a round hole in the fabric. A cough seized her. She bent over, her hips against the back wall of the building.

"With lungs that sound like that, perhaps you should think of giving up cigarettes," said a soft, deep voice. A man in a long wool overcoat and felt hat stood a few feet away from her.

"I didn't know it was a crime to smoke, Herr Nazi. My *Ahnenpass* is inside."

"I'm not a Nazi. I'm sorry, I've been rude." He removed his hat. "My name is Herr Petersen. I'm friends with Herr Grotte. I have, er—documents? For your friend Sonje. She thought it would be best if I brought them to you, rather than to her flat."

Quickly Berni put out her cigarette. "Herr Petersen, I'm sorry. I'm the one who's been rude. It's been a bad day."

"Not at all." He held out a newspaper. It took her a minute to figure out he intended for her to take it. "It's inside." Berni took it between both hands, as though it were fragile. Anita's visa. She thanked God, then remembered to thank Herr Petersen as well.

"Wait!" she cried. He'd replaced his hat and tipped it to her, signaling his departure. "Please, Herr Petersen, I'm hoping you can help me. How can I get a visa for myself?" It was all she needed to plan her departure with Grete. Her passport had arrived, finally; when she'd gone to pick it up at the office, the line of applicants snaked around the block.

"It can be difficult." The man's voice was so smooth and gentle, she wanted to fall asleep to it. "Borders are closing, particularly to Jews. Are you Jewish, my dear?" When she shook her head, he nodded. "You can afford to wait a little longer, then. Why not apply to work in Czechoslovakia, or England?"

She shook her head. "I have to go as soon as possible."

"Then your cough might come in handy, Fräulein. There are tour groups that visit curative places. I can give you the name of a doctor who might be able to write a note."

"Oh, yes, thank you." Her cough! Health sojourns! Why hadn't she thought of it herself? She wanted to kiss him, right in the middle of his fluffy circle of hair.

After he'd written the name and address of the doctor on the inside of the newspaper, she clutched it to her chest. It might as well have been made of gold leaf. "Thank you."

Herr Petersen smiled again and walked away, disappearing into the crowd gathered on the other side of the road, waiting for a trolley. Berni floated back into the bar, wrapped the paper inside a sweater, and pushed it to the back of her cubby.

"Good, you're still among us!" Hansi whispered when she returned to the bar. "Who the hell was that? He asked for you by name. I never like it when anyone does that."

"Oh, no one. Plainclothes SS. He asked some routine questions."

"My God." Hansi put his hand to his heart. "I hope you didn't tell him anything."

• • •

Berni and Sonje did all they could to keep Anita indoors until November 18, her departure date. Sonje bought her magazines full of pictures, recipes, diagrams for homemade faux-flower hats; she found board games, decks of cards, cosmetics samples. She sent Berni to the delicatessen for Anita's favorites: French raspberry jam, whole-leaf Darjeeling.

On Monday at noon, just before Berni left for work, Sonje burst into the apartment with a paper bag under one arm and a manila envelope in her hand, breathing heavily, her cheekbones splotched pink. "Take this," she said to Berni, who finished tying her boots in a hurry.

The bag held a heavy bottle, which Berni set on the table with a thunk. "What's wrong?"

Sonje's fingers shook as she untied the scarf over her hair, the fabric beaded with rain. "A man in a belted leather coat is loitering on Pfrommerstraße. Don't look out the window. Thank God he didn't ask what was in this." She held up the envelope. "From Gerrit. Anita's passport."

The edges of Berni's vision blurred with fear. "What do the Gestapo want with her?"

Sonje touched the outer corners of her eyes, looked at her fingers. "They probably keep an eye on former prisoners. Wake her, will you? Tell her we have something to celebrate."

"What are we celebrating?"

Berni and Sonje swung around to see Anita, dressed in boots and purple harem trousers. In place of the wig she wore a silk turban. Berni wondered how much she'd heard, or if she'd been able to see the man and Sonje interact. Her room faced the street.

"Here, darling!" Sonje's smile stretched wide, like a rubber band. She pulled a bottle of apricot brandy out of the paper bag and indicated Berni should pour, which she did, generously.

"I have something for you," Sonje said, lacing her arm through Anita's. She opened the envelope and spilled a small booklet onto the table. The cover bore a splay-winged eagle and the words *Deutsches Reich—Reisepass* above a series of perforated numbers. "Gerrit did splendid work, *nicht*? Take a peek inside."

Anita paused, then opened it to the first page. Berni slid one of the snifters through her fingers and looked over her shoulder. There was Anita, swastika stamps over her chin and the upper left corner of her wig. Gerrit had used one of the photos of Anita dressed as herself, the red hair rendered medium-gray, the stiff little collar of her blouse tucked inside her string of beads. Berni could tell by the way Sonje's breastbone went up and down, the way she kept dabbing the tops of her cheeks, that she'd told Gerrit to do this.

"And look!" Berni cried. "Metzger!" The name Gerrit had used was Anita Maria Metzger. "We are truly sisters now."

Sonje tucked Anita's turban behind her ear. "What do you think? You can go to New York and still be yourself."

Anita stayed very still, staring at the photograph, holding the passport open with two long fingers. "Thank you," she said, her voice barely audible. "This means something to me."

"Be sure you're very careful," said Sonje in a hurry. "At the border, on the train, hand them your passports as a group, with the rest of the people in your car. If you're lucky they'll just count them and count your heads . . ."

Berni held on to every word, but she couldn't tell if Anita was listening or not. After a while Anita put down her glass and scratched her calf with the other foot, nodding absently.

• • •

Late that evening, Berni heard a knock on her doorframe. When she looked up she expected Sonje, but the pointy knee that pushed the curtain aside belonged to Anita. She wore a shower cap and had washed away her makeup. "I have a present for you."

She came over and lay down on the pallet. Berni made room in a hurry. It had been a long time since they'd lain together. "Ready?" Anita asked, and handed her *The Prussian Housewife's Handbook.* Berni read the title twice, then a third time, mystified. She looked at Anita through the corner of her eye. Both of them burst out laughing.

Berni traced the book jacket, imagining Anita at the bookstore, thinking one day she might need a manual, that she might be a wife. "Does it teach you how to prepare sausage?"

"Oh, yes, sausage. The German delicacy. You have to handle it with love." Anita lay back so that Berni could put her arms around her and kiss her on the forehead. They stayed that way for quite a while, listening to motorcars shear puddles out on the street. Berni wondered why more people didn't choose this, friends instead of husband and wife.

"Won't you sleep with me, like old times?" she asked, her voice thick. She'd begun to doze. Anita nodded, her shower cap tickling Berni's skin. She went to retrieve her pillow. As soon as the lights were out, Berni felt awake again. "You're so lucky," she said after a while, to hide how much she knew she'd miss her.

"I keep thinking of the things I must do for the last time. Eat a frankfurter with hot mustard at Fritz's. Talk you out of seeing whatever silly man you have in your life."

"I have no silly man in my life."

"Good. I'll tell you ahead of time: the next one you meet, get rid of him."

"You, too." Berni took Anita's hand and held it until Anita began to snore. Berni found herself drifting as well, her thoughts becoming thin. A few shallow dreams skimmed past her, like gauze drifting over her face.

In the morning, when Berni woke, she was alone. In the hallway she found Anita's bedroom door open and Sonje standing before the dresser. Anita's cosmetics case, crocodile pumps, and leather boots were missing, and she had taken about a third of the cash from inside one of the quilts.

Berni was afraid to speak; speaking would make it real. Finally she had to ask if there'd been any note, and Sonje handed her a small card.

My darlings,

You have tried and tried to help me, and all I have been is a burden: a little worm, dangling on the hook, bringing the Gestapo jaws snapping at our apartment. There, I can see him now, leaning against the side wall of Lenye's across the street.

I cannot stay. I cannot go to America, either; we've all known it was a long shot, too long, and my best chance at this point is to hide. I cannot hide with you.

I've left a little token of my gratitude for your love and friendship. You'll find it on the bust in my bed chamber, just waiting for one of you to try on. Sonje, I suggest you be the one to carry the mantle, use the passport, the visa. Don't let her be stubborn, Berni; too much has gone into this plan for ungrateful me to put it all to waste.

With love,
Anita

Berni wiped her eye. "What does she mean?" But she already knew. The wig, her precious, shining wig—made of real human hair from the Orient, she always claimed—sat on its dummy on her vanity.

Sonje's voice shook. "She means for one of us to go in her place." Berni noticed then that she held the ersatz passport in her trembling hand. "The damned fool!"

# BERNI, 1935

"Hello? Hello? Yes, I'll hold."

Sonje would not give up easily. Berni sat in the orange chair beside the window, watching sleet bounce off the black wrought-iron balcony, as Sonje called nightclubs.

"It's the damned Olympics," Sonje said, pacing, tangling herself in the telephone's long cord. "Naturally it's given her false hope. Good God, how long can they keep me holding?"

False hope. Because of the upcoming Berlin Olympics, the Nazis had relaxed. Some *Juden unerwünscht* signs had been taken down. Sonje called this disingenuous, yet in the same breath she insisted she could outlast the Nazis.

"Have you considered," Berni said now, choosing her words carefully, "honoring Anita's request? The children need a chaperone, don't they?" She hoped Sonje would. If she went to America, then Berni could emigrate with Grete without guilt, secure in the knowledge that Sonje was safe.

Sonje held up a finger. "No?" she said into the phone. "Well, telephone if she turns up." She slammed the receiver down, then immediately picked it up and began turning the dial. "*Anita* will be the one to use the passport, when she comes to her senses. And I could never leave with her missing. Hello? Operator?" She asked to be connected to the Bar Motz in Prenzlauer Berg. "I'd sooner offer the visa to you," she whispered to Berni.

"Me?" Berni busied herself taking the ashtray to the garbage. Had Grete been someone else, she could have told Sonje there was already a plan in motion. "I couldn't."

Sonje raised an eyebrow. "All I've ever heard you say is that you want to visit London, you want to—Hello? Hello? Yes, I'm looking for a friend who might've come to your bar in the last few days. She's about twenty-two, very thin. I'm afraid I'll embarrass her but I believe she wears a wig. A red one. She's ah, how do I put this, an unusual-looking girl . . ."

• • •

A few days later a bill from Trommler arrived, asking for that month's rent and the previous two months' back pay. Weeks had passed since his last visit, which Berni realized now, with a sinking feeling in her gut, corresponded with the new miscegenation law.

"So, we have a true landlord now," said Sonje.

"Bastard," Berni whispered.

"Do you see what he added at the bottom of the page? 'Landlord respectfully requests that Fräulein Metzger deliver back rent in person, presently.'"

"What does that mean?" Berni asked, but she already knew. She could imagine Trommler naked and bloated beneath her, white hairs on his chest and under his arms. She could almost feel the way her hands would sink into the spongy flesh of his shoulders.

Sonje reached for her elbow. "I'm going to pay him more than he's asked, to keep him at bay. But you don't have to do anything but deliver the cash, *nicht*?" She ran a hand through her unwashed hair, then reached for her coat. "Don't let anyone in while I'm at the agency. Pretend no one's home."

Not five minutes after Sonje left, the telephone rang. Berni made it there just before it stopped ringing. "Hello?"

Nobody replied.

"Are you calling about Anita?" She could hear nothing, no breathing or background noise, as if the caller were sitting inside a closet. Her abdomen quivered, and she waited, waited, until she heard it: three little huffs. Berni shut her eyes and repeated the signal. "Oh, my little darling, it's you."

She heard the squeak of a tiny swallow on the other end of the line.

"Listen, Bird, I've found a way. There are people who arrange group visits to Switzerland, Finland, the United States, for people who need to take the cure. My bronchitis will be our savior! We'll go through Liège. If the border guards at Aachen are as lax as Sonje says they are, we will not be harassed, even if we take some money."

Grete still hadn't said anything. Words spilled out of Berni's mouth with such incredible speed that she had to catch her breath. "We can live in the mountains in New York. Or the pine forests of the Carolinas, in the south. Don't worry, I'll protect you from alligators."

No reply. What if the person on the other line wasn't Grete? "Say something," Berni pleaded. "Tell me it's you and that you have your passport."

After a moment, Grete's voice: "You're saying too much. I have my passport. When can we leave?"

"I still have to visit the doctor. I'm sorry, Bird. So much has happened . . ."

"Please hurry."

"Why?" The need to cough prickled the back of Berni's throat. She suppressed it. "It isn't him, is it? He hasn't turned violent on you?"

She could hardly hear Grete's response. "No. Never. But do please hurry, Berni."

"I'll drop in to the office tomorrow. There's just one thing I have to take care of, and then I'll go. Afterward we'll meet. Could you meet me on Monday, at five? Meet me at the Bahnhof Zoo restaurant. It's loud in there." Berni caught her breath. "You haven't said a word to him, have you, Grete? Have you?"

"No. We need to stop talking now."

"Agreed, my love. We're almost there. I'll see you on Monday, at five in the evening."

Inside the receiver she heard a click, and a moment later, the voice of the operator.

• • •

Trommler's apartment in the Hotel Excelsior, where he met Sonje when he wanted to get away from his wife, reminded Berni of the inside of a fish tank, and Trommler, at its center, an engorged blowfish. Watered silk wallpaper in deep blue covered the walls of the sitting room. Trommler had the maid set the tea tray on the seat of the velvet armchair, so Berni was forced to sit either beside him on the divan or on an embroidered footstool. She chose the footstool.

He rattled a tortoiseshell case. "Shall we play dice?"

"No thank you, Herr Trommler," Berni said, watching snow float past the enormous windows. The doctor could be getting in his car right now, closing his practice to get home to his family in the suburbs. Trommler already had the rent money. She watched the pendulum of his cuckoo clock and decided she would wait ten more minutes.

"How is dear Sonje?" Trommler asked, biting an almond cookie. "The laws aren't getting to her too terribly, are they?"

"She's managing," Berni said, unable to look him in the eye. Sonje had instructed her to act polite, but coy, to turn down his advances, but make it seem as though it were simply a matter of time before she caved.

"I'd like to see her, of course, but you know I was raised to be a law-abiding citizen. You can't fight the law."

Berni took a deep breath through her nose. "This is a beautiful suite."

He puffed up a little and chuckled. "Yes, I saw you appraising the Persian carpet. You ladies know exactly how to calculate what a man's worth. Why, the last girl I invited here, before Sonje, had my annual income down to the pfennig after fifteen minutes. Down to the pfennig!"

A clump of gray snow clung to the heel of Berni's boot; she switched the cross of her legs, and it fell to the rug. "You're making me blush, Herr Trommler."

"You? Blush? Berni, my dear." His thumb began rubbing her skin. "I'm a modern man. I have no illusions about girls these days. It doesn't bother me that you've given yourself out."

Eight more minutes. "Given myself out?"

He raised her hand to his wet lips, leaving a trail of slobber on her skin. "If you think the parlor's nice," he murmured, moving her sleeve so that he could get to her forearm. "You should see the bathtub. It is massive."

"It must be," Berni said. "Otherwise you'd still be stuck in it."

"Sonje is a very close friend of mine," he sputtered. "I doubt she'd want you speaking to me with such—such disrespect!"

She had to get out of here, get to the doctor. "Pardon me, Herr Trommler. I'm not feeling quite myself today. I think soon I should be going, so that I can elevate my feet."

He settled back into the cushions, saucer balanced on his stomach. "I'm not a bad man to befriend, *nicht wahr*? Not only because I can procure the best *Baumkuchen* in the city. I have more serious connections. Reinhard Heydrich is an old friend from university . . ."

"Is that so." She'd heard Trommler rattle off the names of his important friends a dozen times. Six more minutes. Two more days until she met Grete at the Zoo station.

Trommler was still talking, his breath enveloping Berni in a radish and onion fog. ". . . Heydrich's the one who told me the Gestapo are watching Sonje." His beady eyes sparkled.

"What did you say?"

He opened his mouth in mock surprise. "Goodness, girl. Hadn't you noticed any secret police lingering outside your building?"

"No," Berni lied. Since Sonje had pointed him out, she'd seen the man chain-smoking across the street. Cigarette butts were beginning to pile in the gutter.

Trommler's lips pursed. "Herr Heydrich thought I'd be very interested to know my rental apartment showed up on a list. Apparently Sonje has become involved with some Jewish groups? 'Reinhard,' I said—we're on familiar terms—'She's not a concern, just one of these women who always needs to feel involved.' I think I may have had some influence." He put his cup down and rested his elbows on his knees. "You see? I am a good friend."

Berni's body trembled all over. Sonje had kept Anita hidden in the apartment, all the while freely coming and going, taking the trolley to the Jewish Relief Agency with her cello case, her briefcase full of sheet music. Berni realized with chilled detachment that she would have to sleep with Trommler. She had to convince him there was still something for him in this arrangement. And then she had to get Sonje to leave her parents' apartment.

Already Berni could feel a dulling of her senses. The tea tasted like mud. Trommler patted the space beside him on the couch, and as she went to join him, the little walleyed cuckoo sprang through its wooden shutters, mocking her.

Best to get it over with quickly. "Herr Trommler . . ."

He didn't let her finish the sentence. His rib cage crushed her into the divan, her face smashed against a velvet cushion. He interpreted her groan as a moan of pleasure and began kissing her neck, the round drum of his hips pressed between her open thighs. She let her hands drop as she listened to his belt buckle flap open. Her eyes searched desperately for something on which to focus, to take her out of what was happening to her body, and fell on a newspaper folded under the coffee table. The cover featured recently apprehended traitors to the Volk.

"Wait," she said. A last gasp of energy surged through her arms, and she put her hands to his shoulders, locked her wrists, and pushed. "Wait!"

He toppled toward the arm of the sofa. "What the hell is the matter?"

She grabbed the paper from under the table and shook it open. The story was about an alleged putsch planned by a group called the Catholic Action. Two priests had been accused of undermining the government at their pulpits. They'd hoarded foreign cash, according to the *Völkischer Beobachter*, so that they might strengthen the Vatican at the expense of the Reich. Photos of two men who looked like clerics ran beside one of their accused accomplices. She had the jowls of an elderly woman, but she held her blunt chin high above her wimple. The newspaper claimed she'd stored vast amounts of money in a girls' orphanage in Charlottenburg.

• • •

Later Berni had no recollection of how she'd gotten to St. Luisa's. Of course she must have taken the elevator to the lower level of the hotel and walked through the tunnel underneath Askanischer Platz toward Anhalter Bahnhof. When she arrived at the orphanage, her S-Bahn pass was in her pocket, so she must have taken it out to show a ticket inspector, and at some point switched to the U7.

She knocked, repeatedly, on the old oak doors. Finally the one on the right creaked open, a sheet of warm air leaking out. "The reverend mother isn't here," said the girl, the same one Berni had spoken to before.

"Please," said Berni. "I need to see someone. Anyone. Please."

"Just a minute." Berni was shut out in the cold again. Behind her she heard people laughing, the ringing bells of a sleigh. Then there was whispering inside, and the door groaned open again. Now two faces stared down at her.

"Sister Josephine!"

In the time that had passed the old woman had become shriveled, too small for her skin. It seemed all the hair on her face had drifted away. At one time she would have pulled Berni to her bosom, but she kept back, eyes fearful. When Berni tried to cross the threshold she held up a hand. "We can't let you in, Berni. It may be that you had nothing to do with it, my dear, but we have to be ever more careful now."

"To do with what?" Berni felt as though her guts were on fire.

Sister Josephine inhaled, then put her hand on the girl's shoulder and told her she was free to join the others for lunch. When she'd gone, the sister turned to Berni. "All right, hurry in, you'll catch cold out there."

Inside the vestibule, the dark wooden walls were saturated with bright white light coming from the snowy street. Berni blinked hard, trying to clear the spots from her eyes, trying to make sense of things. Sister Josephine stood at arm's length, peering up into her face with both apprehension and pity. "When's the last time you saw Grete?" she asked quietly.

Berni's breath hitched in her throat. "About a month ago, Sister."

"She came to ask for a position as a nurse here, and even though we hadn't advertised for one, Sister Maria Eberhardt allowed her to come in."

"I know. Sister Maria turned her down."

Sister Josephine nodded. "Well, Grete paid us another call last week. She said she wanted to ask some questions about her parents, but Sister Maria said she seemed nervous, asked to go to the restroom and then left in a hurry."

Berni breathed hard. "And then?"

"Two days later the reverend mother was arrested. The Gestapo knew exactly where to look for hidden money. The strange thing is they found a briefcase of American and British currency, thousands of marks' worth, under the desk in her office. But Sister Maria didn't keep money there. She kept it—"

"In the chapel," Berni whispered.

Sister Josephine nodded; she winced as she swallowed. "They took her into protective custody," she said softly.

Berni's ankles wobbled. She'd forgotten how to stand. She collapsed into Sister Josephine's arms, making the old woman gasp. She had no warm feelings toward Sister Maria Eberhardt. But if the SS considered her enough of a threat to put her away, she must have had some good in her.

"The thing is," Sister Josephine whispered, "we were receiving funds. A kind lawyer, part of the Catholic Action, provided us with foreign cash, *verboten*. Sister Maria took such a risk for all of us . . ." Her words ended in a sob. "The officers who arrested her were just boys. I couldn't believe the faces of these boys."

Eventually Sister Josephine pulled away and blotted her eyes with her sleeve. "You mustn't mention this conversation to anyone, do you understand? Not to anyone." Her hand was cold and soft on Berni's. "Stay out of trouble, my dear."

Berni went slowly down the steps under the skeletal chestnut tree. She could barely lift her feet. On the fourth stair she slipped on a patch of ice and went down, her shins crunching old chestnut husks. She lay there for a while, unmoving. Nobody inside her old childhood home came out to help her. She lingered long enough to hear the Angelus bell ring and the swell of a hundred voices, praying together.

● ● ●

Grete arrived at the Bahnhof Zoo on Monday at twenty minutes of five in the evening. Because she was early, and the temperature mild for November, she took a slow walk around the perimeter of the zoo. Children holding balloons dragged their feet through the exit, following parents and nannies pushing sleeping toddlers or holding crying infants. The sun had gone down half an hour earlier but still cast a faint bluish glow on the half-finished rock wall they were building for the penguins. She passed a polar bear rubbing its oily yellow fur on a concrete boulder, looking frisky and happy to be outside in the increasing cold, and as she gazed up at the glistening Indian tiles on the turrets and spires of the elephant house, she, too, felt something: if not happiness, then something close to it. The elephant house reminded her of the wider world beyond Berlin. She knew she never deserved to be happy again. But in another place, with Berni, away from Klaus, she could try to start over. She'd live a better life; she'd do good, to make up for the damage she'd caused. She took one long breath of the fresh, brisk air, and went into the restaurant to wait for Berni.

Berni saw all of this from a train bound for Amsterdam.

Her face, in the window's reflection, looked gaunt against the black branches of passing trees. Somewhere, over a hundred miles away by now, her twin waited, cheeks pulled upward in anticipation, the same shallow divot in her chin. Grete would have ordered her first beer by now. It would be sitting on the copper surface of a table in the Zoo waiting room, untouched, foam still intact.

In the seat beside Berni, closer to the window, the little boy put his head back against the seat cushion and made an almost inaudible sigh. She could see his face in the reflection as well, his brow furrowed from trying not to cry. On the other side of the aisle, the two girls, Herr Grotte's nieces, clung to each other and sniffled. The boy sitting with Berni didn't want her to touch him. He'd recoiled from her, the strange tall woman in the bright red wig, when she tried to take his hand as they climbed the platform in Hanover. She wanted to tell him she felt the same way he did: as if everything inside her head had turned to liquid the instant they'd gotten in the car with Herr Petersen in the middle of the night, a day and a half ago. She knew she couldn't show emotion in front of the children, but she wanted to tell the boy it was all right if he did.

"How about some sweets?" she said, her voice foggy. "You can eat anything you want." As soon as she said it, she knew she shouldn't have; the unspoken phrase was *because your mother isn't here.* The boy shook his head vigorously, pulled his little knees to his chest, and put his head against the window. She let him alone.

What was it Sonje had told her before she left? "Circumstances have made it so that a lack of trust in someone is no longer an insult." The last Berni had seen her, she'd been in Gerrit's spacious apartment in Kreuzberg. Gerrit had been happy to welcome Sonje into his home after Berni told her everything, about Trommler, the Gestapo, and finally, about Grete.

"I told Grete about Liège, and the border crossing at Aachen," Berni said, her voice cracking, in the security of Gerrit's study. "Klaus must know. We are ruined."

"Shh, shh." Sonje handed Berni an envelope. The student visas were inside, with three letters of acceptance to an exchange program in New York, including a note allowing Anita a three-month visitor's permit as the children's guardian. There were also four passports, including Anita Metzger's, and four train tickets from Hanover to Amsterdam.

"The group was never going through Liège," Sonje said quietly. "The only ones who knew were Herr Grotte, Herr Petersen, and I. Not even Anita. Not even the children."

Berni tucked it all back inside the envelope. She had never felt so relieved to learn she hadn't been trusted. "Promise me you won't return to your old apartment," she said, tears catching in her throat. "Let it go. It's Trommler's now."

"Of course," Sonje said, and from her smile Berni could tell this was a lie. She still had the keys in her pocketbook.

"Don't go back for the candy dish."

Sonje burst out laughing. "The golden candy dish! I forgot all about it. Where was it hidden? Oh, don't worry, don't worry, I won't."

It was remarkable, Berni thought now from the train, how easy it was to make a few small decisions that led to something enormous and irreversible. Something as simple as trying on Anita's wig and conceding that she looked passably like the girl in the photo. The sky outside the windows of the train was completely dark now. They were approaching the Dutch border. The boy beside Berni shivered, yet she could feel heat coming off his skin. They both knew what was coming. His pupils ticked nervously over the black scenery they passed, trying desperately to seize onto something. For a moment his gaze and Berni's locked in the reflection, his face panic-stricken, his eyes startled.

The foam in Grete's beer would have dissolved by now. She would have begun to wonder if Berni wasn't coming.

The train started to slow down, and the boy shuddered. Berni wished she could take his little hand, to distract herself from the thought of Grete waiting. *Grete.* She had to have been the reason Sonje wouldn't share the details of the plan with Berni until the very end, yet Berni knew Grete hadn't breathed a word to Klaus. She'd been desperate to get away from him, from what she'd done for him; that much had been evident in her voice on the telephone.

Still. That did nothing to change the fact that Sister Maria had been interrogated for six days. The radio reported one of the two priests had been sent to Dachau. The lawyer had been found guilty of treason and sentenced to death.

Berni felt a tug on her left hand, and she looked down into the brimming brown eyes of the little boy beside her. He pointed outside. Bright lights, a station. They'd come to the border at Gronau. Berni took a deep breath. When the train finally stopped, she heard the doors bang open.

"Anita," the little boy murmured.

"Shh," she said. The corner of the passport envelope was growing soggy in her hand. "Don't call me that. You can call me something else, *nicht*? You can call me Fräulein M."

"Fräulein M.," he said timidly. "You can call me Hündchen."

The enormous, thick-booted guard had burst into the front of their car. He was taking a very long time to examine the first bunch of passports. Her heart would explode. "Does your Mutti call you Hündchen?" she asked the boy, her throat thick.

He nodded.

She had to look away, still holding tightly to his hand. He looked exactly the way Grete had in the courtyard of St. Luisa's, the morning Berni had climbed into the Maybach with Sonje. If she stared at him too long, she knew she would cry.

"Hündchen," she said. She would not cry. She could not let on that she had their money, hers and the children's, sewn into her coat. Her voice needed to remain steady. It had to be a clear and confident and reassuring voice—dear Sonje's voice—so that when their turn with the border guards arrived, she would be ready.

# PART IV

# NEW YORK, 1970

*Break off my arms, I'll take hold of you
with my heart as with a hand.*

Rainer Maria Rilke

# ANITA, 1970

In the beginning, when she first arrived in the United States, Berni had imagined a little machine inside her head that processed English into German, then German into English, producing her halting responses on ticker tape. Long days of conversation, as with the immigration and customs officials in the harbor, left the machine smoking, overused, in need of oil. In time she used her translator less and less. Phrases like "the rent was due on the first of the month," and her response, "I will have the money tomorrow," came naturally. After a year or two passed, she did not have to think *Ich werde morgen zahlen* first. In time, she even dreamt in English.

Changing her first name, on the other hand, happened instantly on paper, much longer inside her mind.

"What is your name?" strangers asked.

*My name is Berni*, she told the machine inside her skull, and after a few beeps and burps the machine chugged out a little piece of paper: *Your name is Anita*. "Anita," she replied, the word as clunky on her tongue as "cafeteria" or "breakfast." For a while she avoided meeting people, greeting people; she sought jobs and landladies who asked few questions. She worked in a munitions factory in Atlanta, and would have gone on unmolested for years, perhaps to this day, if Remy hadn't been so determined to know her. She waited until the day before their wedding to tell him her real name, then insisted he never mention it again.

Janeen's surprise arrival, sixteen years after Anita had arrived in this country, finally made the translation stick. To the new baby girl in her arms she was Anita and had always been Anita. Anita Moore, mother of Janeen Moore, an American child; she'd let the machine rust.

Not even the arrival of Grete's letter had changed that. It was not until she had to tell the story to her daughter, to say the words "I was called Berni," that she began dreaming, not only in German, but as Berni again. Anita was again something she had to put on each morning, like underwear or hand lotion. In the first few moments of every day now, in that vulnerable space between sleep and waking, she was Berni. She was Berni until she reached toward Remy's side of the bed and found it empty. And then she remembered everything she'd lost.

Anita, the true Anita, appeared to her as she slept. She hadn't aged, but her hair had grown back, luscious and brown and shiny. She stood with her legs in their Bemberg stockings twisted at the knobby kneecaps, hid her face behind her hand, and laughed.

"You want to see Grete. And you will go to her not to confront her, but because you hope to find she's changed. Admit it."

The bed sheets were damp. "No . . . no . . ." She reached for Anita, tried to grasp her by the shoulders. "You are my sister." Her fingers closed on air.

• • •

Margaret Forsyth resided on a beautiful, quiet block near Central Park, dotted with buildings with crisp new awnings, brass doors, and waiting men in white gloves. Janeen and Anita had walked all the way from their hotel on the Upper West Side, and now they stood, unsure what to do, in front of a pricey boutique with its doors thrown open to the summer. The space inside looked empty, white, and cool; Anita longed to duck inside and hide. She reached for Janeen's hand and could feel the force of their pulses pounding together.

"We don't have to do this, Mutti." Janeen held Anita's hand tightly between her fingers, the nails painted shimmery white. It seemed only now that the two of them realized the enormity of what they were about to do. "We can still turn back."

"We must keep going," Anita growled, pretending Janeen was not the only thing that kept her moving forward. She winced into the sun as they walked. She'd left her bottle of aspirin on the bedside table. Today she would see Grete. She felt exactly as she had forty years before, waiting on her front steps in Schöneberg on Grete's day off from the Eislers', or at the edge of a Goebbels rally.

*Margaret*, she reminded herself, her temples throbbing. Today she would visit someone named Margaret, who had very little to do with the sister she'd left in Berlin.

The urge to find her sister in the flesh had begun after Anita began taunting her in her sleep, and once it wormed its way into her waking thoughts, she could not ignore it. Less than a week after the letter arrived—after she'd read the scorched pages twice, three times—she and Janeen had boarded a train that crawled up the eastern seaboard toward New York City. Only in Washington, when Anita disembarked to smoke a cigarette, had she considered turning back. But she couldn't, not now. She hadn't seen Janeen so alive in months. It spooked her a little, in fact, how excited Janeen seemed to be to find more of her family. The last thing her daughter needed was to become entangled in the disappointment that was Grete.

In the gazebo in Shortleaf Park, Janeen had waited only a few stunned minutes before her questions began. Anita wished she'd asked about Hündchen first. The news on him was relatively positive. He'd moved to Israel to find his father, his only family member who'd survived Auschwitz.

But Janeen had started by asking about Sonje and the original Anita.

"Sonje and I stayed in contact until November 1938," Anita said, inspecting her palms. She and Janeen had stayed in the gazebo past two in the morning, and by then all of the lights in the park had gone out. "And you know what happened in November of 1938, *Liebchen*."

In the dark, she could not tell if her daughter was crying, but she heard a catch in her voice. "Kristallnacht." Janeen put her hand to her throat. "And the first Anita?"

It had been difficult to formulate an answer. "I do not doubt that Sonje searched for her until the end."

The two of them hadn't moved in ten minutes now, as they watched a truck parked outside Margaret Forsyth's apartment building, its hazard lights on. Movers were attempting to slide a sofa wrapped in padded blankets down the steps, and for a minute Anita forgot herself and almost went to help them. Instead she and Janeen stood numbly by and watched. A man in a black suit and gloves emerged next, carrying a stack of end tables, and finally, behind him, a woman appeared. Janeen put a hand over her mouth.

The woman looked quiet, delicate and patient; she waited for her doorman to ease the tables down the steps, giving him gentle nods. She had thick whitish blonde hair, cut in a full bob like the top of a mushroom. One of the movers took the lamp she held, and she offered him a kind grin, however brief; she did not look like the type of person who smiled broadly or often. Self-consciously she tucked her hair behind one of her ears and then pulled it out again, and in that gesture Anita glimpsed the plastic cover of a hearing aid.

Anita did not realize until Janeen put her arm about her waist that she'd made a noise, a kind of sob. She put her fingers to her cheeks, but they were dry, and when she looked up she saw Margaret squinting in their direction. Her eyes became big and small, big and small.

Margaret seemed to forget her moving truck. She glided toward them, the little blue jewels of her eyes never leaving Anita's face. By the time she reached them, she was weeping.

"I knew it was you," she said. Her voice had become clearer: there was only a hint of a blur to her words now, but she was still

Grete. Anita could hear pure Berlin laced through her American accent. "You came. My goodness. Berni! I knew you were . . ."

Her fingers covered the top half of her face, and she stood apart, crying, not touching either of them. Finally Anita stepped forward and opened her arms.

"Grete-bird," she said, despite herself. She let her head rest atop Margaret's, shocked at how natural it felt to embrace and hold her, as though no time at all had gone by and neither of them had anything to explain. When they pulled apart, she stared closely at Margaret's face, amazed at how little had changed in the pink cheeks, the startled eyes.

"This is my daughter," Anita said, reaching behind her. "This is Janeen."

"Hello." Janeen, impossibly calm, offered her hand to Margaret. "Pleased to meet you."

"My dear." Margaret lifted her scarf to one of her eyes. "Oh, my goodness. You look exactly like Berni." She laid her fingertips on Janeen's flushed cheeks, very delicately, and only then did Anita begin to panic. She could have begun by demanding answers, and instead she'd offered a hug. She'd brought her own daughter forward. It was too late, now, to scream.

• • •

They stood on the sidewalk for a while, not saying much, and then Margaret seemed to remember where they were and muttered something along the lines of, "I suppose I must take you inside." She seemed agitated now, even though she'd stopped crying; her face looked tight.

"No, we will come back later," Anita said, but before she knew it they were all inside the elevator, standing in silence, stunned, as though rendered senseless by an explosion.

They stepped out of the elevator and right into her apartment, onto the black-and-white checkered floor of the foyer, and Anita realized all of a sudden that her sister was rich. The address should have given it away, but her mind had been fogged. Her sister was rich.

"Beautiful," Janeen said in a hushed voice, on tiptoe.

"I'll get you each a glass of water," Margaret said, whispering, as though she, too, was only visiting here. She left Janeen and Anita to stand in the hall, peering into the emptied rooms. The walls were papered in satin, each room a different Easter-egg color: yellow, green, pink. Cardboard boxes full of Margaret's detritus were piled on the floor. Stained outlines of frames littered the bare spaces on the walls.

"Most of the art was my husband's," said a voice behind Anita's left shoulder. She startled so violently that she almost made Margaret spill the glass of water she held out.

"I am sorry about your divorce," Anita murmured, taking a sip.

Margaret sniffed. "It was a long time coming. We had some good years, some bad." Her voice was barely a whisper. "Charles and I split this apartment in the divorce, so we sold it. I will be happier in Morningside Heights. And you, Berni? You're married, still?"

Anita opened her mouth. She was no longer Berni, no longer married. Or was she? She twisted the ring on her finger.

"My father passed away," Janeen said, and Margaret swallowed, her forehead and neck turning crimson.

"Oh." Margaret put her hands to her chest. "I had no idea. When?"

"Last month," Anita grunted.

"I'm sorry, Berni. I truly am sorry."

Anita bristled at the name. Janeen looked at her with wide eyes. "Please, I'd prefer that you don't—"

A young man's voice boomed toward them, coming from a room in the front of the apartment. "Who are you talking to?" he called. "I found the missing andiron, by the way, but I still think you should sell the set."

"I . . ." said Margaret, her face drawn. "Erik . . ."

He sighed audibly. "You don't even have a fireplace in the new apartment, Mom."

All three of them had frozen. Anita swallowed, her throat dry. She hadn't thought about other people, about the fact that Margaret had children, but of course—they'd be here, they'd be involved. They would have even more questions than Margaret did.

"Who's that?" Janeen whispered, and Anita felt her heart ping. The boy in the other room would be her cousin.

"That's my son," Margaret whispered. She led them into the living room. At the far end, two giant windows displayed pure green, the tops of the trees along the park. A grand piano, dust on its shiny lid, sat in the corner, its bench turned on its side. Among a sea of moving boxes sat a young man of about twenty, who looked at them suspiciously over a stack of plain paper and a pile of knickknacks. His hair was ash blond, the same color Grete's had been when she was his age, but darker and kinkier at the sideburns.

"I don't know how to say this, Erik dear." Greeting her son had made Margaret's voice turn nasal. She reached for Anita's hand, as much for support, it seemed, as in introduction; it was the first time they'd touched since their brief embrace outside. "Anita Moore, Janeen, this is my son, Erik. He'll be a junior at Cornell this fall."

Erik put down the tchotchke he'd been wrapping, brushed his hands on his jeans, and came to greet them. He smelled of fresh sweat and aftershave, though his cheeks still had a soft, boyish appearance. He gazed at Anita and Janeen, his face bewildered. Anita gazed back.

Her sister's son. She had a clamp on her voice box.

He grinned at Janeen, lingering on her a little longer than was necessary, and Margaret cleared her throat. "Anita is my sister, Erik. Your aunt. Janeen is your cousin."

Erik's expression changed little, as though he did not believe it. "Your sister?"

"Oh, my goodness." Unable to hold herself back any longer, Anita reached for Erik's shoulder. "Yes, I'm your aunt." He was shorter than she was, and under her grip she felt him puff up a little.

He scratched one of his sideburns. "I'm sorry, I . . ." he said, hand on his chin. "I didn't know my mother had family." He squinted at Margaret, who smiled weakly. "You've got to be pulling my leg. Why have I never met them before?"

Margaret hesitated, and so Anita said, "Your mother and I were separated, my sweet nephew, and now we have thirty-five years of catching up to do."

"Why did you come today, of all days?" he said. "Why haven't I heard of you before?"

Not shy at all, Anita thought—Erik was more of a young Berni than Grete. Had her sister thought the same thing over the years? Margaret still looked pale, her lips near colorless. She opened them, fluttering her eyelids, searching for an answer.

It was Janeen who rescued her. "Don't you have a daughter, too, Aunt Margaret?"

Margaret blinked rapidly after "Aunt Margaret," and Erik turned his eyes sharply toward Janeen. "Yes, Anna. She lives in London."

Erik sucked his teeth. "She couldn't be bothered with this whole divorce and moving thing. Lucky her."

Out on the street, traffic, horns, someone shouting. Margaret looked from Janeen to Erik for a moment, then brightened. "Erik, honey, you have a few boxes to consign. Perhaps Janeen would be interested in helping you?"

He snorted. "What you're letting me sell fills like a box and a half, man. It's not like I need help carrying it. Unless you'll part with more junk."

Margaret ignored him. "Could we send you out with him for a little while, dear?" She put her hand on Janeen's shoulder, and again Anita felt a note of panic inside her throat.

"Sure." Janeen glanced at Erik, then her mother. "What do you think, Mutti?"

Erik chuckled. "Where'd you come from? Texas?" Janeen's cheeks went red.

"I think the two of you should get to know each other," said Anita. "Erik, you can show my daughter a bit of the city, *nicht*?"

The two of them gathered a few of the cardboard boxes, Janeen still blushing, and with a final suspicious glance toward his mother Erik led Janeen back out toward the foyer. They heard the chirp of young voices, Janeen's nervous laughter, and then the elevator door shut with a bang. Anita and Margaret were alone in the stuffy, warm apartment. Margaret inclined her head toward the one remaining piece of furniture, a couch covered in plastic. They took their seats on opposite ends, settling into the cushions with a series of awkward squishing sounds.

"Forgive me for staring at you, Berni," Margaret said. "You look exactly as I always pictured you as an older woman. You're still a work of art."

Anita rested her glass on her knee. It made a wet circle she could feel through the fabric.

"Alone, we are, both of us without men. Though I cannot imagine your pain, Berni. I am sorry."

It wasn't just the name, Anita realized; it was the way Grete—*Margaret*—pronounced it. The name Berni rolled so easily off this woman's tongue, it made it impossible to pretend Margaret Forsyth was a stranger. "I'd rather not be called Berni anymore."

Margaret blinked and sat back quickly, looking hurt. She swallowed and made an attempt at a laugh. "Your accent is something else. It is kind of a Gullah German."

"Lowcountry Deutsch," Anita replied. "Shall we switch to German?" It would be a relief, after all these years, like going from swimming in her clothes to gliding in the nude.

A gleam came into Margaret's eye. "Should we call each other *du*?" Anita couldn't answer.

"*Es ist wirklich du*," Margaret said quietly, shaking her head. "I cannot believe it. For years I told Charles I thought my sister might have made it out of Berlin as well, and he treated me as if I were crazy. Wishful thinking, he called it. 'Why would she leave without telling you?'" She fluffed her fingers in the front of her hair, mussing her stiff blond coif, and her shoulders shook for a moment.

Anita did not move. She had to quiet the devil on her shoulder, telling her it would all be so easy if she'd just open her arms to her sister and forgive.

Margaret looked up at the white medallion on the ceiling where a light fixture had been and let out a hard breath. "I suppose, when I sent the letter, some part of me hoped it would be you on the other end. I did not want to think too much about what it meant if it were you. Now that I see you . . . forgive me. It's as if I am waiting at the Zoo all over again."

Anita snorted. "While you were at the Zoo I was on a train with three children, and as I should have been tending to their needs, I could not stop thinking of you." It was good, in a way, that Margaret had made her angry; it kept her from feeling other things. "After what you did, how could I have taken you with us? How could I have trusted you?"

"I understand. What I did was unforgivable. But I never would have put those children in danger. I never *wanted* to hurt anybody. I hope you know this."

Anita gripped the wooden arm of the sofa. In her heart she knew what Margaret said was true. She could picture Grete on that train to Belgium, comforting the boy, her arms around the girls. "Perhaps you wouldn't have brought us trouble," Anita said, "but no, I could not trust you. I never would have thought you capable of what you did to Sister Maria. Convenient, wasn't it, that Klaus needed to round up Catholic dissenters? You could settle your old score."

Margaret turned away, becoming a silhouette against the bright white windows. "I planned to tell you everything at the Zoo. I took no pleasure in settling old scores. For the rest of my life I will think of Sister Maria and those priests, and the lawyer, every hour of every day."

"You deserve to suffer for it," Anita said quietly. "If you wrote to me in the hope that I'd absolve you, you will be disappointed."

"That is not why I wrote you. Some of us do not deserve absolution."

A chill went through Anita's veins. "Tell me." She reached out with her toe to press a loose flap of tape on one of the moving boxes. "Klaus Eisler. That is he, isn't it, Henry Klein?"

"It is he," said Margaret in a small voice. "I hope they catch him."

"Do you?" Anita stared at the soft creases around Margaret's mouth, the powder blush she'd applied in a stripe too heavy on one side. What would they say to one another, if the heavy apron of the past could be lifted away? They'd laugh about the indignities of their increased age. She could tell Margaret she'd become a librarian and ask about the nursing school where Margaret taught. She could tell Margaret she was proud of her.

Finally they heard the elevator door, like the barred door of a zoo cage, bang open again, and a man wearing a back support tiptoed into the room and gestured toward the sofas.

"I will let you finish moving," Anita said, but Margaret gripped her arm.

"Could we have a few more minutes?" she asked the man, who went back to the elevator. "I want to make it known you were right to leave me behind, Ber—Anita. You did what any sensible and just person would have done. You could have let my letter go unread as well, and it means a great deal that you have come. I want to know you again. If you'll let me. We were once all the other had in the world. Do you remember?"

Loneliness showed in her voice, and Anita wondered who kept Margaret Forsyth company. Did she still, in a manner of speaking, have no one she could call *du*?

She wanted to nod, to take Margaret into her arms. Instead, Anita rose and put her hands in her trouser pockets. "We will come to your new apartment tomorrow evening." Her head pounded as Margaret wrote down the address. She stuffed the piece of paper into her pocket with a nod and barreled toward the foyer. Ignoring Margaret's protests, she went to yank open the iron elevator door, only to find herself staring down an empty shaft.

# JANEEN, 1970

Her cousin was handsome, Janeen thought as he bought her a subway token, even though he had the kind of lips that seemed always to hang open. He was a little cocky, too, had an air of prep-school bravado in his expensive tennis shoes and green shorts. By the way he kept looking back at her, she could tell he expected her to be shocked by how decrepit and dirty the station at Seventy-Second Street and Second Avenue was, especially compared to the relative clean of the streets above.

She kept a straight face when they passed the shriveled woman with her accordion, when they caught the attention of a group of men in sleeveless tanks and dark glasses. They stopped at a portion of the tracks that smelled of something rotting. Erik pushed his blond hair, darkened from sweat, away from his forehead and leaned against the tile wall. "They can't really be sisters. Are they? They look nothing alike."

"I think they really are."

"I'd say I couldn't believe my mother would lie about having family, but I can."

Janeen cleared her throat. "So, do you have to move, too? To wherever your mother said—Morningside Heights?"

"Nah, I got a sublet in Kips Bay for the summer with some friends from school." He crossed his arms. "Have you known about me all these years, or were we both in the dark?"

"We were both in the dark." They gave a moment of bemused silence to the secrecy of their mothers. "I didn't know anything until a few weeks ago. Your mother wrote mine a letter, and I guess I intercepted it."

Erik laughed. "I've been trying to intercept for years. No such luck. Did they know about each other? Were they from the same father? Sorry, I'm just trying to make sense of this."

"Same father. Their parents died when they were young." Janeen found she was enjoying this a little, filling him in on their story. "They grew up in an orphanage together. And then they . . . left. My mother never told me much about it until now."

"Guess she can't. They're carrying a lot of guilt, huh? Their generation of Germans."

Before she had to answer, a hot gust of air began building in the tunnel, and Erik picked up his box. When it arrived, the subway car was covered in graffiti, bubbly white and black letters that made no sense. The variety of people inside took her breath away: a white man in a tie eating a hot dog; three black children and their mother, huddled around a picture book; two young women, one Hispanic and one white, in halter tops and platforms.

Erik chose a pole to lean on, and she grabbed onto it. "You should see what it's like where I come from, in the Carolinas," she said so that only he could hear. "My town, Pine Shoals, and the next one, Carter's Junction—they're completely segregated."

Her cousin gaped at her as though she were some sort of alien, and she saw herself through his eyes: her lavender sundress, the fuzzy brown pigtails resting on her shoulders. A bumpkin. "Where we going?" she asked.

"A pawn shop downtown. Below Fourteenth. It's a good one." He waited, she thought, for her to be impressed about his knowledge of pawn shops. "My mother wanted me to consign this stuff, but she needs the money now. Man, it's been hard to get her to get rid of shit. Most of it she wants to keep. And then there are things she wants me to throw away that clearly have value. She doesn't know where her head is these days. Something's going on with her."

Janeen averted her eyes. He probably knew she was hiding something; she'd never gotten away with lying. A name popped into her mind, something she could share: Joachim, her grandfather and namesake. He must have been Erik's grandfather, too. A man who died in World War I a long time ago, who had so little and yet everything to do with both of them. Her lips prepared to form his name, and then the doors slid open.

"This is our stop," Erik said, gesturing toward the sign above the platform: Astor Place. "You sure you're all right with this?"

She rolled her eyes. "Just get off the damned train, please? The doors are going to close."

It felt good to make him laugh. "Yes, ma'am."

• • •

As they walked toward St. Mark's Place, passing tattoo parlors, florists, head shops, he told her what he was studying at Cornell. "Agricultural science." He grinned. "My father made it clear I could major in whatever I wanted, philosophy, basketweaving. So I picked something he wouldn't get at all."

"Why?" Janeen asked. "I'd like to make my father proud."

"Then your father's nothing like my father," Erik replied. Janeen said nothing. They stopped for a minute to pet some black-and-white kittens a barefoot man was selling out of a crate, then kept walking. "So?" Erik said.

"So, what?"

"What're you going to do, to make your old man proud?"

Janeen took a deep breath. One of the last things her father had asked—begged—of her was that she leave Pine Shoals for a while, then come back and write about it. "Write about the South, write about segregation. But see the world first," he said. He'd been out of breath, but his grip on her hand was still firm. "Gain some perspective."

What would her father have said if he'd known she'd be in New York City in a matter of months, walking with a cousin neither of them had known anything about? "I'm going to be a journalist," she said. "I was working on a piece about the student body president at

College of Charleston hushing up war protestors when they kicked me off the school newspaper staff."

She flushed with pleasure when she saw the look on Erik's face. "Not afraid to make enemies?" he said. They stepped over some hippies on a blanket covered in woven goods.

"I can handle it." They passed a restaurant, and she caught whiffs of fried egg, chive, chicken skin. She tried to look nonchalant.

"Yeah," Erik said. "I think you could."

They found the pawn shop underneath a little ice cream parlor, and when Erik asked if she wanted to go in and get a cone, she blushed; despite the gnawing feeling in her stomach, something about ice cream seemed too much like a date. It struck her again, as they went down the steps to the pawn shop, how strange this was. This college boy who she'd have flirted with if he'd been a stranger was in fact one of her closest relatives.

Inside the store, Erik's arrogance finally melted under the spastic flickers of fluorescent lights. He waited quietly as a bulky man haggled with the owner over a razor-thin gold chain and tiny pendant. "A real fucking diamond," the man kept saying to the owner, a ferrety man in suspenders and glasses. Janeen was trying to look nonchalant, but she couldn't help peering at the watches and handguns side by side in the case, the myriad television sets, the deer head mounted on the wall beside a Buddha-shaped clock.

Finally it was their turn, and the shop owner gestured toward them impatiently. Most of Grete's belongings, he said after a cursory dig, were worthless to him. "Not the kind of shit people come in here to buy." He worked a toothpick in the corner of his mouth.

"What about this?" Erik said, his voice higher than it had been outside. He held up a tiny statue of a cherubic boy leading a goat. The man took it and turned it over.

"Yeah, that's a Hummel. It's worth something. I'll give you five for it."

"Five dollars?" Erik shifted his weight, and Janeen caught a whiff of perspiration. "This could sell for twenty-five or more. I looked it up."

With a shrug, the man handed it back. "Sell it somewhere else, then."

Erik let out a long sigh. "Man. Maybe I should have listened to her." He reached inside the box Janeen had carried and pulled out a thoroughly tarnished metal plate. "She told me to throw most of this away," he said, tossing the plate back inside with a thunk.

"Wait a minute," said the store owner before Janeen could slide the box off the counter. His fingers, yellow around the nails, closed around her wrist, and she felt Erik lean forward protectively. "I just want to take a look," the man said, and finally she relented.

They watched as he took a filthy, greasy rag from under the counter and began polishing the metal plate vigorously. His nostrils flared wide with exertion, and Janeen and Erik stared, mesmerized. The black film came off easily, revealing the dull shine of old silver. Symbols began coming into view. "Uh-huh," the man muttered. "Mmm-hmm."

In the center of the plate a quaint country village emerged; around the rim, strange symbols. *Runes*, Janeen thought, they were called runes. Two lightning bolts, something that looked like a Z with a cross through it. A death's head, a key. A swastika.

Janeen's lungs burned. She realized she'd been holding her breath. When she dared glance at Erik, he was frowning deeply, his eyes bulging from his head. "What in the hell?"

"This," the pawn shop owner crowed, "is one of the plates the Nazis sold on Party Days. Looks like someone got this one at Nuremberg." He seemed excited. "This, son, is worth some money. One-fifty or two hundred, I'd give you."

"She told me to throw it away," Erik murmured, staring in horror at the symbols.

"Ha!" said the store owner. "A Hummel and a Nazi plate. Who is she? The Stomping Mare of Ravensbrück?"

Erik went pale, and Janeen reached out and plucked the plate out of the man's hand. "We need to think about it," she said. "Two hundred sounds good, but maybe we should check elsewhere? Erik?" She waved her hand in front of his face. "Shouldn't we have lunch first?"

The owner shouted after them: he'd go to two-fifty. Maybe even three. The thrill in his voice made Janeen sick; she wondered if he collected Nazi memorabilia.

"Why would my mom have something like that?" Erik said when they'd had a chance to take a few gulps of the cooler, if not fresh, air outside. Still there was very little color in his face. "And why'd she hold onto it, all this time?"

Janeen could guess exactly why Grete owned such an object, and who'd given it to her. "It's a good sign she wanted you to throw it away, isn't it?" She put her free hand in the middle of his upper back and pushed gently, taking over the role of guide. "Let's get something to eat."

• • •

A little while later they found themselves in a hard booth, all right angles and wood. Both ordered reuben sandwiches. As she sucked creamy foam off the top of her pint, Janeen felt the bench wobbling; under the table, both of Erik's legs were jiggling violently.

"You're keeping something from me," he said as Janeen wedged open a gold packet of butter with her knife. "You didn't look surprised at all to see that—those Nazi—" He spat out the words as though trying to flick something off his tongue.

She wanted to tell him everything, become confidantes, but something held her back. It was Margaret's story, and it was only right that she share it with her son. Beyond that—it was Margaret's *duty* to tell him, and Janeen didn't want to let her off easy.

"Help me make sense of this," said Erik. "Please. They started out in the orphanage together. Then what?"

She chose her words carefully. "They did what they could to get by? Sounds like the girls in orphanage had few options besides joining the Order or marrying young. Or the academy."

"The academy," Erik said, shaking his head. "There's one thing I did know about. Every damn time I didn't do my homework she'd go on about *the academy, the academy, I vanted so badly to go to the academy vhen I vas a girl, you should know how lucky you are.* I don't get what the big deal was, she still went to college, am I right?"

Janeen felt almost embarrassed for him, this rich kid. *You don't know she had to sell her soul to go to college,* she almost said, *and you don't know the consequences my mother faced for keeping hers.* "Give her a break, will you? They had it tough."

"Oh, I'm sure you've never given your mother a hard time."

The waiter came then, and she tore into her sandwich. Erik left his untouched, watching her. After a few minutes had passed, during which Janeen felt uncomfortably aware of the sounds of her own eating, he reached under his feet and pulled out the plate.

Janeen recoiled when he put it in the center of the table. The thing gleamed now. Nuremberg, depicted in the center, looked perversely wholesome with its clock tower and cross-timbered houses. Erik traced the occultish symbols as though stroking an Ouija board.

"Tell me this," he said finally. "What would you have done if you found this in your mother's house?"

"I'd bring it to her and ask why she had it." She spoke through her napkin, eyes on her sandwich. "I'd ask who gave it to her. Tell her you have a right to know."

"So there *is* something you know and I don't." When she didn't answer, he blew a hard breath. "You're goddamn right I deserve to know. I've been babysitting my mother all summer as she writes and writes and talks to herself in German. No one else cares." White bits of spit flew from Erik's lips as he spoke. "She even talks to people who aren't there. That's what I thought she was doing this morning—I wasn't kidding. I thought she was talking to ghosts. I didn't expect you two, in the flesh. I'm relieved it was you who showed up. If it had been that old lover of hers I don't know what I would have done."

The noise inside the restaurant seemed to increase: busboys slapping plastic tubs full of dishes on a metal counter, waiters calling to each other. Janeen leaned forward. She tented her hands on the table in front of her, like two spiders. "Old lover of hers. Someone your mother was seeing after the divorce?"

Erik looked taken aback. "No, no—someone from a long time ago. From Germany. He was in town, I think, and they had dinner together. Why?"

"Do you know what his name is?"

He opened his mouth, looking scared now. And then he said what Janeen knew he would say, the name that had been on the tip of everyone's tongue. "Klaus?"

*Don't panic.* Janeen had to focus on finishing lunch, and then she'd go back to the hotel and figure out the best way to tell her mother, if Anita didn't already know. This was why they'd come, she realized now. Her mother must have known this was where Klaus would go.

"Janeen. Janeen!" Erik snapped his fingers. "Do you know that name? You have to tell me what's going on, man, you can't hold out on me."

"Ask your mother, not me. Ask about Klaus. Ask about the plate. Erik . . ."

"Yes?" he replied, looking miserable and defeated.

"I—" She took his hand. "Be prepared. That's all."

After that they didn't have much else to say to each other. He paid for their lunch, said he'd take her back to the hotel, and this time he hailed a cab. Light rain streaked the windows of the taxi, lifting steam from the roads.

"I don't know when I'll see you again," he said when they stood in front of her hotel, having exchanged phone numbers. This, too, made it seem as if they'd just been on a date, though this didn't bother Janeen now. Something had crystallized between them in the last few hours; even though she still couldn't bear to tell him her father had just passed away, Erik was beginning to feel more tangibly like family.

"Come visit me in Ithaca, will you?" he said. "Keep me from gorging out if I keep finding old Nazi props of my mother's."

"I'd love to." She couldn't help but smile.

Erik smiled back. All his earlier bravado was gone, replaced by earnestness and melancholy. "I'm glad I met you, Janeen. Even if you're just as goddamn stubborn and mysterious as the other women in this family."

A worried look came over his face, and she knew his thoughts had turned back to his mother and Klaus. She wished she could say something reassuring. "I'm glad to have met you, too." She opened her arms to him, and he held tightly to her. Her head over his shoulder, she saw their reflection in the cab window. She thought, with a thrill: *Cousins.*

# ANITA, 1970

Early the next morning they found Margaret's new home on Tiemann Place, at the border of Morningside Heights and Harlem. Her apartment building was crisscrossed by a series of black fire escapes like a zipper. Anita stood on the sidewalk, staring at the locked front doors. Beside her, Janeen shivered. "We told her to expect us this evening," she said, a hint of pleading fear in her voice. "Wait, Mutti. Let's think first. Oh, maybe I shouldn't have told you about Klaus."

Anita shook her head, gazing at the windows, wondering which one was Margaret's and if she stood behind one of them, looking out. "Shouldn't have told me about Klaus. Are you crazy?" The news had made it impossible for her to sleep. She'd wanted to come over here earlier, surprise them as they slept; it had taken an inordinate amount of pleading from Janeen to get her to wait until morning.

"Look, there's an intercom. Maybe we should buzz her?"

"Quiet." Anita leapt forward, following an old man carrying a bag of bagels into the lobby, and seized the door's handle just before it closed. He turned and furrowed his brow at her but said nothing. Janeen huffed to catch up. There was no doorman, and so they walked right into the elevator and pressed 8. Anita snapped her incisors, watching the elevator climb slowly.

The hallway was empty, carpeted in faded gold. Margaret had left her door unlocked, so Anita did not even need to knock. Behind her, Janeen made a cry of protest as she pushed her way into the cold white apartment.

"Grete!" Anita shouted before she stopped short. She felt Janeen plow into her shoulder.

Margaret looked up from a small glass dining table. A half-empty pitcher of orange juice sat before her, and a platter of bread and cheese, deli meat, cups of muesli. The table and chairs were set up among a mess of suitcases and half-unwrapped kitchen tools. Loose cables and wires protruded from holes in the drywall. In the midst of it all, Margaret looked like a little gray mouse. She scurried toward Anita. "I wasn't expecting you."

Gently Anita pushed Margaret aside and went into the living room. There were two place settings at the table; a crumpled paper napkin sat on the other seat. The blackened crust of a piece of bread and a sweating slice of Swiss cheese were left on the plate. Anita swung around, her head spinning, to see that Margaret's eyes were open so wide that Anita could see white all the way around the irises.

"Where is he?" Anita whispered.

Margaret did not answer. A toilet flushed somewhere to the right of them, further inside the little apartment, and Anita froze. She could see Margaret's eyes flitting around, onto the bubble-wrapped green plates on the counters and the hardcover textbooks on the floor, the way they did when her tinnitus was at its worst. When the bathroom door opened, light pooled into the small hallway off the living room, then went out, and all three of them flinched.

"Oh!" said the man when he came into the living room, his face relaxing quickly into an expression of welcome, as though this were his house. "Company, Margaret?" He had thinning whitish hair combed straight back, oiled to show the comb lines, and the remnants of a sunburn. His eyes were a very pale blue-green, and he was tall, over six feet, with delicate jowls and a pronounced bump on his nose. He stared down into Anita's eyes, his expression intelligent and focused, and then he glanced toward Margaret, who licked and then bit her lower lip.

"Forgive me," she said. "Anita and Janeen Moore, this is my husband, Charles Forsyth."

Anita could scarcely move, and so the man had to come a bit closer in order to shake her hand. His was cold and damp. When he moved to shake Janeen's, he broadened his lips into a long, toothy smile, and Anita wanted to reach between them and pry their hands apart.

He turned back to Anita. "Soon to be ex-husband," he said through another smile, the skin around his eyes folding into pleats, like closed fans. "But why be specific?" He spoke with no accent, in English that was almost too perfect, his voice dry and bland as crackers.

She had to think quickly. "Charles Forsyth, the famous photographer! It is a pleasure to meet you. What a moving collage you did on the *Kindertransport*. The photos of the children waving over the rails of the ship!" She clapped her hand to her chest.

He acknowledged this with a long nod, and Margaret tried to usher them all toward the breakfast table, but Anita continued. "As a German, I was appalled by our government's barbarism toward Jews." She noticed how he tracked her every move, his posture cool yet alert. "Ah, but it was refreshing to see Americans work to expose the injustice."

"Well." He put up his hands, indicating that he didn't deserve such praise. "You know the very reason the *Kindertransport* happened was the Americans' limit on Jewish refugees. In taking ten thousand, England made herself look very good." He was still smiling, his pale eyes twinkling merrily, but Anita thought she detected something hard at the edges of his voice. "There's barbarism everywhere, Mrs. Moore," he added with a grin. "That is all I am saying."

"Quite," Anita said, and swallowed. There was a buzzing in her ears. She watched his mouth move as if in slow motion as he talked to her, not hearing the words. His face looked newly shaven, but he'd missed a line of hairs, most of which were white, a few red.

He reached a long arm toward the table to fetch his coffee. "Are you here for a visit? From Germany?" When she didn't answer, he asked again: "Are you a friend of Margaret's from Germany?" His face remained bland, impossible to read, as he sipped.

The buzzing noise reached a fever pitch in Anita's ears. "Excuse me," she whispered, the words scratching out of her tightened throat. She attempted a smile. "I just remembered I left something in my hotel room, I—I have to go."

The man cocked his head to the side. "Well, that's a shame. We could have made two more places for you at the table."

"We shouldn't interrupt your breakfast," Janeen told Margaret. She sounded relieved.

"Lovely to have met you," he said, and Anita pinched her lips tightly together, her buttocks, everything clenched so that she could maintain her composure.

"Another time," she managed. She took Janeen's hand and headed for the door, which felt light as she pulled it open, its white paint marred and scuffed. The hallway floor seemed to push away from her with each step, as though she were walking on the moon.

"Who was that man?" Janeen said in a whisper as soon as the elevator doors closed.

"Probably her former husband, as she said." Anita willed the elevator to hurry, hurry. "We shall let the authorities figure it out."

Outside it had begun to rain, cold droplets that chilled Anita's ears and the part in her hair. She hurried Janeen toward Broadway, where they were confronted by traffic and noise. Water dripped from the greenish iron undercarriage of the elevated rail. A girl in hot pants shivered beside one of the iron pylons.

"There," Anita said, pointing to a public telephone on the opposite corner.

"You're going to call the police?" Janeen asked, shivering, clearly distracted by the scene under the train tracks, despite everything. "And say what?" she called. Anita had already crossed Tiemann Place to stand behind the two men who were using the phone, one shielding the other from the rain with his open leather jacket. Both of them glared.

"Mutti, wait, let's . . ." Janeen's lips were bluish. "Think first."

"There is nothing to think about!" Anita snapped. When finally the men abandoned the phone, leaving the receiver dangling by its thick metal cord, Anita rushed forward. Rain ran into her eyes as she tried to think who to call. 911? The FBI?

A pale hand reached out and held down the metal switch hook. Anita turned to see Margaret standing beside her. "It won't do any good," she said quietly. "He's left."

"Left!" Anita cried, and she tried prying her sister's fingers off the telephone. "He couldn't have gotten far. Hands off, let me call the police, you let that *Schweine* go . . ."

"Please do not." Margaret hadn't bothered to lift the hood on her jacket, and her white-blond hair curled and sagged with rain. "He's just gone out for a while. He'll return, God willing. I tried to convince him you hadn't recognized him." She looked back over her shoulder. "He's been staying there a week. Plans are in motion to have him captured. I didn't think anyone else need become involved."

"You haven't even told your son?" Janeen asked, hugging herself, her teeth chattering.

Margaret shook her head slowly, looking shocked. "No, I especially would not tell my son. Why involve him in something like this?"

Slowly, Anita's wrist slackened, and the handset dropped. A train went by on the elevated tracks, rattling the telephone booth and sending sheets of water pouring onto the street. "The FBI would have taken him by now, you know this—if you'd actually called."

Margaret looked up at the waterstained façades of the brown tenement buildings. She sighed and closed her eyes, her mouth becoming slack and tender, and Anita's heart went cold.

"You love-starved little idiot," she said to Margaret, even though they were both old now. "You've been sleeping with him."

Margaret's eyes jumped, and she opened her mouth, but the shout came from Janeen. When Anita looked up she saw Janeen had her hands over her ears. "Stop it, stop it!" she cried.

"*Ach*, Janeen," Anita cried. "It'll be all—"

"No, it *won't* be all right, Mutti, not as long as we stand here in plain view." Janeen's upper lip quivered, showing, finally, her anger; Anita sensed it was directed at both herself and Margaret. "If he's out of the apartment, he could be watching us right now. No matter which of you two is right, it won't do us any good if he sees us here, arguing in front of the telephone."

"She's right," Margaret said quickly. "We need to get inside."

"What are you suggesting," Anita huffed, "that we go back to your place?"

Janeen began nodding, still shuddering violently, and Margaret put an arm around her. She glanced at Anita. "I don't think we'll have company."

• • •

The apartment *smelled* like Klaus. Anita couldn't stop thinking this. A whiff of something from the old country lingered in the air, even though he hadn't been there in decades and neither had she; still she could recognize it, the musky scent of masculine force, of traditional meals cooked by someone else, of the sweat left behind by painful lovemaking. The breakfast table still had not been cleared. She would have bet that if she'd entered the bedroom, she'd find the sheets dirty. All of it made her head ache.

She stood at the glass door to Margaret's tiny balcony while her sister changed in the bedroom and Janeen prepared tea, not quite able to convince herself she was really here. Somehow Janeen seemed comfortably rooted in this nightmare space; she had quickly found her way around the little kitchen and had water boiling, milk and sugar on a tray. Now, for God's sake, she was unpacking some of Margaret's boxes, putting cereal bowls in the cabinet beside the mugs. Anita felt too weary to tell her to stop.

She felt something fall around her shoulders, and when she turned she saw that Margaret had draped her in a weblike white afghan. "You're shivering, Anita." When Anita looked down she realized she was also dripping rainwater on the parquet, but Margaret didn't mention this. She kept her head down, avoiding eye contact. Anita could see she'd put her hearing aids in.

"Come," Margaret said. "Have a seat on the sofa." She gestured toward the same one from the day before, still covered in plastic.

"No, thank you," Anita said, turning back toward the gray scene outside. "We won't be staying long."

The kettle boiled. Margaret gestured toward the kitchen. "She's taking care of us."

"I know she is," said Anita. "She does too much of that."

Janeen brought the tray over, the tea in a white pot. "I hope you don't mind," she said as she removed the lid from a blue tin of butter cookies—she'd gotten it, Anita realized with a bit of nausea, from the breakfast table.

"Not at all," said Margaret. Janeen responded by stuffing her mouth with three pretzel-shaped cookies sprinkled with rock sugar, and Anita realized she'd again forgotten to give the girl breakfast.

The tea poured out dark. "Mutti?" Janeen asked, holding up a thin cup on a saucer. Anita took it but did not drink. She turned away from her sister and daughter, who sat amiably now, sipping their tea. Anita looked out over roofs, at water towers and the emerging sun. Somewhere in this city, Klaus lurked. Or he could have been under one of the rivers, on a bus speeding away from New York, toward Canada or Mexico.

"Erik loved meeting you," she heard Margaret tell Janeen. "He called me last night."

"Oh?" Janeen asked, her voice strangely high-pitched. "Did he say anything else?"

"Anything else? What do you mean?"

As Janeen hedged, Anita watched a sparrow bathe in a shiny pool on the balcony and sipped from her cup, punishing her tongue with the scalding tea. The bird washed its wings. This was the last thing she'd wanted to submit herself and Janeen to. On the contrary, she'd hoped to find her assumptions had been wrong. She would have been very happy to be wrong, happier than she'd ever been.

Behind her, Janeen cleared her throat. "I think you should tell Erik about Klaus Eisler." She said it with no hesitation, but both Anita and Margaret stiffened; it was as if Janeen had turned on a harsh lamp, bathing the once-calm room in glaring, scrutinous light. In any other circumstance, Anita would have reprimanded Janeen for telling an adult what to do. Now, she waited, holding her breath.

"My dear." The plastic on the couch creaked as Margaret resettled herself. "It's a delicate matter. I've been told by the people I'm in contact with not to let anyone in on this plan."

*How dare you*, Anita wanted to say. They all knew there were no "people." It was one thing to lie to her, but another to lie to her daughter.

Still, underneath everything: the desperate hope Margaret was telling the truth.

"That implies you don't trust your own son, ma'am," Janeen said, just a hint of wobble to her voice. "And I think you can. Tell him the story and explain you're preparing to turn Klaus in. I know you will."

Finally, Anita had to turn to face them. Their heads were bent together, Margaret's smooth blonde one and Janeen's frizzy dark one. "And how do you know this, *Liebchen?*"

"You know she will, too, Mutti," Janeen replied, imploring Anita with her eyes.

"Is that so," Anita said in a cold, quiet voice. "Here is what I wonder. You knew exactly where to find me, Grete. How? A letter arrived, addressed to Anita Moore, not long after Klaus resurfaced. You've been quiet about this coincidence, *nicht*? This is why I cannot trust you."

Slowly Margaret stood. She crossed her arms. "Yes. Klaus was the one who found you."

Janeen gasped. "He knows where we live?"

"He knows where we live," Anita said without taking her eyes off her sister, "because Grete told him, a long time ago, that I'd left the country, and she told him to send his SS friends to look for me. Didn't you?"

Slowly Margaret shook her head. "It was not like that."

Janeen's chest rose and fell quickly, her face twisted in anguish, and this was the worst part, Anita thought: Janeen wanted to believe in Margaret.

Margaret licked her lips. "I've been trying to find the right way to tell you. I didn't want to put it in my letter, not the first one—" She stood and came to Anita. "He'll be back soon. I need to tell you this now. Berni, I need you to listen. If you're here when he returns, it will jeopardize everything."

"Just listen, Mutti!" Janeen pleaded from the sofa.

Slowly, Anita laid her hands atop her sister's outstretched palms and looked into her eyes, broken capillaries at the corners. Anita was reminded of a game they'd played as children to see who could slap the other's hands first. Grete had the better peripheral vision; it was one of the few games she'd always won.

"When you didn't appear at the Zoo," Margaret began, then cleared her throat a few times. "I knew something had happened. I went to Sonje's building and pounded and pounded on the door, and eventually a woman answered, a Brownshirt for certain; she called Sonje 'that Jew' and claimed not to know a Berni, nor an Anita. 'Whores flit in and out of that place, who can keep track?' she said, though I could tell she was lying.

"After that I searched all the nightclubs and bars, from the lounge in the Adlon to the seediest basement club. Nobody had seen you. I felt as though the world had been rearranged while I'd been sleeping. Finally I returned to Sonje's, hoping to find you there, but your windows were dark. I'll never know why I stopped in the café on the corner, maybe just to sit in a seat you may once have occupied. When I saw the owner wearing his SS uniform, I nearly left. I knew I had to get away from them. All of them. But then, behind me, I heard a familiar voice. I turned and recognized the sweep of Sonje's pretty nose. She wore a snood, and she did not stand up straight, but I knew it was she, instantly."

Margaret stopped and swallowed. Anita's diaphragm rose and fell rapidly. A metallic taste had come into her mouth.

"She walked past without noticing me and hid at a corner table behind a pair of dark glasses. She looked like a ghost. I remember thinking how terrible it was, the way the government had erased these people who were still there.

"After a few minutes, a man came to join her, a man in a black hat, obviously a Jew. I hid by the cigarette display and turned my ear toward them. They mentioned a group of children who had gone to America to study abroad.

"'They are enjoying their studies?' the man asked.

"Sonje spoke slowly. 'Yes. All three have settled comfortably into their new schools in New York and are finding their lodging agreeable.'

"They clinked their coffee cups together as if they were glasses of beer. Then the man asked, 'And their Fräulein?'

"'Yes,' said Sonje. 'Fräulein M. is well, too.'

"Of course, instantly I hoped the *M* stood for Metzger; it would mean you were still alive and that you'd made it safely abroad. Then my palms began to sweat, my heart race. If you indeed were Fräulein M., it meant you'd found out what I'd done and left me behind.

"For a few unbearable moments, the two were silent. Then the man made his voice very gentle, very soft, and asked, 'And your other friend. What news of her?'

"From my hiding place I could not read their lips. I strained to hear, but saw only Sonje blowing her nose. She hid her face in her handkerchief.

"'A telegram,' she finally blurted out. 'She was taken to Plötzensee this time. Fell out of the window trying to escape, they said.'"

Janeen cried out, the blanket to her mouth. Anita had to compartmentalize the news in order to keep thinking straight. Hadn't she always known her Anita had been killed by the Nazis, in one way or another? Why should it affect her, hearing how it happened? Why?

"I could not help it then," Margaret continued. "I burst from my hiding place. I frightened her, with my desperation, with my Nazi pins. She must have recognized me, for she shrank back into the booth; when I called her name, she pretended it wasn't Sonje. 'Berni,' I cried, 'tell me if it was Berni! Please!' Before I knew it the two of them hurried from the restaurant."

"And Klaus?" Anita said, her voice very far away. "How did he find out about all this?"

"I told him." Margaret could no longer hold Anita's gaze. "We were in a biergarten off Friedrichstraße. Everything tasted like sawdust." She swallowed. "I told him one of you had made it to the United States, and one had fallen from a window. I figured his connections could get me answers, but also I wanted to let him know one of you had gotten the better of him. Of us.

"'Oh, Grete,' he said. 'You know that means your sister is either dead or wants nothing to do with you.'"

"'I pray she is alive,' I told him, 'and I am glad for her if so.'

"'If I hear any news of your sister,' he said then, 'I will tell you.' I suppose he kept this promise. It's why we are here."

"How wonderful of him," Anita said, mouth dry. "And then? You continued to see him."

"Yes. I did. His pull on me was that strong. But not anymore." Margaret's chin dropped to her chest. "Last month was the first I'd heard from him in years. He wrote to tell me he'd found you. When I saw the name Anita I assumed I had my answer as to who died in the prison. I'm sorry, Berni. I am so sorry for her."

Anita hadn't even noticed Janeen rise from the couch, but suddenly there she was, standing beside her aunt, stretching her fingers toward Margaret's arm. At her touch, Margaret flinched, then relaxed. "I also knew," she said, her voice firmer, "that the only way this could end was with Klaus's capture."

Klaus's capture. But Klaus wasn't here now. He'd gone. He was free as a bird. "I should have called the FBI when I had the chance," Anita said.

Slowly Margaret shook her head. "Not the FBI. Think, sister. The FBI will do no good."

The room blurred and tipped. "You are trying to tell me he was an informant."

"A CIA informant, yes, perhaps. I know he was given a visa in 1945. This is why we have to tread very carefully. I do not know what a call to the American authorities would do."

Margaret's eyes were cold, icy blue in the light reflected from the windows. "I beg of you, please. You do not need to forgive me, but you must believe me."

Anita swayed on her feet. She heard her own voice telling Janeen they had to go, to meet her down at the curb if necessary, to say goodbye to her aunt for both of them—she said this as though Margaret was not in the room.

She left the elevator for Janeen and took the stairs, turning down and down and down until she burst into the street. The rain had abated, but everything still felt cool. After her breathing evened, she looked up slowly at a pigeon bobbing its head in front of her, at two young men sprawled on a tarp. Both were too young to live on the street. One wore women's shoes.

*We're the sisters.* Her sister had fallen from a window in a Gestapo prison. She searched for a better image to focus on, a happy one, so that a shape on the ground would not be the Anita that stayed in her mind. Anita at Lake Wannsee, flirting with a burly American. Anita peering into a mirror with her mouth open, trimming her eyebrows with a razor blade.

Janeen stayed inside a long time, long enough for Anita to begin to worry. She had nearly worked up the nerve to find her way into the building again when her daughter came out the front door, her face ruined from crying. "You aren't going to do it, are you, Mutti? You can't call the FBI. Will you?"

"Shh," Anita murmured, gathering her close.

"I know she's telling the truth." Janeen's eyelashes were pulled into points by her tears. "What she just told me . . . I know she's about to turn him over."

"How do you know?"

"She told me more, about Germany, about Klaus," Janeen said, looking stunned, looking like the most tired seventeen-year-old Anita had ever seen. "She had a gun, but she . . . she wants to do right this time. She said that. And I believe her."

"Okay, *Liebchen*," Anita said, too weary to argue or even to ask about this gun. "It is time for us to go home." She expected Janeen to protest, but instead, she nodded and pulled a dark piece of hair out of her lips.

Dark clouds roiled overhead. In the distance, faint thunder. Anita could sense Janeen remembering Klaus at the same time she did, wondering if he was somewhere nearby, watching. Anita hustled them toward Broadway, waving one arm at each taxi that passed, the other wrapped tightly around her daughter.

# GRETE, 1939

Grete had first heard of the Blumenthals, of all places, at the Café am Zoo. She hadn't returned in three years, but everything looked the same: potted palms and fig trees, the three-story ceiling covered in green tiles like scales. Even the crowd, mostly uniformed men and expensive-looking women, could have been the very ones who'd stared at her that night she waited for Berni, the girl with a suitcase under her chair.

Before their entrées arrived, Klaus slid a folded square of paper across the table.

"I wasn't expecting an assignment so soon," she said quietly, her voice lost in the din of the restaurant, the buzz of good news. Czechoslovakia was now the Protectorate of Bohemia and Moravia, thanks in large part to the success of Case Green, an SD operation. "I'm already tracking Herr Reuter."

"I know, darling." Klaus made his eyes pained, sympathetic, the way one might look at a dog. He leaned over the table and kissed her hand. She felt the give of his soft lips, the immediate response between her legs. "But stakes are high—the Poles could invade any minute."

She unfolded the paper. *Mr. and Mrs. Caleb Blumenthal.* "Jews?" she said. "They'll never let me inside. The Winter Relief wouldn't send a nurse to check on a pair of Jews."

"The wife has a condition," Klaus replied. "We think they're plotting to abscond without paying their property levy. A neighbor heard them phone a doctor in Sweden. They'll let you in."

Their wine arrived, and he inspected the bottle, gave a generous smile to the waiter. "In the Republic years," he said, pouring Grete a glass of Riesling, "Mr. Blumenthal was a *Lyzeum* schoolteacher, a known rapist of students, I'm afraid—"

"Stop. Please." Each time he needed her to check up on someone, there was a story; the former doctor was a pedophile, the family of Communists had been plotting to blow up a school. She had to look at the ceiling to keep from crying. A chandelier the size of a Volkswagen dangled in the center. She imagined what would happen if it fell, the crater it would leave in the checkered marble floor. Shards of brass propelled outward like shrapnel.

"I can't do this," she said quietly. "Not again."

"Pardon?" he replied, and he leaned forward, one hand cupped around his ear. "I'm sorry, I couldn't quite hear you." He seemed to know she wouldn't repeat herself. "You know I've brought you into the SD network to protect you, my love. Need we revisit your close calls?"

She shook her head, staring at the heavy chandelier. She saw herself choosing the weakest link in its chain, taking aim, firing.

• • •

*Guns, not butter*: Goebbels' slogan was everywhere in early 1939, to get people to accept the rations. The average German could live without butter; the Reich as a whole would never survive without guns.

Grete had both.

Klaus had installed her in a new apartment complex in Neukölln; all day she heard planes ripping overhead. She did her best to hide the scents of coffee and butter from her neighbors, but she saw the way they looked at her. Late at night, she heard them return from the factories where they assembled electronics or airplane parts as she hid in bed with a cup of chocolate, another gift from Klaus. Through the thin walls she heard them complain about low wages, the tariffs taken out of their paychecks for food, uniforms, time off. They couldn't even change jobs without permission from the Party. They feared war would break out before the end of the year.

They lived like slaves. They questioned Hitler. Occasionally she reminded herself—when she wanted to feel better—that she could have turned them over for questioning the Reich, but chose not to. She only spied on people when Klaus asked.

He visited sporadically, when he was in town, and her neighbors treated him with fear and respect whether or not he wore the uniform. He usually came at night, after suppertime, a paper bag full of rationed goods in his hands, her next assignment in his pocket.

"But I'm a nurse, not a spy," she told him. "My work is to keep people healthy."

"You and I have the same duty," he replied, raising a blond eyebrow. "The SS pledge to uphold the health of the German ethnic body. You and I both must root out germs and disease." He took her wrist into his hand. "You know I've assembled an immaculate file on your service as an informant. I've practically made you untouchable."

He said it as though she had nothing to do with it.

She wished he'd be more discreet about the gifts, that he'd be quieter as they made love. Everyone in the building, she knew, called her the SD officer's whore. She could have told them she wasn't his whore, she was his fiancée, but then they would ask the wedding date. They'd ask how she got along with his colleagues or his parents, whom she suspected knew nothing about the engagement.

The important questions might not have occurred to her neighbors. How many traitors to the Reich do you have to uncover in order for him to actually marry you?

Or—how can you make love to someone who'd have you arrested if you ever dared disobey him?

Or simply—*how do you sleep at night?* Sometimes, looking out her tiny round window at the new, plain courtyard, she imagined Berni asking these things, her voice high-pitched and righteous, her fist in her hand.

Grete tried to stay in her victims' apartments for the briefest time possible. *Stop talking*, she wanted to tell them when inevitably they slipped and said too much. The physician told her his blood pressure might have been high because that morning he'd given some students a hundred marks to print anti-Hitler leaflets. The old woman in bedroom slippers asked whether Grete thought anyone would notice if she withdrew money from her pension so that she might go to Denmark with her daughter's family.

Grete knew why they confided in her. They saw the same thing in her that Klaus did: weakness. They saw a limp dishrag. And who needed to be careful around a dishrag?

It didn't matter that she watered down the reports she gave Klaus after her house calls, that she left out some crucial information. The people she spied on could be hauled in for the tiniest infractions, then tortured, or killed, or sent to concentration camps. And they were.

• • •

She'd been visiting Herr Reuter for two months under the pretext of tracking his heart murmur. An auto mechanic, he'd been a labor organizer during the Republic, but had turned Nazi so enthusiastically in 1933 that he'd ended up on the watchlist with many other March violets. Herr Reuter saw her exactly for what she was; Grete could tell he despised her. He'd never let anything slip when she visited. For this, she could have kissed him.

His garage wasn't three blocks from the Blumenthals' apartment, and so she went past it on her way to call on them for the first time. She peered in at the cream-colored Type 1 he'd been working on the last few weeks. Someone had brought in another car for service, a huge yellow Mercedes with headlights like round spectacles. Both obscured the view of a rusty van without tires, floating almost to the ceiling on lifts.

She'd snuck past these doors in the middle of the night. She'd seen the flashlights, the van lowered, Herr Reuter and his assistant working to put a new engine inside. The tires, she knew, were resting against the back wall, ready to be installed at a moment's notice.

Herr Reuter planned to leave the country, and soon. Nobody else—she knew the Gestapo, too, checked in on Herr Reuter from time to time—seemed to have noticed. All they were looking for was evidence of Herr Reuter stirring up labor trouble, and she could honestly report she'd seen none.

Reluctantly she left, walking her bicycle up a little street crowded with parked cars, leaping over puddles to avoid the trolley. Eventually she found herself facing a smaller street, almost an alley. One side was bathed in sun, the other shadowed. Halfway down, on the sunny side, she found the Blumenthals' building, a five-story with blue flower boxes filled with geraniums. Every time, her heart pounded like this. She prayed they wouldn't be home as she pressed the buzzer.

Her spirits sank when she heard the locks shift and a chain swing loose. The door opened a crack. A man in his late twenties peered out at her. He had full cheeks and a snub nose, long-lashed green eyes. "Can I help you?"

"Good morning, Herr Blumenthal. I've been sent by the Winter Relief to inquire after your wife's condition. One of your neighbors implied she needed help, and we never let these reports go unchecked."

Herr Blumenthal let the door open a little more so that he could peer up and around the alley, perhaps wondering which of his neighbors had brought the Reich to his doorstep. He stared down at her for a minute, blinking. "Yes, come in. I'm not sure what can be done for her, but perhaps there's something."

She followed him up a creaking set of curved wooden stairs. When they entered the apartment she smelled it right away: illness, urine, the odor of an unshowered body. She wondered what Frau Blumenthal suffered from. Klaus hadn't said.

Herr Blumenthal gestured toward the bedroom. "Let me tell her first. She won't like seeing your uniform."

"I understand." Grete waited in the little kitchen, the floor elaborately tiled in colorful squares. Long-tendriled plants cascaded from the window above the sink. The room would have been cheery in another time, and Grete had to stop herself imagining Herr and Frau Blumenthal setting up home here, full of optimism, before everything changed.

She heard whispers from the other room, and at one point a high-pitched cry, but after a minute, Herr Blumenthal emerged. "She will see you."

It took effort, as she entered the bedroom, not to gasp. Frau Blumenthal lay sprawled on the bed, taking up most of the mattress with her pregnant belly and splayed legs. Her ankles emerged from the hem of her nightgown, thick and red as hams; her hands looked like inflated rubber gloves. She watched Grete with quick, hateful eyes as she pulled a chair to the side of the bed. Grete pulled a blood pressure cuff from her bag, but hesitated before trying to slip it on Frau Blumenthal's swollen arm. She already knew what the result would be.

"You're what," she said quietly, "eight months along?"

"Seven," said Frau Blumenthal, her voice unexpectedly dainty and light; Grete wondered about the woman hiding under all of this bulk.

"I'll need to check your blood pressure, but I'm fairly sure you have toxemia."

Frau Blumenthal laughed harshly. "Is that so? Did we need a visit from the government to tell me I have toxemia?"

"Rosi." Her husband hovered in the doorway, arms still crossed. "Let her check you."

She allowed Grete to put on the cuff and verify what she already knew. One-forty over ninety; Grete didn't even read the number aloud. "Well, Frau Blumenthal, the good news is there are ways you can control it. I'd suggest eating—"

"Less salt," Frau Blumenthal said, ticking things off on her bloated fingers. "Drink water, elevate my legs. Stay in a reclined position, to keep the swelling down. Anything I'm forgetting, Frau Doktor?"

Grete shook her head, studying the rickrack sewn along the border of Frau Blumenthal's duvet. She imagined the mother or aunts who would have assembled her trousseau.

"We've been following these so-called remedies for a month, and look at me." When Frau Blumenthal gestured toward her feet, the pent-up water in her arm jiggled grotesquely.

Grete bit the inside of her cheek. Every shred of her medical training screamed at her to do all she could to save this woman, who could be days from death. She cursed the Nazi teachers who'd taught her to preserve life above all else and with the other sides of their tongues spoke of rooting out diseased portions of the populace. As though the Volk really were one body, not a collection of individuals with dignity; as though some of them were indispensible and some disposable—the human equivalents of tonsils or adenoids.

Klaus knew this woman was suffering. Yet he sent Grete here not to help her, but to make sure she and her husband paid an unfair tax before daring to leave the country that rejected them. It didn't take medical training to feel compelled to save Frau Blumenthal. All it took was humanity.

Wincing, Frau Blumenthal lifted herself onto her elbow, her enormous belly shifting and sagging with her effort. Grete thought she saw movement inside, and had to keep herself from feeling for the baby.

"Tell me," Frau Blumenthal said. "What advice would you give me if I weren't a Jew, if I were Aryan like you and you'd come to help me rather than interrogate me?"

"*Rosi*," Herr Blumenthal said, sounding terrified now.

"It's all right," Grete told him. She turned Frau Blumenthal's wrist over and felt for her pulse, as much to buy herself time as to examine the patient. She looked back at Frau Blumenthal's lively eyes. "I'd say you needed to be in hospital," she said honestly. "There isn't much they can do, but they can administer a few drugs that might help, or they could assist if you went into early labor. Your baby or you could die otherwise."

Behind her, Herr Blumenthal let out a moan, though his wife's face seemed to relax a little. She loosened her grip on Grete's arm, winced and flexed her fingers to ease the edema. "And what would you do, if you were me, Frau Doktor?"

"Please, I'm only a nurse—"

"Would you, if you were a Jew—would you walk into a German hospital, a child in your womb, asking for treatment? Would you trust the doctors to save your baby?"

Grete looked around. They had no radio playing, the windows in the kitchen were open; she could hear someone talking in the *Hof*. "No," she said. She didn't even bother to keep her voice down. "I wouldn't."

"I thought not. Is this why you didn't advise me to go to the hospital to begin with?"

"No," Grete replied. The truth surged up her throat, compelling her to let it out. She felt the way she might feel right before vomiting, nauseous but anticipating relief. "No, I didn't give you that advice because I am not here to help you. I am here because they know you're planning to emigrate without paying the property levy, and the SD sent me to report on you."

Once the words were out they seemed to hover above the bed, lulling all three of them into silence. Sitting between them, Grete could sense the Blumenthals communicating with each other over her head, using only the panic on their faces.

"Now you know," Grete said, writing in her notepad. "When I come back, we don't have to pretend. I will return in a week. Meanwhile, do nothing. This is the report I will hand in." Herr Blumenthal came to read over her shoulder: *Nothing of note. Wife too ill to travel.* Out of the corner of her eye Grete could see his fists clenching, and she knew what he was thinking—if he killed her, would their problems disappear, or worsen? Could he kill for his wife and unborn child? Would he?

"They are watching you," she told Frau Blumenthal, whose nostrils flared in fear. "So don't do anything rash. When I return, perhaps we can discuss a better way to get you to that hospital in Sweden."

She left, feeling as stunned as she imagined they felt.

On her ride home she wouldn't congratulate herself; she'd done nothing to help them so far except offer the truth. The image of Frau Blumenthal's ankles and feet loomed before her every time she closed her eyes.

That night Klaus came over long after dinner, late enough to set her neighbors' tongues wagging. As they lay together, her secret lay between them. She made love to him as she never had before, taking control, pinning him down by the wrists.

• • •

In the light of day things seemed different, more precarious. Grete wasn't quite sure what she was doing. All she knew was that it was dangerous, but that she couldn't stop the truth now that it had begun to spill out.

In Herr Reuter's study that weekend, after she'd listened to his valves rasp, she took out her notepad right in front of him and prepared the same report she did week after week: *No suspicious activity.* "Don't you want to know what I put in my log, Herr Reuter?" she asked as he buttoned his shirt. "About your heart?"

"Not really," Herr Reuter replied. He was a pudgy man with great brown nipples covered in hair, and he wore round tinted glasses. "Long as I'm not dying."

She went in front of his chair so that he would have to look up at her and turned her notebook around, putting her finger over her lips. His large face changed little as he took his time reading. Finally his eyes rolled upward, a sneer at the corner of his mouth. "I don't know what to make of this. I don't understand . . . medical speak. You will have to explain."

She nodded. "It just means there's little danger. Good news, *mein Herr.*"

"Good news," he echoed in a kind of trance.

She went to his radio and turned it on as if she were in her own home, then brought a chair close to his. "I am closing my journal," she said quietly, even though he could see her do it and replace it in her satchel. "Now tell me about the van."

"I don't know what you're talking about."

"I think you do."

Herr Reuter's breath charged from his nostrils. "Why don't you just arrest me?"

"Would you rather I did?" She tried to steady her voice. Between the radio, turned up nearly to full volume, her tinnitus, and the hatred on his face—she'd never seen such hatred—she could feel herself losing control. "If you were imprisoned, you would let them down, *nicht*? I think someone is waiting for you to take him or her out of the country."

Blood ticked through a vein on the side of Herr Reuter's neck, but he said nothing and did not move.

"I want to know when you plan to leave. I can tell the SD whatever I want, Herr Reuter. It won't take much to have you arrested, as you have pointed out. If you'll tell me what you're planning, maybe I can help you."

He began chuckling, a nasty, porcine sound. "Help from a Nazi bitch, no thank you."

"I'm the only one who's noticed the van, Herr Reuter. You've done a good job hiding it."

Now he stood. He began pacing behind her chair, and though she couldn't hear his footsteps, she could feel them vibrating the floorboards.

"It is not I who plans to emigrate," he said finally, forcing her to turn to face him, cup her hand around her better ear. "It is my brother. He's what they call one of Berlin's 'warm brothers,' a companion to other men." His lip curled a little. "I'll drive him to the green border one week from now, with whatever of his possessions fit. Minus his lover."

"Not the green border," said Grete. "The Gestapo have caught on about people walking into the Netherlands. They will round him up in the woods with the others and drag him back to Germany. They'll send him to Dachau wearing the pink triangle."

He paled. "I don't believe you."

"Believe me or don't, but I say take him north, to the port at Travemünde. Have him stay there a few days, pretend he's on holiday. Then buy two round-trip tickets for a ferry ride to Sweden." She waited for the music to crescendo. "Have him take nothing with him but a small valise. He can pretend he's going for only one night, so that he and his girlfriend might enjoy the sea air before she gives birth to his child." The speech made her dizzy.

"Sweden?" Herr Reuter asked, looking merely puzzled now. "Girlfriend? Child?"

"Yes. You'll be taking someone else with you; this is my price for allowing you to go. She is expecting a baby, which will look good for your brother. You'll have to hide her somehow on your drive to the coast."

Sweat beaded on his forehead. "Hide her? Is this person a Jew? If they catch me—"

"It is a risk you'll have to take."

He fell to his knees on the floor, his hands in front of him for support, and she feared his heart really had failed him. She helped him into the chair, yanked his handkerchief from his pocket and mopped his forehead. When she returned from the kitchen with a glass of water, he still hadn't opened his eyes. He lay back, his head damp, his glasses askew across his nose and mouth.

She held his chin and coaxed water down his throat until he sputtered. "I like you, Herr Reuter," she said, wishing she could make him believe her. One of his eyes opened a crack. He looked as if he could spit at her face. "I am not doing this to hurt or threaten you. The Jewish woman is someone else I've been sent to report on. I'll be pleased to hear both she and your brother make it to Sweden alive."

"Oh, so I'll still be dealing with you upon my return?" he said, his voice hoarse. "Nurse Metzger, my sweet caregiver?"

"Yes," she said. "I need you to keep hold of that van. When you return, your next task will be to help *me* out of the country."

• • •

The day after, she went to give the Blumenthals Herr Reuter's name and explain that Frau Blumenthal should be ready to leave in six days. If she'd expected them to thank her, she would have been gravely disappointed, but Grete knew better. The three of them sat in the dining room, Grete playing with one of the silk flowers in the arrangement on the table as the couple stared at each other, mouths open, heartbroken.

"Six days?" said Frau Blumenthal. "And you're sure he can be trusted?"

Grete nodded. "He has as much to lose as you do," she said, realizing only after she'd spoken how untrue these words were.

Herr Blumenthal still hadn't moved. His green eyes shimmered and mouth trembled as he studied his wife's hand, turning it over and over on the tabletop. His wife whispered something Grete could not hear, and he shook his head, inhaling with a wet sniff.

"It is the best chance we have, *Schatzi*," he said, stroking her skin. "We'll take an even greater risk if we both try to hide in Herr Reuter's car. Besides, we don't have the money for a ferry ticket for myself and your doctor bills once you've arrived safely. You and the baby go. I will find a way to Sweden as soon as it's possible."

"That's right," said Grete. "Your husband can meet you later, Frau Blumenthal. The important thing is for you to take care of your health right away."

Frau Blumenthal cut her eyes, full of tears, toward Grete, pursing her bluish lips. Grete felt acutely how unwelcome she was in this moment, despite the role she'd played in bringing it about. "And what about you?" Frau Blumenthal said. "How can we be sure *you* can be trusted?"

"You can't," Grete said, getting up to go. "When Herr Reuter arrives it will be very late at night. If you decide not to travel with him, if you decide all of this is a trap, you can keep your lights off and ignore the buzzer. I am sure he will not wait long." She took in Frau Blumenthal's swollen wrists, the skin marbled in red and white, for what she hoped would be the last time.

"I wish there were a code word I could give, something to convince you to believe me." Buttoning her brown jacket, she made her voice very soft. "All I can say is I pray you'll go."

• • •

A couple of weeks later she sat with Klaus, having dinner at the Hotel Adlon, feeling as though everything she'd done behind his back were written on her skin. *Nothing to report. Go through Travemünde.* Part of her wished he could see.

Herr Reuter's shop hadn't opened in days; an *On Holiday* sign hung in the window. The van was missing. At her weekly appointment with the Blumenthals, nobody had answered the door. She'd felt a surge of victory swell in her stomach, then the urge to burst into tears.

"We'll be having champagne," Klaus told the waiter, winking at Grete, or perhaps admiring the view; behind her head there was a window that opened out to the Brandenburg Gate. When the waiter began to list varietals, Klaus shooed him away. "Bring us the best, please," he said. "Tonight we're celebrating."

"Ah," said Grete, her smile thin. Her next assignment, then, would be a difficult one; she'd known as soon as he suggested the Adlon. She, too, had made more effort than usual tonight. She'd painted her lips coral and curled her hair so that it lay on her shoulders, gold on emerald, hoping if she looked especially nice it would distract him from asking questions.

Instead of reaching into his pocket, he took her hand. "You are a sight for sore eyes, darling." A lock of blond hair fell across his forehead, and he grinned with one corner of his mouth, and despite everything a little gasp of love sighed in her chest. She was fifteen, naked under her nightgown on his balcony all over again.

She half-listened as he told her about his most recent visit to Poland and what the SD aimed to accomplish there. "Entirely feasible, we know, because of our successes in Czechoslov . . ."

She was having trouble concentrating. The room swam before her in a sea of cream and plush brown, dizzying her. It hurt, almost, to focus on his eyes, and so she picked a spot somewhere on his forehead, noticing lines in the skin that hadn't been there before. Perspiration rolled down the sides of her torso.

She realized only when she shifted her gaze to his mouth, watched his teeth close around his fork, loaded with ham and beans, that their dinner had arrived. Half a roast chicken, which she couldn't remember ordering, sat before her, untouched.

"I just want you to tell me," she said, gripping her fork and knife without lifting them. "I want to know what my next assignment is."

He cocked his head and lifted his glass. At some point, he'd switched to beer. "But that is what I've been trying to say, darling. Because of my new position under *Brigadeführer* Jost, we need to turn our attention to the move to Warsaw." He laughed once, irritated, it seemed, that she'd missed all of his good news. "Haven't you been listening?"

Grete could see their waiter approaching with a tray of whipped and sculpted desserts. She blinked him away with a nearly imperceptible shake of her head. "We?" she said.

"Yes, that's what I've been saying. We are moving to Poland, at least for the time being, so that I may serve as Herr Jost's undersecretary. This may be the most important post of my career." He leaned back in his chair and gave his mouth a thorough wipe with his napkin. She noticed he'd cleaned his plate. "Why, look at you, little Grete. You haven't touched your dinner, and here I've paid through the nose for it. Whatever could be on your mind?"

With her fingertips she smoothed the fine linen covering the table. Underneath she could feel nubby, ordinary terrycloth. "Where will you put me in Warsaw? What will you tell the other officers—you need to find lodging for your mistress?"

"Look at me, Grete," he said, and when she did, she could tell he enjoyed this. His pale eyes twinkled. "You're being melodramatic. You aren't my mistress, you're my fiancée! We'll be married, of course, as soon as we get there. Before we go, if you'd prefer."

Stunned, unsure what else to do, she nodded.

Klaus laughed. "We'll even do it in church, if you'd like—my little Catholic fool. We'll get you a pair of lace gloves. In Poland, you can surround yourself with Catholics if you want."

"Oh, Klaus," she said. There were tears in her eyes, one slipping down her cheek, but she couldn't be sure what caused them.

• • •

Butter, not guns.

No, that wasn't right.

Grete couldn't sleep. Goebbels's slogan hammered against the inside of her skull. Klaus snored beside her. After his proposal, she'd finished the bottle of champagne.

Guns, not butter.

After a while she got up and pulled the curtain aside, letting in enough moonlight so that she could study him, his long white body immodestly draped in her sheet, his sticky genitals exposed. He'd drifted off immediately after they made love. His penis curled in its nest like a giant grub.

He wanted to take her to Poland. She could tell he meant it by the way he'd attacked her once they were alone in her room. They'd staggered to the bed, attached at the mouths. Kissing before intercourse had been tossed aside months or years ago. Normally he started at her nipples, or by dropping his pants. Tonight he held her, cradled her head between his forearms as he pushed himself into her. He teased her tongue with his teeth. Did it hurt, he wanted to know. Did it feel good? Just these questions were almost too much for her to bear. He'd never asked before.

*Warsaw. Married at a Catholic church in Poland.* She dug around inside the bottom drawer of her desk, careful not to make much noise as he went on snoring. She'd heard the wives, even the officers' children, who went to Czechoslovakia had helped make Case Green a success. They flirted with, hosted, befriended the Slovak nationalists whom their husbands convinced to side with Germany.

She found what she'd been looking for and quietly shut the drawer. In Poland, Klaus had told her, she could surround herself with Catholics. He'd figured out how to give her the biggest assignment of all and offer it dusted in sugar.

What would he think if he could see her now, naked except for her thin pair of panties, her tired hands pointing a gun at his face? Hers was a Mauser C96. It hadn't been difficult to obtain, not after the Night of Broken Glass; the government's ban on Jews keeping firearms resulted in a surplus for everyone else. All the salesman told her was that it was preowned. She'd never fired it, or even held it for so long; it required both wrists steadying the wooden handle, and still the barrel shook.

As delicately as she could, she cocked her weapon, keeping her eyes on his face. Soon he would ask about Herr Reuter. He'd ask after Frau Blumenthal. He was smart enough to put it together. She either had to leave him or kill him. She took a step closer, watched his chest rise and fall. Her sweat took on a different smell, something animal. Her neighbors would hear and come running. She would have to take care of herself before they could break down the door.

She couldn't have known, not at this point, just what she might accomplish in killing Klaus. The annexation of Poland still sounded fairly innocuous. She could not know where Klaus would be in three short years, his boots caked in Lithuanian mud as he watched an endless parade of Jews, stripped naked and holding hands, march toward Soviet-dug trenches. Watching his brows lift innocently as some dream took him by surprise—he let out a faint whimper—Grete could not have imagined he'd be one of the men standing on the perimeter of those pits. That on command he would empty his weapon into the crowd.

She did not know what was to come, and yet she did.

Spit foamed in her mouth, leaking from her lips and mingling with her tears. Even if she convinced Herr Reuter to take her to Sweden tomorrow, even if she never committed another evil act for Klaus, she wouldn't have done enough to stop him.

These would be her last thoughts on earth, then. One she offered to God, a prayer for forgiveness that she didn't expect to be answered or even heard, and one for Berni. Wherever Berni was—above her, watching; abroad, living another life—she'd want Grete to pull the trigger.

*Do it, little bird. Squeeze. It'll be over in a second. One squeeze is all it takes.*

Counting, Grete thought, might help; she'd count to three, and then she'd do it.

Eyes pressed shut, she got to three, still stood there trembling.

First she would touch him one last time. One caress, and then she'd end it for both of them. She chose her favorite place on his body: the hip, white and smooth, blue veins under the skin. When she felt how warm he was she realized too late that her hands had frozen. He jolted, eyes fluttering, and she stumbled backward, the gun dangling in one hand at her side.

"What is it?" he said, smacking his lips. He rolled over, facing the wall. "While you're up, bring me a glass of water, will you? Then come to bed."

She stood there with the gun pointed at him, waiting for him to turn and see her. "Yes, Klaus." Her chest heaved. What would he say if he could see her? Would his pulse even rise, or would he know she wouldn't go through with it?

After a while his snores began again, and slowly, slowly, her arms fell. She felt as though her spine had been yanked from her, as though she were a fish who'd been gutted. The Mauser returned to its drawer. Perhaps she'd have another chance, tomorrow, or after he returned from his next trip abroad. She spread her limp body onto the mattress, and Klaus draped a hand over her waist.

# ANITA, 1970

Anita stood at the motel window, watching the bleary landscape of Levittown, Pennsylvania, bend sideways in the wind. Between the sheets of rain and frothing trees the hardware store and sad strip mall across the street became almost beautiful; she could imagine them as little white castles at the bottom of an aquarium.

"The news is on, Mutti!" called Janeen from one of the beds, and Anita turned, reluctantly, back toward the television. Her bowl of fluorescent orange macaroni and cheese, purchased from the diner downstairs, had grown cold and hard on her bed.

As expected, the anchors began with scenes of hurricane devastation, the reporters in the field blinking under the hoods of their yellow raincoats. Hurricane Curt, via mudslide, had killed over a dozen people in the Caribbean. Much of the South had lost power as the storm grinded its way up the coast, and train travel had been shut down at Trenton, forcing Anita and Janeen to find a motel the night before.

"Look at that," Anita said now. "It's turning." The satellite image showed Trenton under one of the storm's long fingers, its eye poised to follow a dotted-line path out to sea.

"That's a relief," Janeen said, chewing the straw of her Coke. The lights flickered, and both of them tensed, but the electricity held.

Neither of them said aloud what they both hoped: that the news would shift to other stories, that they'd hear Klaus had been apprehended. With every minute that ticked past, Anita wondered how much closer he could have gotten to freedom. A full day had passed in which Margaret could have turned him in, and hadn't. The two of them could be on their way to a remote island—would the storm have stopped them? He could have driven west. By now he could be close to Alaska. In any case, Anita knew that wherever he went, this time, he'd be careful. He'd ensure nobody would ever find him.

After the storm coverage ended, the anchors relayed the news of a failed mission in Vietnam that had taken the lives of thirty-six helicopter pilots, then a report of a fire in Philadelphia at the home of four Penn students: fortunately, nobody was hurt.

"You see?" Anita said, swigging Coke. "Candles."

When the broadcast ended, again with no mention of Henry Klein or Klaus Eisler, Janeen dropped her head. She sat cross-legged on the bed, her bowl in her lap. "*Liebchen*," Anita began, her voice cracking. What to say? Apprehending Klaus will not bring your father back? "I do not want you to be disappointed if Grete lied to us."

Janeen shook her head. "That's not it. I'm worried about her and Erik. What if Klaus found out about her plan and . . . did something to her?"

"So you still believe she will do what is right. How, Janeen? How can you be so sure?"

Janeen opened her mouth, but only a few sputtering sounds emerged. After a minute, Anita went with a sigh into the tiny bathroom to brush her teeth.

Rain washed over the hotel through the night, and though they didn't speak to each other, Anita knew neither of them slept much, if at all.

• • •

The bathroom window, like a porthole on a ship, revealed fair skies the next morning as Anita showered. Branches and debris littered the motel parking lot, and a few men stood beside a truck with a smashed windshield.

"Tracks south are clear—" Anita began, trying to sound cheery, but when she came into the room she found Janeen sitting on the bed, phone to her ear, a piece of scrap paper in her lap. She looked up at her mother with worried eyes.

"Well, when's the last time you saw him?" she said into the receiver, then nodded a few times, rubbing the little piece of paper between her finger and thumb. "Okay, thank you. Would you tell him, when he comes home, that his cousin called?" She hung up. "Erik's not at his apartment, Mutti. His roommates haven't seen him in more than a day."

"We hardly know him."

Janeen's spine stiffened. "He's our family. I don't care what Grete did. He is."

"You misunderstand me. I mean we do not know this boy's habits. He could have spent the night out, with friends or a girl. Or a boy!"

Janeen shook her head, brown eyes solemn. "They said he doesn't normally do this."

Anita went to her suitcase and turned her back to Janeen. "Tracks south are clear," she repeated. "Now, let us get our belongings up from this awful floor, *nicht*? I fear there are fleas here. I am going to bathe everything in Lysol when we are finally home."

She began zipping bags, shaking out clothes, and slamming suitcases loudly, aware of Janeen's complete silence behind her.

• • •

The station in Trenton wasn't built to handle such a crowd. Locals glared from the pay phones at the tired travelers sitting on their luggage in front of the counters, waiting to be reissued tickets that had been canceled because of the storm. Janeen went to buy a candy bar from a vending machine beside the police station. Anita found herself staring up at the flip board above the tellers. In white letters on a black background: train number 72, Palmetto to Charleston, leaving at 10:32 A.M.

Train number 358, Federal to Pennsylvania Station, New York, would depart at 10:10 on the opposite track. The clock on the wall read 9:52. She watched the letters flip as another train left the station, the remaining schedule bumped up one notch.

"Excuse me?" the man behind her whined. "You going to move up?"

"Maybe sometime soon," Anita said to irk him, then pushed her suitcase forward with her foot. She wasn't sure why she felt so edgy, but it might have had something to do with the dog. The policeman beside the ticket counter wore knee-high, shiny black boots and held the leash of a dog, a massive German shepherd with ears erect, big as a man's hands. Its tongue lolled from its mouth, draped on jagged teeth.

The police in Anhalter Bahnhof had dogs that day, when she and the three children awaited the train that would take them away from Germany forever. And at Gronau, dogs boarded the train with the guards, hunting for deserters.

That day, too, she had been preoccupied with thoughts of Grete.

When Janeen returned, her chocolate bar half-eaten, Anita handed her some change. "Go to one of the pay phones," she said, gesturing toward the cluster of shady characters hanging around the booths. "I'll watch you. Go and call your cousin's roommates again."

Janeen turned the dimes in her palm with her thumb. "What should I say?" she asked, but in the quickening of her eyes, Anita could tell she already knew.

"Tell him we will not be going home quite yet." The line had cleared in front of her; she was next at the counter. Anita reached for the handle of her suitcase. "Tell him we must make a detour, back to New York."

• • •

Anita wasn't sure what she'd expected to see at Margaret's building: signs of a struggle, or blue police lights whirling outside, but the place appeared exactly the same, the same two homeless boys camped at the base of the façade. Dark puddles, full of cigarette butts and trash, streamed toward the drains in the street.

Janeen shivered. "He could still be in there, Mutti."

"We do not know her telephone number," Anita repeated. They had gone over this during their brief train ride and in the taxi uptown. "It is a risk we must take."

They waited a little while in front of the doors, their reflections distorted in the glass, legs wide, mouths pulled even deeper into frowns. The doors reflected the sun's attempt to burn through the clouds, a weak gray circle.

On the train, Janeen had asked how Anita knew Margaret and Erik were in trouble, what she'd thought happened to them. Anita shook her head. "I have never been able to read my sister, to know what she's done or will do. All I feel is a pull on myself."

Eventually a young man came out of the building with a pair of skates knotted over his shoulder, and he held the door without question as the two of them dragged their suitcases inside. They rode the elevator up to the eighth floor, anxiety so thick between them Anita could feel it buzz, like the beginning of a storm.

At Margaret's door, Anita knocked loudly, Janeen standing behind her, wringing her hands. "Margaret?" Anita called. "Open the door, it's me." She found she couldn't say her name. "Open the door, Margaret," she said, her voice cracking.

Janeen chewed one of her knuckles. There was no answer. They could kick down the door, or find the superintendent, tell him they thought the people inside needed help. Anita felt blood pounding in the hand she used to steady herself against the door. What would they find inside? What devastation, what trauma? She knocked again, harder this time, and heard a small dog begin barking in the apartment next door. "Margaret," she tried to shout, but what came out was mostly air. She needed a paper bag to breathe into. Margaret was her sister, her own flesh and blood. Despite everything, how could she have walked out on her once again?

A hesitant voice came from inside. "Who is it?" A boy's voice.

"Erik?" Janeen came forward, put her fingertips to the door. "Is that you?"

"Who's there?" he said, sounding fearful. "Why are you covering the peephole?"

"Mutti!" Janeen cried, moving Anita's hand.

"It is Anita and Janeen," Anita said, looking straight into the peephole. "What's going on in there—is your mother safe?"

"I—" Erik said. "Something happened with . . . him. I think she might need a hospital, but she won't let me take her."

"Let us in, Erik," said Anita, trying hard to sound as if she were in control. "Let us see if we can help."

She heard him undo every lock. When he pulled the door open, he looked young and scared in his socks. Janeen took his forearm and held it for a second. "I thought you were going home," he said, shutting the door behind them, relocking the deadbolt, the knob, the chain. "I tried asking her what happened. All she would say is they took him. They took him early in the morning, yesterday, I think—that's all I could get her to say."

"Where is she?" Anita said softly, and he pointed, swallowing, toward the bedroom.

Inside the room the blinds were drawn, the light gray. Margaret lay on the bed, her tiny, curled-up legs creating scarcely a bump under the covers. Her breathing sounded shallow. Only her eyes, large and icy blue, registered their arrival.

Anita went to her, kneeling on the floor, as Janeen and Erik hovered on the threshold. Anita felt her sister's skin, which had a yellowish cast, and found her forehead cool. Out of habit, she tapped the cleft in Margaret's chin and tried to smile. Margaret continued to breathe in short gasps, a slight rasping sound in her lungs, as Anita felt for her pulse. After a minute she tucked her sister's wrist back under the blanket.

"Call an ambulance, please," she said as calmly as she could, and still her daughter and nephew looked as though she'd just told them to prepare to jump. "She will be fine, but I believe she is in shock." Janeen hesitated as Erik went to make the call, and Anita went to her. "Stay with him, will you, *Liebchen*? Give him strength."

Janeen nodded, firming her jaw. When she'd gone into the living room, Anita closed the door behind them. Despite their fears, despite the fact that neither of them deserved to be part of what had happened here, Anita didn't doubt they would be all right.

A knitted wool blanket hung on a chair; she brought it and tucked it around Margaret's shoulders, smoothing back her hair, which was damp at the roots. She brought a glass of water from the nightstand to Margaret's lips and coaxed her to drink.

"They took him," Margaret said, her voice nearly inaudible. "The Mossad agents. In the middle of the night. They threw a hood over his head. They will put him on trial. And then they will kill him."

Doubts sprouted in Anita's mind, weeds she'd pulled without taking care of the roots. How did she know for certain Margaret was telling the truth? How could she know Margaret hadn't let Klaus get away, that the pain she felt now wasn't merely lovesick grief?

Doubts would always be there. But the ambulance would arrive soon. They would not have much more time together. Anita put a hand on Margaret's forehead.

"It cannot have been easy for you to do," she murmured.

"No. In a sense it was easy. It is what he deserved." Margaret's voice sounded high, nasal; her hearing aid sat on the nightstand.

"But he cursed me, you should have heard the way he cursed me. He promised he'd tell them everything I did. And the agents said . . ." Margaret's body convulsed in weak coughs. "They saw my records, from the SS," she croaked. "If I hadn't cooperated, giving them Klaus, they could have . . ."

"But you did cooperate. You gave them Klaus."

"You didn't believe I would." Margaret's eyes fell closed. Her voice turned airy. "It is what he deserved. It is what I deserve."

"Hush," said Anita, a lump in her throat.

After this they did not speak. Anita went to the window and twisted the cord to make the blinds tighter, darkening the room. Then she came to the bed and, after waiting a moment with one knee on the mattress, she slipped under the covers beside her sister.

It would only be for a minute. The paramedics were on their way. Anita felt herself struggling to hold something inside, something that threatened to burst from her chest.

A soft knock sounded at the door. Then one of the kids whispered something to the other, and she heard them retreat.

The bed felt narrower than she'd expected. She found herself pressed against Margaret's back, her lips touching the ends of blond hair that smelled of milk and honey. Anita closed her eyes. She felt the blankets shift, and she peeked to find Margaret facing her now, eyes shut. Her face had regained some of its color. Their breathing fell into a rhythmic pattern, their ribs expanding and contracting in unison. Under the covers Margaret's feet tickled Anita's shins, the skin freezing cold. She left her toes there, borrowing Anita's warmth.

When Anita smiled, her tears ran into her mouth. She tasted salt. Poor Grete—she never did like thunderstorms. As soon as she could toddle, she would climb from her trundle into Berni's bed in their room in the attic, under the eaves.

Sirens were approaching. She could hear them whining up the avenue. "Tell me a story," Berni said, though it was usually she who spoke while Grete listened, and she knew neither of them had anything left to say. But she watched the corners of Grete's mouth lift—lines, now, running from her nose to the corners of her lips—and so she said it again. "Tell me a story."

Grete smiled back at her. It was enough, it seemed, just to say the words.

# ACKNOWLEDGMENTS

Writing a book set in another time and another country can feel impossible. I owe a great deal of gratitude to the many people who helped me find my way in the dark.

Thank you to Shannon Hassan, my amazing, tenacious agent, and everyone at Marsal Lyon Literary Agency for finding the perfect home for Berni and Grete. Thank you to Benjamin LeRoy, Heather Padgen, and everyone at Tyrus Books and Adams Media for making this novel the best it could be. I could not be happier to work with all of you.

I never could have done this without my professors in the creative writing program at Boston University: Leslie Epstein, Xuefei Jin, and Allegra Goodman. Thank you for believing in these characters and in me.

To my Sheilas—Jordan Coriza, Joseph Fazio, Kathleen Foster, Jill Maio, Jessica Ullian, Farley Urmston, and Jennifer Cacicio—thank you for reading this so many times. Thank you also to: Stacy Mattingly, Lauren Sorantino, and Bekah Stout for offering your fresh eyes; Kate Hollander, for sharing your extensive knowledge of the Weimar Republic; Quinn Slobodian and Michelle Sterling, for letting me text you at odd hours with German usage questions; Grayson Mills, for teaching me about teenage life in South Carolina; and Daphne Kalotay, for being a tremendous friend and mentor.

Jim and Julie Kerr, thank you for believing in me and for raising an incredible son.

To my four fantastic grandparents: Mom-Mom and Pop-Pop Woods, thank you for the lovely, much-needed respites in Florida, and Nonna and Poppy Apostolico, *danke schön* for taking me to Germany twice. Nonna, I will never forget sharing beer and schnitzel with you in Alexanderplatz. Who knows us?

Stephanie and Michael: I love you even more than Berni loves Grete, and I feel very fortunate that our story is much simpler. Consider me your sidekick for life.

To my parents, who didn't bat an eye when I said I'd rather be a novelist than go to law school: thank you for your faith in me. My father, Jim, has taught me so much about language, especially the German I needed here. And my mother, Susan, gave me the priceless gift of a love of reading. Mom, I can never thank you enough for always surrounding me with books.

Camille: it's you and me, kid—we did this together! You are my shining star. I am so lucky to be your mommy.

And to Colin, who has believed this would happen from the time it seemed, to me, a distant possibility: I am grateful for you every single day. Thank you for supporting my dream. I love you.